BORROWED DREAMS

To request permissions, contact the publisher at LEWAROROAD.com

Paperback: ISBN 978-1-737-4087-0-3
Ebook: ISBN 978-1-7374087-1-0
Library of Congress Control Number: 2021811741

September 2021

Printed by in the USA.

LEWARO ROAD

The odds against her could not have been greater and yet through faith, perseverance and extraordinary resilience she became one of America's greatest Daughters.

JUSTIN SWINGLE

ADAPTED FROM THE SCREENPLAY

WHITE SHADOWS, BLACK DREAMS
BY JUSTIN SWINGLE

JUSTIN SWINGLE

Lost Beginnings

1

THE BURNEY PLANTATION was the entire world for me. I was born at Grandview two years after the Civil War, that bloody struggle the white folks blamed us for, and after which they sent us packing to nowhere.

As a child I was convinced the moon rolled over the big house cooling it on hot summer nights. I'd been told by the old 'croppers that the nightglow reflected off the big house was to keep out the heat and the field dust the 'croppers stirred. White folks readily assured us that this was the natural order. The Lord meant for the fields to hold the burning sun by day 'cause that's where the coloreds lovingly toiled alongside the farm animals. If that sun wasn't up there ready to blind, they reminded us, a colored might lift her eyes from the rows of cotton and get to wondering what could be out there that might replace the drudgery? I yet wander back to my lost beginnings looking for answers, even if the questions are yet tangled.

My folks' place was on the swampy side of the Burney plantation close to the river. We all knew the shadows down there were inhabited by the tortured souls of those who came before; their spirits never stopped wandering our memories. Were they yet searching for that part of their soul that had been wrenched? Well, the Burney place might have been a stone's throw out of Delta across the river from Vicksburg, yet it remained deeper in the heart of the South than you can imagine. So, early on I sent my imaginings to that beyond, even if I didn't know where that place was.

My daddy was born to Grandview, and never left till death provided an escort. He was still young and yet old when the day came when he could not rise from his stone sleep. Owen was tall and soft-spoken. He never got worked up 'cept maybe when Minerva was. Oddly, Daddy getting worked up is what seemed to soothe Momma. He could pull her back into his warmth just by turning down the corners of his mouth. It was a signal that he'd had enough of her fussing over things—things that she could never have fixed anyway. Caressed by his gentle words she'd finally let loose of the moment that had tormented her. It was the only serenity that Momma ever knew, the surrender to his powerful arms.

My daddy and Samuel, Ella's cousin, went fishing most Sundays and sometimes late summer nights. Alex trailed along when he was old enough. I remember once asking Brother if they talked to the fish down there. He claimed they only talked about not talking to me. Like my daddy, Brother didn't say much. Still, he heard every word I uttered. At times it seemed that he could even hear between my very thoughts. I remember Alex saying Daddy and Samuel talked about having an acre of their own one day, when the credits owed Burney were paid off. But, Lord, that date would never be found on no calendar printed in the South. It was only a borrowed dream. Still, I learned early that borrowed dreams get us to the next day.

Momma was a tiny woman. Granny said Minerva was the runt of her kids and that's what made her tough as pig's hide. Guess you got to be to hold your place at the table when you're barely five feet tall and got three brothers a foot taller. What food there was went to those who reached the quickest. Ain't that life anyway? Momma learned early to grab what she had to. Well, some claimed Minerva was known to keep a pinch of nightshade hidden back somewhere.

Nightshade, the poison of the South, made some white folks jittery just at the thought. One that surely seeped through their nightmares. Yes, Momma could sure give folks the eye. She'd look at me, my brother Alex, or even Owen, and you knew real quick what was what. To stay clear of Minerva's temper you'd quickly take the path she meant for you. But it wasn't just my family. Nobody seemed to mess with Minerva, a person so small she could be put down with one blow, yet folks knew she was tough enough to somehow, some-way strike back. Didn't ol' Isaac go running off mad to escape her? One day I'll tell you about that.

Up in the big house where my friend Jackson Burney lived and Ella, his nanny, worked and slept, it was always cool, wasn't it? Through Ella's eyes I could see through the vistas of her fantasies of life up there. She once told me that in the big house there was the purest of white clouds that drifted through a hundred rooms to cleanse them of the powdery field dust that sifted through our lives and seemed to settle at the bottom of our dry throats come sundown.

"Just like them snow-white clouds," Ella told me, "they comes with the summer rains and fills up the rooms in the big house and float gardenia petals all the way up them stairs to Miss Burney's bathin' tub like she tol' 'em to."

Ella's explanations came like the whispered hush of some sacred truth nobody ever understood. Or maybe it was the kind of untruth that bound our lives to the plantation class.

"You carry water up for Miss Burney's bath?" I asked.

"No, chil'e. This is the way it is; sweet summer rain pours into her bathing tub bigger than a pond. Comes straight from heaven through a secret window ain't no colored can see through. Then it lifts all them white petals till they near float over the top of her tub. But they never do, 'cause they ain't 'pose' to."

Ella knew that nothing happened at Grandview unless Melinda Burney decreed it was to be.

"I bring 'er white linen towels beaten soft as silk. That I do."

I believed everything Ella told me. Wasn't it a version of the truth, that Melinda Burney's world was a whole lot closer to heaven than to mine?

"Don't the rains down at the shacks come from the same clouds?" I wondered out loud.

Our conversation quickly drifted to another place just out of reach, one where silky clouds could never cleanse away the unpleasantness.

Most mornings Jackson's daddy sat out on his white veranda looking at his paper like there was nothing else to do. I was sure that man never truly saw us—he sure never looked us in the eyes. It seemed he only spoke to coloreds out of the sides of his mouth, us trailing a respectful distance behind. I was so scared of Master Burney, him with those pale blue eyes. I thought with them eyes he couldn't see us. Yet my friend Jackson could sure see me. He was my age. He had brown eyes. Maybe the color of coffee with cream. How many times did I look up at the big house and see Jackson climbing under the table and through his daddy's legs while Ella stood silently behind Burney fanning him with a turkey feather fan? Why'd she do that? Wasn't it already cool up there? I figured it had to be one of those things poor colored women did—fanned white folk that were so cool they looked to be drenched in whiteness. Up there was a world where warm white suds laundered the white linen shirts Master Burney favored and where he sat on that white veranda, ten times the size of my shack, waiting for a breakfast table to be set with glistening white china. You know that table was drenched in so much white linen it pooled at the bottom of the table legs. And up there close and yet so far from me was my friend, a white child with white hair playing in all that fragrant white gardenia scented coolness. From the shadows under the magnolias where I'd watch, I could see him, even if his white world chose not to see me. So, I figured that meant they couldn't see me inhaling the fragrance of their big gardenias. How I twisted my thoughts wondering how I might smell even more. Those softly scented blooms were bigger than my hand and grew in well-tended pots on that veranda. White flowers cut daily to float aimlessly in a crystal bowl as clear as tears, so much like their lives at Grandview had floated from day to day for a hundred years. Why? Why did I wonder if Jackson could smell them gardenias? He never acted like he could smell nothing. But what was there to smell in his world other than fragrant flowers? I never stopped asking myself why my world was so close to his yet still so far? Such thoughts have a hold on me and still tug me back to my beginnings.

But, Lord, the heat of them fields; didn't it feel white hot on our backs? Was out in that dry dirt our Promised Land? There the heat was sure guaranteed us, and the white folks promised it would never run out, even as everything else did by the end of the month. Even when the salt of my brows burned into my eyes, the old folks whispered their own sacred truths, which vowed we should never stop thanking the white folks that the burn in our sweat-filled eyes was different from the rock salt that burned in the wounds of those who'd prayed as the lash crossed over their backs. Well, maybe they were only recalling the voices of those who haunted the shacks begging for answers that would never come—like why were they denied a dream, that sweet smell of freedom, a taste of dignity? I guess it's all in the figures. Ain't it always?

After breakfast, Master Robert Burney never seemed to do much more than look at his horse as Isaac brushed it, while Miss Burney stood on her veranda like a porcelain doll wrapped in fragility. Melinda was that certain kind of plantation woman that evolves from the deepest secrets of the South. Her up there cooing at him as she tossed her fine honey-colored hair back, waiting for Ella to fetch the brushes to arrange her hair high to reveal her long neck. I heard Ella tell Momma that Miss Burney's gaze at her husband suggested she was truly longing for him to stop riding his horse and come ride her. It would be many years before I could read a woman's broken but carefully punctuated sighs to understand such things. But no matter how sugary Melinda's voice was standing in the shade of her veranda, she never seemed to capture the master's absolute attention. No, word down at the shacks was that Burney took to a different kind of fragility. Whereas Miss Burney could always deny the master what she teased with a toss of her hair, some of us could not, and had to surrender what he lusted after. You see, the kind of fragility he took to was pounding his dirty deeds from behind. Like I told you, he never looked us in the eyes.

One summer night, peering through the bottom of a glass of bourbon he was tipping, Burney swallowed an eyeful of my older sister Louvenia. She'd blossomed that spring, along with the peach trees on Orchard Hill. Lord, didn't we pay a high price to the same people who banked that our lives had no value? Seems that Miss Burney saw the twinkle in Burney's eye and told ol' Isaac to send that girl-child packing. It was all done quietly. Louvenia was sent off with nothing but her lost innocence to inoculate her for a life off the plantation she was born to. Like a stray dog, Isaac prodded Sister with a stick all the way down the oak-lined drive that led away from Grandview. She never saw Owen and Minerva again. Them acts tend to shadow you like the nigger dogs. Yes, they slip up on you to nip at your heart, gnaw at your hopes and tear at your soul a bit more.

We were all driven by the lash of his tongue to hate Isaac, a mean ol' man. Seemed like Burney's overseer always knew what Jackson was up to; it was his job to watch over this plantation prince. But then he knew what we were all up to because he had eyes all 'round his head. The white folks told us so, and snickered at our bowed faces when they did. Once I tried to look up under the back of his greasy ol' hat, but couldn't see no eyes up there. Nonetheless, I knew they were there. Down at the river's edge, ol' Clara preached that the devil's got eyes back 'a his head to see if Jesus is coming at him with a stick. We all waited for the Lord to beat the hell out of Isaac. Then Momma did it for Him.

Jackson didn't seem to care 'bout no eyes anywhere on Isaac's head. No, he didn't. He'd walk past that man paying him no mind, 'cause he was walking proud with a special task Ella had given him of toting down to my folks a tin of meat renderings she'd spirited out of her kitchen. Guess that freed him of her apron strings long enough to find some mischief. Like me, Jackson was only five or six, but unlike me he'd learned early that his world didn't require that he address servants in passing or explain his actions to nobody. Ol' Isaac was powerless against this white child, 'cause if he messed with Jackson, his daddy would put an end to Isaac being overseer. Had to be that way to prepare Jackson for the day he would be master of Grandview. He had to grow up knowing he answered to nobody. Those were the rules, and nobody dared to say otherwise. Well, I guess Jackson knew it from the beginning.

"Young Master Jackson, where you goin' with them burlap bags?" Isaac inquired in a tone of silky politeness that never tidied up his words to us.

"I takin' a walk, don't it look like? And it ain't none of your business, huh?"

"Why, no, but maybe yer daddy, he be wondering whereabouts you're headed, 'cause he tol' me to keep an eye on you. You know yer momma don't want you down with them dirty niggers! Heard her say so. Yes, Sir, I sure did."

Jackson looked him in the eyes, the front ones. It was surely a moment that gave Burney's overseer heartburn. "I reckon my daddy's wondering why his horsey didn't get brushed this mornin' like he tol' ya."

Isaac knew when Jackson was mimicking his daddy. He got a daily dose, and by his expression it was mighty bitter to swallow.

"Now, Jackson, you saw me down there brushing yer daddy's horses, 'cause you was talkin' real nice then."

"Maybe I did, but now I forget."

Jackson had one hand on his hip like Ella did when she was about to smack him for sassing.

"I'm tellin' my daddy you been talkin' strange like you been at the bottle again. That's gonna get my momma to work up a cry when she hears what I gots to say. You know what happens when Momma sets herself to bawlin' on things she don't want 'a hear 'bout. Daddy's sure gonna come after somebody!"

"Now, Master Jackson, you'd be lying then. You'll go to hell for it!"

"My daddy ain't gonna like you tellin' me to go to hell."

Jackson was disinclined to further discourse and walked off. He'd communicated his position often enough for Isaac to know when to capitulate and step aside. Ella also knew 'bout Isaac, 'cause if she'd done the pilfering from the kitchen, Isaac would'a ripped her back open. He must not have thought thrashing a woman would send him any deeper into the hell he was destined for. Jackson and Ella understood that unique place they held in those tangled shadows of the big house, shadows that sometimes drifted all the way to the shacks. Each, in their own way, made that knowledge work for them. Seemed at times they had ol' Isaac dancing to their convoluted tunes, as though he was being chased by wasps. Yes, they had their ways of dealing with his daddy's overseer, Jackson and his Ella. These two were united in their need for each other. It was a love that seared through those white shadows, sparked off his folks' Southern sensibilities, and left them all singed up at the big house.

JACKSON'S GRANDVIEW

2

WHEN I WAS five or six, I'd wander from the fields up to the big house—that place where no coloreds but the house servants ever ventured. I'd go to meet my friend, and in so doing stepped over an invisible barrier that the rest of them always seemed to see.

Jackson and I loved playing in the dirt in Miss Burney's garden. Dirt is where I lived anyway, but Jackson wallowed in it, maybe 'cause Melinda hated it so—him getting soiled and all. Jackson defied authority as a ritual. I was in awe of that defiance, knowing that at the bottom of the path where I lived nobody ever heard of authority being defied without a lash or lynching rope as witness. Jackson would break Southern rules, get dirty, get nigger dirty simply to defy the order he lived in. White princes break rules and live to tell. Colored kids learn early that a backhand could be settled on us without any justification. There were no such consequences for Jackson. Playing with me near the veranda, he'd cover himself in dirt and then crawl up on his daddy's lap, covering him with the fresh chicken manure that Isaac had spread over Miss Burney's rose garden that morning. Burney would holler for Ella to come take care of the problem. He never yelled at Jackson; he was never the problem—Ella's inattention was.

Jackson always got what he wanted or needed, because Ella was there to see to it. Yes, it was Ella who hauled Jackson in, stripped him of his soiled clothes and bathed him in the warm white suds and then wrapped him in white linen towels as she hugged him. Yes, hugged, 'cause Ella was the only one up there who really loved that child. He survived on that love, because for the Burneys, Jackson was only the heir. They didn't love each other; how could they love their child? But there are reasons for all things. I'm gonna tell you 'bout that one day.

Jackson and I started playing together nearly every day till I was sentenced to the cotton fields. Jackson also had tasks to perform. He was being groomed to be a Southern prince, for the day he'd be joining the others who reigned over plantation society in those post-bellum river parishes. Most days, he had riding lessons. As a child, I always thought it was strange how white folk thought of riding horses as fun, and even dressed up for it. We knew it only as work. We never got dressed up to ride horses or mules—what would we get dressed up in? As I recall, it seemed like Melinda Burney always made Ella dress Jackson like a toy doll. When he wasn't riding, he'd come out in his white short pants and shirt and sit in the dirt to line up his toys, waiting for me to join him.

"Your daddy don't mind me playin' up here?" I asked, knowing that Master Burney couldn't really see me, but knew his ma sure could.

"My daddy's out ridin' his horses. Ella never tells."

"What 'bout mean ol' Isaac?"

"He's out huntin' nigger problems."

"What's a nigger problem?" I asked.

"Don't know, do I? Guess Isaac don't know, too, 'cause my daddy keeps tellin' 'im the same ol' thing. I heard 'im!" Jackson jumped up and put his hands on his waist, mimicking his daddy. "'Isaac! Get on up to the orchard and take care of that nigger problem!' Guess Isaac just don't never mind what my daddy tell 'im, do he? 'Cause my daddy's gotta keep telling 'im like he do my momma all the time."

Even as a child I had to stop in my tracks to sort what came out of of white folks' mouths. "Your momma's a nigger problem?"

"I guess, 'cause my daddy keeps sayin'." Hands akimbo, Jackson re-assumed his daddy's posture. "'Melinda, don't be comin' back from Vicksburg with no more new dresses! Hear?' I know ol' Isaac hears my daddy, but my momma, she don't hear nothin' she don't aim to! That's what my daddy says. Then my momma says right back ain't nobody in Delta cares what my daddy say 'bout nothin'."

"She brings back lots of dresses? New dresses?" I asked, utterly perplexed.

Sometimes I'd go off wondering about our talks for the longest time. Like, where do dresses come from? What's out there beyond those fields that pretty dresses are waiting? Like all kids from the shacks, mine came from flour sackcloth sewn together by ol' Clara when Momma was in the fields.

"Nobody hear your daddy, even when he's callin' you?"

"Nope, and I don't hear Ella when I don't want to, do I?" he said with a mischievous grin. "But I can sure make Momma hear me good when I aim to, huh? Don't I? I put mud on my shoes and go walking on her fancy ol' rug ain't nobody 'pose' to look at."

"Don't Ella hear your daddy?" I wondered.

"Guess she hear ever'thing, even when she don't, and do what he tell 'er even when she say she ain't gonna."

Jackson continued: "When Momma gets home from Vicksburg, she kisses my daddy's face all over, then he don't see all them dresses up in the attic. But I do, and I don't believe a word Momma says 'bout no damned ghost gonna get me if I get into things up there." Jackson's voice dropped to a conspiratorial whisper. "I told my daddy my horse stunk like Isaac. Now Isaac gots to give my horsey a bath 'fore I go riding, don't he? You know what?" Jackson whispered in my ear. "Once my daddy—he kissed his horse! I seen 'im, too!"

We fell over laughing.

"I ain't never gonna let my daddy kiss me! Are you?"

Again, I had no answer. Back then, I didn't worry 'bout Master Burney wanting to kiss me, 'cause I was sure his pale eyes kept him from seeing me. But Lordy, Melinda Burney sure could! Later that morning she ventured out onto the veranda where her breakfast waited. She'd just bathed, and Ella went to weaving freshly cut jasmine through her mistress's golden hair. Miss Burney suddenly got an eyeful of her boy all covered in chicken shit. Seeing us playing together put her in an awful state. Numb with fear, I wondered if I ought to run and hide in the fields. Could she reach that far? Nobody ever seen her past the veranda 'cept in her rose garden.

Jackson, his white shorts covered in chicken shit, never looked up when his ma stormed off the veranda like she was gonna wring his neck. But then the words she hurled were really meant for me. She aimed herself at me like a tornado and stomped down them steps as hard as her delicate feet were able, only to freeze when she realized she'd soiled her shoes in all that chicken shit we'd scooped up. She looked at me as if I was filthier than her slippers, and stomped over to Jackson. He didn't seem to care 'bout Miss Burney's fit coming on. Still, I knew the way that woman was hissing that she was gonna backhand me for being in her garden with her child. Nobody had to tell me what was in her head. Coloreds cultivate a keen intuition on these matters.

"What are you doin', Jackson Burney, playin' down with that nigger girl?"

Jackson was squatting close to the nest ignoring her such as he always did. But then wasn't it quite apparent he was laying an egg? Jackson was quick to change tack when he was in trouble.

"Momma! Why you got flowers growin' out 'a your head like that?"

A wiry sprig of jasmine had loosened and bounced about her neck gone red from rage.

"You know very well Ella arranges these flowers for your daddy."

"Chicken shit is what makes roses grow, don't it? We want flowers growin' out 'a our heads, too, don't we Sarah?"

"What? Why you little… You're in big trouble now, mister!" she hollered unconvincingly.

Miss Burney yelled for Ella like the bed bugs was eating her alive and clutched her long skirt up off the soil. "Ella! Get down here!"

Jackson paid her no mind. As he squatted there waiting for the egg to drop, he took a handful of chicken shit and dumped it on his momma's white kidskin shoes. Then he went to grunting like we'd heard ol' Isaac do in the outhouse behind his shack. I ain't never heard no hen grunt when she was laying. Well, I wasn't gonna stand and run, not within smacking distance of that woman. Thought to hug the ground till the storm passed. But Lord he wasn't finished!

"Daddy say there's a nigger problem, Momma. Them niggers gots too many new dresses, and they's gone to hiding 'em in the attic so Daddy can't get into 'em. Bet he's gonna get ol' Isaac to go up there and clean up that mess, ain't he Momma?"

I never looked up at that woman so she couldn't see me. But then out 'a one half-closed eye I squinted a tiny peek. Miss Burney's face, that never been in the sun, had turned scarlet. It left me wondering if white folks catch on fire when they get worked up real bad.

"That's what I said, Jackson! You're down here all filthy from playing with one of our niggers again!"

Jackson put his dirty hands on his waist and, mimicking his momma's spun-sugar voice, echoed her. "Ain't it what I been sayin' first, Momma! Don't you ever listen none?"

"Well, actin' like that aren't you your daddy's little Burney through and through? Yes, you are!" She looked towards the veranda doors for Ella to finally appear. "Ella, if I call you one more time!" she squealed like a tethered piglet.

About then Jackson dumped his whole pail of fresh chicken shit on Miss Burney's shoes and then did one better by polishing them with it. I just hoped when the blood squirted out of her eyes it wouldn't get on me none, 'cause I could hear Ella's feet come thumping down the stairs of the mansion as ol' Isaac, hearing Miss Burney's commotion, came running from the orchard to protect the mistress with his pruning shears. But done no good. She already gots her shoes ruined, and her child was down in the rose garden making chicken-shit nests, playing with somebody not even 'pose' to be past the lawn of the big house, let alone in the mistress's presence. Ella was in trouble! The only thing left for Miss Burney to do was to kick the loose chicken shit off her shoes and onto me, where I 'magine she intended.

"Jackson Burney! You awful little monster!" Melinda squealed in defeat.

"Now you're a big nigger Momma!" he let out.

Oh, Lord, what could come out 'a that child's mouth? Guess Miss Burney got him thinking having dirty clothes was near to being a 'cropper. She gave one nasty look at Ella who stood moping her brow with her dish rag and stormed back into her white palace where things would always stand down to her temper. And Isaac, he could only stand there sweating fear till the ground at his feet stank.

"Isaac! After you scrub up my horsey, you best get Momma up on 'im and scrub 'er down, too. 'Cause she smells like chicken shit, don't she?"

Yes, the prince had directed Burney's speechless overseer to bathe his ma. But Jackson didn't scare Ella none. She slapped her hands together, signaling Jackson was getting smacked the same, and swept him up, swatting his hinny good as she did. Jackson wailed like bloody murder had caught up with him, but it was just an act, 'cause he turned and grinned as he was being hauled in, leaving Issac there mopping his brow in relief. That man was so relieved, he didn't scat me out of the garden, and wandered back to his pruning mopping his brow. Jackson's diversionary tantrums had again saved me from a slap.

I sat there shivering, praying that Jackson wouldn't be lynched come nightfall when nobody was looking. See, back then I thought people got in trouble for being bad. Didn't know people were lynched just for being colored. Of course, Jackson wasn't lynched. Pretty much everyone wanted to buy peace with this six year old who so easily defied the rules we all lived under. Didn't mean he wasn't severely disciplined, though. According to Ella, Jackson was put in a shiny white tub filled with white suds, a supreme torture for him, then shuffled off to spend the evening in bed. There he'd secretly work on teaching Ella the alphabet, them both eating the hard candy Jackson had stolen from the big jar on his daddy's desk. It was the form of punishment they both loved to inflict on each other.

Once again I'd learned that there are different kinds of justice in this life and different ways to get some for yourself. I would carry these lessons and memories of my friend with me forever.

STONE SLEEP

3

THE MOONLIGHT THAT cooled the big house on those summer nights seemed to cool nothing down at the shacks. Still, enough found its way through our only window to lighten the deep shadows on my folks' weary faces. Through the dim light I saw that anguished look, the look of their tortured sleep—the sleep the utterly exhausted are driven to. Never serene faces lost in slumber; just hard like stone. No, sleep was never a release from our reality, 'cause even in slumber the white shadows throbbed at our bodies always for more. Then, seemingly moments later, the sun seeped through the cracks in the boards that made up the door to our place, a shack not fit for chickens. Strange how white folks claimed we were luckier than the chickens. Maybe because we had a fireplace, but come winter there'd be little wood for a morning fire, and surely never enough to warm away our stone sleep.

Every morning I woke to the smell of cow manure that filtered in—fresh steaming manure deposited by the ol' cow that tended to wander up through the shacks come dawn. Yes, the door was shut, but never locked. We were denied locks because the shack didn't belong to us, even though we'd paid for it many generations over. Nothing at Grandview belonged to us but the misery. We could have our fill of that, and always come by more if it ran out. But, Lord, it never did.

Our days started in deep darkness when Daddy got to smelling that cow too. If he didn't, he'd soon feel Momma's elbow.

"Get up, Owen. Alex, mornin' time."

Daddy struggled to get his breeches on; his boot somehow got on first in the darkness his eyes had first opened to. Or did that really happen in the sheer fatigue that devoured him that night and he never got them off? How many times did my folks collapse from exhaustion only to fall asleep half-dressed? Folks learned young that sharecropping meant one thing: after sharing with the plantation class, there'd be little left for us. Not even the rest we'd earned from our labors.

Alex slept near the fireplace on planks elevated by wood crates. Seemed like Brother had a hard time believing it was truly morning. It was it too easy for his body to deny the truth. Time fits differently after wearing it on your back thirteen hours in the sweltering heat of them cotton fields, where the white shadows stalked everyone but shade was nowhere to be found. Hard-worked muscles beg for more rest even if none is gonna come your way. It was easy for Brother's young body to deceive him. Still, he'd try to swindle a few more moments of slumber out of the waking hour. Was it restitution to make up for the abuse the fields had imposed the day before? Maybe just enough that his wronged body wouldn't ache so when the fields laid another day's labor on his tortured young back. The pains slashed through our calendars that nobody was ever gonna see, and then our days were no more than watching ourselves grow old before your time. Who asks a mule if they've worked too hard that day? Need more rest mule? Never would we hear that tendered. No, not ever. Folks had to somehow survive the day if only to see another. Got to be easier by keeping our thoughts contained and never letting them venture beyond the fields transported by those dreams of a better life. But was there really a place where rest was granted as easily as the

Lord's absolution? The dreamless realities we lived under were ever constant. The tale we kept telling ourselves was that if we could only see our way to a far-off place, maybe to that Promised Land, things were gonna be better. That's what Momma always prayed: "Lord, deliver us from 'em!" This daughter of slaves discovered mighty young that the dreams of 'croppers are like rotting meat. They only turn blacker as the days passed us by, taking our hopes along with the yesterdays. Our lives in their white shadows smelled no better.

Momma's first words in the morning seemed to push out like she'd slept with a throat filled of cotton fiber. "Owen, get me my apron, I tell you…"

Had she really said that, or were the words leftover from some past morning? For the chronically weary, mornings can easily blur into all the days before. You see, we all knew that ol' Isaac would soon be coming to drive the 'croppers to the fields. To this day I still hear that snarling nigger dog screeching.

"Up, up, you damned worthless…. Anyone not ready for workin' loses a month's food credit!" His garbled words spewed as easily from his half-drunken mouth as whiskey poured down a throat.

Daddy might be hopping 'round the shack when Isaac was coming, his boots still not cooperating enough to let him pull his pants up over them while he struggled to reach the window and untie the apron that made as a curtain—the apron that would serve as my daylong companion. Momma would tie one of them apron strings to my wrist and the other to the bedstead, all the while reciting Bible verses in the dialect of the half-asleep.

"The Lord is my Shepherd, I shall not want…"

If Jesus was listening could He hear our supplications through my wailing?

Alex pulled a dried apple out of the old burlap bag that kept off fruit flies and handed it to me—well, at least dropped it into my lap, him not having time to wait for me to clutch it. No, ol' Isaac would soon be there pounding on the boards of our cracked door just as he pounded on our splintered lives. What good were my sobs of terror? I was a colored baby, a nobody more trouble-some than the farm animals, according to ol' Isaac's scriptures. While Momma's verses promised that the nobodies were somehow gonna be the somebodies in the Lord's Orchard if only we could cross over to where His bounty waited. But it always seemed to be Isaac's verses that ruled our days and then laid siege to those nights of stone sleep. One of Isaac's gospels was that 'croppers worked better in the fields with no kids to fret over, as young'ens couldn't be sold for profit ever since that Lincoln made a mess of things. You see, the time wasted on babies came right out of labor that could be better spent tending Burney's interests. No, that wouldn't do. If you wanted to get in good with the overseer to get a bit more credit to stave off starvation in a bad year, you'd do best to abandon your baby girl late one night along the river's edge so nature would take its course and sweep her under the muddy currents. It was a horror forced on many up and down that river. Let me tell you sometime 'bout the momma who carried her baby down to river's edge, thinking she could keep the rest of her chil'ren if she'd only surrendered that child, and then returned the next morning to weep but found her baby still there smiling. The currents of life can quickly change. Do you look into your child's eyes for another tearful farewell and then walk off again? Never underestimate the power of hunger when it's beating on your kids' bellies as they sit looking into an empty bowl.

As a baby, I spent the day alone in the shack tied to a bedpost. You ask if it was bad for me. Well, maybe 'croppers' kids don't feel time pass in the stale silence of our shacks. Still, you know it was bad for my folks. Like most 'croppers whose kids were born in this new kind of slavery, they knew they could return at night and find their child tied to the bedstead all but dead. Wading through the cotton all day wondering on what you might find back at your shack could bring you to your knees faster than the heat and humidity of them fields. As a 'cropper you prayed hard that this wouldn't be the day your rickety door came open and a pack of those feral dogs living at the edge of the shacks wandered in for a kill. You knew ol' Isaac's drift when he heard your squalling kid and reminded you which path led to the river. Didn't we all know Isaac fed them dogs to keep them around and drive his point harder? The nigger dog that fed the dogs was that man.

Momma's dark skin was still so very hot when she returned late with Daddy, him nearly holding up Alex by then. Her mahogany face had turned red-brown like only a day of Southern sun, dirt, sweat and hunger can render. The first thing she did was free me from the apron and hold me with tears streaming down the channels of her dusty face. We'd survived another day. But could we survive the night? Some nights were longer than others. Longer than most babies' lives. How many times did Momma return sick and puke all evening while Daddy held her head? He'd fix his arm 'round her stomach so's it wouldn't come out when she retched out the heat of the day that had thickened in her gut.

"Is Momma gonna die?"

"Alex, go fetch some water," he mumbled in reply.

Owen shook his head as he glanced about. His own exhaustion had pounded on his back and numbed his words into blurs that still remain crystal clear in the tissues of my memories.

"Momma sick?" I asked.

Motionless, she sat there as though she was waiting for something to come up. But what do you puke when you don't got nothing in your belly but dust?

Owen would ease her from the basin, where he'd tried to clean her up, and over to the bed. There she sprawled motionless and stared at the timbers above. What was she looking for? Blinking the dust away, yet still seeing nothing. Didn't she see me then? Can't she hear me crying for her? I can't count the tears because they're still rolling down my cheeks. We learned young that even our loudest cries only crash into the silence of our exhaustion.

"Ain't no cryin' gonna help yer ma, Sarah, so stop fussin'." Daddy's voice was quiet-like. "Go help your brother fetch water from the well. Go on now."

I still see him going about, picking up this or that only to set it aside with the other hand, all the while looking strangely lost in our one-room shack.

I followed Alex, wondering if white folks in the cool white world throw up when they're exhausted. Maybe they never get that way. Is that 'cause they got us? So they don't have to throw up when the heat and dust is thick in their gut? But who'd ever seen white folks out there in the fields? I never understood why misery was such a part of our lives. Lord, didn't that misery shadow Owen's life to the bitter end? And yet never once was he so miserable that he seemed to smell the puke as he held Momma's heaving head. No, he couldn't, because she was his wife and the mother of his children.

But I still do.

❦

Isaac's shack was at the bottom of Orchard Hill, which he was entrusted to keep us away from when the peaches were ripe or he'd soon find himself walking backwards down the road that lead to nowhere. Ella told Momma that Burney told Isaac to tear down the hog's house and build a new one for them fine hogs he'd just brought in, and then said for Isaac to take the scraps from the old one and build himself a shack. The message was clear enough: Isaac was no account to Burney and could be replaced as easy as building a hog pen. Well, Isaac's place was nothing but a pile of splintered wood, but it had a tin roof that probably didn't leak much unless it rained. Folks at the shacks said under that tin was where ol' Isaac hid from his nightmares. Momma was sure he was the first born of Satan himself. Said she knew 'cause he smelled like he had to be. I knew how bad ol' Isaac smelled and that made me think twice about taking any path that might lead me to hell.

You see, Isaac had the same pale blue eyes as Burney, and that silvery hair that made him metallic looking. Metallic, like that broken mirror that ol' Clara found tossed away with the scraps of the big house. Clara told us that the devil must 'a lost that very mirror and he'd steal your soul away if you looked at yourself in it and then flipped it upside down. There you'd see Satan grinning back. "Devil gots your soul for sure," she claimed. Isaac walked hunched under the weight of the hatred that fueled him. He walked stooped like he was hauling the devil himself on his back. Momma got me to think that all blue-eyed folks were the progeny of some devil. She didn't know any better. I still believed it till years later when Sally, with her kind blue eyes, saved me from more than a few devils and many a hell not printed on any map.

Sometimes I heard Momma shake Daddy Owen awake in the middle of the night if she thought she'd heard ol' Isaac on the prowl between the shacks. Was he on the run from the demons that chased him? For that ol' man it all got lost somewhere between those bottles stacked behind his shack. So many he'd drained trying to reconcile his hatred for my people and his need to find pleasure with one of us, one who had to give it up, give Isaac his pleasure as payment to keep her children from starving. You see, ol' Isaac was more than a drunk, he was as rabid with hatred as any nigger dog. That's all he was to the plantation class, a dog to be beaten into biting; tearing the flesh off the coloreds for bigger profits. Some said Isaac's hatred induced him to take his pleasure while her man was forced to watch the quick copulation. It was a way to rape the body, mind, and soul—the desecrated trinity of the slave-owning classes. Colored folks knew what starvation was, and that if you got thrown off a plantation, you'd be branded a vagrant—the sentence for which was yet another slavery, the chain-gang. Think your life's in the lurch? You were good as dead when they came with the manacles. Then it didn't matter no more, nothing did, even if you thought it once had.

One summer evening when I stumbled back home from

playing too late with Jackson and cut through passing by hog's house, Momma yanked my arm and yelled.

"Never, ever, are you hearin' me chil'e, go near ol' Isaac's shack!"

"But, why, Momma?"

"'Cause he works for the devil!"

"He don't work for Mas'er Burney?" I asked.

"Like I say, he work for the devil!"

"Stay vigilant," womenfolk in the shacks said under their breath. Late nights I could hear their murmuring as they sat on the porch mending the rags we wore; them looking out while the men were down at the river catching something to put on the table. You could drift into sleep when your man was gone and fall victim to ol' Isaac. His lust could drag you between the shacks where his nightmare awaited. Lord, let me tell you, vigilance is a crushing weight when piled on all the others.

One morning, when I was a child of just five summers, my daddy and Alex slipped outside to wait for ol' Isaac, but Momma had slipped down a different path that her exhaustion had dragged her to. She landed on that stool where she sank over the table asleep. Hers had been another long night of heat sickness but them things don't matter none to Isaac. Only thing that did was getting the cotton in before prices fell and he'd for sure lose his hog's house.

"Minerva, get on out here! Isaac's comin'," my daddy pleaded as Isaac's glare settled at Owen's doorstep looking to scorch his pride.

By the time Momma roused and got out the door ol' Isaac was standing there. No, he didn't work for the devil; Isaac was the devil. He glared with hatred at the sight of a colored woman who didn't tremble in fear of him. His was more than hatred of 'croppers who worked for him or had to bend over for him. He surely hated himself for not being part of the plantation class he serviced on his knees. Only one more hired hand the camellia class used up like the rest of their livestock. Yet Isaac had a special hatred for Minerva, a tiny woman who looked at him with the silent courage that only a man taking on a she-lion with cubs could know. In the back of his whiskey-drenched mind, he knew that Minerva Breedlove was the only 'cropper on Burney lands who would have the guts to show up at his shack in the middle of the night to cut his throat and then sit on his bed grinning as his last breath gurgled away. Momma had more guts than most men 'cause she believed the Lord was behind her. Or maybe it was 'cause she knew Isaac's secret., that he took to girl-chil'es, and that gave her the strength of a she-lion.

"Here I am!" She glared like she towered over him as her contempt cut him down.

"That so?" Isaac demanded and licked his lips. "Thought you'd sleep in again, huh?" he growled. "You not 'memberin' or is it a case of you not appreciating Master Burney's generosity lettin' you'uns stay on after the war?"

Minerva's steady demeanor crazed Isaac. Yes, he knew she wasn't afraid of him, and that the other 'croppers were witness to it.

"I'll tell you one last time—we still keep the laws of the South!" he barked. "You caught with no work, you a vagrant. We all know that. You a vagrant, you go to jail like that!" Starring at Minerva, Isaac snapped his fingers. But it was in Owen's face he did it.

"That's what them jails is for, ain't it? Then what 'bout you kids? Huh? You in jail, they get taken who knows where? Yeah? Who gonna get 'em then? There ain't gonna be no vagrants at Grandview. Owen, you'd best make sure this woman sees to cooperating with me. We gonna have it Isaac's way, me and your woman. Ain't we now?"

Looking proud, Isaac chuckled as if he'd just served an uppity nigger her just deserts. But it was a false grin. Still, Minerva wasn't gonna let it be. Not while the other women looked on. She nodded at my daddy, loosened her jaw like she was gonna lash Isaac with her tongue, and hurled spit at that ol' man's back. Yes, she did, too.

Isaac paused, but then pretended he never knew spit was dripping down his vest. No, he didn't want to turn back for more. His nights wandering hell were already too long for him to stay awake fearing a visit from a nigger woman in rage. So, he moved on with that plaster grin of his. Owen held his hand over Minerva's mouth so her words wouldn't chase after him. Isaac surely thought he'd wait for the right time to retaliate—for that sweet moment when Minerva would be vulnerable enough to give it up peacefully, if only to see another day with her family.

But my daddy, he saw things different, and like most men of the shacks feared what Isaac could do to his family. What does it take out of a man to suffer motionlessly while his wife is browbeaten, and his boy stands there drenched by the shame of it? He so well knew what Isaac had been preaching was true; if you were suspected of being without work, you were put on a chain-gang along the county roads. It was a fact to the camellia class; if you strayed from the plantation you were born to, you were inciting trouble. It 'a be like burning a Confederate flag in their faces! There'd be no putting a foot down on the road to your dreams in the new South. Slavery wasn't over; it had just found a new label, licked and pasted over the sins of the plantation class. One I reckon would be more palatable to the good Christians in the North. Lincoln had been dead two or three years before I was born and couldn't vouch for what he'd meant in that Emancipation Proclamation that had caused such a furor among plantation folk. Clarification for these issues would preoccupy generations in the South. Meanwhile, best take any work a white man offered and tell him he was mighty Christian, whatever the pay, if there was any. Yet at our shack, the vagrancy laws gave ol' Isaac no power over Momma, 'cause before she'd be branded a vagrant and lose her kids, ol' Isaac would be gurgling blood under her nose. He knew it. Minerva's eyes told him so, and his every nightmare surely reminded him that come one day, Momma would surely be paying a visit to hog's house. And ain't that what happened?

After the moon had long slipped from sight and the sharecroppers
had gone to the field, Jackson's momma would descend through all
the misty clouds of her white palace and drift down the grand stairs.
Her pastel dressing gown looked to float from one step to the next.
Melinda was a beautiful woman with pale brown eyes and honey-
blonde hair like Jackson's. But her beauty was only a thin veneer and
could wither as fast as the gardenias plucked to float in bowls next to
her breakfast turned acid brown. In utter silence, without so much as
a rustle of her dressing gown, Melinda would enter Jackson's nursery
brushing her long hair. It was the only thing Ella remembered seeing
her do for herself. Like a hunter, Ella said, she came down to the
nursery looking for a kill. There, summer and winter, Ella slept
nights on a rag rug at the foot of Jackson's bed. Do you know how
it feels to awaken having slept on a cold floor with your arm twisted
up for a pillow? Well, didn't we all know what stone sleep was? By
stealth, Melinda entered, intent on catching Ella asleep. When she
did, she'd deliver a kick to Ella's head to fix that problem clean. Yes,
it was a cold hard floor, and a colder kick that started too many of
Ella's days back then. Don't matter none if Ella was up all night with
colicky Jackson. Nobody asked why Ella had them bruises. They only
asked why we didn't have a smattering of black marks to demonstrate
we were at heel. Life let up on you when nobody looking? So, then
what was Isaac doing with his time? Somebody's had gots to pay, and
that somebody was always dark-skinned in those white shadows we
carried on our backs.

"Ella! Are you sleepin' again when my son's awake? I'm thinkin'
I best carry a switch with me all the time! You know how that makes
me feel?"

Melinda's voice was not like spun sugar when she spoke to Ella.
No, it was sharp enough to cut blood.

"No, ma'am. Nobody ought not to put a switch to ya so's ya
knows how it feels," Ella said, distancing herself from another jab

of Melinda's pointed slippers. "Jackson kept me up with the colic. Couldn't get no sleep."

"You think you're here to sleep? Is that what? One more time and you'll be out in them fields again. A day with the sun and mosquitas and you'll see what a blessin' you got in my house!"

"Yes, ma'am. I start tomorrow countin' the blessin's when I see 'em," Ella said.

Well, Ella knew how to speak between the words, because Jackson had taught her how to talk back. And so much more.

Melinda Burney was young and inexperienced at keeping her household. A white house in plantation country had to be kept like everything else, in a thick tradition much of which was unspoken secrets—much like she kept herself a secret from the real world beyond her rose garden and from that other world down by the river where I lived. The house slaves were not white, but they were considered blessed by the blessed class to live in those cooler shadows of the white house, because it was a bit closer to the scraps they were tossed. Like Jackson, Ella bridged the world between the big house and the 'cropper's shacks. It was a jagged contradiction that bridled Miss Burney till the day she died. There came a day when Ella told me about what she done to ol' Miss Burney.

Truly, Melinda seemed only as real as the clouds that filtered through the many rooms of her mansion, wafting the fragrance of night blooming jasmine as easily as the field dust swallowed our shack and penetrated deeper into our lives than any fragrance from the Burneys' gardens. Real women get hot. But the rules of Melinda's world required the coolness of a Southern white woman. The maintenance of the appearance that life was effortless, even seamless. It was complicated balancing the contradictions, trying to look fresh and soft like the petal of a magnolia and smelling like jasmine cleansed by a summer rain. Yes, looking luscious enough to want to fornicate with, but too innocent to really know about all that not-white-woman stuff. Only farm animals and coloreds had unbridled passion—despite the bridles that yanked at our lives.

You see, Melinda's world was more complicated than Minerva's. Momma's life was bound by only two passions: making sure her children didn't starve, and that her man didn't get taken off in the dead of night to be lynched. Dealing with few concerns, day in and day out your entire life, makes things simple, don't it? Because that is your life. There ain't nothing more to be looking for when you're a 'cropper. Your best jab at hope is only day-to-day survival. The thought of jasmine woven through her hair surely never entered Momma's thoughts. But for Melinda Burney, deciding which three or four dresses she would wear on a particular day could be confounding enough to send her to bed with head throbs. Ella told Momma that sometimes she stayed up till dawn ironing Miss Burney's pastel linen dresses before she was able to fall on that rag rug at the end of Jackson's bed for a few moments of sleep. I wondered if Ella ever slept long enough to work up a dream that one day she'd have her own bed. If she did, it had to be a black dream, the kind you rub out 'fore it strangles your thoughts leaving you feeling mean 'cause you know it ain't never gonna be for real. "Oh, Miss Burney, please sleep in a bit when the sun come up," was her mantra. But prayers of the dark-skinned could not be heard in the heavens. Perhaps the Lord had pale blue eyes and could never see us to know who was calling. But then perhaps we were turning to stone from sleeping too rough on the hard realities of our lives.

ORCHARD NIGHT

4

WHEN I TURNED seven, I'd trail off from the fields and head back to the shacks, where I'd try to own a chore or two for Momma. Come dark, I'd be standing at the door impatiently watching for my folks to drag in. It was a mere pat on the head, nod, or touch of their eyes that greeted me.

Momma's words sounded dry, as though they were coated with the field dust she'd inhaled that day. "Sarah, you soak them beans like I tol' ya?"

Daddy sighed and looked about as if he saw nothing. Even young, his eyes were going bad. Said the glare of the sun had put a haze over them. Was there enough wood at hand to cook a pot of beans, he asked? Like so many other nights, his question went unanswered, as simple utterances were lost in our shuffling about. It had been another day that had fallen under the weight of the shadows, where it crumbled under our exhaustion. If we somehow got to it, the next day would bring only more of the same. Yet a small portion of that night awaited and would deliver sweet morsels of the Lord's bounty.

"Yeah, Momma. Picked ever' bit of rock out of them beans like you tol' me."

"Alex, go find some wood and get the fire goin'. Your daddy is tired sick tonight."

Her words had barely escaped her chapped lips before she collapsed against her intentions. She could only fall over their moss-stuffed bed motionless, her legs dangling over the edge stiff and frozen-like. My daddy reached for her worn shoes to ease them off without paining those swollen ankles and raw toes. He poured out jagged rocks the size of peas and cursed every one. The voice that came out quiet most times wasn't gentle that night. But I knew it was only anger that his wife ached so and he was helpless to gather the drops of salty blood that burned between her raw toes.

"Why you in such a hurry, woman? We ain't gonna be hungrier if you rest a bit."

Holding on to Owen, Momma struggled to her feet despite the weight her eyelids had taken on.

"Tonight…" her words stumbled. "Tonight…me and Sarah… We's going up to Orchard Hill. Gonna make this family some peach jam for Preachin' Day. We gonna…"

Minerva could have just whispered halleluiahs so only the Lord could hear and still I'd know. It was orchard night, and the summer fruit was waiting.

Still, there were no halleluiahs coming from Owen. He looked at things differently and knew that Momma being in the Burney orchard could provoke Isaac. The thought of Burney's overseer at his wife's throat got him worked up. His voice strained lower, maybe as though Isaac might hear should he be stalking the night. "Minerva, you know what Isaac'll do if he catches you in his orchard 'gain." It was as though his words emanated from his flaring nostrils.

Momma's voice was not strained to a dust-ridden hush no more. No, it came from her depths, like she meant for Isaac to hear should he be prowling between the shacks. "And he knows what I do back at 'im!" she said. "Isaac done seen me cut up a hog with a butcher knife before it even knowed I been followin' it! Sarah, go pull some of that salted pork out. Just size yer fist, chil'e—no more."

Later, as I lay on my pallet, Momma's words put me back to the times when I heard the door creak open and saw a shadow of Momma slip out into the darkness. Still, she'd be back in her bed when I awoke. So, then had she really gone? Dreams can blur when they're layered over our exhaustion.

We were down at the river one day when Alex told me. He said late, when Momma's aches wouldn't let her be, she'd wander down to hog's house to pay Isaac back for prodding her family like mules that day. Through his broken window she'd glare at him till he looked up and saw a shattered glimpse of Minerva standing somewhere on the other side of his nightmare. Maybe one more swig and the apparition would leave him be. Brother said I was to never tell nobody. He'd promised Momma he'd not say something or else somebody might go put a word in Owen's ear. Well, I reckon the apparition of an abused 'cropper stalking his dreams gave ol' Isaac many sleepless nights. I heard Momma tell Ella that Isaac didn't deserve no peace even in his sleep; no merciful rest that would release him to the mind-numbing stupor he searched for at the end of a bottle. No, for our survival Momma had to be at his throat just to keep him off ours.

The summer of our last walk up Orchard Hill remains the most vivid of my childhood. I wasn't sure if it would happen, because as soon as I picked up my first spoonful of beans, Momma seemed to collide with her exhaustion all over again. Still later she stirred. I watched from my pallet till she stiffly pulled up from her bed. She looked to be waiting, too. Waiting for her thoughts to come alive again. When her head stopped weaving on her weary neck, she nodded and then gently touched my daddy's cheek to know if he was deep enough in his stone sleep that he wouldn't notice her pulling her old boots back on.

Used to be Alex came with us, but not that last time. Still, he heard us rustle about.

"I too tired, Momma," Alex moaned from his pallet and turned over to catch the tail of a dream that probably hadn't waited.

"Go back to sleep, Son. This be a time just for Sarah and me," Momma whispered and patted his dusty hair. "Like when you go with your pa and Samuel down to fish. Like that."

"Stay in the dream as long as you can," Momma's kiss to the back of his neck signaled. She was right, because a few moments of sleep was the only reprieve we had. I was glad Brother got to stay in bed. By then the ever longer days of cotton picking had started working his young body hard. His only compensation was nights that worked him all the harder to make up for the hours of abuse the fields put on his back.

In his half-sleep, Daddy heard Brother stir. "Isaac gonna cut the blood out 'a you, woman!" He turned over and his eyelids followed.

"Then I cut 'im's throat good! That's what!" she whispered. "Now don't be worryin' none. I gots to show my girl how to survive—survive a whole lot of Isaacs that 'a come her way one day!" she said. "Come Sunday this family's gonna have us some biscuits and jam from them ripe peaches the Lord saved from the pickers this morning."

The real moment began when Momma took down the apron that no longer tethered me to the bedstead, but now curtained our only window. It would carry our bounty from Orchard Hill. She gazed out the window up to the attic of the big house. Finally, Ella signaled she could see Isaac's candle had gone out at hog's house.

"We's goin' to the orchard now," Momma said like we were readying ourselves for the passage over Burney lands to the promised one. "We's goin'!"

On the way up the hill I could feel the soil clinging between my toes where Isaac been watering that morning. I reached for Momma's hand at the moment we were hidden under the canopy of the peach trees. Their branches arched up over us like angel wings that protected us from view of the big house. Momma smiled as she put her hand over my eyes and whispered for me to see where we were simply by inhaling the sweet smell of ripe peaches. Then she pulled one apart, held it to my nose. How I still love fruit fresh off the tree that holds on to the sun long after it lets go of the day. Those peaches were so ripe they 'bout melted in my hand. Momma squeezed one and told me to lick the peach sugar. I still see those moments, all caressed by her look of joy as we partook of this ritual, the sharing of the Lord's bounty. Come Preaching Day all of us down in the shacks would share that jam with hot buttermilk biscuits slathered in the fresh butter the neighbor made. This sacred place up on Orchard Hill may have belonged to the camellia class, but truly the moment belonged to us, and I would lay claim to it for the rest of my life.

Picking up them peaches as fast as I could, I asked Momma why her voice hushed even in the stillness of the night?

"Go on now and keep recitin' yer verses," she whispered.

But why whisper? Who but the Lord could hear?

I recited the verses Momma taught me as I gathered the peaches she was hitting to the ground with a stick.

"Though I walk through the shadows, Jesus will see me forever in His Orchard. Momma, what's forever?"

"Today, tomorrow and all the days come af'er."

"Will you be here, Momma?"

"Yes, chil'e, just like Jesus. Gonna be with ya deep in yer heart, I be there waitin' and listenin' for your call."

Then Momma swung 'round like the whisper of an angel had cautioned her Satan was on the prowl. She grabbed my hand and led me to the edge of the orchard. Up there at the big house Ella appeared on the veranda where she slowly waved a candle like a warning from the Underground Railroad. The angels tell 'er to do that? Or for Momma to be vigilant against the one who always stalked us?

Minerva tugged me back to where the apron held our peaches and grabbed up as many as her small arms could hold.

I broke the silence. "But why the verses?" I struggled to hold on to as many soft peaches as she.

"Yer life's gonna be a long journey. Only the Lord knows how far he wants ya to go or where he wants ya to end. Along the way these verses gonna protect ya from evil." Soft peaches rolled out of her apron as she dropped to her knees and took my hands into hers. "The verses and my dreams for a better day for my chil'ren is all I gots to give ya. Ain't my dreams so big nobody can steal 'em? Maybe that be the only thing they can't haul away with 'em."

"Why you cryin', Momma?"

"Why, I ain't chil'e! No need for it, 'cause we got the best dreams in the world. No matter what comes at ya in life, folk's gots the freedom to dream on anything they can set their mind on. So, you gots to set it big."

"Where I get a dream then?" I asked.

"I tell ya what I knows. What my own mammy tol' me. Sometimes ya got to run and catch yourself a dream even if the currents is pullin' you under. 'Cause maybe they's all gonna float away. Them dreams will. Maybe like when you try to catch a fish in the stream with your bare hands. You gots to run hard and fast all your days to catch up with a dream. Then when you catched a big bunch you bundle 'em up to make 'em bigger. As many dreams as you can. Big as a bridge to get yourself to the better side. Sometimes, now hear me chil'e, the other side is the place they don't want folks like us, 'cause that's the good side and they's savin' it for their own. So, you got to be keepin' plenty of dreams bundled up tightly in yer soul."

"What's a soul, Momma?"

"Ain't it a place to hide your dreams from the white folks?"

The spell was shattered with Isaac's cursing. Likely he'd crawled out of a nightmare and awakened to a room with only an empty bottle staring back.

Momma looked up and saw Ella on the veranda, where she snuffed the candle out. That was her signal there was a reward on our throats. She knew the Burney overseer was sure determined to collect on it. She held her hands over her mouth so fearful was she that a yelp would escape and set the nigger dog to barking. Wasn't it true that howling dogs always heralded white Satan's entrance into the halls of our lives?

"I's dreamin', too, 'bout havin' an orchard so's we can make jam ever'day." I struggled to hold my skirt filled with peaches. "Momma, how come we only pick fruit at night?"

"I told ya. 'Cause it's better for us. The Lord protects us at night. And 'the Lord is my Shepherd…'"

"Where's Jesus waitin', Momma?"

"In the Lord's Orchard…"

Yes, I truly knew it was His bounty we were hauling down the slope, even if the price tag was stamped 'Burney'.

"He keeps me out 'a troubles and out 'a shadows, don't He Momma?"

About then Isaac stumbled over his rage. We could hear the nigger dog yapping.

Momma took us deeper into the darkness yet through his drunken agony, Isaac could still decipher our scrambled movements. It must have stirred his ugly imaginings as we could count on Isaac's rabid hatred to vanquish his inebriation long enough to put him stable on the path that could lead him to inflict the horror of his severed soul on to ours…if he caught us.

"Minerva! I know it's you up there in my orchard 'gain. Huh? Now ain't it you up there?"

Momma tugged me to the shacks down the slope the other way.

"Come, yer daddy's waitin'!"

Daddy might be there for us, but if Jesus had been waiting in the Lord's Orchard, I was sure ol' Isaac had surely scared Him off. Well, Momma told me the devil is ugly, mighty ugly; would scare anybody off. She knew I would face him disguised in many forms along the journey ahead. Some forms filled with running blood gone toxic with hatred and then, too, some devils as empty as a stack of whiskey bottles in an alley waiting to be shattered over my hopes and dreams. I would find that getting through those broken shards would let blood over and over again. But then didn't we all bleed in torrents looking for the bridge to that better life?

From the sounds of Isaac's boots crushing the twigs he'd pruned that morning I knew this nigger dog was as near as his rage.

"I finally caught you, woman!" he yelled. "Now what are you gonna give ol' Isaac to keep your shack?" His voice crackled and hissed like it was from the very depths of the sputtering hell he would pull us down to; down for his lusts to gorge on.

Momma grabbed my arm and dragged me down a path of weeds that scratched my legs and stuck to my thin dress. She looked behind for the nigger dog. I could hear his boots pound the hard dirt like he pounded on our door. Nearly there, a peach dropped from Momma's heavy apron. But as I pulled back to grab it, she yanked my arm and hauled me into the shack. That very door we'd fled behind had but one defense to the outside world and Momma went for it. She kept Granny's big scissors hidden under the bed.

"Now get to bed! Don't make a noise no matter what ya hear out there," she commanded. Her glance pierced my thoughts more than the severity of her whisper. "And don't get your pa up for nothin'!"

I retreated under my blanket where my thoughts quickly fogged over from fear. What do I do now? Why for? Don't know. Don't even know if Jesus can hear my fears.

Momma rustled about and then slipped out into the darkness. I crawled up on the table to peek out the naked window, but Minerva had disappeared into the shadows between the shacks. Up on the steps of the veranda I saw Ella wringing her hands in prayer. Our glances swam back and forth, hers enormous with fear. "Oh, Lord, no! They's gonna lynch ever' one of us now!" Ella's eyes seemed to yell.

But I wouldn't let her see mine and covered them with my hands. No, I'd keep my fears to myself, like Momma said. Still, I kept at the window and watched between my shaking fingers. I knew I would. If Momma fell from sight I would disobey and yell for my daddy.

And then there he was. Standing there licking his lips and growling in a dialect of obscenities that Satan had taught him good—words I did not know but felt the meaning of nonetheless. Momma came out of the gloaming to face down his intentions and then waited while this nigger dog sniffed at her shaking flesh and undid his breeches for the feast. She held Granny's rusty scissors open behind her like two jagged knives: one to stab, and the other to follow till the bloody deed was done.

"You been stealin' from the Burneys 'gain," Isaac slurred. "I caught ya this time!" His tongue was thick from whiskey. "You accustomed yourself to gettin' away with it, huh? Yeah, you been messin' with me a long time, ain't ya?" His lascivious toothless grin was followed by a wink and another lick of his lips with his brown tongue.

"I ain't stolen nothin'! It be our sweat that tends that orchard," she declared, her head raised high. "We got a right to some of the fruit."

Isaac's voice got hard so's to punctuate his slurs with the distinction of a man wielding a stick in a woman's face. "Woman, is you blind? Can't see the color of your own skin? Ain't it the color that say you don't got no rights? Now come out of them shadows so I can see you clear. Yeah, come over here and show ol' Isaac what you gonna give me to fix this between us. Come on now."

Minerva's hand trembled until her skirt fluttered at the tattered hem where the points of Granny's waiting scissors gnarled the broken threads. "No! You come get. That's what you been aimin' for, ain't ya? Now I's waitin' for ya, Satan!"

Isaac chuckled through his imaginings and headed for the gorging he'd so longed for.

But just as I turned for my daddy, Isaac stumbled and passed out at Momma's feet. This was the moment. Momma pulled out her rusty scissors to deliver her promise swift and hard. I would rely on the verses to clear the fog that came down on me like hot steaming gravy. The Lord is my Shepherd. He leadeth me to quiet pastures. But where are them quiet pastures, Lord? I knew not near the Burney orchard.

Momma took a pail of water from the mule trough and tossed it hard at Isaac's face, laughing at the nigger dog as she did. Then she did it again.

On the ground Isaac groaned and twisted his face in the mud till it oozed up his nose. When he came to, Momma was on him. Her open scissors jammed under his jawbone ready to penetrate that ol' brown tongue that had abused her family so many times. At his first flinch blood trickled down the scissors.

"Well, ain't it like I always tol' ya? Your big ol' mouth, it ain't got nothin' to say no more? You thinkin' you'd steal from me what you stole from my oldest girl Louvenia, huh? You fouled 'er and then you put her off with nothin'. You too drunk to 'member, but I ain't. I think on it ever'day."

With Isaac's every flinch, Minerva's scissors let out another bright red blotch of confession that trickled down his hoary throat.

"No! I don't know nothin' 'bout that! I never did nothin' to your girl that I 'member," he gurgled.

But the blood smeared over Minerva's hand said he'd lied again. Yes, he remembered every moment. Probably reused the memory again and again when he found himself with only an empty bottle as companion and relied on his past sins to pleasure himself.

"Maybe that's 'cause what you did to Louvenia ya thinkin' is nothin'. Is that yer meanin'? I told ya after what you did to my girl, if you ever messed with my family I'd cut yer throat, sit on top of yer stinkin' carcass and smile in yer face while ya choked on yer guts comin' up. Don't it look like I's smilin'?"

"Huh? No, no, it don't. She never meant nothin' to me. That's why I let her off the Burneys' like I did," he lied again.

Not wanting to see what was coming, I ran back to hide under my blanket. I was crying when Momma came in. She lit a candle and waved it back and forth at the window, indicating to Ella that Isaac's throat been slit, and then blew it out. I was so scared I shivered, wondering why being in the Lord's Orchard was so costly to my folks?

So ended another day for us in the flaming white shadows.

JESUS AT MY DOOR

5

DON'T KNOW IF I ever fell asleep that night so fearful was I of what awaited the next morning. Would Jesus be waiting at our door where Momma had surely dropped ol' Isaac's head?

The next morning did come, but was different from most: we all slept in. Well, I didn't, 'cause I always woke up first. I looked over to see Momma still in bed staring at the timbers above. There next to her Daddy's face had turned soft and serene like only hours of contented rest can bring the unaccustomed.

"We be gettin' up now," she said softly.

Daddy jolted up. He looked puzzled as the room was filled with light. You see, nobody ever slept till light filled the room 'cept on Preaching Day.

"It's Sunday?" he asked and rubbed his eyes from the light streaming through the window. "Huh?"

"No, it ain't. Knew you had to have some rest."

He jumped out of bed like they'd just put the roof ablaze and ran to the door to see if Isaac was coming. But only dead silence waited on the other side of our door. Not much more than rustling was heard inside during those long moments our glances crisscrossed.

How could I not wonder if my daddy had seen Isaac's head out there? Or maybe the Lord holding that head by the ears waiting for Minerva Breedlove to come talk to Him 'bout the happenings of the night before. Owen's hope waxed high.

"Isaac, he drunk? Never got up, huh? That what?"

"Maybe he still up at hog's house. Him on his knees up there!" Momma declared with the self-righteousness of one thinking themselves in good with the Lord from their deeds against the wicked.

"Yeah, I reckon that man still talking to Jesus."

"Huh? What's you talkin' 'bout?"

He looked away from Momma's air of proud silence to see what my eyes might reveal. Again, the chaos of our glances darted back and forth as I didn't know what the truth was. Still, I was certain certain ol' Isaac was burning in hell by then and could only wonder what that was like.

"Ever'thin's fine," she said. "I done made it so."

I pulled the blanket back up over my head, wondering what my daddy would say to Jesus waiting outside the door to hear why Momma cut that mean ol' man's head off. Well, Minerva could always defend herself. I could see she might step forward to acknowledge that cutting throats is a sin, but is it a sin to cut Satan's? What would Jesus say 'bout that, himself always fighting with the devil? I reckoned she'd best chat with ol' Clara to work out the best angle. Yes, my thoughts were going in circles and yet still heading nowhere, least of all out the door where I was sure Jesus was waiting!

"Sarah, come out from under that blanket," Momma hollered as the grits came to a boil. "We gots to go up to the big house while your daddy and brother eat. I got somethin' to tell Ella."

"What's you been at that you need to go up to the big house? You know they don't want us up there," Daddy asked, gulping his food so he could get to the fields.

Well, if I couldn't figure out what happened, and I was mostly watching out the window, then how could he? But I didn't have time to figure nothing, as we was gonna pay Ella a hush visit. I jumped up with feelings of self-importance as Momma and I had something going on even if I had no idea what. Daddy shook his head like he was flicking off a fly. Or maybe like he didn't understand no woman-talk and didn't aim to bother.

Momma pointed me towards the door. "Come on now, Sarah."

We left with me wondering if I'd have to step over ol' Isaac's head. If I did, would he wink at me? So I closed my eyes as I always did when Miss Burney stared at me in her rose garden. I still half figured that Isaac would look up at me like that hog Momma butchered once did. The one that stared at me for the longest time till I went screaming to Alex who been in on it with that hog 'cause he was carrying its tail in his pocket and he was the one told me to go stare at it till it winked. And when it did, I screamed till my daddy dragged Alex over by his ear, smacking him even though it was that hog that done winked at me.

No, I sure didn't want ol' Isaac, the man that lived at hog's house, to wink at me none!

Momma jerked my hands from my eyes as we headed up to the big house. "Why you got your hands over your eyes and you're stompin' on my feet?"

Did that mean she didn't see ol' Isaac wink at her none? Or did she just kick his ol' head aside when he did?

⁊

It had rained that night, so the path up to the big house was clean of the powdery dust that usually rolled over our feet on the way to the fields. Before Minerva could even knock Ella was at the door, aghast. Then she'd probably never opened it for 'croppers, 'cause none ever ventured up there before. I was antsy to hear from Momma why we were up there.

"Oh, Lord, no! You still here? They's gonna lynch us all now!" Ella whispered loud enough that Jackson stopped slurping his grits 'n' cream and came over to get in on things.

"Be still, woman," Momma commanded, pointing to the heavens like a plaster saint. Still, Ella looked a bit crazed and kept glancing about her kitchen like Miss Burney might sneak up on her.

"What's you doing up here? You knows Burney gonna see ya up on his veranda. You got to get yourselves down to the river quick. No, no! You take off, they knows you done it for sure! Ain't that right? Huh? Ain't it now?"

"Done what, Ella?" Jackson asked as he pulled her apron strings to tie on the doorknob like he told me he tied down them Indians the time they come to the door on the hunt for cookies.

"Isaac, he ain't dead yet, 'cause he gots no place to go what with no head!" Momma said to clarify the matter. But it hardly did.

All Ella could say was, "Huh?"

"I said, the debil, he wouldn't take him, and you know the Lord won't have 'im. Ain't that the truth? So, I reckon he best fall on a pair of scissors and cut himself good in the neck. Ain't that what happened? That what you're a thinkin', Sister Ella?" Momma dragged her finger across her neck to mark where Isaac got his throat cut and winked at Ella. "You know what I mean, don't ya now, Sister Ella?"

"Huh?" was all Ella could utter from her gaping mouth.

Only news of the Lord's Second Coming via Vicksburg could have impacted her more. She looked my way, but I had no idea who was coming and who was going, 'cept Isaac was sure to be stuck in the mud someplace I could only imagine.

All the same, we were still impressed with Minerva's bit of a sermon. As good as ol' Clara's preaching any Sunday. But not Jackson. He groaned from behind Ella's apron and rolled his eyes like a heathen who'd been hit upside the head by the preacher's words too early on a Sunday morning. Jackson went back to slurping his grits. That's because there's a language secret to us womenfolk and I was working hard to decipher it. I figured whatever was really going on I was on the righteous side of things and expected Ella would soon join in. After a long pause and penetrating gaze first at Momma, then at me, Ella did come 'round.

"He near dead down at hog's house? Huh? That what? You put them scissors to him's throat like we talked on that time?" She whispered so's Jackson couldn't hear over his slurping. That's the way heathens eat their grits, don't you know? At least that's what Ella said when she went over and smacked the back of his head.

Lordy, didn't we all have our chins high nodding with satisfaction like the preacher's wife every time the traveling preacher said Amen! We'd vanquished Satan's truest disciple, ol' Isaac himself. When were the angels coming to thank us?

Well, Momma went on whispering in the voice of divine sacredness she kept for Preaching Day down by the river, or maybe just 'cause she didn't want Jackson hearing, so he went slurping all the louder so's she'd speak up. He already forgot Ella's smack upside his head?

"Isaac, he on his knees prayin'," Momma announced.

But how'd she know what Isaac was doing down at the hog's house? Then I got to thinking, how'd he get his head back to his shack anyway? Seemed like most days he could barely see where he was going with it bobbing on his shoulders.

"Prayin', huh? Well, he best not pray to Jesus," Ella announced. "'Cause the Lord don't want to hear nothin' from 'im 'cause he's no good."

"Maybe Issac's prayin'. Him prayin', 'Thank you, Lord, for saving me from that Minerva!'" Momma declared, still nodding up and down. Dear Lord Jesus! Ella had gotten better stories from Jackson on how the cookie jar got emptied by them Indians.

"Amen, Lord, Amen!" Ella added, declaring her allegiance to our side of things.

Still acting like a heathen, Jackson knocked over his milk. It spilled over the table and onto the floor. Heathens drink out of their hands down at the river, Ella once told me. Then he jumped up hooting and hollering like he was gonna gallop off.

"Stonewall Jackson, save us all from Isaac gots no teeth! Huh, Ella?" he yelped.

Ella and Momma looked at him like they was 'bout to smack his face. First time I'd ever seen Jackson shut up without the usual prolonged discourse of which mouth was likely to shut down first. Surely that was a thing the South had never witnessed. Guess Ella figured if anybody was gonna save us from a lynching, it would hardly be some dead Confederate general Jackson was named after.

Still, Ella panicked when Momma pulled the big scissors out for her to hide.

"Now white folk gonna know you're figuring on killin' that ol' man 'cause them scissors. They's knows ever'thing we're thinkin'." Ella grabbed the scissors and remarked to Jackson: "You ain't never seen these here scissors of Minerva's, hear me, chil'e!"

"I still seen 'em, Ella. But near forgot if you give me a cookie!"

Ella lifted her hand like she did when she had smacked him minutes before.

I stood there thinking on Ella's notion 'bout white folk getting in our minds and all. If they be in our minds, how comes they ain't in our hearts? They certainly didn't spend much time in our empty bellies where there was always plenty of room for strangers. I started to get lost again in my thoughts when Momma's words tugged me back on the trail that she was prodding us on.

"White folks lying when they say they knows what we thinkin'," she said. "No, they never knows what's comin' from our folk. That's what protect us from the lash. They's afraid we might up and get 'em in the night. Right in they's own bed! Ain't that right? Now take these here scissors and hide 'em."

"Hide 'em where?" Ella asked, looking to see if Jackson was still plundering the cookie jar. He was stuffing cookies in our pockets; one for me and one for him, two for him, two for me.

"Hide 'em where the menfolk won't never look," Momma whispered.

"Where's that, Sister Minerva?"

Ella looked about her kitchen for the best place before smacking Jackson's hands off the cookie jar again.

"Under Miss Burney's pillow!" Momma said. "You think that woman's gonna let them men traipse through her things with they's dirty hands? Tell ya what, hide these under her pilla. I bet she thinks twice 'bout opening her big mouth at you when she sees how close you come to her throat with these here scissors!"

Guess Momma was right. The men would hardly be climbing through Miss Burney's bedchamber searching for a rusty pair of scissors that had met Isaac's throat. He'd for sure go howling that a colored woman from the shacks near killed him with them and ought to be strung up for it.

"I gots to go to the fields and pretend nothin' happened last night, 'cause ain't nothin' did. Did it, Sister Ella?"

Ella nodded to the whole mixed-up recipe Momma expected Ella and me to keep stirring. "No, I ain't seen nothin' or heard nothin' 'bout Isaac's head been near cut off like it ought 'a be! Amen, Lord!" Ella bit her lip to keep from laughing.

"That's the truth. Ain't it?"

Then she nodded to confirm that our tales were all consistent. Jackson only groaned. Don't know if it was because he didn't believe us 'bout cutting Isaac's head off, or because he was too busy stuffing cookies in his mouth with both hands before Ella could grab them away. Heathens eat with both fists; that's why they're heathens, Ella reminded Jackson. So, I quickly put one of my hands behind my back to keep from turning heathen, but then nearly swallowed a cookie whole.

That was the proudest day of my life. I walked back to the 'croppers' shacks holding Momma's hand. She held her chin up high like a preacher's wife leading us to the Promised Land.

 formlet

Daddy and Alex were long out in the fields by the time Momma and I got there. Seeing us come along, the 'croppers paused to gauge Isaac's disposition on somebody showing up late. They could remember all too well that before emancipation this brazen conduct would have been rewarded with a lashing. They wiped the salty sweat from their eyes at the sight like they'd just seen a vision.

Right away Momma went to rubbing a different kind of salt into Isaac's wounded ego. The rag he wore on his neck to cover his meeting with a certain pair of scissors was brown from dead blood. He wasn't up for no more. No, he sauntered over to the edge of the fields, pretending he never saw Minerva coming along like the Queen of Sheba herself.

The humidity in those fields along the river can near kill you, but you never paused your labors to take water while the overseer watched. To make sure desperate thirst didn't cut your time away from the rows of cotton the overseer kept a lid on the water till feeding time. Then we'd line up for a swallow or two from the same can everyone else struggled to get theirs from. On a good day, you could get enough good water down to eat that day-old cornbread they fed us; scraps from a table in a big white house. You see, pure water, like everything else it seemed, belonged to the white folk. Still, they told us we could have all the water we wanted, so long as it came from the swamps and not when the sun was up and working us; that time belonged to them. Fever could kill folks after one sip of swamp water, after two days and nights of the purest agony the fever generously provided. After that, you'd soon enough welcome hell if Jesus had yet to come for you. Best wait for the clean water when it was given out, 'cause hell had to be a bit worse than life in the overheated shadows of a plantation. Yet how many were left wondering?

Minerva walked up to the water barrel, took a pitchfork and knocked off the heavy lid and filled a big tin of water. She lifted it high to the sun like a sacrifice, drank from it slowly and then turned in a circle, gazing at the others over the top of that tin. First Alex wandered over to Momma. Looking agitated as hell, Isaac reluctantly followed. He was eager to subdue the confrontation Minerva had manipulated before the others caught her fever. Speechless as beasts of burden, the 'croppers gazed at each other and then slowly walked a *pavane* towards the barrel of clean water.

"Momma, can I have some water now?"

"Yes, Son. We can all have our fill, 'cause this here water, it don't belong to that ol' man. It belongs to the Lord."

Minerva filled the tin and handed it first to ol' Clara, who'd been working the fields since she was my age. Clara passed it to her son, Samuel, and he to Owen and on around.

Led by my daddy, Isaac found himself surrounded by sharecroppers who closed in 'round Minerva. They held their pitchforks and scythes like butchering tools. Fueled with Momma's courage, they glared at Isaac in a fashion nobody'd ever seen. His hand dabbed at that rag tied around his neck to see if he was bleeding again. He was, even if he wasn't.

"Why, Isaac, I'm thinkin' ya sleepwalked out 'a yer bad dream again. Or did ya just cut yer throat shavin' cause you been in a hurry fer Mas'er knows ya been drunk all night?"

Isaac never been talked down to by no colored woman. Sure not in front of colored men, some bigger than him. He glared at her and tightened his fists as his rage sucked in his toothless mouth.

Their message didn't come in so many words. It couldn't; them kind of words are frozen in the toxic fears that inhibit the thoughts you been keeping down. You see, these folks had never experienced talking to white folks direct-like, so tied up in fear were they. No, their message was sent from the tines of their pitchforks aimed at the empty cavity where Isaac's heart had never been. Were they thinking they'd stick them pitchforks in his gut, bind his carcass in corn stalks and let him disappear under the currents of that muddy river? No, there were too many angry souls lost in the Mississippi for that. Lynched, cut down with only their last gasps left for the kin to claim, and only then to be swallowed by the muddy waters of the Mississippi. That river was a sacred burial ground for so many of my people.

"Now you come by my place come Saturday," Minerva said standing tall, "'Cause that's the day we're butcherin'. I give you another close shave then. Yeah, you just might disappear in what they grind up. Ain't it so?"

Momma got up close to Isaac's face. He backed up against them pitchforks that helped him hear just as good as Minerva's scissors had the night before.

"Look here," she said. "I smilin' 'gain."

The 'croppers all grinned at him. In all their years at Grandview, they'd probably never looked Isaac in his face. Those grins surely brought his icy blood to a rolling boil.

"You get your damned water—then get back to your hoes 'fore Burney come by." Isaac's eyes pleaded for peace even as his nostrils flared with rage.

The sharecroppers took their time finishing off the water before they slowly drifted back to their task of nourishing the white shadows with their labors. The water we'd taken would still be squeezed back out of our pores before the sun settled the accounts.

Minerva's position in shacks had risen that day. There was now a peace between Isaac's oppression and the oppressed. It was a bitter peace, yet it helped lighten the load that let us crawl over to another day where a borrowed dream might be waiting.

SILENT CRIES, BROKEN WHISPERS

6

THE MORNING OF that last summer at Grandview was unlike any before. A stillness hovered over our shack that jarred my young thoughts from the moment my eyes opened. What was wrong? Why hadn't Daddy gotten up to head to the fields? Momma went about getting a pot of grits on like she was sleepwalking.

"Alex, you and Sarah go down by the river and pick your daddy some them wild grapes. That 'a make 'im feel better. Go on now."

"What's wrong with 'im, Momma?" Brother didn't seem to expect an answer.

Silently she shuffled about, shaking her head at nothing, till she finally pointed us to the door. That was always her signal she wanted us out of the way. There'd be no grits that morning.

I always loved to meander down to the riverbank with my brother where there'd be a thicket of wild muscadine grapes or berries waiting. I squatted for the low vines as Brother reached for the higher. I loved listening to his tales of when the river would one day carry him off on some adventure. At the water's edge I chattered on 'bout this or that. Alex barely grunted at my notions. Even so, we put a bit more grapes into the basket than our mouths. I remember asking how many basketfuls we could eat in a day. He said nothing and that silence spread like a ground hugging fog. You see, Alex had stopped picking and was gazing up the slope to where Samuel stood staring back. Why'd he come down to the river? He and Daddy only went fishing with Alex on Sunday and they never let me come.

"Alex, you and lil' Sarah come on back," Sam said. "Your ma be needin' you. Come on now."

Alex didn't move. It was as if he couldn't. Still, his eyes followed Samuel. Sam's boots snapped the vines that lay over the path as he headed back up.

"Why'd Samuel come? Daddy up there waitin'?"

Most times Alex would rather jab me with a pointy stick than hold my hand. Yet he said nothing as he gripped mine.

Up ahead Samuel turned to see if we were following. His expression never broke loose from the haunted look he'd come with. I looked up at my brother, but he only mirrored that fear. You see, nobody had ever come looking for us down by the river. Why would they? It wasn't near dark and the river wasn't swollen from the rains. Our eyes darted back and forth looking for the comfort that would not be found. In crashing moments, the reality of that morning would hit me like a belt across my tender face.

The door to our shack was wide open and 'croppers, most I knew, were staring in. What were they looking for? Their heavy silences were deeper than the one I awoke to. Jane, Samuel's wife, was working near where Momma fiddled with some old bent tins. She stared into their emptiness like she was hunting for something she'd lost. Jane worked at the fireplace and mumbled bits and pieces of her thoughts to Momma. I figured it was woman-talk as I didn't understand the half of it. Still, I searched their sorrowful glances for something their words hadn't revealed.

Momma dropped her tin cans yet did not reach for them. She

looked down at her feet like she'd simply lost them forever. Lost what, I wondered? Lost forever is a frightening feeling. I felt that fear as Momma's eyes strayed from mine, looking lost.

Jane finished filling a poultice with smelly bits of roots and herbs, which she dipped in vinegar and squeezed over the fire. Our shack quickly filled with ashy steam. She took the poultice over to my daddy and dabbed it on his forehead and looked to be telling him a secret. He flinched, but still only gazed at the timbers above as if he was searching for something he'd lost. Or was he merely trying to hold on to what he was losing?

I went to show Daddy our basket of wild grapes, but Jane shooed me back with one flip of her wrist.

"Back away, chil'e," she said.

With her finger pointing at my face she looked hard into my eyes to make sure I minded. At that I knew for sure there was trouble even before Momma gasped and put her hands to her mouth like something was about to fall out. I guessed she didn't want nobody to hear if the sadness in her eyes drained through her lips that couldn't close because of all those heavy sobs about to fall out. Again, Momma's hands cupped her mouth when she heard Jane telling Daddy a secret about Jesus and that it 'a soon be over. I guess Jesus heard her prayer, as on her last word my daddy's eyes stopped blinking forever.

I knew what had arrived at our door that day had brought the silent cries of one who has nothing and nowhere to hide from the void of it all. Who might save us? Who even would? Still Momma reached out.

"Sarah, go up to the big house. When ya get to the lawn, yell for Mas'er Burney to come."

Walking about the shack like she was in the wrong place, Mama's voice faded to whispers like somebody done wrung her throat.

My broken thoughts pounded to whispers in my head. Why'd I need to go up to Jackson's? What was I gonna tell Burney? I ain't never said a word to Jackson's daddy.

Jane wanted me gone, too. "Go on chil'e."

Momma's chin trembled when she noticed Alex sitting in the corner with his arms twisted about his head as though hiding his eyes could push it all away. What was it he so feared?

More alone than I could have realized, I sifted my silent cries, wondering why I needed to stop at the lawn up there at the big house? Did Momma forget that I'd long been past the lawn that moated it to play with Jackson? Or did she know I didn't really count—that to the white folks up there I was just as invisible as the fever that had visited my shack? Only a nobody; one of those who ain't 'posed to go that far into the shadows of the big house, I recalled Ella saying, unless the white folks are tossing scraps on Christian day. Yet I don't remember them tossing much of anything our way but misery. Still when I came close to the lawn for some inexplicable reason I stopped. There I yelled over the invisible barrier that now pricked at my fears. My feet felt strangely anchored on the dirt side even as my shadow loomed over the soft green lawn that ended steps from the white veranda; that certain boundary that I'd never seen before now held me back. So, I yelled over it.

"Mas'er Burney come quick! Hurry, come quick!"

I yelled for my daddy so Jesus would come and pull him back from Momma's sorrow and deliver us from the silence he'd fallen under. I yelled till I thought my throat might come out. It didn't, but Jackson did. Maybe Jesus could hear me then.

Jackson looked deep into my eyes as he teetered over the banister. I said no more, as the words wouldn't come. Jackson said nothing back, and ran to his door, yelling even harder than he'd ever yelled at ol' Isaac. He knew something was wrong, too. You see, there was no distance between Jackson and me.

"Daddy! Come out! Sarah's here!" Jackson yelled through the open door that was always closed to us.

What could I do to get Burney's attention? If my voice gave out like Momma's, would he hear my fears?

Still I knew, knew that only Jackson could get his daddy to come out, 'cause never before had any 'cropper come to the big house yelling for a Burney's attendance.

"Daddy, I said come out! Your horses got loose again and they's eatin' up Momma's roses. Daddy!"

Jackson knew Burney didn't like dealing with nothing but his prize horses, and didn't take to his son's manipulations, against which he was as defenseless as his momma's daily brew of tales she'd long dunked him in about her shopping. Nevertheless, he had to keep an eye on his former property, even if it was only driven by his son's foot stomping for attention.

Burney stepped out reading his newspaper with scant intention of going beyond his fragrant world. Now as I look back, he never really did.

"Daddy, your horses got out again!" Jackson pointed down to the shacks but that didn't fool Burney none.

"Where's my horses, Son? I bet they're in the stables where they belong, ain't they?"

"No, they's down visitin' Sarah. Go see!"

Jackson glanced my way to convey that his strategy was working as usual. But Burney didn't look to me for confirmation of his son's tall tale. I doubt if he even knew my name, or to which of his former slaves I was kindred.

"Now, Son, how are they eatin' your ma's roses if they're down in the shacks? That where your ma does her gardenin'? With our niggers? If you interrupted my breakfast for nothin', I'm tellin' Ella to whoop your butt good!"

"She already done it. You forgot," Jackson said.

In their convoluted ways Jackson and his nanny always covered for each other.

"Between you and your ma my memory sure seems to fail somewhere, don't it?"

Jackson always knew how to direct traffic at Grandview.

"Yeah, down by Sarah's," he replied.

Burney headed down the path to the shacks, all the while mumbling something mean about the 'croppers; the very ones whose backs provided him with a life that floated ever so seamlessly on that cool veranda hanging with the scent of jasmine.

Burney walked past me like I didn't exist. I knew to him I didn't, 'cause his eyes, like ol' Issac's, were that cold shade of near colorless blue. About the color pond water reflects on a winter's day. He couldn't see me, so how could his heart feel the anguish of those crumbling moments? Burney yet had to follow me, as he had no idea where Owen and Minerva, born to his property, dwelled.

I glanced back to see if Burney followed, as he looked all so blind to everything but the inconvenience of it all. The corners of his mouth told me so. They'd turned down so hard his young face appeared crimped. Still, he followed me to my door. There the 'croppers swayed an open path for the master—their eyes respectfully downcast as he walked up nodding to nobody. But then he probably couldn't see us.

All was silent in that dark ashy shack 'cept for Momma's wailing at the foot of the moss-stuffed bed. Then, choking on her sobs, she struggled onto the bed and across my daddy's legs. She grabbed on to them as if she could pull him back from the other side; But she could only lay there wailing tattered pieces of her heart. I stood wondering why my daddy couldn't pick up those pieces like he had so many times when the heat of the fields had sunk her low. Hold her sobbing head? Wipe her tears away? Because only her silent cries were left and even those were all but spent.

My daddy still stared up at that small hole in the timbers that surrendered a glint of light over his brow. Alex yet sat in the corner where he'd pulled himself tighter into his arms. There was little to go.

"Why ain't you out in the fields?" Burney demanded. "This ain't Sunday. Isaac's knows to get them crops in before the first rains. I'll cut you off all food credits if you don't get out there, and I mean now!"

But we knew what he meant even before he spewed the words. His glaring eyes spoke louder than his voice. Burney's words were hard, mean and therefore true to his deepest heart—that part of his soul that could not follow Jesus to the doorsteps of the downtrodden. So why do I yet look back after all these years searching for a glint of tenderness in his eyes, a drop of humanity somewhere in his uttering? 'Cause there was so much from his seven-year-old son? The heat of his anger singed my thoughts for I quickly realized where the ugly words that ol' Isaac openly spewed at the 'croppers came from; they were born from the very depths of the soul of one Robert Burney, former slave owner. And I also knew why he didn't mouth them himself. For those deeds he had Isaac around so his Christian mouth remained unsullied by the coarseness that his wife would surely claim to be offended by. But then maybe a mouth roughened by coarse words can't savor a mint julep. How could I have known?

The 'croppers withdrew in silence. Minerva moaned and choked as Burney stared on. His mouth twitched and his words fumbled as they reloaded.

"Owen, he dead…" Momma whispered.

Now like Alex she cried with no tears.

"He gone to Jesus. Now you ain't got 'im no more. No, you ain't!"

Her words were tangled in her sobs but still hit the walls like an ax hits dry timber and landed, splinter by broken syllable. I stood there fearful of my heart bleeding me away till nobody could see me. Not my daddy for sure. His still open eyes could see me no longer, and I yet begged for him to.

Burney jolted the way Miss Burney always did at the sight of me in her rose garden.

"Fever! Damn you!" Burney yelled. "You brought me to a shack with the fever! Look at you, you got it too!"

He reared back from Owen's stare.

"Owen dead…" Momma repeated; her sinking eyes still pleaded. But Lord, it was all too late.

I always cried when Alex did—figured I could rely on his instincts. That day I would have cried all the same as I struggled to sort the whys. Why was my daddy sleeping with his eyes open? Why was Alex sobbing so pitifully? Why did Momma seem lost and so far away?

"Don't…don't separate my kids. Don't run 'em off like stray dogs. We been workin' all our days fer you. Jesus is watchin'!"

Momma lilted to her knees, like she always did when she prayed, but there was no prayer left. She crawled over to clutch at Burney's ankles and beg for something that was too broken to possess again. Her twisted body folded at his dusty boots, which brought the look of terror to Burney's ashen face. Still I wondered how he would comfort her? Wipe her tears on the sleeve of his white shirt like he did Jackson's nose? Was he gonna sit a spell to offer thanks for all the years of work he'd squeezed out of Owen Breedlove? No, that was not why he'd come to our shack. There were no flowers hidden in his clinched fists or tenderly arranged somewhere his bitter words.

"Ain't nobody in the world watchin' a nigger die!"

But, Lord, somebody was watching. With my own eyes I'd seen much, and no, there was nobody counting. Not the life of Owen Breedlove; nobody but Jesus that is. Tell me what dying is? Why is Burney mad at Momma? I could no longer cry as loud as my brother, yet I still tried.

Momma mumbled broken whispers to comfort Alex and me.

"The Lord is my Shepherd. Though I walk through the shadow of death…"

But I reckoned the words were too brittle for the Lord to hear, even if He wanted to.

Momma's face screamed, but her words only crumbled to the ground next to her mouth. "God is watchin' you!"

Minerva Breedlove died the next day.

Something was gone, but how could I have known that it was my childhood?

DARK DEALS

7

LATER THE DAY Momma passed, Ella came down to bathe my folks for their final journey. She whispered something 'bout the cleansing was so the filth of the plantation wouldn't keep the Lord from recognizing them among the dusty faces gathered at the gates of His Orchard. My folks' faces would be wiped clean of the field dust their lives were hidden under. No, no one ever heard their silent cries of desperation or their broken whispers of fear. These were held in trust for the next life along with their souls.

The winding sheets that shrouded Owen and Minerva seemed so strange to me. My folks never wore anything but homespun and sackcloth, but now were wrapped for eternity in the finest sheets woven of imported Irish linen. Jackson had pulled them down from Melinda's oak linen press and hid them under the veranda for Ella like she'd told him.

With Granny's rusty old scissors, Ella hacked out the Burney monograms and tossed them off like they were dirt. They lay strewn at her feet, these large circles of roughly cut fine cloth with those beautifully monogrammed "B"s in royal blue silk thread needled by former slave women who'd probably never slept under a sheet. I gathered the cutouts, the size of large magnolia flower petals, and gazed at them transfixed, thinking that in my very own hand I possessed something of infinite beauty. I gathered up these scraps of sheets as Ella sang the spirituals. But Ella's warm voice couldn't bring Alex to the same place. After listening to my sad sighs long enough, Brother fled our wake to go off and scream his anguish alone. Then there was pounding on the door.

I thought it was Jane and her Samuel come to help. But Ella seemed to know it wasn't. She reached for Granny's scissors and aimed them at the door, as if it couldn't be opened against the rusty points. Did she sense the evil that lurked out there? Isaac walked in all the same and looked about uneasily, as if death might still be lurking in our shack. Ella pulled the Burney sheets up over my folks' faces. Isaac stood there glowering. But the flotsam of grief his appearance could so easily have brought was soon to be fixed by Minerva. Yes, even in death she protected her family. I'm telling you the way it was; them dark deals that came with Isaac that night. Ella knew why'd he'd come, because she knew how black his soul was.

"Sarah, go on down to ol' Clara's and help 'er get her biscuits on. You and Alex gonna be there tonight—then at Jane's tomorrow. Go on now, chil'e."

She aimed Granny's scissors in Isaac's direction as she spoke to me, and never took her eyes off that man.

"What Burney say?" she asked.

Isaac eyed me as I lingered near the door. His glance was like the hot breath of a nigger dog against the cold sweat of my fear.

"Burney, he say the boy's gonna stay. He got to work off the food credit. Yeah, that Owen, he borrowed plenty. It's gonna take a mighty long time to get things paid up. Yep, he sure belongs to me now," Isaac declared like a slave owner.

"What about Sarah. Then she stay on too!" Ella declared.

"No, she ain't! Miss Burney want 'er gone! Told me to make sure it happen no matter what Burney say. She say that child just like her ma and she don't want 'er 'round Jackson no more."

"She a baby, not even seven summers," Ella said.

"Now why that matter to me?" Isaac replied. "I do what I told. She gone tomorrow, or the next night and I be taking her off myself!"

Isaac tossed a grin my direction, chuckled and wiped the drool from his toothless mouth.

"No, that ain't how it's gonna be!" Ella announced.

"Who say? Huh?"

"Minerva! That's who!" Ella replied.

Isaac howled with laughter. But then his face turned on him and he looked as though he'd been smacked good and hard. He had been, and it was soon to be a fatal blow. "She dead. Dead, right there in front of you." Yet he wondered, didn't he?

"Minerva, she tol' Burney not to scatter her chil'ren. She means for it not to be."

Isaac chuckled at the notion that the same woman, cold with death, could still face him down. "Boy's gonna stay. That's all there is to it," Isaac repeated.

"Then what's gonna happen to the girl?" Ella asked suspiciously.

"She come with me. That's all." Isaac winked at me the way that butchered hog once did.

"I tellin' ya, it ain't gonna be that way!" Ella reaffirmed.

"What's that Minerva gonna do?" he asked. "Wake up from her dead and put some ol' scissors to my neck and say it ain't gonna be that way?"

"No. Jackson gonna do it."

"Jackson?" The color in Isaac's face evaporated. "He a boy. I ain't 'fraid of no boy."

But Ella knew better.

"Huh?" Isaac grunted and waited for more bad news.

"Jackson. He gonna crawl up on his daddy's lap and fill Burney's ears with lots of things he heard his Ella say 'bout 'ol Isaac, him's daddy's overseer. He gonna do that." Ella grinned ear to ear. Maybe like Minerva was smiling in his face again. And wasn't she?

"So what?" Isaac sputtered. But he knew what the what was and how much more rotten it'd be for him once things finally sifted over to Melinda's ears.

"Minerva, when she come up to the big house to get 'er scissors back, she told me things you ain't never goonna want Miss Burney know. Is ya?"

"Huh? What things Minerva say 'bout me?"

"She say, Minerva do, that you got blue eyes like the devil himself. Cold and gray like stagnant water."

"Huh? What that woman say 'bout my eyes? It ain't none of her business 'bout my eyes!"

"Yeah? That so. My boy gonna say somthin' Miss Burney ain't never gonna want to hear."

"Ain't nobody gonna tell Miss Burney nothin' 'bout what happened back then!" Isaac growled.

"No? Then you go up to my kitchen door 'morrow and call for Burney. You do that. Then ask 'im what Jackson been sayin' 'bout you. Where you get them blue eyes. Then ask 'im what Miss Burney gonna do 'bout it now that she knows the truth. Yeah, you a big man. So, go ask 'im if you still got a place here come a day er two."

"Miss Burney'll cut the blood out 'a you for making mischief she don't wanna hear! You ain't nothin' to her!" Isaac said.

"Miss Burney do that? Ain't never 'cause I gonna wrap 'er in winding sheets when she dead just like I did Owen and Minerva here. No, I ain't 'fraid of that, 'cause Jackson gonna scream bloody till ever'body in Vicksburg comes if I whisper that his momma gonna put me off Grandview. But Burney, up in the big house, he call you his hog-man. You think he gonna let his hog-man be after what Jackson tell 'im? No, he gonna come for you!"

"What Jackson say 'bout me? Isaac demanded. "What he know then?"

"Jackson? What it matter? I know 'bout you. Minerva give it to me! Ever' bit of what you done back then! But Jackson, maybe he twist things. He a chil'e. Yeah. But maybe he wanna make sure it go deep into his daddy's ear. You don't gotta know no more. That 'a be the way it is."

"What's you want then, nigger?" Isaac blurted.

It wouldn't be the last time Isaac found himself capitulating. Yes, he must have known that Minerva, even dead, had folded his cards again.

"You see? Minerva, she still got you, ain't she? Yeah. And she gonna keep gettin' you for the rest of your days. And all along, I still be here with my boy watching when she do it!"

"I said, what do you want, nigger woman?"

"Heard Burney tell you to go into Delta in the mornin'. Pick up his seed come over by boat from Vicksburg. In Delta, you gonna send a message to Louvenia Powell. Say her younger brother and sister is comin' to her. Both 'em. Yeah, they's coming together, like Minerva meant for it. No, Burney ain't gonna turn 'em into mules. Not even a gruntin', boot-lickin' hog like who's standing in front of me! Then you gonna go buy some ferryboat tickets for these kids to get over the river to Vicksburg. You gonna do what I say."

"I ain't got no money!" Isaac whined. "Where I get money for tickets? Then what happen when Burney finds out I let that boy off 'fore he work off them debt his folks owe?"

Isaac's heart must have beat harder than it had in years.

"You go tell Burney you're wantin' to lick his boots. You get down there and lick 'em good and he give you a dollar. If he say no, 'cause maybe you stink too bad, Jackson go get into his daddy's desk and get one, then go tell his daddy you stole it. Anyway, why'd a boy steal a dollar he don't need? Him's daddy's gonna ask me 'bout that. I say 'a course Isaac steal it! Burney knows you gots to have yer bottle, don't he? You drunk up all your wages already, ain't ya? Gone to stealin' form Burney now, ain't ya? Yeah, right from the big house you done it 'cause you're hurtin' for the bottle, huh? But that ain't my problem. Now you go do what I tol' you. Kids be ready after they folks buried proper."

"Yeah, well, you better get 'im buried quick," Isaac said. "'Cause Burney say get rid of 'em."

"No, hog-man," Ella said. "You gonna do it!"

"Me? I ain't got nothin' to do with 'em," Isaac said. "Burney, he done told me to dump 'em in river. They ain't no more to him than dead dogs! So, the 'croppers best do it quick 'fore Miss Burney catches her sheets is gone."

"Owen and Minerva, they ain't gonna be hauled off like some cart of manure. I say it ain't gonna be," Ella said. "They kids gotta know where they folk is buried. It's right they do. They was born to Burney lands and they gonna stay here forever to remind Burney of it."

"What in hell are you talkin' 'bout, nigger?" Isaac demanded.

"You gonna go tonight. I be standing there with the candle. You gonna dig two graves up top Orchard Hill. That's where they gonna be."

"Burney would shoot me dead if I let them niggers be buried up there. That orchard was planted by Burney's granddaddy himself."

"You decide if you more worried' bout Burney, or Jackson comin' for you, hog-man!"

Ella knew the answer.

Through his hatred, Isaac snorted long and hard before conjuring a new lie. "I tell you what, nigger woman, we'll wait and see 'bout that lil' girl standing over there. But that boy, he gonna stay put. Burney ain't gonna put a bullet in my head. So, I help ya get them niggers buried, 'cause I don't want you 'croppers up there making noise that brings Burney down on me. I help you bury 'em, but you ain't puttin' no grave marker there! I'm tellin' you, you ain't! Then you send the girl to me! That 'a be the deal. Hear?"

"Okay, Isaac. You keep the boy and take the girl off on your own.

Guess there ain't nothin' I can do 'bout it!" Ella said, but it wasn't what she meant.

"Now you're hearin' good, nigger woman!"

Still, she'd really heard another voice more clearly, and that was the direction Isaac was about to find himself tossed.

✥

It came about the next night. Down at the shacks the 'croppers waited with candles lit. We were at Jane's and standing there next to Brother was Ella, holding Jackson's hand. They'd crept out of the big house to come join us. Attended by all, Owen and Minerva would be delivered to their final resting place up on Orchard Hill.

You see, it seemed that earlier Ella told Jackson, again and again, till he figured something was up, that he best not sass his momma none at the supper table. Being Jackson, he kept mouthing off till his pa sent him to bed. The Burneys had no sooner retired than Ella and Jackson went through the house collecting every candle they could get to, all of them 'cept the ones high up in Melinda's crystal chandeliers. At Jane's, these candles were cut into pieces and passed around. Then we all proceeded to the top of Orchard Hill where the view back over the river and way off to Vicksburg was clear as the night the three kings went looking for the Christ child, ol' Clara pointed out. Even now, as I look back at that night, the wonderment remains. The moon, that I was sure only shone above the big house, guided us. It was like a hundred flickering stars traveling up the hill to the knoll atop, that sacred resting place of the Burney family.

Way up under the peach trees, ol' Clara led the' croppers in prayer. Then I heard a whisper that moved like a quiet wave from those down the hill up to the top where Ella held on to Jackson and my hands. Ella cupped Jackson's ears to his mighty annoyance. I couldn't hear what they was whispering, but I knew that ol' Clara's nod to Ella was some kind of message. Ella smiled and nodded back. Then ol' Clara lifted her hands up to the heavens and we gave thanks to the Lord for taking Owen and Minerva's weary souls unto a final place of peace, and for protecting their children from evil.

But what kind of evil? Well, among we 'croppers, evil always meant ol' Isaac.

We started back down to the shacks as Samuel, Jane's husband, suddenly appeared in front of us with his shovel in hand and started shoveling the soil over my folks' graves. Jackson and I helped Jane gather up dry leaves to scatter over their place of rest till it disappeared from view. Standing there alone except for his dry tears, Alex reached for my hand as Ella and Jackson disappeared on down the other way toward the big house.

Motherless Morning

8

THE NEXT DAY at Jane's I woke up early. Standing silently by the window was Alex looking as though he was waiting for someone. Didn't know why, but I wondered if it was for our folks.

"Who you waitin' for?" I asked.

"Who say I waitin'?"

"It's me here talkin'."

"Samuel, he ain't come back yet. Been gone all night. I waited up to see."

"See what?" I asked.

Jane stood at the open door gazing out towards where that old well was and then turned and smiled. She took a seat on the porch steps.

"You get yourself a biscuit then come sit with me."

"Where's Samuel?" I asked, wondering why Brother hadn't if he'd been looking for him.

"He comin' when he's finished."

I ate my biscuit waiting for Samuel's return sitting next to Jane. Alex only stood there at the door. Guess he didn't want to sit out on the porch with no jabbering women.

Later that morning I wondered up to the big house. I stood at the edge of the lawn to see even as I had no notion what I was looking for. Up there Ella had Burney's breakfast laid out nicely. She stood fanning him on the veranda so the humidity wouldn't bother him as he ate. Up close I could hear them.

"Isaac, he gonna bring yer horses 'round?" she asked.

"Don't mess with me, Ella," Burney replied without taking his eyes off that fine plate of ham and eggs. "You best go see if Sam has that well filled in like I said. Water gone bad. You know my wife can smell somethin' unpleasant all the way from Vicksburg. You tell 'im Miss Burney wants it finished today!"

"Yes, Mas'er. I tell 'im what you say."

But Samuel already knew.

By the time Ella got Jackson dressed, Samuel was all but finished. That well, the one my daddy told me never to go near, had disappeared. Nor was there a trace of Isaac from then on. Nobody ever seen him again. Word was that he must 'a gotten drunk and fallen into the river. But that talk was followed by a snicker or two. Who knew for sure? The tales on ol' Isaac got to be as tangled as the growth along the river. But what we all figured, talked about in nods and whispers, was that it was surely Minerva who'd tripped Isaac into a grave of his own, wherever that lay. From then on Isaac was only one more of Grandview's many secrets.

The next day I felt so afraid for Momma and Daddy that they'd be alone up there on Orchard Hill that I promised myself I'd come ever'day to talk to them. Still, I felt utterly lost. I was sure I'd hear my folks' voices if I could only make my thoughts quiet down long enough. But who would hear me? Then I heard her: Momma's voice as crisp as the air up on Orchard Hill the night the two of us gathered peaches.

"These Bible verses and all yer dreams, that's all I can give ya, chil'e, my dreams for my chil'ren!"

A couple of days later, I guess after enough time to get things worked out, Ella slipped down to Jane's. She looked at Alex and then me, but as hard as she tried, the words wouldn't come for her. It was left for Jane to tell us that we'd be leaving Grandview forever and would do so quietly, like runaways, with only Samuel as witness. It was a blessing, Jane murmured as I cried. Still I didn't understand why the women standing about offered their own tears. Or why I was a motherless child. Could Daddy still be looking for me from someplace? Where then was that place? Alex had no answer. Where was my home if not near Jackson's? Ella went silent. I can't remember the verses… Can you hear me, Momma? Say them again then. Where do I hide my dreams from the fears chasing them down? It all got quiet, except for the voices in my head.

The next day Ella came to help Jane get our things together. We had nothing, and Alex put it all in one burlap bag. I heard that Samuel would be waiting out of sight under the oaks at the end of the drive to take us away. We were leaving the only world we'd ever known and going to one we had no conception of. One that would possess us, like the Burney plantation, but still not want us. We were told there'd be a cart ride over to Delta. From there a ferry would transport us over to the docks near Vicksburg, where a short train trip would take us to that part of Vicksburg where coloreds lived. There, somewhere, awaited a woman whom I was told was my older sister. But what was a train? Alex tried to describe it, but he'd never seen one either. I knew he was only reciting what Samuel had told him.

Shortly I was to take the first steps on the longest walk in my life; a gravel drive only traveled by white folks driven by a colored, to the gates of Grandview. There it hung close to my face as we walked under the oaks—the long hanging Spanish moss that Jackson and I loved to pull down for Momma to stuff her bed.

We were only a way down the drive when I heard the screen door slam and Jackson run out hollering for me to wait for him. I could see Samuel up ahead fidgeting nervously as if ol' Isaac might suddenly appear and curse at him. Jackson chased after us under the hanging moss, screaming his fears and kicking at the gravel when Ella tried to pull him back.

"How come you're going somewhere?" he asked.

He freed himself from Ella's clutch to chase after us. I couldn't look him in the eyes, but didn't know why.

"We're goin' to live with my sister Louvenia in a big white house," I said to comfort my only friend.

I kicked the dust up something awful, anything to slow us from the direction we were headed. Alex jerked my arm to stop. Did he, too, want to slow the avalanche we might face? We could never have known what was waiting for us, and perhaps that saved us from the moment.

"But why? I got a big house, don't I?" Jackson said.

Ella dabbed his face with her apron to catch his tears. "You and Alex gotta live here with me."

I plied Jackson with other notions I'd created from my fantasies. "We's gonna have jam ever' day." Don't even know why I said that, as I'd never had a notion that there were folks that had jam ever' day.

"I like jam, don't I?" Jackson escaped Ella's clutch again. "Can't I go, too?"

"But Ella'd miss you," I told him. Would Ella come to know how much I would miss him?

"Who's gonna play with me till you come back home?" he asked wiping tears.

Ella ran to stop him from following after us. Her tears were not of happiness. No, her eyes had that same look as the time she told me 'bout walking from one end of hell to the other. I could only wonder why she was scared, like we were. What did she know? She didn't say, but held Jackson close to keep him from escaping the cool shadows of that fragrant world he didn't know he owned, only to escape to the scorched one that awaited us.

Samuel was there at the end of the drive with his wagon. He waved for us to come quickly.

Alex lifted me onto the straw in the back and climbed up next to Samuel. They had things to say and things that needed to be heard. See, Samuel had been Daddy's best friend. They were both real quiet, 'cept when they were down by the river fishing with Brother. Then their quiet voices worked up a howl over tales about things the womenfolk got into. Then Samuel went quiet before talking about our daddy and what a good man he was and how much he loved his boy. For the first time, Alex cried as Samuel went on to recount their times on the river and the stories those catfish had told them.

Samuel kept his arm around Brother's shoulder till we reached the docs at Delta. Alex climbed down. He averted his gaze, guess 'cause he didn't want me to see his eyes red and wet. After tipping his hat to the white men who passed, Samuel lifted me down and kissed my forehead. It was like my daddy did. Then he pointed to the ferry that blew steam and handed two pieces of paper to Alex: tickets to our exile. Samuel dabbed at a tear like it wasn't no tear and climbed back up on his wagon and left.

Alex seemed to know where the train was that Samuel had directed him to. Brother could not hold my hand, as he was clutching those train tickets like our lives depended on their safe conveyance to the ticket man. Then he gestured with his head. Over there waited the steaming monster that would take us somewhere, and to that someone named Louvenia.

For what seemed like forever we sat on those hard wooden seats on that monster train that terrified me beyond words. Even more so when that old white man came up to our window, his eyes glaring like ol' Isaac's, and spat at the window as if the glass would not shield my face from his brown tobacco spittle. As a child I wondered if his stare might cut through that very glass? He spat again to punctuate his hatred. But the window was closed and sealed despite the heat and humidity. See, coloreds could only buy seats behind the engine, which spewed smoke and cinders. Two orphan children in the South. The man stumbled off, tipping his hat like a gentleman to a passing white woman.

Despite the old man's greeting, I was stuck wondering if we would ever eat again. Didn't know. Neither did Brother, or he'd answer me when I asked again and again. Maybe his mind had taken him back to the river where he always went to figure things and he could no longer hear me that far off. Nobody else could either. I was sure of it. My empty stomach kept reminding me.

At the next stop, another old man came up to the window. I ducked down into my seat. These instincts develop early for young coloreds. Alex wouldn't budge, but I knew he was scared 'cause he held my hand like he was gonna break it. Then another old man ordered us to get off the train and pointed the direction where he probably thought hell was waiting for our arrival. We got off and stood there lost till she walked up, this woman who looked as frightened as us. And just like Daddy. I didn't know who she was, so I looked at Alex. He only looked off maybe to find our future, perhaps the sight of which caused his head to quickly turn so his eyes wouldn't reveal the nothing he saw in all that noise and confusion. She waved to Alex, that woman, and a faint smile came to his face. First one I'd seen in days. There were tears in those eyes of hers that were just like Daddy's. This was surely my older sister, Louvenia.

Lost in the Shadows of Jesse's Alley

9

I NEVER SAW SO many people out and about as when we stepped off the train in Vicksburg, just across that great Mississippi River but farther off a plantation than anyone in my family had ever disappeared to. As a child this city was terrifying. Who were these people bustling about the station? More people than I'd ever seen, and from Brother's darting glances, more than he had. How far from home are you when you're truly lost? How far even is far?

The noise pounding off those buildings, some taller than the Burneys' big house, where did it come from? I'd never heard such a roar, even when the river was pounding the banks and breaking off pieces. Why were people talking so loudly? Were they trying to say something over the roar of that river we'd crossed but could no longer see? And why did they walk along shoulder to shoulder talking yet still never look each other in the eyes? They seemed to gaze ahead like they knew where they were going yet still meandered along like maybe they didn't.

Louvenia broke the din of my chattering thoughts. "Ain't ever been at a train station before, huh?"

"We ain't been nowheres," Alex announced.

But I had. I'd been under the veranda playing with Jackson Burney.

"Now Sarah, you're a big girl now." Louvenia noticed what Brother seemed to deny.

"I almost eight," I said in case nobody ever told her. I learned later that when we tried to work out how old Louvenia was that she couldn't count.

"How'd you know? You're a girl. You can't count nothin'," Alex said. I had to think on that.

"I can count! My friend Jackson teached me."

"You ain't got no friends 'cept that corncob doll, and I cut her head clean off so's she won't be talking back to me no more!"

So, it was Alex that done it! Jackson and me with all the chickens we could corral along with a duck held a wake for my baby. The one with the hemp hair that daddy had carved from a corncob that wore a dress sewn by Jane from the pockets torn off Burney's old castoff shirts.

"Jackson and me buried my baby and told Jesus you did it!"

But that was a lie, because we really told Jesus the devil did it, 'cause that's what Ella told us to tell the Lord when we prayed so He'd be sure to notice my baby in heaven even if she didn't have a head. But then later I revised my prayer when I found my baby's head where it had likely fallen off.

"I'm going back to live with Jackson. Yes, I am."

When Jackson was 'round nothing bad ever happened to me and my pockets were near always filled with hard candy or broken cookies.

"Then you don't know nothin'! Jackson's ma eats nigger kids!" Alex informed me. "You'd be sittin' down with Jackson for suppa and Miss Burney's gonna come up and cut yer throat good like she done all them coloreds come up on her veranda and sassed 'er. Before you quit yer whinin', you'd be in that old pot where they boil hog's heads! And you know sissy Jackson; he's gotta eat ever'thing Ella puts on his plate! Jackson's gonna eat you for suppa! You still wanna go back there?"

I knew Alex spent lots of time down at the river figuring things out, him being near two years older. Still, that wasn't the picture I had, 'cept maybe 'bout Miss Burney slipping up behind me and cutting my throat. She always looked at me as if she was of a mind to do that, didn't she?

I was working out these thoughts with one hand holding my throat in case Miss Burney slipped up on me if she was shopping in Vicksburg. That's when Sister-woman boxed Alex's head. Why was Louvenia mad? Or was she only as frightened as Brother and me? She looked as if something was about to slip up on her, too. Did all that noise on that street pound her thoughts too thin, too? Well, I was soon to learn that the one who led by his fist was always slipping up on Sister.

"Ain't nobody eatin' up nobody! Now I want you to listen good," she said. "Mr. Jesse, he don't want ya livin' with us. Yeah, we been together just a few years now and it ain't been easy. No, it ain't been nothin' but a hell! Don't even think on what I had to do for him to take you in. And if he don't take to you, where you think you're going then? Huh?"

Not really moving and yet feeling bustled, my head started to spin from the fear I read in Sister's eyes. To anchor my thoughts, I looked at the ground. Down there my pinched toes hidden in my borrowed shoes seemed to stay put even as visions of what Louvenia had said jostled my thoughts. I stood there feeling torn between that white veranda where I knew Jackson was surely waiting for me to play and the dirty street where I stood feeling lost. I clutched Alex's sweaty hand. Got me to thinking: maybe I best hug the ground till the storm passed and I could hear through all the noise again.

"I go live with Jackson!" I mumbled, with one of my fingers trying to hide somewhere in my mouth. I mumbled to my feet telling them to run! All my toes could do was squirm, like the rest of me. Them not knowing if they should go back or forth, up or down.

"No, Sarah, you ain't never gonna see Grandview or Jackson Burney 'gain. Not never, hear?"

Why wouldn't I? Sister words hit me in bits and pieces that I couldn't hold together to make sense of. Along that river was my home. What about Momma and Daddy up there on Orchard Hill?

"I tell you where you're goin' if Jesse don't take a likin' to youse," Louvenia began. Then she looked as if she was about to tell us the most awful thing we'd heard since Owen and Minerva passed, and would rather have bitten off the tip of her tongue than say these words. "He say he take you where they take all colored kids gots no home. Jesse take you where they take ol' horses got no work lef' in 'em. Yes, he will, too. He say it all morning and then some!" Sister wiped away another tear. In the dark days ahead there would be times when she couldn't even do that for us.

I truly had no real idea where Sister was talking about, but I could rely on Alex to sort things. One glance from him told me we best not wander in the direction Sister-woman was talking about, 'cause I knew the fear in Brother's eyes was real as they never deceived. Still I was thinking: Why wouldn't Jesse want us? Back then I held that only Miss Burney never wanted us.

I never walked so far in my life as that first day in Vicksburg. How far could somebody walk in one day on the very same feet? Then how far could somebody walk and still nobody know you? I was sure we'd walked a thousand blocks to get to Louvenia's, but then I'd never walked a block before to know. What could be waiting that was so far off from where I'd come that we were not yet there? My thoughts mumbled on, but still couldn't keep pace. Like me, they only wanted to walk backwards.

After what seemed like hours of walking down one alley after another, most so narrow no sunlight touched the old black brick walls, we finally reached our destination. But I tell you plain, there was no white veranda with a table of refreshments waiting. There was no white anywhere to be seen. The door we were marched to looked to be down a long shadow that I would soon learn ended at Jesse's place. It had to have been one of hell's dead ends.

Louvenia tugged us on down this service alley stacked with trash, broken bottles and reeking of the stench of fermented urine, to a screened-in porch. There, she shoved the old door open with her shoulder. That kitchen door seemed reluctant to admit anyone. Or, I'd soon learn, let anybody escape. Sister bustled us into her world and its moldering darkness.

I'd never seen a kitchen before, and couldn't figure on the purpose of so many laundry tubs stacked on the porch we'd passed through. Turned out they were tubs that I'd soon be dipping my hands into and spending the rest of my childhood trying to avoid touching the bottoms where that greasy, gritty filth waited. It wouldn't be the only thing I'd avoid the touch of.

Sister hurried us further through her kitchen to another room smothered in darkness that hissed with the creaking sounds of the old floorboards that taunted our every step. It was a room surrendered to the dark so a man's sins would be harder to decipher. Cardboard was packed against the only window and the walls were a collage of stains in hues of filth that only desperate living can layer up. Yes, this room was dark enough to hide the wickedness it was witness to, and where I saw Louvenia's husband for the first time. A cold chill went down my sweaty young back at the sight of that ol' man.

There he sat sputtering grunts and scratching at himself like he was eaten by lice. This was Louvenia's husband, the man who might not find us acceptable. He slouched in a torn old chair strangely situated in the center of the room. Like a throne it was, with oddly placed doilies covering the chair's gutted upholstery—the spilled inners that had long turned dirty brown. Yes, there was Jesse, sitting like ever'thing revolved around him. I was soon to learn it did.

After a stammer or two, he looked up. He'd been so preoccupied with the whiskey bottle he was trying to conquer that he hadn't notice us standing there, me holding Sister's hand from fear. She looked at that old man as if he might have something to pull out at us. A stick? Yet her pause seemed to tell him to take another swig—like it 'a clear your head, ol' man so's your vision's less muddy. He tipped the bottle and emptied it to the bottom in one guzzle, then wiped the thick drool from his mouth. I could smell him, and he smelled like a rotting form of ol' Isaac. I thought he had to be the oldest man in the world. Him with those worn old pants with suspenders hanging at his sides and that filthy yellowed sleeveless undershirt. There he sat with his empty bottle standing court as it surely waited for the next one to arrive and relieve it from duty. He held it tightly like it was a golden scepter. His horny hands were stained ochre from nicotine—as though he'd kept 'em buried in the yellow clay back along the riverbanks at the Burneys'. I would soon find that Jesse kept 'em buried alright. Buried in the swamp of lies he conjured so they'd never be exposed to the truth of hard work.

I could never figure how this man could be as black as that alley at night and yet never spend a day under the sun in any field. But Jesse's life was the night. A life where the bars and bottles could so easily entice him to flee the shadows of his own scarred soul. He stared up and down at me. I stared back and then looked up to Louvenia, having no idea what he was. She heard my thoughts and answered to help situate us on this man's good side, like it might assure us of our survival.

"Go on in kids. Don't be afraid. This be my husband, Mr. Jesse."

Jesse didn't get up; I figured he couldn't. Surely, he'd been in that old chair for ages and like an invalid, it now held him prisoner. He looked hard at me as though he could see something right through me. And he could. I was too young to know my innocence was glowing, and Jesse was salivating for a lick.

"These them nobodies you went clear 'cross town for?" he demanded, tipping his bottle for the last drop he'd already swallowed.

"Leavin' me with no meal on the table? I tol' you, they's nothin' to me but two empty stomachs wantin' my food!"

The rest of his greeting melted into slurs that still needed no translating. No, every snarled curse fell on my ears crystal clear.

"Alex, you go put your things in the kitchen," Sister said, her voice soft and gentle like Daddy's. "Then have a piece of that pie, Annie, the nice neighbor brung it by."

Alex had carried our valuables all day, his other shirt, my other blouse and a corncob doll, and took them to a place that offered no safekeeping in the corner of Louvenia's kitchen.

Jesse looked me over, not noticing Louvenia squirming at the sight of his tongue twisting to get out of his gaping toothless mouth to lick at his brown lips. Then, in a blink, he was at the edge of his chair, pulling me to his rancid body.

Louvenia lunged to wedge her arm between Jesse and me. He dropped me to grab that arm and twisted her to the floor so hard I figured he'd broken it. He'd rehearsed this dance before, hadn't he? Just like she'd rehearsed springing up from the floor to distance herself from his fist on the next round even before counting her cracked ribs.

"Why ain't you a sweet lil' thing?" he said. "Crawl up on Jesse's lap so I can get me some sugar, lil' girl. That's what you be good for now, ain't it? Ain't it all you's good for, too? I know you done showed up here to take Uncle Jesse's mind off things. I be needing takin' care of, little pleasure now and 'gain, 'cause Louvenia here, she ain't good for nothin' that could please a man. Is you, woman over there? You don't got no work to get to, Louvenia? Then go get me a bottle! I got me some business here gonna keep me busy, ain't you, lil' girl?"

Sister wrung her hands and shook her head at Jesse defenselessly as he slobbered grisly kisses on my cheek and then neck. But when he twisted my head to find my mouth, Sister somehow wedged her body between Jesse's and mine.

"Jesse, let her be now, she don't know you. Let her be, I tell ya."

Louvenia wormed and twisted between Jesse and me so's to lessen his grasp.

How easily he could hold me and reach to slap her down again, a *pas de deux* that would be encored many times in the years ahead. All I remember is flailing as hard as my small feet could to land a kick in a place a man don't wanna feel no heel. He moaned and dropped me to raise his fist just as Alex reappeared. Praise God, Alex had Momma's eye. He looked at Jesse with a glare that caused his nostrils to flare. I don't 'member much after Louvenia hit the floor again. Only that I cried, Jesse bellowed, and so I cried louder. Alex twisted his fist into a confused knot hearing Sister's pitiful sobs, which were thick enough to slice the fog that shrouded me in confusion. Tears came down her sad face like rock salt done been pelted in her eyes. The initiation into the shadows of Jesse's alley life was complete.

Yes, a tidal wave had rolled over me. One of wrecked emotions that so easily drowned my young senses into all the nothingness we'd arrived at that day. What could I grab on to? The floor was too far away to hug and, anyway, Louvenia had already staked claim to the spot under his feet. Even through the fog that blinded me that black night it was crystal clear that we'd sure not moved into a big white house as I'd proclaimed to Jackson, and there'd be no jam waiting on our table.

Such a long journey on that train to have gone nowhere and I would be staying there for years to come, and even afterwards pieces would follow me along my journey as tightly stitched to my spirit as a shadow is to my heels. Yet all through these times I could still hear my momma's voice.

Momma, why do you keep whispering if you know I can't hear no more?

What are the prayers and the prospects of a child lost at the dead-end of a dark alley? I was lost in Jesse's shadows, and it would be years before he would find me—the man that would take my hand and lead me away from it all.

LOUVENIA'S BLACK DREAMS

10

I DIDN'T KNOW MY sister as a child back at the shacks. I was a still a baby when the day came when Louvenia disappeared from our lives. But from time to time I'd hear Momma speak of her and cry to my daddy 'bout what had happened. "Where's my girl now?" she'd beg. He shook his head but never could offer nothing large enough to catch her tears. No, how could he have known where his oldest child had ended up? He'd never left Burney lands himself. I didn't understand much of the story back then, just felt Momma's tearful rage.

You see there came a day when Sister was old enough to catch Burney's eye, and this sighting bludgeoned her childhood innocence on the spot. Momma had been able to fend off ol' Isaac but she could do nothing about Burney's lust. That put Miss Burney in a quandary. Melinda Burney knew how to maintain her facade of delicious innocence but still not crack the hard lacquer shell hidden beneath. She spent her days leisurely cultivating that most Southern female talent yet could turn on a dime to deal with anything that might insinuate on her life in the shade of them magnolias. The sweet jasmine Ella wove in Miss Burney's hair was a signal for Burney to come and pleasure himself. But she was only pretending, and he knew it. Knew most times there'd be a roadblock to her bed, and he wouldn't have enough for the toll she demanded. The attic was already filled to the brim with bright-colored tea dresses. Still made Burney mad when he came up against one of Melinda's roadblocks, as he must have figured he'd already paid a high enough price razing them as fast as she'd re-erected them. There was only one way left for him; she forced the issue, hadn't she? Burney simply meandered around her roadblocks to fix his needs elsewhere. That meant trips down to the shacks.

We weren't good at the kind of negotiations Melinda Burney knew so well. Not that we didn't take to weaving jasmine in our hair, but the only thing we had to negotiate with was our lives. So much easier to fold them; then your kid gets to see another day. Burney's arousals, which had no place to drift to but the shacks, left Melinda with only one recourse. Yes, when Burney went riding, she summoned his overseer up to the big house. The message was always understood even before it was sent. Isaac had best be at the back door by the time Melinda got downstairs. She had a bitter peace to brew and would not hesitate to toss her frothy rage on any servant not heeding her wishes. Long before this day, Melinda had already worked out a few dark deals with Isaac. It was easy enough for them to partner up. He might have been worthless as an overseer, but so long as Burney took his pleasure in breeding his horses and no more than that, she'd make sure Isaac had a bunk down in the hog's house. Keep an eye cocked for Master Burney's doings down at the shacks, the mistress com-manded—then come up to her back door for the nigger dog rewards.

Isaac was told by Melinda that Louvenia was to be put off the place before Burney got back for supper. Otherwise, Melinda would take a switch to Sister herself and drive her all the way to the end of the oak-lined alley. For sure Isaac knew he'd then be walking that gravel path next. We all knew that the end of that drive only led to nowhere an unescorted woman would want to be come nightfall. It was checkmate for Burney. Melinda didn't have time for her own kid; there were to be no mulattos coming to unsettle her rose garden and incite chatter up and down church pews on Sundays. The Burneys had their name carved on the first pew reserved for their use only. Sitting up there, she'd surely hear the tittering behind her back. I 'member Momma saying it was Ella's job to run down to the shacks and see if any newborns were half-pale. If they was, she was to drag it from its momma's breast and sling it into the river. Sacrifice for the sins of the father? Or eternal freedom for the child? 'Course Ella never hurt no baby. But some said maybe Isaac did. The fear of finding a half-white baby in your rose garden was at the top of the list of secrets that ruled plantation folks up and down that river. Christian souls tend to be jarred when unpleasant details show unexpectedly, such as a pair of soulful eyes that wait at your backdoor for the scraps… or maybe asking to take your family name.

"Just fix it!" she'd exclaim when Isaac stood in her presence. That ended her instructions for the day. Her expression easily communicated the seriousness of the situation, with not a speck of sweat drawn to her delicate brow despite the furor that must have been stirring in her head. It was all that was needed. Ol' Isaac might 'a gotten around Master Burney, despite his messing up after he'd drifted to the bottom of a bottle and failed to get the 'croppers to the fields before the sun come up. But he knew there were two covenants to Robert Burney's faith he best not violate: invoking the displeasure of his wife, and allowing anyone to conjure a notion that Jackson would not be master of Grandview come one day. Isaac knew his own fate teetered precariously on how low he bowed and scraped when she appeared on her veranda in her Southern regalia. Hers was a carefully arranged crown of jasmine that she could so easily unwind and lash his face with, leaving more marks on his nightmares than Jackson's daily taunting. His was surely a miserable black dream of being lost out on some county road, passing a chain-gang or two looking for new recruits even as he stumbled from ditch to ditch along them back roads looking for a whiskey bottle with one or two drops left.

Isaac was clear on the things his mistress meant him to do: get rid of Minerva's girl Louvenia, and do it cool and seamlessly, like white-flowering jasmine should look when woven through a white woman's golden hair. But the thing is, this man had long survived on their scraps, and the scraps also meant the women Burney cast aside. It was how things worked for plantation menfolk. He knew how to obey his mistress and still get his rewards. Yes, Isaac, he finally got to Sister too, didn't he? Play some cards? Roll some dice? Spin the bottle and see who it aims at. It pointed to Louvenia's young face.

He made a bargain with Sister that Momma never found out about till it was too late. If Louvenia gave it to him, like she had Burney, without fuss or protestation, ol' Isaac would let her stay on with our folks so long as she kept out of sight but still at his disposal for conjugal visits. If she showed herself at the big house's back door to tell the secrets, Isaac promised he'd cut the blood out of her, starting with her face. The point was made by stretching her mouth open with a knife. What could Louvenia do?

Sister told me she laid down for that filthy old man with no teeth till his grunting was over. Said she let her mind fog over till the deed was done. The only other option was to lay down and starve to death somewhere off the Burney place, just hoping Jesus found her before somebody picked her up for vagrancy and initiated her into a chain-gang. And best make sure your near-dead body ain't close to the big house when you get used up. That'd be untidy to white Christian sensibilities and could get you hauled off for loitering to some dark basement jail at the county courthouse. Lynching ropes are tied at both ends to make sure ain't nobody ever gonna leave the place alive. No coloreds ever did.

Louvenia loved Momma and Daddy and didn't want to leave them, and she didn't want to die all alone along some county road after the laborers had finished with her, so she went to the hog's house when Isaac bid her to come put some flesh down on her bill. It was her secret, one wrapped in too many layers of shame to count. Surely, when you're starving not to be vagrant in the new South, your mind tends to drift into that fog quick when called upon to do so. That's what happened to young girls that got kicked off plantations with or without their kid.

Did she ever ponder if Isaac would keep his part of the bargain? Well, Louvenia was sent away, wasn't she? It was the very day Miss Burney noticed Louvenia was with child. You see, there came the hour when Isaac confessed in a drunken stupor that he'd had her. But the coda to his confession was that Burney had Sister first. Miss Burney sought blood for the betrayals. Yes, we all heard the shouting from the upstairs windows at the big house. Louvenia was barely fourteen and had lost the baby, a little girl. Nobody 'round the shacks talked about it. Anyway, how was Sister's story different from all the others dredged through our collective shame?

Louvenia wasn't a strong woman when her life away from the Burneys' put her on shaky footing that would head her straight for Jesse's alley. No, in most ways she was fragile, but she had a strong faith that kept her from selling her body like so many women were reduced to doing. But then she already knew what that was all about. One sale to ol' Isaac to stay with her folks had already netted her off the plantation with less than nothing. After somehow getting herself over the river to Vicksburg and days of wandering the alleys with nothing in her stomach, Jesse didn't look so old and ugly. Hunger makes you see things differently, because it all gets veiled in that thick fog stewing in your head that keeps your thoughts numbed.

Well, it had been a long time since Jesse Powell had been a young man, but my sister went with him anyway. She knew she was headed down her very last alley, and he was the only thing standing there with that "Come on over here and let's do some plain talking 'bout you and me" kind'a look. Turns out, he'd long been waiting for someone like Sister; spirit broken and head bowed only to see his dirty shoes staring up her dress at her marred innocence. A woman who was at the point where there'd be no turning back for something less frightening than what she saw standing in front of her. Men like Jesse

can smell hopelessness before they even fork up a helping. To Jesse
Powell, it didn't make no difference whom he picked; a woman had
little value beyond what services she provided.

∾

Soon after Brother and I arrived at Jesse's, Louvenia started washing
down the kitchen walls. The scrubbing left them a bleached-out ochre
color maybe like old shellac; yellowed from years of the nicotine left
by Jesse, his older brother, their men friends, whores, gamblers and
the hustlers that made up his sacred choir on gambling nights. They
all knew Jesse's place was good for a laugh and to freeload whatever
food Louvenia had somehow come by.

The kitchen was where Louvenia spent most of her time working the tubs to earn enough to pay our weekly rent to the landlord
and the bribes to Jesse for the rent on our throats. I didn't do much
back then but listen while Sister worked her tub. Sister's words could
be razor sharp. They were meant to teach me 'bout surviving in the
alleys. But then it was a sharp life out there that ate up those not
already too lacerated by it all to be ready to survive.

Sister was a gentle soul, but I think she knew she wasn't surviving
and was determined that somehow, I would. Over the years bent over
tubs at Jesse's there were scattered times when we managed to sort our
lives out from under the weight of our days—days made heavy as a
coffin weighed down with the debris of his life.

Yes, time was worthless as most of our days poured into each
other as quickly as we poured out that brown tub water in the alley.
Late, soon after Jesse returned from the bars, Louvenia would scream
and moan somewhere in the depths of her nights when he slapped
her against the walls that jailed her. No, there was no one outside
Louvenia's place who could hear it; there was too much screaming and moaning going on out there already. Another life broken?
Can't fix nothing you can't see, so why open your eyes to some other
woman's wailing? Everybody down that alley had her own wounds to

decipher. "You still ain't seen my husband yet? He been gone for days now," a neighbor once asked with a shadow of terror hanging over her, knowing if his life was spent, hers would soon follow. It was always the same mantra we heard bouncing from those alley walls; dark thoughts penetrating deeper wounds aiming to break apart hopes. Uncountable were the nights Sister and I held our hands tightly over our ears to protect us from that familiar loop: one, two, three, four, smash, crash, collapse, plead and then the beg-again chorus. "No more, please no more!" she'd beg. "Please, no more!" How high can Jesus count the terrors ringing in my ears? Days follow each other in an ever-deepening haze when you don't count 'em. And no one did at the end of Jesse's alley. But then nobody had much to count period.

Deep in his sleepless nights Alex would lie on his pallet staring off somewhere deep in that corner of the room, his face hardened with rage. Him looking for that place I knew he wanted to go, needed to go, but like Louvenia and me, couldn't find a way out. How do you fix a soul? So much harder than the breaking of it was.

During these eternally long nights, Alex would pull his blanket over his head so he couldn't hear Jesse's gospels being taught Louvenia upside her head. Jesse, he figured he had to preach his gospels hard with his fist so's his meaning would more easily penetrate Sister's seeming reluctance to learn proper. Alex's chest could still hear what his ears denied. It heaved up and down just like somebody jumping on it—pushing all those scrambled dry tears out into the open. He had to hide these tears in the daylight where he knew a man couldn't admit to crying himself to sleep every night. That kind of admission puts a man face-to-face with his own impotence and the fear that those lurking in shadows of Jesse's alley would swallow him whole. What did Jesse fear? Who would get him his next bottle? Did that fear beat the life out of him long before Louvenia showed up, or would he have lost his soul somewhere at the bottom of a drop of bourbon all the same? My brother, he couldn't cry no more, not even in dry tears. Now he had to be a man, deal with Mr. Jesse. Yes, it seemed that his childhood had been hammered away along with his hopes and dreams.

Come mornings Louvenia would shuffle her bruises into the kitchen to get the water boiling for the tubs and then near mid-day we'd get Jesse's breakfast going before he headed out clinking his dice. What money we were able to collect from our tubs went to feed him first. Alex and I didn't mind missing meals. We'd gladly do anything to keep Jesse satiated so he'd stay away from our throats. Almost anything. Sister would never leave me alone if Jesse got up early and I was still sleeping in the corner of the kitchen. When he'd finally return from the bars, she'd sit on my cot as I slept till she heard Jesse snoring in the back room. Only then would she go back to her ironing. As I look back now, I truly don't remember my sister having slept in peace an entire night at Jesse's. From her labors bent over the tubs, to Jesse's stalking in from the bars at ungodly hours, where were the precious moments hidden that she could claim for herself?

Sometimes late, after Louvenia wrung out the last rag for hanging, she'd shuffle into the bedroom and collapse somewhere deep in her exhaustion. With Jesse gone, I'd go back there and fan Sister while she rested, just as Ella did Burney, or at least in my mind it was. Maybe not really. Why isn't Sister moving, I wondered? The very thought jolted me. No, she ain't dead, Lord. She moved her shoulder, I seen it. She's just breathing irregular again. Yet as my thoughts simmered in fear, I yet wondered as the distances between each breathe seemed to grow longer. My thoughts ran wild. I'll fan harder, then. I'm not that tired, am I? No more than the night before.

While I fanned, I seemed to always go back to wondering—what would Momma think of us now, so far from any dream she gave me on orchard nights? Would she find pride in us? But where would she see it? No, I best not try to see some for myself. Not now. Don't have time for pride anyway. I'll just let my thoughts drift somewhere better. What was Jackson doing now? No, I won't fall asleep across the bottom of Louvenia's bed. Hell couldn't be hotter than this here room and Sister needs a few moments' peace, so I'll keep fanning, yet I can't help but thinking there's no sight of a cool white veranda at the end of our long monotonous days. Just the same ol' humid steam from our tubs that sucks our breath and singes our thoughts when we dared to think about something else to make the day go easier. Things like how long will Jesse stay gone tonight, Lord? How long do I have to stay awake wondering, 'cause I sure need the rest? I could just shut my eyes here for a few moments, but if Jesse come back looking for more of our wash money on his way to another craps game and discovered Alex was up on the roof eating the food I'd fixed for him, there'd be no way down for Brother but a last jump. In those days, when we had a notion of jumping, we all knew there was only one direction. No, we didn't jump for joy. Not ever.

"I be gettin' up soon. Just some more to rest my eyes and I go finish my ironin'."

Sister's eyes never opened to see if I was nearby.

"You stay and rest, Sister; Jesse gone now," I said mopping her brow. Her thin worn blouse had turned to thick paste against her back.

"No, he not gone," she winced.

"He gone, Jesse gone. Left hours ago—won't be back till morning." I rubbed her rough hands gone cold even in that stifling heat.

"No... He not gone..."

The aches in her body told her he was still hovering over her life like a curse from Satan hunts down the vulnerable. She couldn't escape Jesse's shadow. No matter where he was, he could still menace the peace her soul hungered for.

Yes, Jesse was Louvenia's black dream, and he stalked her like a shadow forever.

LYE SOAP-BURNED DAYS

11

FROM THE FIRST days after I landed at Jesse's door, the clearest notion I owned was that my days would be spent over a washboard. Being only eight, I had no concept of what a decade was. That spared me from the horror of knowing that I'd be working the tubs for years to come.

I know you don't want to hear about washing no clothes. You done it, we all done it, so what? But with your raw hands did you do it for thirty years and then some? Because, Sister, that's where I been. Come, roll up your sleeves, wrap your forehead to keep the salty sweat out of your eyes and follow me to that place where the air gets mighty thin even as the sticky steam is thick enough to slice.

It's a complicated process, at least the part that helps you numb the drudgery. First, get yourself some strong lye soap, strong enough to eat a layer of skin off, got to get them clothes clean, but still not so strong your hands bleed and ruin your white woman's things. From the minute your hands touch that stinking water you learn to set your thoughts so you don't mind spending hours wearing out your washboard. But then you can challenge your mind on where the next meal may come from. I tell you, you can stand on your feet till it feels like you're standing on hot rocks just wondering on a plate of food alone. That's far enough away from the moment to keep your mind working alongside you. How do I get there, that plate of food? What if my white woman don't pay me tonight? Well, there ain't gonna be no white veranda with a table set for me at the end of my day. But could there be a decent meal up ahead? So, if that table's a real place, why is it I can only get there through some conjured daydream? Why can't I just buy me a ticket and go stay a spell; that place where we could eat ever' day? What if it's just outside our part of town? But then what if it's far deeper into the white shadows than I will ever get to? Keep yourself wondering so the time passes. Got to, but then you ain't got no option, do you?

How many times did these trails of thoughts lead me to thinking I may have to jump to find it, find some peace of mind—the ultimate end to the drudgery. Is it possible I'd survive a jump from the roof? Does the Lord deliver cripples got nobody to care for them if only to free them from their misery? How many times did I ask myself over the years? Who would care if I jumped? It wasn't the person that just put his foot on my back stepping over me 'cause he was looking for that same place, a place of bounty free of the worries that we were both told was just up the road a block or two. Because, Sister, when you jumped out of your place in that alley you get yourself slapped back down. Those were the rules that weighed down my days. Never even thought of scrambling them to make them work better for me. But why not, for heaven's sake? I'll tell you why: 'cause when you're a child you don't ask yourself those questions, and then when your childhood's worn out of you, you're too hardened to care.

Back in those first years at Jesse's, I asked myself why I couldn't be out in that alley playing with the other little girls skipping and singing. Well, ain't got time for no playing, I'd remind myself. It became my mantra; such a strange tune for a child. Got to get the tub water hot no matter how hot this damned kitchen is. "Sister is waiting" was the chorus that rang loops in my head; "Sister is waiting, Sister is waiting…Lord, Sister is waiting." What will become of me if I ever get my hands on a stolen moment to reach for a borrowed dream or two? Well, today I won't think, on it and maybe then it will hurt less.

Back then hard-working folks wore their things for a week or more before they sent them out to one of us tub women. You don't figure a white woman with any money did laundry herself, do you? No, washing was for colored women, because we have strong leathery hands that don't bleed as bad from the lye soap burns. That's what one white woman told me, whose hands were so delicate they couldn't touch mine even with a stick. To pay me, she dropped her dime to the ground and stood there like it would give her pleasure to kick me if I didn't come up with a smile of thanks plastered on my face.

Some days, when Jesse was gone, Annie from across the alley would come by and drink sweet tea with Sister and me. She was married to the preacher and already had three little ones when I came to Louvenia's. Still Annie treated me like I was one of her brood and always greeted me with a hug. Sister so loved Annie's kids her eyes seemed to swallow them up when they came 'round.

While the laundry was drying on the porch, Sister and Annie would pull out a bag of rags and sit around the kitchen table making rag dolls for Annie's kids. Some days they'd only get an arm or leg double-stitched and stuffed before another tub load beckoned. I'd watch and listened to their woman-talk as I helped stuff. Other days little dresses or breeches were made from old shirts given to Sister by one of the white women she washed for. When the doll was finished, and a little mouth stitched on, there was a hunt in an old tin for two matching brown buttons for eyes. Buttons sewn on the doll would get a big kiss from Sister before handing it to one of Annie's kids. Their expressions of delight was all Sister sought for those hours of sewing. Few things delighted her more. Louvenia's gaze over Annie's kids told me so.

Days for my brother on Jesse's alley burned him badly, too. There'd be no more trips to the river's edge to fish with Daddy and

Samuel. It was like Brother woke up one morning to find Jesse now hovering over him like another ol' Isaac there waving his fist in his young face. Jesse wasn't ol' Isaac, but he was a mean drunk with no room in his heart for a young boy brimming with vitality and eagerness for life. Surely not a boy soon needing to figure out how to be a man among white folks who would not countenance a colored standing up like one.

But then Jesse was no man. His pride and virility was long spent when I arrived even as his life lingered to feed off ours. I long figured Jesse had lost his soul by yanking ours down dead ends to keep us tethered to him. Belts to women defined his manhood and this dominance was the only thing on his mind 'cept whiskey and whores. Yes, it was an endless cycle of yanks his way to tend his daily needs. No, we never went far from that alley. Jesse's game was all diversionary, wasn't it? He had to have known that if he didn't drag us along on the skids of his life we might up and head in the opposite direction, leaving him with only an empty bottle to bitch at. Drowning folks cling to anybody to get to that next drink. Jesse held our heads under the currents till the bitter end. Even that young, Alex easily reminded Jesse he was a bit of a nothing. Surely that gnawed on the ol' man. From the first day he threatened to toss Brother out, till he did.

My Brother, he'd never be caught doing woman's work like laundry, but was always there to help us get the white folks' things back to their side of town. Sister couldn't get out much by then, as all those cracked ribs and sprained ankles from slipping on Jesse's wet rage kept her home like a prisoner. But Brother, he couldn't deliver by himself to the white woman's door, so we both had to go the distance. The holes in our shoes never lied that somehow, we had. Just Alex and me along those dark dirty streets with him carrying the folded things piled all the way to his chin. See, if a colored man walked across town and knocked on somebody's back door the wrong way, the door might 'a been answered with a shotgun blast for his proximity to the white woman's virtue. Seemed like so much violence for so little virtue, but guilty as charged nonetheless. Was there another verdict? No, but there was always another rope at hand. Alex would carry the heavy load of freshly washed clothes real careful so's not to wrinkle and give the woman an excuse not to pay me. Then he'd hide from sight when I walked up to her backdoor. There I'd be paid a few coins, pick up her dirty things she'd likely toss at my feet and we'd head back across the tracks. Even with Alex himself carrying her rags, I'd 'bout gag on the stench of the woman's dirty laundry. No wonder we couldn't eat some nights, even if we had food.

Don't ever 'member one of them white women offering a sip of water. Guess the charity her Christian Bible called for did not extend to coloreds. We were too primitive to understand charity, so why waste God's blessings on us? That what she thought? Best save it for the horses then. They value a sugar cube, don't they? Anyway, weren't there plenty of horse troughs for coloreds to drink from? Brother knew well enough even before I was old enough to understand, that colored women weren't safe walking at night. You could be robbed of your wash money, innocence, or life. Alex made sure I got home safely, or at least as safe as he could till I was delivered back to Jesse's porch, the trapdoor to his hell.

Deep in his sleepless nights, Brother would lay on his pallet in the corner of the kitchen trying to figure the ropes of his new life off the plantation. His face would go hard with anger as he stared off somewhere into the dead-end corners of them kitchen walls. Him looking for that place I knew he wanted to go, needed to go, but like Louvenia and me, couldn't find the path to get there. How do you fix a soul? Let me tell you, it's so much harder than the breaking was. I'm reminded by those long nights before Jesse threw him out, nights when Jesse wound Sister's head tight around his fist. Alex would pull his blanket over his head so he couldn't hear Jesse's preaching being taught Louvenia upside her head so's its meaning would penetrate her reluctance to learn proper. In anger, Alex's chest heard what his covered ears tried to muffle and would heave up and down like somebody jumping on it, pushing all those scrambled tears into the open. Tears he had to hide in the daylight where he knew a man could never admit to crying himself to sleep. Surely that kind of admission can put a man face-to-face with his impotence and the fear that he might soon lose his soul. Maybe the blackness of it all would crush his manhood into pool of drunken self-loathing like the kind Jesse was drowning in. So quickly came the day when Alex couldn't cry no more, not even dry tears. He had to be a man, deal with Mr. Jesse. The devil comes in many forms, Momma told me so. And Jesse knew the devil well enough to call in a favor or two.

No, it didn't take Jesse long 'fore he tossed Brother out and told him never to come back or he'd get the law on him by claiming he'd been stealing. Never could figure out what Jesse might say was missing. Our laundry money? Who stole that but Jesse himself? Sometimes, if Jesse was passed out in the backroom, Brother would sneak in to eat something Louvenia had set aside for him. Then he would snatch some sleep on my cot. Other times when Jesse was up, Alex would head off walking all night, hiding in the cold shadows where he was safer from being picked up for vagrancy, his crime being not having a job as a boy-man. Why'd it always seem Jesse slept fine 'cept on the nights that it froze hard out there, or rain pelted the tin roof over the porch so hard we couldn't sleep anyway? Those nights Jesse was guaranteed to get up and wander about the kitchen wanting us to fix him another meal. These nights there'd be no sleep for Alex over in the corner, even hidden behind our tubs. Still, we managed to get Alex out the back door many times before Jesse was sober enough to know Brother was sleeping on his kitchen floor again.

As the months bled into years, Louvenia and me came to feel no better off than a pair of mules. We dreamed, but our prayers were never heard. It was that old loop again: somebody wouldn't pay us for our ironing, or Jesse drunk us up, or one of his women needed a new dress and the money we dreamed might one day buy us a ticket out of Jesse's alley was gone again. Gone again! Gone again…gone again. I can still hear it ringing in my thoughts. These things don't never go away. Not ever.

Still, by the time I was a girl-women, I'd gotten sick of all that. So, I started taking the wash money and hiding it 'round the place where Jesse might not get to it. Made no difference; Jesse didn't need to hunt the money down himself. He knew where to find Louvenia easy enough. That's all it took to assure himself of another night at the bars. When he found her, I had to give it up—put our money in front of him and apologize for keeping him from his appointment with a bottle, or he'd beat the air out of Louvenia till she found the money herself. Sometimes I'd pull out ever' cent I'd hidden and throw it at his yellowed face. Louvenia, with her cracked ribs would scramble over the floor to retrieve every cent. Then Jesse, with a smirk pinned on his face, would disappear again. He'd head out to swaddle his women in the lies our money bought while I swaddled Louvenia's ribs in the same tattered cloth that barely held our lives together—I guess the kind rag dolls are made of. And you know, no matter how many times I wound that old cloth around our wounds, I never saw a beautiful blue silk monogram on it reminding me of the Burneys. Why are dreams so hard to build and yet so easy to wrench out of you?

They were different from mine, but still the rules weighed heavily on Alex's young back. He never took to learning to read or write; he just couldn't sit still long enough, and had the notion only silly women wanted to read and all. No, Brother had things he wanted to get done, places to go, his own special dreams brewing of how he was gonna save Louvenia and me. He shared this notion, 'bout saving us, to give me something to hope on. The thing is, he couldn't read the signs to know which doors he needed to knock on to open up a new way. Ever' day I learned from Louvenia and what she didn't know, I had to go find for myself. Even then Sister was there prodding me along and turning my face from the view behind to the one ahead of me. But Alex didn't have a man to protect him from the Jesses of the world. Nobody to tell him that what he saw in them alleys was seldom real, or even what a real life is built on. Yes, things were sure hard to decipher under the layers of ashes from the lives burnt out on that alley, 'cause there's a sleight-of-hand in life and if you don't know where or who it's coming from you lose over and over again. Then what nobody ever tells anybody is when you lose long and hard enough, before it's all over you've already given up. Yes, in all the dust stirred from folks slapping you on the back for being such a damned good sucker, you don't even know it's because you done lost it all and it's already deep in their pockets by then. Then all the folks that stood by the side feeding you lies have one more back to walk over, clawing their way to their dreams one way or another, one back to the next. It's nothing personal—that skin off your back, it's just one more dollar for nothing, a simple sleight-of-hand. Let me tell you, I would swerve from many such folks in the years ahead.

I go into a rage when I hear the hollow sound of a hand across the face of somebody not expecting it. No time to duck or run, that is if you're not already run out by then. Jesse beat Louvenia bad. He beat her 'cause he was hurting inside and needed whiskey to ease his agony. He beat her 'cause she had no respect for him, and he knew it. If you're a colored man and your woman don't respect you there ain't nobody else who will. But along that worn path to his own hell Jesse kept drinking and beating the life out of Louvenia. No, he didn't hit me much. Just now and then. Louvenia said it was 'cause I had Momma's eye, yet he beat my soul, didn't he? Just fixing Sister's wounds was enough to do that, let alone what I knew he'd try to do to me if he could. Bodies can heal; don't know if souls ever really do. Maybe they only go on bleeding till you're dead inside.

The days somehow, somewhere, became years for us marked in the ledgers of our memories by the hundreds 'a tubs we bent over. Too soon I was no longer a child and hadn't been for most my childhood. Our lives had quickly become a carousel of Jesse's abuses riding our souls up and down and then down to depths deeper than anybody could have imagined. No, you don't think about escaping much, 'cause you turn off all the thinking you can. It's part of survival. Right after thinking comes those feelings that plunge the knives deeper. Like: why me?

Seeing the Tinker's Deal

12

WHEN I WAS near to being twelve Sister let me deliver the folded clothes by myself. But never more than five or six blocks on the other side of the tracks from where we lived.

I loved the freedom I felt making those deliveries. I could loop around as many blocks as I wanted and gaze into windows of the stores where white women shopped. I always took as long as I could to get home to be away from that alley but also to be away from Louvenia and Annie, 'cause they'd both been at me. It seemed like Annie hardly ever looked my way that she didn't pause in her tracks and ask if I'd been reading the Bible. Even when she didn't ask her eyes followed me about. But she knew I couldn't read, barely knew my alphabet, that's why I was sure it was Louvenia who put her up to it 'cause I'd been sassing her. I knew it was coming; Annie telling me the Bible said I'd go to hell for sassing. But I wasn't too worried 'bout going to hell. No, I wasn't, as I figured Louvenia would never tattle to Jesus 'cause she knew I'd for sure tell the Lord right back that she'd been smacking me when I sassed. Ain't nobody gonna win on that, so we best keep it out of our prayers.

It was after I'd finished delivering when it all happened. I would have sold my soul for a jar of cool sweet tea it was so hot. I paused to wipe the sweat from my eyes and saw an old white man perched up on a cart wrestling with his merchandise. What was he fussing over like that? I stood and watched the commotion. The barrels piled up on his cart were wobbling so they nearly fell over and all the while he was giving his horse the low-down. I could see that horse was having problems understanding the man's thick accent. No, nothing would stay up piled-up on that cart, and he looked too old to be climbing up and down to fetch things. That's what I heard him say to his horse, and the horse never uttered a word to disabuse him. Reckon that ol' swayback was thinking they'd get home quicker if he kept his mouth shut and didn't get into it with that ol' tinker.

But no sooner had he climbed back up in the seat than a big barrel tipped off the back of his overloaded cart and rolled near in front of me. Stuff spilled out all over and that old man, he didn't look like he was none too happy, no, and his horse just turned the other way.

"What's all this stuff?" I asked. "Any of it still good?" I always heard Louvenia ask the same question, wanting to know what the value is 'fore she pulled her purse out. She said she could read a person's eyes to know if they was lying or not.

"Them mostly books, Missy, nobody wants 'em. So, you get a good price, but only today," he said. "'Cause if I have to pick 'em up again, the price goes up."

"If nobody wants 'em, then why I want 'em? I can't read none."

"Why not, colored girl, you blind, or somethin'?" he asked, looking right into my eyes looking right back at his.

"Now if you ain't blind, then you can for sure see I ain't blind!" That's the way I told folks off. And no, that ain't sassing.

"I can see good enough," he said, "and what I see is you can't see nothin', Sister."

About then I got a feeling that this man had gots to be a crazy. Like them ones hanging 'round the corner from the alley. I wondered if that was why his horse was looking the other way. He was embarrassed at what come out of that ol' man's mouth.

"Sister, huh?"

I walked up closer so's he could see I sure enough had two good eyes and they was working him over good to see what he was up to and he best see I sure as hell wasn't no sister of his! Well, up there close I could sure see that his mouth worked better than his eyes. He squinted and furrowed his brow till his nose wrinkled to the top of his forehead, which seemed to trigger his mouth all over again.

"There's different kinds of blindness," he said looking at me like the sun was blinding him, 'cept the sun was near down by then. "And I reckon the kind you're afflicted with feels good, don't it, Sister?"

"Yeah, what kind you talkin' 'bout then?"

"Ignorance! You know it like a sweet friend, don't ya? Can't read no fine books like these here I'm offering at a special discount. That's why I brung 'em 'round for you today. Didn't ya see 'em comin'?"

"Yeah, I saw you deliver 'em to my feet. Heaven help us if I took the other way home! Then you gonna tell me that barrel been rollin' up and down these streets lookin' for me?"

"You ever seen books roll up to somebody ain't ignorant and then stop to help 'em fix that? Now that don't make sense, 'less you're ignorant, I reckon," he said.

I wondered to myself when was he gonna pass the collection plate for that sermon. I patted his poor ol' horse's head so he'd feel less humiliated.

Well, I had my own view of the situation. But I didn't want to get into it with no crazy ol' white man. So, after looking at him long and hard, I decided to tell him off like Louvenia did the butcher who sold her a pound of gristle that time. No, I wasn't gonna let this tinker take up more of my time and think he was gonna get away with it.

"I ain't ignorant and it ain't my best friend! How much them books, in case I ever wanna know?"

Ain't used books like day-old bread? They got bargains on stale bread, don't they? Anyway, that proved I wasn't no ignorant colored girl. Silly fool!

"A silver dollar and they's all yours, Sister!"

"What?" At that I got to thinking he ain't half as crazy as he been acting, that ol' man.

"A silver dollar! I ain't got no silver dollar, do I? Anyway, I can see they ain't worth half a nickel and you know it!"

"No? Well, there you have it. Them books down there, all for a nickel, and the rest on credit. Yep, you take 'em! Then if you don't read 'em up in a year, you can bring 'em back to get your money back. All five cents of it."

While I was thinking on the deal, I moved my head side to side to see if his eyes followed. I got to thinking he might be working the kind of deal like Louvenia told me some of her customers had. Them white women asked her for credit but then just paid with more of their filthy rags 'fore they hit and run out of town, not paying for weeks of ironing. Maybe this tinker's deal was different. Didn't know, but I knew I had to think on the terms and keep an eye on him eyeing me.

"You get slow to thinkin' when you're half blind, ain't ya Sister?"

"I ain't the one that's blind here!"

Still, I started thinking there had to be a reason that barrel near rolled down the street and right up to my poor tired feet. These books meant for me then? Would I be blind if I didn't recognize a good deal when it near rolled over me? A nickel down and the rest on credit like Louvenia worked out at the grocer's?

"Well, then take a good deal when it rolls your way."

He talked like he'd read my thoughts. Stupid man. After handing him a nickel, I picked those books up, dusted them off and started off. I'd never worked a deal on credit before, and was eager to tell Sister all about it, thinking myself quite the businesswoman!

Then I got to thinking and yelled back, "Hey, Mr. Tinker Man, how I know you're gonna be here in a year if I wanna return these here books and get my nickel back?"

"If I ain't here, my cousin sure will be. Get your nickel back from him. Anyway, I seen yer kind, you can't think ahead that far, Sister!"

Well, well, he was thinking he sees things better than me, but still thought I was his sister even after I told him off!

As he loaded up his stuff he yelled, "You drive a hard bargain, missy!"

And I knew I had, too.

I headed back and didn't stop for more wash soap like I 'pose' to, 'cause I was too eager to tell Louvenia 'bout the big deal I'd made. Figured I'd leave them books on the table to prove to Louvenia and Annie I was the best deal maker 'round Jesse's alley. Sure, I thought, there stacked in front of them was proof.

Sister was finishing the last of the ironing as I walked in. I piled them books on the table and waited for Louvenia to figure out what I had going. Then, without a word I went to pour us a jar of sweet tea. Sister stopped her ironing, looked at me closely and sat down. I told her 'bout them books rolling off his cart and over to my feet where they near tripped me! Louvenia looked as though she'd never heard of such a stupid man in her life.

"He was the stupidest blind man I ever seen!" I continued.

But then I began to wonder if I shouldn't have just stepped over them books and ran, not walked home! Yes, ma'am. I could have skipped this meeting with Louvenia and gotten to bed without the grief that was waiting for me as Sister and I struggled over the damned deal I'd just made. You see, she kept on patting them books and saying "My, my," like they were gonna give her their side of the story, and that being different than mine!

"My, my, don't we got the deals goin' on 'round here?" she said again. "Sure looks like it," she replied to herself. "If you hadn't hauled his books away, then he'd have to get down off his cart, pick 'em up and then go back to sellin' 'em all over again the next day. Wouldn't he? That right? And he never got it right today, huh? So, don't know how it's gonna be any better tomorrow."

I could see Louvenia understood the situation, and expected her to ask me if I told that tinker off like she did the butcher who sold her the gristle.

"So, I gots the better deal than him? Did I? Huh?"

"Well, it would sure seem. But then only if you don't end up haulin' them books all the way back 'cross town a year from now to get your nickel back. That be the case, he's gonna say you're the stupidest colored girl 'round to keep haulin' stuff that's worthless back and forth and, well, who knows where it could all end? You followin' me, Sister?"

"Don't know, do I? That means they's worthless and he gots the best deal and my nickel?"

"Well, you don't know how to read is the thing. But that didn't keep you from haulin' these here books down the alley along with a bag of dirty laundry. What was he thinkin', I wonder? Now, let's see here. We gots to figure this out. Don't want any stupid ol' man getting the best of my sister. No, I won't have it!"

"That's right!" I replied, yet really had no idea to what.

Louvenia picked up one of my books and examined it carefully, like she was looking for the value of the deal. Like pears from a farmer's cart was the way she looked them over. Don't want pears with bruises gonna go bad on you the next day. She looked close at them books and then even closer at me. What's that all about? She can't read none herself. She expects that book to tell her something? That ain't no pear. You got to be able to read to know what that book's got to say, I was thinking.

Then it hit me why Sister seemed to be working over the terms a bit too hard, like there might be a bit of gristle hidden in there. So, I grabbed that book and tossed it back on the table, so she knew, too!

"Then I just learn to read and them books gonna be all used up, and I gots the best deal and don't need to do no haulin' cross town to get my nickel back 'cause they's useless, huh?" I blurted in one breath.

"Well, you see then, he ain't as clever as you, Sarah. When you see 'im down there again, you tell 'im you ain't gonna be bringin' no books back 'cause you used 'em up already. He shouldn't waste his time trying to work a better deal. Not with my sister, that's for sure. See what he thinks on that. That silly ol' man!"

"Yeah, that's what I'll say to him. See what he thinks on that for sure!"

"Don't even know how a man can stay in business who is so simple-minded."

Sister finished her sweet tea like the meeting was over. Still, I was left wondering if Louvenia and I were truly traveling on the same side of the road. You see, I always got suspicious when we agreed on anything without rolling in the dirt first. So, I looked at Louvenia long and hard to see if she'd figured something out I hadn't. She went back to her work shaking her head at how unbelievably stupid that old man was to try to cut himself a better deal off of me.

On the other hand, maybe she wanted me to think something like that. Well, what did she want me to think? So, I went to bed that night wondering. But the next day I knew for sure. Sure did! Sister come back from Annie's with an arm full of dirty clothes, walked onto the porch where I was hanging wet clothes like she was aiming to get into it with me.

"Annie gots a couple of loads of her kids' things we got to help her with."

She stood there holding them things as if she had something hidden in them. Like maybe a stick. What's she got going on, I wondered?

"Yeah, so put 'em down over there, Sister. I'll do 'em after I finish Miss Brown's uniforms."

"She wants to pay you."

Louvenia kept holding onto that pile and looking at me as

though she knew something I didn't. Or maybe I'd sure enough not want to know and she knew it, too.

"Pay us? She ain't got no money with all them kids," I said. "Just put 'em down there, 'less you're gettin' attached to 'em the way you're huggin' 'em."

Sister looked at me like she always did when I sassed and was about to head my way with the flyswatter. She shifted the pile in her arm and glared at me as if I didn't hear her the first time. "Annie says she gots to pay you! But she gots no money—that's what."

Then she started looking down her nose at me like she was ready to roll in the dirt for sure. I knew that look! "Yeah, so Louvenia, I do up her things and she pays me with nothin'. That suit you?"

"Yeah, that'll be fine. But not for Annie. She gots to pay somehow. You know how she is, Sarah."

I gulped and jumped in quick. "Now, don't take one of her kidney pies, 'less you're gonna feed it to Jesse!"

"See, that's what I was thinkin', too. We always think alike, don't we?" Louvenia announced.

"Yeah? Since now? And why are you clutchin' them dirty clothes like that? They gonna get away from you, or you got something hidden in there? Like one of her kidney pies you can't stand the smell of?"

"Best let her do what she can and keep her kidney pies home, huh? You're right, I agree with you, Sarah. You know what's best then. So then Annie's comin' over some afternoon when Jesse's gone, to start you on your readin'. That's what we'll do 'bout this. Hear me now?"

And I sure enough had. "Readin'? I got no time for readin'!"

I tossed some dirty shirts I was sorting into my tub, churned and pounded them on that washboard to show her what I would do to her and Annie if they fussed at me while I was trying to get my work done.

Louvenia closed in like she wanted to see if I'd gone crazy on her or maybe deserved a smack. She looked down into my tub and shook her head, for having no water in that tub where I was wringing the necks on them shirts.

"I ain't never heard of washing with no water. Have you now, Sarah? Well, I guess you have now, huh? Nope, not a drop of water in that tub."

"Then what do you want me to do with her kids' things?" I asked.

"Well, you might as well haul 'em back over there," she said, "'bout like you're gonna do with them books in a year 'fore your credit run out and tell her, her kids best wash 'em them little selves, huh?"

Louvenia looked down into my tub again like I was sure missing the point, so I knew for sure she was getting in my face. That's how Louvenia always starts things with me; she comes from behind and then asks me why I's standing in her way.

"How's Annie know how to read anyway?" I thought if Annie didn't really know how to read, then I'd stop this nonsense cold! We'd just sit there at the table over our sweet tea like any other day and talk 'bout that tinker man that's just plain stupid as can be. Then we could all agree I gots the best deal and be finish with it.

"'Cause her husband's the preacher and he teached her and you know it, too! Now you're the big deal maker 'round here. You gots a better notion? You been pickin' them books up day after day and lookin' 'em over like they was gonna teach you to read just by handling them."

"No, I ain't been pickin' 'em up 'cept they was in my way. And you been puttin' 'em in my way. I seen you do it, too!"

As Louvenia glared I went over and grabbed Annie's kids' things, tossed them in a tub and commenced churning the hell out of them like the devil been in that pile hiding and I was the one gonna cleanse his black heart with lye soap. Amen, Lord. Never once did I take my eyes off Sister so's she'd know I was on to her good. But that damned water she poured in my tub was so hot I started thinking it would be easier on me if I just learn to read some. Yeah, you don't know my sister—hell of a lot easier!

So I figured I'd only go to pretending to read, thumb through them old books, just like I seen her doing ever' time I looked over at her, looking over at me with a book in her hand. That would fix the problem. I was sure gonna teach her to mess with me!

"Then I just learn to read. So, Annie be happy that her bill got paid and her kids got clean clothes and we don't got to choke on no kidney pies."

"I don't see any other way out of it," Louvenia declared as if I'd fallen to the bottom of that tinker's barrel and she was the one who'd saved me! Hallelujah!

"You do cut a mean deal for sure."

Still I had the feeling them books were gonna cause me nothing but grief, no matter how good the deal was. Sister stood there quite pleased with herself. But then she'd won again!

It was 'bout two days later, before I'd even got the chance to burn them books out in the alley, that Annie showed up—should I say sneaked up? She was looking quite official like she was on a mission to save souls and I was next in line. She walked in while I was finishing ironing her kids' things and stood there without a word. She could not have pinned her eyes on me better if she had Louvenia's clothespins on her.

I turned to Sister and got some of that eyebrow of hers, the one that arches like it wants to fly off her face when she's mad. What's wrong with these here women today, I wondered? They was giving me the eye 'cause they suddenly can't talk no more? I heard their big mouths flapping like crows out in the alley just moments before. 'Cept Louvenia, I could read her a bit better. She was giving me the "I got a stick and I'm gonna put it to your head" look again.

"Annie, you got something to say standing there eyeing me, or you just come over to make snortin' noises?"

Annie stood there with her mouth wide open, acting as though she was so insulted she'd turned speechless.

"Now, you know better than talkin' like that," Annie said, but looked to Louvenia.

Sister was sure looking high and mighty while I burned my fingers on that iron, watching them act like they was aiming to get me to the ground to get the kinks out 'a my hair—that's the way they was looking at me. But I didn't care none, 'cause I knew how hot my iron was and could fight them both off if they ganged up to pull my hair for sassing.

"Louvenia, you got something goin' on here that you want me to figure out before the Second Comin'?"

Then I poured the last of the sweet tea and drunk it up in front of 'em so they'd know I was on to them good.

But I wasn't, was I? I was just acting foolish 'cause I had a feeling Annie come over to get me to the table and force-feed me printed words. Kink by kink, wouldn't bother Sister none. I could see that plain 'cause she had a notion I was embarrassed not knowing my alphabet. But you see, I did know some of it, 'cause Jackson Burney teached me. He ran out of hard candy bribes at the letter "U", so I refused to learn more till he stole more from his daddy's jar on his desk. But he said I'd never need the rest of the letters anyway, so we went to doing something else, like laying eggs in our chicken nests in Miss Burney's roses. But Annie here, I could tell she been talking to Louvenia behind my back. They knew how to get me to the ground even without a stick in their hands. Yes, Annie hit me right upside my head with her sermon about white folks getting better stuff than folks on our side of town.

"Now, Sister Sarah, you know white folks don't want us to read none. You drink up all that sweet tea, honey? 'Cause if we can read, we just might be expectin' the same stuff they gots on their side of town. Now, you know they ain't gonna take to that business, 'cause they like feelin' they gots all the good stuff comin' their way and we're only here to clean up, right, Sister Louvenia?"

Louvenia stuck her nose in the air to confirm that business 'bout white folks.

"If you want to stay on the good side of white folks," Annie continued, "don't learn to read none. Hear me? They like us simple and ignorant."

Annie never looked at my sister, but I was still watching her out the corner of my eye. I knew they'd rehearsed this out in the alley. But they surely had a stick upside my head just the same, one on each side. Like damned book ends, the two of them were squeezing my head in a vice 'cause they knew I wasn't gonna take to white folks thinking I was no better than to clean up after them.

"You learn that sermon from the preacher?" I asked Annie.

Sister didn't take to my disrespect none. So, she moved closer to Annie's side to make sure I could see her glaring at me better.

Thank goodness it wasn't pouring rain in our kitchen, 'cause Sister would have drowned her nose was up so high. So, I sat down across from Annie and picked up one of those damned books. Sister must not have believed my intent to learn, 'cause she moved the ironing board over there near the kitchen door like a stockade and then went to get the iron heating off the stove for reinforcements against my possible escape. Well, Annie opened a book and started pointing out the alphabet and we started writing it down.

That's how all that got started; me reading and all. I guess I'd been thinking reading was something for folks who planned on going someplace in life and that never included girls like me, so I best just get my hands down in my wash tub so we could eat that day and forget about tomorrow. Dreaming was for others who had the time to waste on it. And yet from then on, I never moved ahead on the journey without a book nearby to help me find my way to something I'd only wondered existed out there.

Climbing in a Box
to Get Out

13

LOUVENIA HAD BEEN imprisoned in Jesse's jail for nearly ten years by the time my brother and I came to her. She was convinced that what Jesse had told her could only be true: if she left him, he'd get the law on her the moment she squirmed out his door. He warned that she'd go no further than the chain-gang he'd convinced her had to be all but waiting just around any corner she might turn.

Sister must have heard an echo of ol' Isaac in Jesse's words. When you live in brutality long enough, the layers of scars blind you to your options. There were precious few at the end of that alley, so best stay at your ironing board with the curtains pulled tight so you don't look out and only see yourself slowly dying.

We seldom left that hell hole of a kitchen 'cept to deliver our ironing or go buy more soap to pour into more tubs. Sure, it was easy to blame Jesse—a poor soul also a slave, slave to his bottle—but we had to find a way out, Louvenia and me. Mind you, I knew the two options for our women: bent over the tubs or being a whore. Got nothing against whores, but my momma put the fear of the

Lord into me, and if there's anything I feared more than the Lord, it was Minerva up there with Him. That's the only thing ol' Isaac and I had in common: Don't want to cross that Minerva.

I kept thinking and daydreaming on it but still not really knowing for what. Guess it was only pieces of thoughts I'd strung together in my imagination. Like maybe dreaming of where a life of dignity awaited. Where is that? Didn't matter what the place was called. Momma told me a soul is a place to hide your dreams from the white folks. What she never knew was that we had to hide our dreams from plenty of coloreds, too, like the folks who stalked them alleys as well as Jesse, the man who stalked us in his four walls not much bigger than a wooden box.

Mornings when Jesse was snoring in his backroom, Louvenia and I started whispering. What 'a we do? We had that laundry business going good—why did we take it from him day in and out? Him busting our hopes as easy as he busted our lips like we was nobodies—but still nobodies good enough for him to live off. I figured if Jesse was not there at least what pennies we made would be ours. But Louvenia told me she done seen chain gangs and was scared he could all but rise to shackle her—the only promise he ever made that he was sure as hell to keep. How many times had he suddenly risen from a drunken stupor and put her face on the floor? Strangely, she didn't seem to be as scared he might one day up and kill her to make room for one of his whores whose names he blurted in his drunken sleep. Hard to understand how terrifyingly deep that dry well a colored woman can fall into when she's face-to-face with her own door and knows the only thing truly waiting on the other side is her final prayer what with no money, place to go and nobody to turn to. And yet all the same, even when you're kicked to the ground, life can keep booting you ever closer to that dark bottomless well, the one filled with the stench of rotting desperation, a place where no prayers are ever uttered.

"Look at them whores outside Jesse's alley," Louvenia challenged. "They know what I's talkin' about!"

Whores getting beaten in them alleys is what she meant. Life had taught us that when you jumped, it wasn't for joy. No, best not chance it. Stay put. Hug the ground like Jesse admonished, so the next storm wouldn't put you into a pine box six feet under. But even the whores figured they was better than us 'cause they didn't have their hands down in no tub of stinking brown water.

Most of the time Sister and I knew where each other stood on things, and we seldom stood far apart. But she'd somehow survived those years with that ol' man before Alex and I fell into her life. From those dark times I would come to understand that there were things she couldn't put to words. Things still too scabbed to pick open again. Why is shame the wound that resists healing?

One morning while Sister was ironing, and I was twisting the water out of shirts to hang, my jabbering about going on without Jesse got Sister cross. I still recall a saddened look of frustration and anger that seemed to weave through her expressions. She put her iron down and pointed to the table for me to take a seat.

"What?" I asked.

"Sit down over there. I got things to tell you. Things I should 'a told you before," she said. "Ugly things I don't want to go back to but now I reckon it's time. You got to know now."

"Know what, Sister?"

"You're always goin' on like all we need to do is stuff a pillowcase with our things and step out that kitchen door ridin' on nothin' but a big smile. Maybe like we ain't never gonna have to beg Jesse to take us back. But I know better, and I'm gonna tell you what I know, too!"

Louvenia paced the kitchen shaking her head like she was cursing at the very recollections she didn't want to look at again. I sat down to hear what she had to say.

"Not long after I came to Jesse, he told me he was gonna rent a buggy and we was gonna get out of town. Go for a picnic."

"Jesse take you on a picnic? When did he ever rent a buggy?"

"You just hush and let me tell you 'bout Jesse's picnic," she said. "He told me to make up a basket of food. And I did. Baked fresh bread the night before; fried us some ham and Annie give me some mustard she'd made. Even baked a cake. Never since I met that man had we gone nowheres I recall. Then I carried the basket to the stables. Jesse say I carry it 'cause his back was hurtin'.'"

"Jesse's back hurt so bad he couldn't carry no basket of sandwiches?"

"He rented us a buggy. Went all the way out of town and then down some dusty county road."

"Where was that?" I asked.

"Don't know. Just figured he knew a place where we could eat under some trees or maybe near a pretty stream. But then I seen for sure where we was headed. Way up there, in a cloud of dust there was these folks workin' a ditch. They was all colored and Lord, there was women in with 'em. I asked Jesse why we was headed over there. He told me he had somebody he been wantin' me to meet. Jesse stopped where them folks was working their picks and shovels. Them poor folks looked up but couldn't hardly see 'cause they was so blinded by that hot sun and the dirt covering their faces wet with sweat."

"What were they doin'?" I asked.

"They was diggin' a drain ditch along the county road. I tell you, there'd not been a hotter day that summer! No, ma'am." Sister paused like she needed to catch her own breath. "Hard labor, I 'magine. I was watchin' when a man fell over on the side of the road. Don't think he ever got up. Nobody done nothin' for him. Nothin'. Not even give 'im a swallow of water."

"Lord, Louvenia, why'd Jesse go there for a picnic?"

"Then Jesse waved to a man standing there watchin' over 'em all. You know that man was like ol' Isaac that watched us in the fields at the Burneys'. Jesse nodded to 'im. That man, with a grin on his big ugly face headed over. Lord Jesus, I got to thinking that he had that same evil look that Jesse does."

"Were you scared?"

"Jesse, he say to me, 'I want you to listen to me and listen good 'cause I ain't gonna say it but once. There ain't but one reason I took you in, and it ain't 'cause I wanted to look at that face of yours. No, Ma'am, it sure enough ain't.' He say, 'I only married you 'cause I gettin' old and gonna need somebody to take care 'a me when I need it, and that's all you's good for. You got nothin' else that interests me. No, you sure as hell ain't. But if you ever figure on headin' out, you be right down there in that dirt with them other niggers. Look at 'em good, 'cause you'll be down there yourself digging your way back to me with a pick and shovel. And Lord, you know I mean it, woman! You be digging your way back to where I told you never to stray and then be on your knees thankin' me for what I done give you, marryin' you and all.'"

"My Lord, Sister!"

"Just as that man come up to the buggy, I asked Jesse who them folks were. Jesse, he grabbed the basket off my lap and handed it over to the man with the ugly grin. He yanked the rag off the top and tossed it to the ground and went to eatin' my sandwiches like he'a hog. Jesse say to 'im, 'You tell Louvenia here who them folks yonder are. She gots to know to keep 'er straight with me and doin' what I tell 'er.'"

"That man, with a mouth full of my food, he say, 'Sister, that there is a nigger chain-gang. They's worthless. Owe the man money. But they ain't got none, so they come work the roads or the county ditches. They earn a quarter a day, and ever' cent goes to pay off the boss. Yeah, done lost me one just now. Think he's dead over there from heatstroke, that one,' he gestured to the man covered with so much dust you couldn't no more make out his face."

I was speechless.

Sister continued, "Jesse, he say to that man, 'Tell Louvenia 'bout them women over there!' The man grinned, and with his dirty hand grabbed a fist full of my cake and shoved it in his mouth, nodding to Jesse as he swallowed it down. 'Them women, they's whores, ain't they Jesse? Yeah, look at 'em. Dirty whores is all they is. Sure they are. They don't work hard enough out here. Ain't that right? You can plainly see for yourself. So, they got to give me overtime. End of the day, they service the men here. Yeah, they sure as hell do! The man that works hardest and gives me no grief, he first at 'er while the others watch. Then they gets their turn on her. Don't make no difference, she a whore.' That's what that man said, then went to laughin' like it was at me. Jesse, he laughed with him and turned the buggy 'round and headed back. That was my picnic that day. So, you still think it's easy movin' on? I got nowheres to go. Got no money, and after living in this alley I got no name people gonna respect. You see, Jesse and me, we weren't never really married, and you know what that makes me! So, now where we go? Huh? Well, you ask Jesse. He'll tell you where we had that picnic, 'cause that's 'bout where we'd end up!"

"But where we headed if we just stay here?" I replied. "We're climbing into a box. A pine box Jesse gonna nail shut and put six feet under the dirt," I said. "Ain't that also a 'where' you can't find on no map?"

"Let me tell you something else. That man, that nigger watching the others like a white slaver, you know who that was?"

"You know 'im?" I asked.

"That man is Jesse's brother, Fred. That Fred Powell. After that day, he started comin' 'round here to eat my food till he and Jesse got into it over a whore. No, he ain't no better now. Workin' for the man and his chain-gang off the backs of folks like me, he was back then. No, he ain't no better, 'cause I know what he does now with them women at the bars! He works the alleys with 'em!"

❧

At times I wondered if maybe Jesse could read our thoughts; we were sure he could. At least there were days when he seemed to sense there was something stirring behind his back.

Sister was still ironing one night, and I'd just washed my hair in the kitchen sink when he come out from his sleeping room like he was on the prowl and maybe wondering where he could situate our next helping of bruises. Yes, he watched night and day like he watched over his bottles. We were his bottles. That night, just as I was headed off to deliver our ironing, Jesse stopped cold, looked about as though something was amiss. Angrily, he looked as though he was gonna belt us.

"What's that girl doin' gettin' dolled up 'round here?" he asked Louvenia, standing next to me with the brush. "That a new dress that girl's got on? Huh?"

"That ain't no new dress, Jesse. You know it ain't," Sister replied in barely a whisper, as she knew he was looking for a fight. "Just one the neighbors passed down." Then she jumped to defend against his next accusation. "Where would we get money to buy a piece of fabric? I only put a new collar on it cut from an old white shirt one of my ladies give me. That ol' shirt was too small for you to wear," she said. "Sarah, hadn't you best get on with deliverin' your ironin' 'fore it gets dark. Go on now."

"Yeah, then bring me back a bottle or don't come back through my door, lil' girl. That's all I got to say to you!" Jesse snorted.

"Now, Jesse, you knows Sarah can't go buy you a bottle. She only twelve. I go get it when she comes home with the money, 'less you want me to go and leave you alone with your supper burnin'."

"That girl gots too high opinion of herself. You seen that? Yeah, well I sure enough have!"

"I sure seen lots of things, Jesse," Sister responded.

"Huh? If that keeps up, she be out on the streets like that boy, Alex. You remind 'er what I done to him for not respectin' me!"

"Don't worry, Jesse. Sarah ain't never gonna forget what you did to Brother that winter."

And the hurts piled up like lash scars; layer upon layer crisscrossing the backside of her soul. Jesse easily reminded me there were nigger dogs of all colors.

"I ain't in the mood for you," Jesse announced for the third time. "I'm goin' over to my brother Fred's. Yeah. May not come back tonight. You think on that!"

And, Lord how long had we? We'd been thinking on him walking out the door with his stolen laundry money and borrowed pride and getting so damned tripped up on his own life that he never found his way back. Yes, we prayed hard that before it was too late for us there'd come a day we'd step out of the box we were in—the pine box that might soon be our coffin if we didn't move fast enough.

DAYDREAMS IN THE NIGHTSHADE

14

ELL, THE CHANGES came even if slowly. Our days were like standing tiptoe on a wobbly stool as Jesse was once again in good with Brother Fred. They'd teamed to court bottles and the women that followed the good times. Sometimes Jesse never made it back from Fred's place after the bars closed. That meant a bit of peace here and there for us. Even hours without curses bouncing off the walls and reflected off our swollen lips. Sister and I celebrated these mornings when Jesse never come home by pretending he was really gone for good. Amen, Lord. Amen, he gone!

You see, by then Louvenia and I had worked things out; we left food on the table for Jesse so's he had something to do with his mouth when he got up, which quickly put him in the mood to find the door and head to the bar. At the table with his plate of food Jesse seldom spoke to us and, Lord, we never answered when he did. By then his days were so blurred he never knew what direction he was swerving to or from. Monday was a full bottle, after a few drinks and nap or two and he'd somehow landed himself on Friday night all over again. Or had he really just gotten through the last Friday? "Who said that?"

he blurted from his many stupors. But he had yet to realize that there was no one there to answer his knock at the door.

The day came when my hours over an ironing table got me counting more than the piles I had to get through. Mind you, the numbers were never large, but I counted things that meant something to me: a bit more laundry money hidden away, or just a day not pulled down by utter exhaustion long before night came. Even a nice pie good Annie left us could bring one of those splintered laughs from Sister. Made me smile, too. I thought about these rare moments of happiness and wondered where I could find more of the same.

Back then Alex would come by from time to time when Jesse was most likely to be passed out or still lost somewhere in a jute joint hunting the furrows of his empty pockets for the money he'd stolen from us. The money he'd already spent. To signal Brother it was safe to stop for a meal, I'd put the saltshaker in the window. It was our code things were safe in Sister's kitchen. However, one day I'd forgotten to take that shaker down and here comes Brother up on the porch though Jesse was still back there and Louvenia was paying the price of him having emptied his last bottle the moment when he badly needed another drink. Who gots to pay for that? You see, Sister had scrapped together enough to pay off the grocer for six months food bills. That left nothing for whiskey to slosh on Jesse's daily drought. Them times you know it was Louvenia's head that had to make up the shortage. When he was without a drink, the blackness of Jesse's existence quickly reflected off Sister's blackened face. Brother had committed to killing Jesse the next time he sent his fist her way. Now the time had arrived.

Alex walked in with his usual big smile. But when he heard Louvenia's shriek from the backroom his smile turned upside down as his fists turned right side up. Lord, Lord…Jesse was for sure gonna die that night! Brother's grimace told it.

"Alex, Jesse gonna see you here!"

He rolled up his sleeve readying to kill the ol' man. Sister's howls of anguish were shaking the cardboard-patched walls.

"I'm gonna kill that ol' man!"

Alex' face hardened with rage and his shoulders heaved as if he was gonna pounce right through the door to Jesse's head.

"Stop and hear me now, Brother. You know there ain't nothin' we can do. He say he ain't never gonna let Sister out of this house alive. Don't let this be the night he makes good on his promise."

"You gotta get out of here!" he said.

"That was Sister's head you heard lookin' for the door. I leave, then who gonna bandage 'er? What'a he do to her then?" I knew I had to think fast to stop Brother from killing Jesse. "You go on now 'fore he knows you're here and comes at you," I whispered. "Go buy me some wash soap at the corner grocer. Maybe he be passed out by the time you get back."

"You talk like you're oldest. I's the oldest, now ain't that right?"

I knew Alex's talk was aimed to cut through his powerlessness. Course Louvenia was really the oldest, but she was gone from the Burneys', so Alex maintained this somehow made him oldest.

"Well, it sure enough was when you stepped into this kitchen. But if you don't go he gonna get the law on you. He gonna say things so they take you in. You know he will, too."

Young men put their lives on the line and then pause to think afterwards—after their broken egos have settled in the ruins they brought down on themselves.

Louvenia came into the kitchen. Her face was already blue—or was that still from the last beating?

"Lord, Sister, Jesse busted your lip open again! You're bleedin' down your blouse."

"Get me a chip of ice. Glass 'a water." Her trembling hand dabbed at the blood dripping from her mouth.

"You best go now, Alex. Jesse, he possessed by Satan himself tonight. He gettin' dressed to go out. He gonna walk right by us swinging any minute."

Alex yammered 'bout Jesse needing to be put down for good.

"I ain't runnin' like no woman!" he said.

"Oh, hell, Alex, he kill you worse than any woman! He know how. Ask 'im about Fred's chain gangs." Sister worked her yanked-out back onto a kitchen chair where I met her with a chip of ice for her lip.

"He gots to have a woman bring 'im the pot to pee in and fill one on the stove to eat from!" I reminded Sister.

As I wondered how many were the times I'd put ice to Sister's face, I felt a pall come over all three of us. In silence, we could do no more than look at each other and dab ice that quickly melted from all the rage at that table.

"You go on Brother; need that soap so's we can finish up this laundry and eat tomorrow," I pleaded.

Alex murmured something gruesome he wanted to do to Jesse, and left to hold his sanity together while I attempted to calm Louvenia's exposed nerves and fix her flayed flesh. It took a spell before she had enough breath to say much more. Don't that always happen with a punch to the stomach?

"It's not that bad, honey. Worse last time—I know it was. Yeah?"

I gasped, seeing her new collection of bruises as I traced the ice over her face. They turned bluer as we spoke.

"Jesse say I got to fix him some eggs 'fore he leaves."

"What?" I bit my tongue when I heard that. He near killed her, and then reminded her she was his maid. It was 'bout then that Brother's urge to put Jesse away for good seemed to come over me, too. I wondered how I could pay Jesse back? Was Alex so wrong to want him put down for good? Is it a sin to kill Satan? Or even stab at him?

I knew these thoughts were looking for something to ignite, and figured if Sister had to recover from Jesse, then maybe he should recover from me. In that other room was a man I wanted dead, and here I had to serve him one more meal so he could hit the road with a pocket full of our laundry money.

So, I got to wondering: why not then offer up a Last Supper to ol' Jesse—a few bites for him to gag on for eternity? What would do it? A thimbleful of nightshade, the killing herb of the South mushed into his food? I knew there was a reason why slave owners had their slaves taste the masters' food. It ain't a quick and easy death, not from nightshade poison. No, you agonize from hell and back before your last breath. I try to believe Jesus watches over us, but since He already knew that killing Jesse was in my heart, I thought maybe He'd look the other way if I made that mean ol' man real sick, 'cause I didn't have no nightshade anyway. But I could torture him enough he'd sure think I did! Sick enough he'd wish himself dead, but not so dead the law might come for me. Jesse and me, that's where the two of us were headed.

"I'll fix 'em," I told Sister, and lifted her hanging lip with another chip of ice. "You stay here with this cold rag to your face."

Yeah, I was gonna fix him good! Louvenia looked at me quizzically, yet her throbbing lip kept her from asking what I was up to even as her eyes followed after me.

"He say he want his eggs right now. I'll help you."

"Don't need no help," I said calm-like so she'd not know I was worked up. "You keep that ice to your lip. I'll take care of him! You know I will, too!"

And, Lord, I meant to do some business on Jesse! I know Minerva would have taken Granny's rusty pair of scissors in there and teached Jesse the fear of the Lord like she done ol' Isaac. No thinking 'round this and that like Louvenia and me always did.

Then from the bedroom came more bellows from Satan's angel. "Where's my God-damned eggs? Hey, I'm talkin' to you out there!"

But he wasn't really talking to me, 'cause I didn't listen to him no more!

"Hey, what I say just now?" Jesse conveyed with his usual sweetness as I dumped every bit of cayenne pepper and near a whole box of salt into a mess of eggs that I'd cooked in rancid bacon grease along with more than a few jagged broken eggshells. Then I reached under the counter, pulled the garbage tin out, stirred with the spoon till I pulled up them blackened tatas I'd tossed out the day before, and mashed them up good in that skillet. Jesse gonna pay this time with a plate of food poisoning. I was sure gonna make his belly feel worse than Louvenia's lip did!

But then I got to wondering. Had a strange thought of what if I should have left the salt out of that stirred up pan of rot I was scorching? Don't they use salt to preserve hogs? The salt and all that alcohol Jesse already done pickled himself with might keep him going forever.

About then Louvenia, holding her ribcage, came over to the stove to see why I was taking so long. Mostly when I had to fix that man's food, it was a toss in a skillet and a dump on a plate for him. He ain't gonna get more from me.

"Here, baby. You know Jesse likes plenty of salt 'n pepper. Go on now, put some in them eggs 'fore he curses me they ain't the way he like 'em."

Sister reached for the saltbox and poured even more into that man's skillet of fried garbage. I was thinking ain't nobody on earth can eat six eggs cooked in rancid bacon grease, cayenne, rotten tatas and that much salt and live one more day to belly ache; it ain't never happened. Still, I figured if Jesse died from salt poisoning, we might end up with him staring down from the wall where I was gonna mount his stuffed hog's head. But then maybe we'd go to pickling him into jars so the law could never find out whatever ever happened to Jesse Powell who once lived at the end of that alley. Yeah, I had the picture of us putting those jars up in Louvenia's kitchen window then when his friends come by, all his gamblers, drunks and wife beaters following along behind Brother Fred, they'd know we'd had it with Jesse and they best not come to our door no more. I could see Jesse lying over that table where I wrapped Louvenia's ribs and we'd be carving that hog up like Minerva was guiding our hands. Then we'd stuff the butchered pieces down into jars, an eye in one and the other in the jar with his big brown liver lips. What would the neighbors think? Annie across the alley, her looking through her kitchen window down to Louvenia's and seeing Jesse smiling back from a jar! Lordy, he never more than growled at Annie in the alley when she said hello.

After I handed Jesse's plate to Sister, I was so excited about canning him that I decided I'd refresh myself with some sweet tea. Sister looked me in one eye then the other like something was amiss. Don't know if she was expecting a confession, but she only got a tail end of my mischievous grin.

Well, all the same, Louvenia took the plate back. I could hear Jesse grab it with a curse for taking so long and wolf 'em down like some hog that sure needed his head mounted on a wall! For Jesse, six eggs was only two or three bites for his big mouth ain't got no teeth. He never chewed any plate of food, just swallowed it near whole. I was sitting back there at the table thinking Jesse gonna be dead 'fore I drink my sweet tea down and then our lives was gonna change for good! Lord, we's for sure crossing over from Jesse's alley to a sunny day without bruises! I wondered what folks would think if we celebrated by putting a Christmas tree up in the middle of July and then handed out jars of pickled Jesse to his whores. Got some big red ribbons to put on them?

Lord, it sure felt like an early Christmas on Jesse's alley!

THAT BOY'S EYES

15

Bᴜᴛ, Lᴏʀᴅ, ʟᴇᴛ me tell you what happened next!

I knew I'd just committed murder even if Jesse was yet dead. But Jesus had forgiven me; I was sure of it. Because it was about then that this boy walked through the kitchen door and could only have been a gift from the Lord Himself. Was this my reward for putting Satan's progeny to torture? Yes, there in front of me stood the boy that Alex been calling Riverman.

The haze inside my head cleared at the very sight of Alex's friend, Jeffrey McWilliams, the boy he worked with at the stables. Never seen shoulders like his. Never seen lips like his, and what's the twinkle in his eye for? That glint was aimed right for me, I knew it was. This stranger walked in with a smile as big as any bouquet of spring flowers.

Well, Brother was sure not standing there offering no flowers. No, he plopped a box on the table like it was the answer to all our prayers. Alex motioned Jeff to a chair. But this boy's glistening eyes never moved from mine. I took mine off his long enough to look at that box. I could see it wasn't no box of wash soap. You see, it had a picture of a big fat dead rat on it! It sure did. It was rat poison that Alex meant for Jesse! Oh, Lord! I got to thinking this whole family was headed for hell, and then we'd never be rid of Jesse 'cause he surely had property homesteaded there. No doubt just down the way from Satan's place! Lord, Lord, I was 'bout to put Jesse up in canning jars and now there was this boy smiling at my breasts!

Alex introduced me, but I tell you plain, something came over me and I done changed into somebody else! Somebody that sure sounded like Minerva echoing in my ears!

"Jeff, this here is my sister, Sarah Breedlove." Brother shook his head like I was sure something else. "She's real strange like she's lost her senses. But we pay 'er no mind 'cause she can cook some when she puts her mind to it. But then she don't got no mind, I mean a whole one."

"I ain't worried none 'bout what she's missing. It's what she gots that counts. Yep, Sister, you're sure lookin' fine for a woman that ain't got half 'er senses!"

Those were the first words to me coming out of those pretty lips. Still I knew what he really thought was looking fine was my peaches, 'cause he could hardly take his eyes off them! Then that voice took over again. "Yeah? Then Mister, you're missing both halves of your senses if you're thinkin' I'm your sister!" I told Jeff. "I'm Miss Breedlove to you. Hear?" But that wasn't really me saying that. No, it was my momma. I knew it was. What she was gonna say next, I wondered?

Alex rolled his eyes like maybe he was wondering too.

"Sure got a lively one here, Alex."

"You ain't seen the half of it!" Brother moaned like he had a sudden case of indigestion.

"Real lively! Like a cat in a burlap bag. I can near feel them cat claws up 'n' down my back. A saucy woman makes me shiver all over like that."

That so, I thought.

Meanwhile in the backroom my deeds had taken hold of Jesse's poor ol' stomach. Guess that salt was stomping his gut good and hard. From the table I could see Louvenia in there standing barely out of punching distance watching Jesse moan pitiful-like and then hurl more puke her way. I 'magine Sister's thoughts were surely romping 'round that dark room, too, as Jesse's stomach surely was trying to crawl out aiming to squeeze somebody's throat. She could only have been thinking that if she helped that ol' man, he might live on and on, just like the ol' devil himself. And yet if she didn't help him, she might not live long herself once he came for his revenge. To me, all Jesse's puking was sweet music I could listen to forever. With her foot, Louvenia pushed the basin across the floor to catch what Jesse's mouth was hurling.

Meanwhile, back in the kitchen I filled Alex's ear with what I'd done to that ol 'man. Well, he was hardly impressed. No, he sure wasn't.

"Well now, ain't you a hardened killer? No wonder God made you a girl! He couldn't know what else to do with ya! Ain't that right, Jeff? Sister, you think Jesse's a snail? Salt ain't gonna kill nothing but snails in the alley. Now you only done made 'im meaner! What's he gonna do to you and Louvenia tomorrow?" Alex wasn't whispering. "Jeff, forget about what I said on Sarah's cooking."

Then Alex shoved that box of rat poison my way. "Now go do it right and put a spoonful of this in some mush for the ol' man."

"So, then who's a sick hardened killer again?" Jeff seemed to ask my peaches which he couldn't take his eyes off. Yes, my breasts seemed to get the boy near cross-eyed, didn't they?

"Want me to fix up somethin' real good to eat now?" I said to be polite. Jeff sat at the table, him grinning ear to ear and those eyes beckoning me to come sit on his lap. And I know they were, too.

"Yeah, that 'a be fine, Sister! I'll taste anything you put out!" he said.

Then, almost like a light had gone on the moment I'd been waiting for had come. It was time to call the undertaker to haul

Jesse off. Yet all I could think about was that fine boy wanting to taste something that I figured had nothing to do with food. Momma! Come quick and say something for me! And sure enough she did. Yes, Momma's spirit filled me and lifted my arm to grab at that box of rat poison and shove it right in front of Jeffrey like I was gonna feed it to him. Jeff looked at that dead rat on the box and winked.

"Yep, this woman sure gots spirit in 'er, Brother Alex! And don't I like it!"

Right to the very beautiful boy with those lovely liquid eyes that followed my breast around the room, Momma said through my wicked mouth: "Want a big spoon, or you want me to feed it to you with my fingers a pinch at a time?"

"Now how am I gonna know, Miss Breedlove, 'less I taste your fingers?"

That boy stuck his tongue out and wiggled it at me. Now ain't that just like a dog doing that?

Alex guessed well enough that this had to be Minerva's spirit working my big mouth, so he tugged on Jeff's collar and headed for the door.

"Reckon we best be gettin' on. Yeah, for sure something come over Sister here."

"Lookin' forward to eatin' with you soon," Jeff said, looking into my eyes. What else he said, I don't even 'member.

With Jesse moaning like he was desperately holding on to the last ounce of his borrowed life, Louvenia came out, kicked his door shut and sat down safe in knowing Jesse'd be in bed for days to come.

"Jesse, says he must 'a ate somethin' gone bad over at Fred's this afternoon," she commented. "You think?"

Sister's grin was bigger than I'd seen in days. Thank you, Jesus!

Knowing we had a few days reprieve while Jesse' stomach was on the run, I stopped worrying 'bout what we was gonna do next.

It was the first time in the six years I'd been living at Louvenia's that I'd stopped looking over my shoulder to see if Jesse was sneaking up. There was a light in my life, and it warmed me like the sun that never appeared in that dark alley. I was sure that boy Jeff had brought it on the tips of his fingers as though he held it like a kite on a string.

"Why were you so nasty to that boy?" Sister asked. "I could hear you sassin' the men even with Jesse back there howlin' 'bout Fred poisonin' him.

"Me? You heard me offer to fix him a meal. Ain't' that nice enough for now?"

⁂

Well, for five days and nights poor Jesse was at death's door and we sure hoped that it would be the last one to open for him! I ignored him when he moaned for a sip of water. He hungry, he cried like a baby and went back to snoring only to find a scraped-clean plate waiting when he awoke. I'd eaten every bite myself and prayed he'd never wake up.

"Jesse, you already eat up that big lunch I fixed for you a while ago?" I hollered. "Best not eat too much, gonna get sick all over again. Ain't that the truth if you ever seen any?"

It only took three or four days of this abuse before Jesse was rearing to regain his lost territory. Yes, he was back to waving his orders in my face again.

"Hey, get me some real food! Fred got me sick with his cooking last week. Huh?" Jesse moaned. "Fetch me some eggs scrambled the way I like 'em! I's real sick in here!"

"You hear that jabberin' I hear?" Louvenia asked as she walked in from hanging clothes on the porch.

"No, ma'am. I ain't heard nothin'," I replied as I took a big pan of buttermilk biscuits out of the oven.

"Well, then it must be the neighbor's dog wantin' kitchen

scraps." She snickered. "This ham be ready by the time you get the grits to a boil. Annie give us some blueberry jam her momma put up. We gonna have it with our hot biscuits."

"Ain't she sweet?"

"There's too much food here for two people, but I know Jesse's too sick to eat nothin'," she said loud enough for him to hear. And for sure he grunted like he was 'bout to gnaw the table leg off but still couldn't fix his feet on the floor to get at us or the food.

"You come on in here Jesse and get yourself some hot biscuits and blueberry jam," Sister taunted. "That what you're back there gruntin' for?"

"No, Sister. Don't you know, he gonna get better quicker if we don't mess with his poor stomach and let 'im starve," I said.

"Starve to death?" Sister asked. "Ain't he there yet?"

We laughed.

"Hey, get in here; I ain't eaten in a week! Maybe a month!" Jesse's words spilled slowly like the last gasps of a life well overdrawn.

"Who that?" Louvenia looked about for a ghost.

"One of them crazies in the alley, Sister. Don't mind 'im and he'll go away like a bad smell after the winds come."

After breakfast, and while Sister was over at Annie's, I started hearing them voices again.

"Get in here," he said. "I need me something to eat!"

I looked in on Jesse's hellhole. No wonder that old man wasn't dead. The Lord wouldn't want to look over anything as pathetic as that man lying there in his stinking brown bed.

"I'll go fix you some eggs, just as soon as I buy another box of salt. Maybe next week if nobody steals my laundry money!" I could say that 'cause I knew Jesse wasn't gonna get out of bed any time soon to swing at me.

"What? You know I gots the fever, I's real sick here," Jesse whined like he could wring a bit of mercy out of me.

"Yeah, Jesse, you been real sick, but that ain't nothin' new."

"What's you talkin' 'bout like that? Where's Louvenia when I want 'er to tend to me?"

"You know how Louvenia is. Bet she's gone uptown again. She sure likes shopping in them big stores, don't she? Some man she met wants her to pick out a new fur coat to wear while she ironin'."

"Shut that crap up!" he snorted. "Louvenia don't want to take care of me and I gots the fever bad. Had the runs, too," he whined.

I could only wonder; is it a sin to taunt Satan? "Tell me Jesus and I'll stop," I asked. But the Lord kept silent on it, so I opened my mouth all the wider. "No, Jesse, you don't got the fever." I yelled back. "You know that comes from swamp water. The closest you ever been to a swamp was back when you took a bath. 'Member? The color of that water after you dunked your tail in it? Now that was some real stinkin' swamp water!"

"What? Huh? Then why I dyin'? You kill me when I ain't lookin' and I'll tell Louvenia to put the law on your back! That's what!" Jesse tried to snap his fingers, but that was broken, too.

"Now, Jesse, you'd be real mean gettin' Louvenia on my back for killin' you, even if she paid me to do it!"

"I don't want to hear 'bout it. Just go bring me a pot to pee."

"Yeah, I'll do that. You just put a knot in it till I get to it! And tie it tight, 'cause I ain't in no hurry!"

I'd had enough of Jesse and went over to shut the damned window on him. It was July and had to be hot as hell in there. I figured I was just getting him accustomed to his final resting place on Satan's lap. Returning a favor, like all the ones he'd handed me.

Soon as the window was closed as tight as a coffin, I headed out to join Louvenia who'd been in the alley talking to Annie, and we headed off with her kids to buy ices with Italian syrup.

Hiding Behind a Cracked Jar

16

A T TIMES I was jarred by the strongest feelings, as when my thoughts were chasing an iron over an old shirt. Like what would happen if Sister stepped out one afternoon and never returned? Because why ever would she? What was waiting at Jesse's but another tub of brown water and more bruised grief? Headed out to the grocer's one day, why wouldn't she just keep going as far as her feet would carry her? Well, I had to become a mother before I had any answers. Yes, Louvenia always returned simply because I was there waiting. That weighed on her more than notions of her escaping to a better life. I knew from my first moments at Jesse's, Sister was the only thing that saved me from that ol' man, or any ol' man.

The screen door slammed behind her. "Where's Jesse?" she asked as she walked in wiping her brow of sweat. She put the wash soap she'd gone for on the table and sighed as she looked at the piles of stinking clothes that waited.

"He dead," I said. "Undertaker done dragged 'im off already!"

"Think Jesse make good fertilizer?" Sister tittered.

I couldn't say nothing. But Sister could always read me and

patted my hand to let me know she saw through the fears I'd been brewing. Maybe the way a mother looks at her child and knows where her baby's thoughts are taking her. Her smile quickly sent my fears packing even as Jesse was still very much in our midst.

"I ain't dead yet! You know I ain't for real," he whined from the backroom.

Sister yelled back: "Now don't worry yourself none, Jesse. We'll tell the undertaker to come 'gain in the mornin'. You be finished by then. Hear?"

Whiskey numbs the memory and quickly erases days off the calendar. Louvenia could tell we were safe from Jesse's fist by the way he was grunting back there sitting on his pot. While we were sure he'd not 'member any of our abuse afterwards, we kept asking him what he'd eaten at Brother Fred's that had caused all the agony.

Sister had been sleeping in the kitchen since Jesse threw Alex out and Jesse couldn't swing that far even when he was sober. At least that was the lie we told.

"Ain't you finished pounding that ironin' board over there?" Sister asked.

I could tell Louvenia was planning on us having a sister talk. She poured us jars of sweet tea and pointed to the chair I was to take for the duration of her sermon.

"Why don't you ever let Jeff in from the porch when he comes by with Alex for a meal? Now why is that?"

I knew then I'd done a miserable job of hiding my secret. Yes, I'd been thinking of that boy for days. Near as many days as the shirts I'd scorched that week. Was that what clued Sister in? Yes, Alex had been bringing his friend over for a meal and they'd been sitting out there on the stoop to eat 'cause I was too shy to let them in.

"You're gonna let him in to eat proper-like at the table. I'm tellin' you, you are."

"What for?"

I wasn't really trying to start something. All the same, Sister squinted at me like she thought otherwise. Yes, she gave me the eye, which meant that she'd be the one getting the upper hand in this little chat of ours, or else I'd be getting it upside the head.

"What for, huh?" Louvenia said real huffed-up-like. "Alex says Jeff is the finest friend he ever had. A real good man that works hard over there at the stables."

Louvenia and Alex been talking, huh? That why she was so long in getting back? She was down at the stables telling Brother how easy it was to read my mind?

But there was more to it, and Sister knew. How could I tell Louvenia, who struggled with assaults to her dignity ever'day, who wore the color blue wound around her eyes like a target, that I was just too ashamed to bring that pretty boy on in? She might think I was ashamed of her. What Jeff was gonna think of us? I seemed to sputter around that cracked jar working up my defenses, yet all I saw was me covered in sweat from hovering over the tubs all day and hands looking like 'gator skin. Don't even got any kind of pretty dress. No, I didn't want the boy close enough to see what I saw in myself: a weary, confused, frayed and shy girl-woman; one afraid of looking into my own heart, let alone that of a man's. I think I figured I'd stay hidden from it all behind the old cracked jar I held up to the light. I couldn't look at her, 'cause she knew well enough that my heart sang a different tune. "Don't know why I should talk to him, Louvenia," I mumbled.

So I could catch her eyeing me and read her mood, I fiddled with my jar of sweet tea; held it up to the light as if I was looking for a nat in there. Or maybe I figured being hidden behind that jar she couldn't look into my eyes and see into my bared soul.

My mouth went numb as I kept on the trail meandering in my head, wondering what Jeff thought seeing Sister all black and blue after one of her all-night chats with Jesse's fist. These fears had looped 'round my thoughts for days. But maybe I was afraid he might think all them beatings…well, maybe he thinks that's the way it is. Nothing shocking about a woman getting straightened out by a man in those dead alleys. Is that what he thought? Couldn't just like me. No, who could like somebody so beaten down like this girl-woman? The one I saw reflected off an ol' cracked mason jar. Yes, I knew her well even through the pieces of her broken dreams.

I'd never known a man before and didn't understand that at times our men were as beaten down as we were; sometimes beaten into just being an ol' drunk like Jesse. Is that where Jeff was gonna end up? Poor Jesse, where did he lose his way? The day he put a foot down at the mouth of that alley? Was his own vision of what lay ahead for him clear, or clearly muddled as he glanced through his empty whiskey bottles looking for all them days he'd gone and tossed away?

I went back to hiding behind my jar of sweet tea.

"I know you can still hear me if you're not holdin' that jar up to your nose!"

"What did you say, Louvenia?"

"I said, he keeps comin' 'round all the time, don't he?" She peered 'round my jar so's I'd know she knowed there'd be no hiding behind no damned cracked mason jar. "Yeah, your cookin' been gettin' real good lately, ain't it? You notice? Huh?" She moved that jar away from my face again.

Still, I wasn't gonna capitulate. No, I didn't have to notice nothing I didn't have a mind to, even if Louvenia knew my story all the same. Yes, clearly, she knew that boy had captured my heart. "What's you mean by that, Sister?" I asked. "You never pushed a plate of my food back before."

"Honey, I'm ain't tryin' to start somethin' with you. Only you been settin' out there food for two hungry men and then runnin' back in 'fore they step up on the porch. Yes, you have, too. Best cookin' ever, and then you're not steppin' out there to see that fine boy lap it up. Huh? Why, now? Well, I think I know."

At that I came out from behind my jar of sweet tea. Yes, if Sister could read my thoughts even when I shielded them behind a cracked jar, then I figured she could just as easily put a thought or two into Brother's head! And I knew she had, too, because the very next evening Brother showed up right after that ol' man disappeared down the alley. A bit like clockwork. Both the men came like twins tied together at the waist with a rope so's they could get into trouble together! Howling and laughing, they were. Yes, I knew for sure there was something going on. You see, that morning Louvenia had decided she was hungry for Jeff's favorite meal and sent me out to the grocer for a chicken, some fresh onions and tatas. That night Alex and Jeff ate near a whole fried chicken and all them buttered tatas in half the time it took me to peel them.

Then when I thought they was both out on the stoop eating, Brother sneaked into the kitchen. He shook his head at me and nodded to Louvenia like it was the right time to put a flyswatter to my head. I knew Alex was gonna cause me grief and Sister, she'd be right there telling where to lay it on!

"Riverman say he ain't gonna leave this time 'less you come out. Why he even wants to talk to you is beyond me. But that's what he's set his mind to."

I waved Alex off like he was a fly buzzing around my head, and went back to washing the dishes.

"So, what's your problem this time?" Alex looked to Louvenia for backing. I knew that Louvenia had put him up to this.

"That what the boy say, or what Sister say?"

"Now, you stop that being rude to our guest, Sarah!"

"Hell, she don't know no better!" Alex added. "You best keep her locked up in here."

"Why?" I asked, "So no dogs get me? Like the one you brung that stuck his ol' tongue out like he gone rabid?"

"Yeah? So who gots the big yappin' mouth 'round here?" he asked. "Yap, yap, yap, that girl sure know how to yap up a storm!"

"Now you go out there and talk, and I don't mean talkin' no nonsense about dogs!"

Sister's eyes clearly held a flyswatter that I knew she'd soon be putting to my head. She grabbed that big bowl out of my hand.

"I'll wash the dishes tonight, so you can find some time to be polite."

"You comin' out then?" Alex persisted, but not nearly as much as me!

"Why would I do that? Go out there with two men who talk too much and eat too much?" I whispered that part, not wanting Jeff to hear, and then peeked through the curtain to see him out in the alley pacing.

"Sister, there's good men and there's bad," Louvenia cautioned as she dried that bowl.

"And then there's rabid dogs, ain't they?" I replied, but looked at Brother. "With their tongues waggin' at you! Well, ain't they?"

"Like I said, he ain't gonna leave till you talk to 'im," Alex said, all huffed-up-like.

He never had much patience for women, and was getting Louvenia's squinty-eye signal to hold the line no matter what fuss I slung at them.

"Then you best call the dog catcher man! Unless you need a pet dog to talk to. He sure follows you like one, don't he?"

It was about then that Sister near came to slapping me. I could tell by the way she pursed her lips, which always preceded a sound smack.

"That so?" Brother said. "Hey Jeff, best bring your plate on in here now," Brother yelled, then turned—I could have killed him—and winked as he yelled again, "There's pie in here waitin'! Yeah, poison Sister here baked it up just for you. Maybe she's sweet on you!"

Alex is just as stubborn as Louvenia any ol' day. Never could figure who they took after acting like that, Momma or Daddy, 'cause I don't have a stubborn bone in me.

I stood there feeling defenseless with my hair kinked from all the steam and my blouse damp from standing over the iron while I got their supper on. Satisfied with his deed, Alex stood there grinning. He was, too! If Louvenia was gonna swat anybody, righteousness would have it that Brother got the first smack. At that I heard Jeff's big feet stomping up the porch steps, Feeling beaten at my own game, I jumped behind the hanging shirts strung across the kitchen so Jeff wouldn't see me so frazzled. Louvenia jumped to bustle him back out to the porch.

"No, not this time Jeff. You best go on for now, I guess. But you take a pie back to the stables for later," Sister said. "I think that's best for tonight. Yeah."

Louvenia couldn't set up roadblocks to save herself, but still she could come to my defense with one. As soon as Jeff was out in the alley, Sister turned to Alex to work up something else.

"Now I got a plan here," she announced. "You tell your friend that if he wants to thank Sarah for her good cookin'—ain't she just a good cook, too—then he best come to the square in front of the First Baptist come Sunday, where you always go strollin' with your sister. After church, don't you know?"

"Go strollin'?" Alex blurted. "With my sister?" I guess he'd had more than enough of us. "What I know is I ain't never gone strollin' with no two sisters I ever knowed, and don't go to no church and you know it!"

I peeked through a hole in an old tea towel I'd just hung to dry see what Sister was gonna do to Brother for starting something with me. I figured he deserved at least a swollen lip. Louvenia put her hands to her hips and delivered her terms.

"Oh, you been strollin' up the wrong side of the street with this here sister, I tell you plain!" she said. "If you don't have Jeff in front of the First Baptist on Sunday, I'll be feedin' you Sarah's recipe for blackened scrambled eggs. The recipe that near killed Jesse, bless his rotten-to-the-core heart!"

Oh, if Momma couldn't speak through me 'cause I was holding my hands over my mouth to stop her, it was plain she'd go to talking through Louvenia's all the same.

Well, Alex didn't take to arguing with a couple of women, so he stomped off with the Riverman and my pie. It was still warm, too.

Sister watched out the window as they headed off. We could hear the men howling to the end of the alley even with their mouths full of pie.

Sister bustled me to the kitchen table. Lordy, by then I was sure tired of landing in that ol' chair for one of her talks.

"Sit down. I got a plan here: tomorrow we're goin' downtown," Sister informed me in a tone I knew meant the conversation was to have only one speaker and one listener, me being the latter.

Still, I couldn't keep my mouth closed. "Downtown? Why would we go downtown? I got no ironin' to deliver downtown and there's three days of laundry piled on the porch."

"Oh, I see plainly what's you got piled. Nothin' but piles of nasty attitudes is what I'm callin' it!" she said with that nose of hers in the air again. "You're goin' downtown and you're gonna buy yourself some kind of new dress."

"You're talkin' like a crazy woman," I said, but didn't get smacked for it. "I gots no money for a dress." We'd worked all those years just getting by wearing near rags—mostly things people left off at the church.

Louvenia went over to the woodpile, as was her habit; she knew to look over her shoulder to see if Jesse had sneaked up on her. Then she knocked about that pile till she found a rag all knotted up and pulled it out jingling coins. She looked back at Jesse's door again before spilling those coins out across the table like a crapshoot had just started up.

"Here it is. Least enough for a dress and maybe a pair of shoes. Don't worry 'bout Jesse; I take care of 'im so he don't notice nothin'. You're gonna look pretty when you see that boy come Sunday. In front of the First Baptist. I mean for Alex to see to it, too."

"Yeah, where I go strollin' ever' Sunday with him, huh?"

"Never mind, you! I can see in your eyes that he's special to you."

Sister pushed the coins towards me with a wink. What she'd tied up in that ol' rag was months of back-breaking labor. Louvenia had so little hope in her own life, but still she'd just handed it all to me to buy a dress, a silly piece of fabric to swaddle a dream in.

"I don't know if he's fine, do I?" I said, feeling confused.

"Baby, don't start out thinkin' all men are like Jesse," she whispered. "You ain't gonna meet somebody if you never leave the tubs, especially not with that attitude. You got to be nice and talk to that boy. I'm tellin' you, you are so's you can see for yourself that no matter what you think he's lookin' at, your peaches already sittin' nice and high, he's already seen what's in your heart, 'cause he's a good man. Really don't matter much else, do it? So, I'm tellin' you, you got to take the first step away from these tubs yourself."

Standing in the Sun

17

As soon as Jesse woke up the next day Louvenia had something going to divert his attention from our plans to escape shopping. She was fixing his favorite breakfast of bacon and eggs with biscuits and gravy. Same meal we'd feasted on pretending we were celebrating his wake when he was dying from my fried garbage pail scraps. I reckon the smell of that hickory bacon done brought Jesse to the table thinking he'd slept in from July to Christmas morning and maybe Sister had somehow finagled more credit from the grocer. Louvenia had something else for that ol' man. She'd slipped out early and bought Jesse a bottle. You see for the longest time Louvenia had refused to buy his whiskey. But she'd worked it out thinking by the time I got back from town, Jesse's head would be too numb to know I had something new. A new dress never figured in Jesse's mind, unless he could barter for a whore with it. No, self-pride had no place in Jesse's world; after pride comes thinking big of yourself. Hard to keep somebody bridled if they take that tone.

Well, I fussed about going downtown so long that Sister finally tossed her dishrag down and went to get Annie. Sister and Annie decided they'd go get the dress without me then. You see, I'd never gone shopping like that, and it scared me. I was wary that Jesse might suspect something was going on and come home unexpected-like, as was his habit. For days he'd been looking at us strangely as if we might be keeping back our laundry money.

I spent the morning anxiously wondering what they'd come up with. What color it would be, and would it have some fancy trim or something. What might Jeff think about all this? Maybe every girl Jeff ever looked at had a real pretty, even store-bought dress. But were these girls so pretty he didn't even notice what kind of dress they had on? All these thoughts got me to biting my nails. Yes, I was getting scared of Sunday coming and started wondering how I could conjure a way to skip over to Monday to save myself the grief the day would bring. I was suddenly feeling sick-like, I knew I was, and thought for sure I had a swollen lip from chewing on it all week from nerves.

So, I came up with a plan to save myself. I figured if I worked hard enough, come Sunday Sister and me would be so tired the day would roll by without anybody noticing. I figured then we'd never even make it to the church. Anyway, I was sure that Jeffrey would forget he knew Alex because I was his sister and that was sure enough all the reason he'd need. He'd probably have left town long before Sunday even came.

But as you'd 'spect, come Sunday, my sister got up extra early to press my new dress again—she not liking the way she'd done it the night before. I was already wide-awake on the cot but pulled the blanket up to my eyes so she couldn't hear me good.

"Huh?" she huffed again.

From that I knew she'd not take to the notion I'd worked up to face her with that morning.

"Huh? What did you say, Sarah?"

You see, I'd long figured sassing her was less objectionable if I scrambled my words under bated breath. Then I could more easily recant before the flyswatter headed my way. After all, Sister was apt to misunderstand me giving her lip when I mush-mouthed the words. At least it worked sometimes. Or maybe Sister just let things pass.

"I can't go to church. Just can't," I mumbled.

Blanket pulled up over my mouth or not, Sister heard me all the same, and never paused with that iron in her hand to ask me to repeat my whining. I could tell she wasn't gonna take anything off me that morning. Louvenia never even looked down at me wallowing on my cot deep in the throes of my conjured predicament to see what I'd worked up. Nope, she'd not give a damn no matter!

"You're goin'!" she blurted. "You look fine in that new dress, and them new shoes ain't nobody worn before. You're goin', honey. Best head down the road I say to, 'cause I'll be waiting with a stick on all them other paths you tend to wander when you're trying not to hear me good."

"What did you say, Sister?"

"I said, you be up 'fore I get the grits to a boil. Or you're gonna find a boil upside something you ain't gonna want to put down on no hard pew at church."

But I wasn't gonna surrender.

"I just can't though. Something's comin' over me that I never felt about before. You think I'm sick?"

Fever in my head or done gone deranged like Alex said, made no difference to her. Thank goodness I didn't cut my hand off the night before cutting up that chicken. No matter to her, I'd still have to go to church. She'd only tell me to carry my severed hand 'round in a bag or she might drag it behind us tied by a rope!

"Why do you think you can't go to church? You always go to church. Now get up like I done told you, and for the last time!"

She been takin' roll at the church or somethin'?

"My nerves got me to bitin' my lip so bad all week—just can't go out there with it all red and ain't it gettin' swollen, too? I know it is. Go get me a mirror from Annie's," I pleaded unconvincingly, thinking Sister would get caught up chatting with Annie and she'd let things pass. But nothing was gonna work to save me from facing the fact Jeff would not be there, and if he was, it was only to see my gangrened lip hanging near to the ground.

"Your lip don't look half as bad as your head's gonna look if I take a stick to it. And even after I do, you're still goin' to church. Then we'll see who looks at your lip when it's pinned to the back of your head!"

Sister was acting more like Minerva by the minute. Anyway, I wasn't worried 'cause I was pretty sure she didn't have a stick. Still, I looked 'round the kitchen in case there was something else she could get her hands on.

"Jesus hears everything, Sister!" I warned. I figured Sister wouldn't want to mess with the Lord, especially not on a Sunday, and reminded her that words on the Lord wasn't sassing, or so I hoped. But my hopes were dashed with Sister's response.

"Yes, He sure enough did hear me ask Him where the rollin' pin is. Bottom drawer over there is where Jesus reminded me I left it. Do I need to show you He was right and then put it to your head?"

So, I guessed I'd be going to church all right. To save my soul or my head from a prayer meeting with Louvenia's rolling pin. Anyway, I was convinced that on most issues the Lord was already on Sister's side.

Louvenia finished ironing my dress and stood there waiting for me to finally get out of bed and put it on. I got dressed special that morning. Even felt special 'cause Jesse hadn't come home that night. He'd probably slept over at his brother Fred's where he tended to pass out after the bars closed. Maybe Jesus did answer my prayers. Still, I was sure only when Sister asked Him to.

My dress was so beautiful. My favorite peach color and covered in tiny little green apples, little bitty ones, and the buttons were shiny like pearls and the white collar made my face look a deep mahogany. We didn't have no mirror; all them got broken when the whiskey bottles were in transit for our heads. So Louvenia escorted me down to Annie's to look in hers and show off the dress she'd helped pick. What would people think of me at church? Lordy! They all were gonna laugh at me for getting all dolled up? They knew I'd never had a new store-bought dress. Didn't they? Wouldn't they all gawk when I walked in the church house? Who was I trying to be?

"Don't even look like me, do it?" I whispered to Sister as we stood in front of Annie's dressing table mirror.

"Sure it do. Just the outside different," Louvenia kissed my cheek and whispered as Annie touched up my hair with her brush. "And you know what? Look down deep into that mirror, even past your pretty smile."

"Why?" I asked.

"All them rabid dogs you're always goin' on 'bout is gone, ain't they? Just your pretty smile I see, and that's all that matters."

∾

Well, we made it to church despite the fact I was sure my shoes were lead-filled or maybe aiming to head some other way. I knew folks were staring, 'cause I was dragging my feet so much I might scuff my new white shoes, or maybe I was hoping I'd make us late so we'd have to sit in the back where nobody would notice I'd dragged my lip in behind me. Was he gonna be there after all?

Sister shook her head and mumbled something about me always mumbling.

When we paused to buy some paper fans from the boy on the corner, Jeff walked up and handed me a fistful of pretty white daisies. I didn't know what to do. Nobody ever gave me flowers. Sister elbowed my side to pry open my mouth.

"Ain't that sweet, Sarah?" she said. "Jeff you comin' in with us?"

"No, ma'am. But if Sarah has nothin' to do after, she might want to sit a spell in the park. If it's alright with you, Louvenia."

Still nothing would come out of my mouth.

"Sure it is, Jeff. She'll be right here on the front steps," Sister replied on my behalf. "Just standing in the nice sun. Ain't this day a blessin' from the Lord?" Louvenia looked at me and nodded.

Well even if my mouth could work, Jeff couldn't have heard me plainly 'cause I was hiding behind my paper fan, just sure my lip had swollen to twice the size since I looked in Annie's mirror. You see, I never believed Annie when she said there was no such thing on my lip as a bad ugly lump! Maybe it had turned black even, 'cause I knew she was just being nice.

Sister and me went into the church fanning ourselves, but not like the big-hat women who acted like they was waving off a swarm of horseflies. Sister dragged me and my lip up to the front row where I took a seat and went to praying. Praying hard, "Oh, Lord, Lord, Lord," I chanted till Louvenia jabbed her bony elbow in my side again.

"What are you doin' there snortin' like that?" she whispered loud enough so all them big-hat women spun their heads to see my condition. But I was not snorting! Them were coded prayers to Jesus 'bout Him getting Sister off my back!

"I'm tellin' you, you bite that lip one more time!"

I paid her no mind 'cause I knew she didn't have the rolling pin with her. You see, I pulled it out and hid it under my cot to teach her a lesson. Sometimes the Lord can be wrong about where He hides things. Anyway, if she had a stick hidden, I knew she wouldn't use it on me, not in front of the preacher. But just in case I rolled my eyes at her till I was near crossed-eyed. Everybody in the pew gawked at me, so I moved down a few inches where it had to be a bit safer from her reach.

Sitting in front of us, the big-hat women's heads spun again like they's tops to see what Louvenia was fussing over. Sister's eyebrow, the left one, almost flew off her head at them. But I guess Jesus did hear my prayer this time 'cause Sister kept her mouth shut and let me be.

The preacher finished preaching; don't know 'bout what, 'cause

I wasn't listening much. Probably about the devil being in our midst again. I was in a sorrowful state. The devil was near, and I probably lured him with all my thoughts about Jeff—and in my thoughts, what Jeff and me was doing wasn't praying. I looked back at the church doors knowing that Alex brought him just to abuse me, and they were surely out there just waiting to complete the humiliation Sister had commenced that morning.

Church ended. I looked at Louvenia. She must have known my thoughts were muddled and looked behind us at the church doors as though Jeff war surely there smiling.

I thought at first to sit tight and pray till ever'body gone, and then Alex and Jeff would surely have wandered off, too. But Louvenia wouldn't have it. She kicked me in the ankle, smiled big to all the big-hat ladies like she'd not even done that, and bustled me from the pew.

"Is there a reason why you were just sittin' there?" she asked. "You weren't listenin' to a single word the preacher said. No, you was sittin' there snortin', and then you stay put when he's done. My, Lord, child, what's come over you?"

Well, I followed her out wondering how much bigger my lip had gotten. Folks looked at me for looking at them to see if they'd noticed. Does a black lip turn green when you're in church? I tried to pull my lip out to see. Louvenia smacked my hand down.

As we neared the back doors, I could see the sun peeking in. Reminded me there was truly something warm and good out there and perhaps he waited for me. Jeff *was* waiting, and walked right up to me in front of them big-hat women always congregating on the steps outside the church doors to see who sees them with their fancy hats on.

I will never forget his smile. That morning I thought Jeff was the handsomest man in Vicksburg. He had a nice clean shirt on, not ironed, but clean. Louvenia proudly glanced at all the womenfolk looking on at Jeff's good manners. Still, Sister heard not a word on Brother's manners!

"What's on your feet?" Alex asked. "You get them shoes off some dead white woman?"

"Oh, you like Sister's new shoes?" Louvenia squinted at Alex. "Ain't they beautiful? Sarah sure knows how to dress fine, don't she, Brother?" she asked Alex, but tossed a smile Jeff's way.

"That right, huh? You read that in the papers this morning?" Brother asked, but got no smack from Louvenia like he sure ought 'a had.

"Miss Breedlove, care to join me down at the square for some lemonade?" Moses Jeffrey McWilliam, the man Brother called the Riverman, offered his arm and led me away from the church step. Unbeknownst to me, they would be my first steps heading to a new life.

Over the hours that followed that bright day, Jeff made me feel ever more special. It truly seemed he never saw nobody but me. Don't know how many white folks passing saw I had white shoes on like them, 'cause ever'body seemed to vanish but him.

On that first stroll around the square, Jeff and I talked and talked. I found out that, like me, he was the child of sharecroppers, and that his grandparents were also slaves ripped from Africa, thinking they was being savaged away by the white slavers to be butchered for meat, only to be hauled up to the white shadows still somewhat alive albeit with severed souls.

It was near dark 'fore Jeff walked me back down Jesse's long alley. I kept telling him Jesse not gonna like him coming near his porch. But he kept holding my hand as though Jesse didn't mean nothing to him, 'cause maybe only I did. For the first time in my life, I felt like I'd stepped out of a deep dark shadow and was standing in the warmth of the sun, where I'd caught a glimpse of dignity dressed in a dream all my own. Still I wondered how long it could last?

RIVERMAN

18

Yes, I was floating in that soaring place where you can only fall hard; I'd fallen in love with Jeffrey McWilliams—the Riverman, and not just because he'd been hanging on my gate all those weeks.

For days I'd been right there listening to Alex tell Louvenia 'bout the man at the stables. From the beginning Brother and Jeff's friendship knew no bounds. In our world where folks only looked to peel a layer off others' backs, I'd never heard of selfless giving like this man's. Through Jeff's serene eyes, I began to see beyond my world to the one Sister had been pointing towards yet didn't know how to get to herself. Her deep faith had told her it was out there somewhere and someday, and somehow we'd get there.

He said his daddy called him Riverman even when he was a boy. His ma claimed it was because Jeff was big for his age and there was nothing he enjoyed more than fishing with his daddy. During those days when Jeff and his folks lived off the land, there were no fields to be harnessed to, no begging for credit from the plantation masters and no overseer pounding on their door and backs for more. With nobody bothering them, they clung to their only dream, to live free, and that's what they did for three years or so. Time travels quickly when your life is ripe with happiness, and there ain't no dread 'bout what tomorrow might hit you with.

Jeff, he was near six years older than me. I was born two years after the Civil War, so I never knew what being a slave was as my folks had. Sure knew that sharecropping was. Near to being the same shackle even if it was called by a different name. As slaves my folks knew that if they walked off Burney lands there'd be some kind of nigger dog pursuing. After the war, it was the chain gangs that barked for free labor along the drain ditches in the rebuilding of the new South. Knowing this kept many folks from looking for something better, yet it didn't stop Jeff's folks.

When the war ended, Jeff's ma and pa left the plantation they were born to in the dark of night even though they were free. Didn't even take a pot; didn't want to give the master cause to come after them with a pack of nigger dogs. Laws still don't mean nothing in the South. They was gone for good. That was all they needed to take with them, his daddy declared, as they headed to a dream of their own for the first time in their worn lives.

Many plantations along the Mississippi were deserted during the war with the North when white folks moved to cities as the South was near burnt to the ground. Towards the end of those bleak times even some white folks barely escaped the Yanks that stormed the South hungry as wolves. During those days, late at night Jeff's daddy went foraging on abandoned plantations for things they needed to survive. He piled up the goods he found: a few bowls, a wooden stool, some tools, bedding, a chicken or two, and carried off what he could haul in a cart. Never so much that he'd need a horse 'cause they was all gone by then. Jeff's pa led his family down the trails that followed the river as far from the plantation houses as they could, farther and farther from any sign of white folks. They worked their way to where the land was wild and untamed and where it would be easier to hide in the thickets if it came to it. Out there they lived freely for the first time. Every day Jeff's ma got them on their knees to pray that the white folks would never come to haul 'em back the way they'd hauled back everything else they'd lost during that war that unchained us from the shackles that we'd soon be wearing again in the new South.

Where the growth was thick Jeff helped his daddy build a shelter of sorts. Way out there, yet close enough to hear that muddy river crash the banks after the rains. They got by on hunting, his ma's berry picking, and fishing for hours just like Alex did with our daddy and Samuel. At times I wondered if was possible they'd seen Jeff and his daddy with their poles over on the other side of that mile-wide river.

Jeff said his pa told stories on how that river turned mercilessly on folks 'cause the white folks owned it and they was mean and that made the river jump and twist like a snarling rope, the kind that runaway slaves jerked against to escape from being dragged back. Still, the river took its revenge and one bad winter the banks broke off till Jeff's shack lifted and was carried away with the mud, along with everything they'd collected over time: a hearth of their own, a pot of fish stew and a few hand tools. There'd been barely enough time to scramble for higher grounds.

Time was done, his pa mumbled to his ma. Time was done… You see, that last flood had broken Jeff's daddy's spirit for survival. It too was done. Nothing left for them to scratch out a living with and no strength to forage a new life again in this new South. All done.

Jeff was only 'bout thirteen or fourteen when he had to bury his daddy. Jeff said his ma sat there under a tarp pelted with rain still talking to his pa as though he wasn't truly gone. Jeff, he had no shovel to dig, and the strength for digging had gone missing, too. He buried his pa by winding him in his tears and the last worn sheet they had. After their farewells, Jeff let his daddy be swallowed by the muddy waters.

I got tears in my eyes when I heard about that sheet. Those sheets may not have been monogrammed with blue thread like the Burneys', but in the end, our lives weren't so different.

After a few days, Jeff's ma kept talking 'bout how she couldn't get no sleep what with the aches that had settled in her joints. She gonna get better, Jeff kept telling her. But his better was not the same she longed for, nor the one she was resolved to slip away to. His ma struggled for the words to tell her boy where she was aiming for, but they never came. But do they ever come for any of us? Pain numbs the tongue to silence, the pain of love.

Jeff told me that one night he suddenly awoke to the sounds of an eerie silence. The woods, he said, had suddenly gone stone quiet. What is the sound of the cold quiet you see in your blackest dreams? Maybe it's the sound of death searching for someone in the depths of the moment. It was the sound of that silence that brought terror to river people 'cause the icy waters can rise in silence all the way up to your neck waiting for you to swallow.

He rose from his blanket only to see his ma standing there in the moonlight looking back at him—a smile on her silent lips as she stood there knee deep in water—that river unrolled behind her like a glassy comforter. When he yelled for her, she crossed her arms over her chest as if she was arranging herself in her coffin and lay back over the glassy surface and drifted to her final sleep. Yes, that great river had answered her prayers and carried her off to be with his pa. Jeff then understood what she couldn't say to her beloved only child. She couldn't take no more. She had to be with her husband and didn't know how to ask her son to forgive her for leaving him an orphan.

From then on Jeff made his own dreams, and one was to have land far away from the floods of the Mississippi and the plantation folks always pointing to their feet for coloreds to come kneel for the day's orders. Nobody was gonna break his soil off and carry it away like that river done. To own his own plot of ground was the promise he'd made to his folks after they'd slid under the water on their last journey. That dream of a boy of thirteen summers never went cold on him. With his tears hidden deep in his empty pockets, Jeff headed off the banks of the Mississippi for the last time. There were to be many miles trundled before our eyes met for the first time.

Days after his ma's passing, Jeff dragged himself along till he made it to the docks at Vicksburg. The colored stevedores told him he best make it into the city 'fore they picked him up to work the county roads, 'cause there'd be no dock work for a boy too young to lift ten tons a day. Jeff told me for any kind of wage, them dockers looked mean enough to kill. Somehow Jeff managed to make his way to the heart of Vicksburg where he worked when he could get it and, I guess, stole the horse's food to stay alive when he couldn't. You see, apples for horses were plentiful even if opportunities weren't. Stable work was the lowest and paid miserably, so there were always jobs to be had at places that smelled like horseshit. Jeff got him one that didn't pay enough to feed himself. That's the way it worked for a colored man. After working the stables for all those years, Jeff still didn't have enough money to buy a decent pair of overalls. And yet at the stable he brought Brother under his wing and gave him a portion of his meager wages, even if that delayed his own dream. And if Jeff and Alex couldn't save for an acre somewhere, someday, at least they could swap dreams of what it would be like to own a piece of dirt to farm one day. But one days don't always come. No, they're mostly just borrowed dreams.

Still, it didn't happen like a poem, Jeff and me. It took a lot of hearing 'bout him from Alex to finally see a vision of the Riverman's soul. You know I needed to filter what I saw of men through my day-to-day life with Jesse and the kind of men that hung 'round that alley.

Back in those first days after our arrival at Jesse's, Brother kept his mouth shut, but then when Jesse took out his anger on Sister, Alex came after Jesse with his fist, aiming to put him down for good. One time I thought he'd knock Jesse's jaw through the top of his head with a right-hand hook. But at the last splintered moment, Brother let his fist collide with the wall instead, leaving a gash. Jesse looked stunned like I'd never seen before. He was only accustomed to us taking his blows. When he realized his head was still on his shoulders, he yelled about getting the law on Brother and fled like he was. 'Course, we knew he was really headed to Fred's to lick the wounds he didn't own. Fred was always good at stirring the blues and helping Jesse find a new woman to bandage things. Got a bottle, Fred? What was that woman's name again? 'Member? Well, them kind don't need no name, was Fred's singular reply. "'Cause ain't nobody care 'bout 'em!"

Alex knew he had to hit the road quick. Jesse still had his head and Brother his fist, and he knew the next round it would be Sister and me who would lose. So, he packed his things and left us to the lonely wails of that alley. He had only a thin coat and even thinner hopes to take with him.

Before Alex left, Louvenia and I pleaded with him, begged for him to stay put. Just stay out of Jesse's sight a bit, we would cajole and set things right, as we'd learned that life under Jesse's rule could be fixed with a bottle. "Ever'thing gonna be okay," we cried. But we knew better. There never was an okay at Jesse's.

That night I helped Sister dig through Jesse's things till we found some coins he'd stolen from her that week. Louvenia handed them to Brother sobbing, 'cause she had nothing else to give him. Alex walked off into that night as terrified as we. Him, only a boy of fifteen. The door closed, Sister and I covered our mouths so our sobbing wouldn't tug at Brother's last steps away. We knew that most people driven into dark shadows of them alleys were never heard from again. The price of freedom is always dear, and sometimes you're reduced to eating your foot off to escape the many traps. Working till late after Brother left us, Sister stuffed strips of old rags she'd dipped in laundry starch into the hole in the wall that Alex's fist made, should the law come for Brother. Yes, at Jesse's even the walls had wounds and bandages.

Jesse returned the next morning still drunk. He'd forgotten about the swing he'd barely ducked from the night before and never noticed the patched wall. Probably never saw the wall.

Louvenia wouldn't speak to Jesse for weeks, but that hardly offended ol' Jesse. Don't think he even noticed. He never heard her anyway, particularly when she pleaded mercy from his fist. Jesse was accustomed to laying out his needs in monologue; Sister best know her place was to fill those needs. Breaking her back over tubs or that old stove making his meals was the order of the day. A big mouth deserved a big lip, and when your lip hangs low enough, you learn to travel the way Jesse intended before the last swing weighed things down to greater depths than any soul can bear.

⤙

Then after days of silent sobs in our aprons, Alex appeared on the porch. The Lord had heard our prayers; Brother had not been devoured by the winter's cold. He'd survived by wandering between the shadows of that heartless city till one morning, even before the farmers' carts rolled in with their produce, Brother came upon the stable where he met the Riverman. That morning, when Jeff opened up, he saw Alex across the way hunched under the eaves of the gro-cer's—his life trickling away like the rain trickled down his young cheeks, one tear at a time. The hunger had long disappeared, like it does when your belly finally goes small from emptiness.

"Hey, you shivering over there. Come on near the fire. I get us some coffee 'fore the boss come." These were Jeff's first words to a Breedlove.

Alex, shivering from the morning rain, followed him in where Jeff got a fire going in an old stove. He tugged Brother over to the heat before disappearing. Alex said the place was full of horses and smelled as bad. Jeff returned and tossed a shirt to Brother along with that big smile of his.

"Put yours over that chair. Be dry 'fore the boss come 'round, if he do." Jeff went over to where the food was stashed and pulled out some bread, cheese and apples. "Boss buys these apples for the horses. Charges the customers a nickel for two but never gives 'em to no horses. So I eats 'em when he not 'round and tell 'im they gone bad."

Alex said Jeff had the whitest teeth of any grown man he'd ever seen.

"Why was you over there, wet and all?" he asked Brother. "You don't know the grocer gonna chase you off when he opens? He been sayin' coloreds outside his place bad for business."

"I know. Was thinkin' on it," Alex said.

"I tell you what. I need me some help here anyways. You help clean up but stay low when the boss 'round and I share my wages. Ain't much. Don't get my wages then 'least you got a dry place to sleep up in the hay loft. Boss don't look up there. See? Don't got to think on nothin' now. Just gotta get on with it."

A body can only spend so many rainy nights out in the cold before you stop worrying about somebody gonna grab you by the ear, call you a vagrant and yell in it that you ought 'a be in the chain-gang. It don't matter no more 'cause you've already got one foot in a pine box and death couldn't be any colder than standing in the rain night after night. It didn't take but a day of working together, mucking out stalls and all, for these two men to become fast friends. Jeff's boss already laid the work of two men on his back, though he paid wages for only one, but at least they had a roof over their heads and all the bruised apples they could eat.

Three or four days after Jesse escaped Brother's fist, he came back to tell us 'bout the Riverman. We were filled with joy at Brother's return. Every day we'd wondered if he was gone from our lives for good. We were happy he'd found work, some kind of roof and a friend who knew where he'd come from and offered a hand to share and not one more backhand.

Got to be that Brother could figure the hours when Jesse was likely to be at Fred's or the bars and started coming by to eat. Annie, whose kitchen window faced the mouth of that alley, kept watch in case Jesse lost track of time, or lost enough money at craps and headed home early. If Annie saw that ol' man coming down the alley, she'd tell the preacher to yell out the door with his loud voice for his kids to come in. We could hear the preacher and would quickly hide Brother behind the tubs or somewhere. With Jesse back to his brown bed snoring, Sister would soft-foot over to close his door, then brace a chair against the wobbly knob, which could hold Jesse back a few moments in case he heard us and got up to tell us to close our God-damned mouths and then go bring him a plate of food. His kicking at that bedroom door that was always 'stuck' would give us enough time to bustle Brother out the back door.

I recall that the three of us had many whispered suppers this way. It was during these meals that I came to know about Jeff long before Brother started bringing the boy around. Yes, during those hours of hearing Brother's experiences with this man and through his love for his friend, I saw this man Alex called Riverman.

"He a good man, that Jeff, bringin' you in out of that rain like that," Sister commented many times. Then she looked at me with the most serene eyes I'd seen for ages, like she'd heard some real good news. Nobody ever heard much good on folks in them alleys. A good man? She seemed to want me to hear over and over. A good man, ain't he, Sarah?

Yes, Lord, somebody had saved our brother and with him, my sister and me, because I knew that Jeff's spirit and kindness helped us all not to give up.

With that bag of apples Brother had brought over, I baked a big apple pie and sent some back to this Riverman. Guess through Alex, he was hearing 'bout me, too.

BROKEN SHARD OF HOPE

19

I**T GOT TO** be that Jesse stayed out most nights so he could sleep well on all the days he never remembered. Late afternoons he'd call out for a meal or to empty his pot, but we didn't hear no more.

"You hear that?"

"No, I ain't heard nothin' no more!" Sister said.

"Must be somebody out in the alley then."

These were our cautious whispers as we gathered our hushed thoughts and bundled them into the daydreams we'd share on those nights we worked our irons over miles of old shirts.

Then sometime in the evening, Jesse would crawl out of the bed, put on his old suit, grab any money he could get at and head for the good times. He was still having them good times 'cause our wash money was coming in good, real good, and he figured he was getting most of it. But he wasn't. We worked hard, pressed and folded things like no other tub women 'round them alleys. It made us proud when we could pay Annie's boy, Tom, to deliver the clothes for us. Tommy earned himself some money and gave some to his momma. We all helped each other get by. Yes, life let up on us a bit down at the end of Jesse's alley.

But the day came when Jesse started looking at things more closely. Him looking down into our laundry tubs to see how much work we had. He surely noticed how hard we worked, so he figured there had to be something going on. Then one day, without a word, he went to the cupboards to see if they were bare enough. In all those years, I never 'member him opening them before. What was Jesse's thinking, and what would it cost us? Them cupboards were still mostly bare. Where'd we put it then, all that money coming in? Had he missed something during his last three-day binge? So, what was this business going on in his own house? Were we really putting all the money out? He surely wondered, and that made the bile at the corners of his mouth drip all the more.

But we weren't. Not no more. We only put out enough to keep Jesse drunk enough to be numbed off our backs. Then the rest we were putting in a hidden place. Jesse, his life was getting ever so desperate back then, had to have it. But equally, our own survival depended on him not getting at our laundry money. You see, he could smell a dream, too, and I bet she cost all the more the worse he smelled. When you're an ugly ol' man who lives off bottles, you gots to have plenty of money or no woman gonna pay mind to your offer. It's all gonna be a waste of her time. Ain't enough money in the world for his ugly ol' business, Louvenia whispered to me one night when Jesse cursed us for having only a dime sitting out for him when he took off. We'd decided that the next night it would only be a nickel. And it was. Jesse threw it back in Louvenia's face and left for bigger change.

Guess it was about then that Jesse got himself into some trouble trying to get at the big-man money he was desperate for. You can't put down a half bottle of whiskey and keep your head on straight at the craps. No, your life starts rolling faster than the dice, till it hurls itself back at you. Jesse always surrounded himself with folks, like Fred, just waiting to walk on his back, any back, for any amount. They were kindred in their ugliness right to the bottom of their rotted-out souls. When his pockets went dry, these same folks started pounding on Jesse's back to see if anything would drop out of his empty life. When they figured nothing was left, they still knew which two backs to stomp next. Word gets 'round who's not so down and out and might be good for a quick take down. Therefore, I knew it wasn't Annie pounding on our door late that night. A courtesy call from Jesse's caroling choir of drunks?

"Who'd come down that alley to our door this late?" Sister whispered like a runaway slave.

She walked over to the door knowing only somebody delivering grief would be standing there. She peeked out.

"I from the city here." The man's voice was loud, like he wanted all the alley to hear. "Yes, ma'am, the city sent me to this here address. This Mr. Jesse Powell's place? Huh?" The city inspector looked past Sister into her kitchen like he needed to see what we had.

"Yeah, but Jesse gone," she told him. "He say he don't want to talk to nobody."

Louvenia wrung her hands as she did when frightened. I stopped ironing and put the iron back on the stove to heat in case I needed to press my own message to this caller's face if it came to it. Then I walked over to Louvenia standing at the door with her foot fixed to it, so he couldn't push it open wider.

"What's you want?" I asked. "You don't know what time it is to do the city's business?"

"It don't matter none. I from the city. City inspector, I is. Official business here. Seems like they's been lots of complaints 'bout all these here bottles stacked up outside your laundry porch," he warned, jabbing his finger at the direction of our faces.

"Ain't there ever'thing stacked up and down this here alley?" I told him. "Ain't nobody ever come from the city 'bout it before, have they, Sister?"

Sister shook her head and looked towards Jesse's bedroom. Probably hoping he'd jump up to see who was in his kitchen. But not a curse came from him. He was too deep in another nightmare and couldn't have known another was unfolding at the door.

"Well, you bet they is now," the man from the city said. "If Jesse don't show up with the money tonight, this very night, I'm tellin' you the city's gonna put 'im in jail till he pays up."

"What money be that?"

Sister put her hand over her mouth to cup any puke her fear might bring up. I held on to her arm to still her trembling.

"That's all I got to say on it." The man turned to walk off, but then hollered back, "He's got 'bout forty-seven dollars in bad gamblin' debts some ornery men at the city done paid off for him. Now they wants their money. He better come up with it tonight if he knows what's good for him, 'cause they's people out there with friends who sure knows where the jail is."

He walked off shaking his thick finger at Jesse's thicker stack of bottles piled along the walls near as high as his jagged lies.

Louvenia locked the door and fell into the kitchen chair to sift the implications. I could tell the fog had rolled in on her bad 'cause she held her head with both fists and stared at the kitchen table-top like right there was the bottom of a well she was about to leap down—her trying hard to think straight in the confusion that man had dumped on her.

But there was no fog come down on me this time. No, I started seeing up ahead what might be a clearing of sorts. Yes, even looked like an oasis of calm if we could only make it there. And I meant for it to be.

Jesse was still asleep as I pulled his door closed and sat down next to Sister to talk it out. She was trembling all over by then. That word jail was the same word Jesse threw in her face all the time. Jail for her, that is, for not minding him, because jail for Jesse could never have been a notion that would fit into her battered thoughts.

"If they take Jesse to jail, then they gonna come after me for the money. That right? They gonna come for me?" I held Sister's hands so they'd stop shaking. "What am I gonna do? We only gots 'bout six dollars saved up. Took us months. Ain't that near to being two train tickets to somewhere far?"

Louvenia was sorting her fears aloud. We sat there motionless to look at our options one by one, 'cause we never had two anyway.

"We just gonna do nothin'!" I announced. "Jesse cut his deals with them at the bar. They knowed he don't got money but they still played the dice like big shots. Let 'em work it out between 'em. No, we ain't pullin' our money out to pay down Jesse's gamblin'. And nobody gonna come for you tonight, not never, 'cause you got nothin' to give 'em."

"We gots near six dollars, I think. Got it for now, anyway."

She looked over her shoulder at Jesse's door like he might spring out and find her throat and use it to get at the money; six dollars hidden somewhere behind our secrets.

"No, we don't got no money. They can search the place but we ain't go it 'cause I'm takin' it over to Annie's. I know she'll hide it for us."

"Best go now then, 'fore that man come back. Or comes back for me! He gonna do that?"

I patted Sister's hand without another word. How could I have known what might happen to us? But I was determined we'd be ready for it.

Later Jesse crawled out of bed to go out. We'd been biting our nails as we waited for his exit to a jail cell. Sister had cooked up his food and laid it out extra nice. Jesse came in, looked at that nice plate of food sitting there and then at me like I'd dusted it with pinch nightshade poison. But I hadn't. Just wanted him to sit down and fill his mouth so he'd not be talking at Louvenia, as I was scared her trembling would alert him that something was amiss. If he figured there was some kind of trouble brewing out in the alley, his instinct would be to head over to Fred's till things cooled down as he did when he got into it bad with the whores' pimps.

Jesse looked hard at Louvenia. She kept her head down at her ironing. Then he looked at me. But I couldn't help but give him a real big grin so's he'd know something was up for sure! He quickly figured as much and pushed his plate back after only two mouthfuls. Eyeing us hard, he hit the road without his usual curses on our worthlessness.

Louvenia fell into the kitchen chair and slumped back into her old familiar fears. "What's we gonna do now?" she asked the tabletop. "Come away from that window and lock that door good!"

I did, and sat down next to her. "Let Jesus figure out what's gonna happen to Jesse." I knew if Jesus was in on it Sister would rest easier, 'cause she didn't take to my notions on Jesse most times, saying I best not tell Jesus what I wanted to do to that man.

We didn't talk much the rest 'a the night. Just went to bed wondering what the Lord would come up with. Was He gonna answer our prayers?

He was.

⋘

It was the next morning when Jesse's brother Fred showed up. It had to have been the earliest I'd ever seen him.

"Listen to me good! Jesse, he done got picked up last night at the bar," Fred blurted anxiously, or maybe already desperate for a drink. "He got put in jail and couldn't sleep a wink 'cause the noise. I just been there. All them whores hollering across the hall and the like. And it stinks down there. Nobody to empty the crap pots."

Fred kept eyeing sister's scrambled eggs like he expected her to go fetch him some.

"What Jesse do?" Louvenia asked and glanced my way. "He in trouble?"

"Like I tol' you, cops say he been fined by the city for not cleanin' up your damned pile of bottles out there and they ain't gonna let 'im out till you get that mess cleaned up. Then he gots to pay a big fine and I tell you, that fine gettin' bigger ever' day!"

"That what the city man say?" Louvenia asked. "Jesse get out when his bottles get hauled off?"

"Him fine 'bout fifty-seven dollars. You got that kind of money? Let me see it then," Fred looked longingly 'round the kitchen. "How much you got for me to take to 'em this afternoon?"

Guess he expected to squeeze us for any money he could above Jesse's fine.

"Him fine not forty-seven dollars?" I asked the old liar.

"How'd you know? The city man already told you, ain't he? City man said he come by and warned you what'd happen if Jesse didn't take care of things," Fred said, sinking in his own swamp of lies.

"Louvenia, you ever heard a man say that?" I asked.

"No, nobody ever come 'round knockin' on our door and he never said nothin' 'bout no fine I can 'member," Sister said. "Now you say he owes 'em twenty-seven dollars."

"I said forty-seven. You messin' with me?" Fred asked.

"No, Fred, I ain't. But you know how noisy it is out there in the alley. Can't hear a word most the time," Louvenia told him. "But I sure heard you say Jesse gone. You hear that clear, Sarah? Lord, have mercy! If he ain't locked up somewhere, too! Nobody done gone and lost the key over there had they? Huh?"

I stood up to Brother Fred in a way that would have made Minerva proud.

"Maybe somebody did come by, Sister, but you couldn't hear 'cause your hearin' got cut off from being hit upside your head by Jesse's fist."

Then I turned to Fred and put Momma's eyes on him till he flinched.

"Fred, you gots a heap of concern for your brother; he ain't eatin' good down in the city jail and his whores is annoyin' 'im something awful with their snorin'. Or is Jesse locked up with the same whores he owes money to? That what this is all 'bout?"

Fred never did take to me.

"Huh? What's that? 'Course I got concerns. Jesse my only kin. He my blood," Fred snarled.

I was thinking I'd never tell nobody that Jesse was my blood. Anyway, how can you drink that much whiskey and still have blood in your veins? It made no sense to me, but I could smell an alley rat, and this one's name was Fred.

"But you got no concern 'bout Louvenia here gettin' her head knocked against these here walls?" I asked, real nice, too.

"Now don't start up with me, sister-girl. Ain't none of my business what Jesse does to any damned woman. It be his house, ain't it?"

'Bout then Fred and I were scrambling to opposite sides of the road and I aimed to set a few rat traps along his side. "And it ain't none of my business if Jesse in jail. And Louvenia here, she's broke! Ain't you, Sister?"

"Don't shit me!" Fred said. "Jesse say he sure Louvenia gots it comin' in good! He say there's got to be enough hidden someplace to get him out of jail. Then he pay 'em back the rest with interest when he gets his hands on it."

"No, Fred. Louvenia spent ever' penny we made on men, craps in the alley and whiskey. But ask me real nice-like if I gots it comin' in good. Yes, I do, Fred. Jesse wants to borrow some money from me? That be so, then he's gotta come 'round and talk terms face-to-face. Maybe we work out a good deal on credit, but only after he clears up some past debts. Like eight years of borrowed drinking money you and him pissed out in the alley."

"How's he gonna do that, sister-girl? Come by and talk 'bout your situation here? Ain't I just told you he's in jail? Maybe you don't know what that means 'cause you're plain stupid?"

"Fred, I ain't gonna take issue with you. So, you best head off now, 'cause fixin' your problems is too hard for me. We talk again one day when I get smarter."

"Then Louvenia, you gots to come up with that money so's we can work somethin' out with the city folks and get our Jesse out. He don't like it down there, I'm tellin' you plain, he sure enough don't!"

Sister stood up and pointed her finger at Fred. "I real worried 'bout Jesse. Sure I am. Who gonna bring that man the pot when he don't want to get out 'a bed? Or fan 'im all night when he gets hot?" Louvenia feigned sorrowful grief and wiped a tear with her apron. 'Cept I know Louvenia; she was really hiding a grin and gagging down a laugh by biting the corner of that rag. "But the thing is," she continued, "I gots no work 'cause Sarah here stole my customers out from under me. Didn't you Sarah? Sure you did!" Sister looked at me like I was pure wickedness.

"Yep, Fred. That time when Jesse hit Sister and she had a bandage over her eyes and couldn't see what I was up to, I cleaned her out. Guess a bit like your brother Jesse done to her. Ain't that right, Louvenia?"

Fred stood seething from our mockery. I could see his fist twitching to belt his reply.

"Guess Jesse gonna have to stay in jail till you get a job, Fred, and then you can go down to the city and pay off Jesse's problem, a few cents every week or so. That's what I'm thinkin'," Sister said, hiding her grin in her apron.

Fred was in no mood for us. He no doubt saw a picture of himself suddenly unwanted at the bar where they took no credit and Fred's only cash came from Jesse's theft of our money. "I don't know what you're up to, but when Jesse gets out, you best expect he'll be mad as hell and come lookin' to backhand you with some of it!" Fred announced, like giving us hell was some new torture we'd never come up against. "And we just see what your big mouth gets you then. Don't expect it 'a be right side up like them bottles out there. You think, sister-girl?"

"He ain't out and we ain't gonna worry 'bout nothin'," I said, but that was a lie.

We were worried plenty, but Momma taught us to hide our fears; we'd let Fred figure out what Sister and I had going. But then we didn't know ourselves. I was thinking Fred was just gonna head off to hunt down a borrowed drink and probably wouldn't fuss 'bout ol' Jesse till he needed more whiskey money. After a day or two of stupor, he wouldn't even 'member he had a brother in jail.

All the alleys 'round here end up at the same dead-end: The bottom of an empty bottle that gets tossed onto a pile nobody wants to admit exists.

"When I comes by again, you best have them bottles out there in Jesse's alley hauled off," Fred said to Louvenia, but looked at me.

"I know you gots to go, Fred. The whores are gonna be fussin' for you. You best take some good cookin' over to poor Jesse on your way."

I contorted my face to look sorrowful about Jesse's situation. Louvenia went back to hiding her grin behind her apron. She had to know I wasn't finished with Fred yet.

"Now, that's better, sister-girl," he said.

I went over to the garbage pail and, with my back to Fred, pulled out two dry-as-board biscuits that Sister had tossed out, wrapped them in newsprint and handed them to Fred.

"What's you thinkin', girl? Jesse don't like biscuits none," he snorted. "You go fix 'im some cornbread right quick. I want me some, too."

But I took them biscuits, dropped them to the floor and stomped them hard and handed them back to Fred. "But he loves crackers, don't he? Here's two. Fresh from under my bare feet."

Fred left in a huff without his brother's biscuits, but I reckon he did take my message. I smiled, thinking how hard Jesse would have to swallow on it.

Before Fred got too far, Louvenia stuck her head out the door and yelled, "Fred, you gots some money I can borrow? I's broke and don't like Sarah's cookin'! You seen her biscuits! Near killed Jesse the other day, her fried eggs did. Need some money to buy a meal. You know I'm good for it, don't you?" Then she slammed the door and started laughing like a crazy woman.

Yes, we laughed and laughed like we hadn't laughed in years. Just like two crazies that had just made it to the other side of freedom. But then we fell into each other's arms wailing in fear and panic. What would happen to us next? Sweat broke out on my face. Sister turned silent thinking on our prospects. It was not a prospect that Jesse would one day return to take his revenge. It was a certainty.

We didn't hear from Fred for a few days and never heard no more on Jesse's situation. We didn't want to know. As that haze of fear evaporated, the days then followed in calmness and we found serene sunny mornings where we sat lost in all the quiet, drinking our coffee with not a snort from the ol' man to break our thoughts. Strange what life sounds like when you're not listening through the crash of whiskey bottles over layers of thoughts you hope to ride out to that somewhere better.

Picking the shards out of your borrowed dreams, the shards from our shattered and broken lives, is what hope is born of.

LIVING ON HORSE SHIT LIES

20

ALEX AND JEFF worked hard at the stables. Still, sometimes the owner, Mr. Harold, claimed he didn't make enough to pay them. He'd say maybe next week be better, but it never was and never would be 'cause it was all just a tale Harold used to rope their lives in. Brother said he knew it was a lie because he could see Harold had lots of customers handing him money; he just didn't want to pay their wages. When Jeffrey tried to talk to Mr. Harold 'bout getting paid up, he told them they could go get work elsewhere if they didn't take to the situation. But things are different for coloreds. If the men headed off for new work, they'd sure be asked for references from their last job. Got no references, maybe you're just out of jail; don't need nobody today. Best get yourself lost looking for work elsewhere. We all carried the weight of our days under such rules.

Truly it was no lie that if you didn't have references, you'd get no job. Sleeping in the hayloft was bad, yet you knew come winter you could freeze in them alleys or be picked up as a vagrant. That's a destination where you'd share a pallet to sleep on with a filthy stranger alongside a shared slop bucket to feed from. Yes, chain gangs always afforded employment. Harold knew letting the men sleep over the horses in the hayloft was the only thing Alex and Jeff had to keep them from being lost out there. Got to be the men had to swallow hard their pride so they wouldn't gag on Harold's horseshit lies.

⁓

Annie and I got to be good friends during the hours Jesse was gone. She couldn't come 'round much when he was home 'cause her little ones followed her ever'where and she didn't want them seeing that ol' man spewing his gutter-talk at Sister and me.

At times I helped Annie stay on top of her laundry for those kids. When Jesse was gone, she enjoyed visiting with Sister and teaching me to read better while Sister ironed their things. Those times Louvenia would pour sweet tea and listen to us talk about things that were in the books. She always loved to hear how some folks had lives so very different from ours. How did that happen, she often wondered out loud.

"Now, Louvenia, Sarah here's gettin' good with learning new words. When are we gonna get you goin' readin'?" Annie asked.

But Louvenia didn't like to hear 'bout it. She jumped to finish ironing that shirt. Still, I knew she was afraid of how words could tangle her thoughts. Maybe like having the key to your jail slid right in front of the very bars that held you back. The key to your escape close enough you could reach down and grab it, but you also knew you still really couldn't. What waited for you outside your prison may only be another borrowed dream, one blacker than the one you still bled from. Sister put her iron on the stove to heat.

"When Sarah comes home from deliverin' the ironin' she reads the verses," Louvenia told Annie. "She reads the Psalms while I'm ironin'. It soothes my nerves, don't it Sarah?"

Sister looked at me with pride. Once, late at night when she figured I was sleeping, I heard her praying. Telling Jesus that I'd read to her that night. No one in our family had ever been able to read before.

Louvenia had fixed up a nice dinner late that evening. Jeff was eating with us as he did whenever he could get away from the stables and Alex would cover for him. Sometimes Alex would come over while Jeff covered and then he'd take back some home cooking. It was one of these nights when Fred walked into our kitchen like he owned the place.

"I gots some real bad news here," the old liar announced. "Jesse gots big problems. The folks down at the jail done decided he ain't gonna get out for thirty days, maybe more 'cause he can't put his hands on no money to put down on his fines."

I had to bite my tongue to keep from thanking the Lord for this truly delightful bad news. Jesse paying for his sins for once! Louvenia almost fell into her chair as tears of joy welled in her eyes. But I didn't want Fred to see how happy we were and then go tell the devil's captive! I jumped to pull Fred's attention my way.

"Sister, them onions you chopped still botherin' your eyes?" I asked knowing better. "Go back there and rinse 'em good. I take care of Fred here."

Fred wouldn't have cared if Sister was walking around with both eyes hanging from their sockets after having collided with Jesse's fists. He situated himself at our table as if he thought himself a guest waiting to be served. He probably wondered why I was smiling ear to ear. You see, I had that box of rat poison down there in case he got too comfortable.

"Yeah, and Jesse say bring 'im some decent food. Him not eatin' good down there and gots the runs."

Fred kept eyeing Jeff.

"Who's this here boy in Jesse's house? Huh?"

"I'm Jeff McWilliams."

Jeff glared at Fred like he recognized the demon for who he was. Fred went to acting like he was now Jesse's shadow.

"What's he doing here? Jesse, he don't want nobody in his place."

Nobody but gamblers and drunks, I guess.

"Then who gonna bring 'im the pot?" Louvenia snickered.

Maybe she didn't count even as a nobody to Jesse and Fred.

"Fred, you best take some food to Jesse. You know he must be real hungry. I sure know how that is 'cause I been hungry right here in this kitchen after his friends stopped by for a meal, or two."

I got up and put a tin of food on the table for Jesse. Nothing but garbage I was 'bout to throw to the cats in the alley. When Fred not looking, I poured most of a shaker of salt in it before covering the plate.

"You best take this down to Jesse. Don't let it get cold now. You know how mean Jesse gets when his meals stand too long."

Fred was about to run off at the mouth when I bustled him out.

From out on the porch, I could hear Louvenia break down at the table and cry like her dam broke—that dam of emotions she had pent up for years. Lord, it was an avalanche, too. Sister wailed so hard she choked on her tears because her throat, so wrung with Jesse's hands, was now even more constricted with fear. But this time there was no thumbprint on her flesh.

"Jesse be gone for a whole month?" she sobbed to confirm Fred's news. "That what, Sarah?"

Sister needed my help to sort the implications. It was like she'd finally awakened from a real black dream that was yet nipping at the corner of her lip like the bite of a nigger dog. The sight of Sister so suddenly broken-down scared Jeff. Guess he'd never seen a woman undone over something he couldn't see to protect her from.

"Jeff, Sister needs her rest; you best go back to the stables for now. She be alright."

I was sorry for Jeff. Louvenia's weeping throbbed at our hearts. Yet I knew well enough that through this surge of pain there was also joy cleansing her soul of the years of Jesse's dirty dealings on her. Jeff read my eyes, nodded and then got up without a word. He stood behind Sister's chair, put his arms around her and kissed her temple. His own eyes were filled with tears when, in silence, he walked out into the lonely night.

I went to get Sister a moist cloth to put to her throbbing head and prayed. Louvenia gonna be better in the morning, Lord? We're still here, I reminded myself of our blessings. Then I sat down to read the verses.

"Yea, though I walk through the valley of the shadow of death, I will fear no evil…" At least I'll try not to for now.

Yes, we had survived, and there awaited another day ahead, and we would sure as heaven own it.

Stolen Moments, Borrowed Dreams

21

ON THOSE SUMMER evenings when we headed home from delivering the ironing, we'd steal a few moments here and there to window shop. One night Louvenia paused in front of that hat shop a few blocks from our place. At first, I couldn't think why, as we'd passed it many times without lingering. I could see it was the kind of shop them fancy big-hat women from church likely shopped at. It was on our side of town, but undoubtedly the finest store 'round there, maybe finer than any I'd ever been in. I stood next to Sister and watched her gaze through the glass. All the weary lines on her face eased and there was even a slight smile on her lips where too often only bruises hung. Hers was the kind of soft smile one has while watching a child at play. Her furtive gaze through the shop window revealed that she had glimpsed something that took her away from her troubles if only for a few stolen moments. Was it all them beautiful hats displayed in there that had captivated her? More ribbons, bows and flowers gathered in more colors than I'd ever seen.

Then I noticed what had put a gleam in Sister's eyes; she was fixed on that one particular hat displayed on a fancy pedestal—the one with the feather bird that was prettier than all the rest. The little brilliant-colored bird seemed to peer back like it desperately wanted to fly away with Sister. I was sure it was a tiny glimpse of a dream she'd shared with me long before. A borrowed dream of being a fine lady for a moment or two. Like Sundays when the big-hat ladies tossed aside their cleaning rags, put aside their irons and got dolled up to sit up there in the front pews like royalty.

It seemed as we ventured along that street Louvenia always paused to gaze through the window yet never went in. Only stood there looking at that particular hat with the little feather bird nesting in some pretty gem-colored flower petals. I'd imagined it was like a secret between them, Sister and that little bird. Yes, she had a dream hidden where nobody could steal it away. She'd never had such a fine thing. Probably never thought she might one day. We had no time to borrow dreams like that—but this time was different, because I decided to do more than follow Sister follow her borrowed dream; I would capture that bird and pleasure her with a few gilded moments.

A week later, after delivering' our ironing, I headed over to the milliner's with coins jingling in the purse I kept hidden in my blouse. Couldn't spend all I took in that week, but figured I could put some down on that hat. Enough to hold it till I could pay the rest. I stepped into that shop, but quickly felt it was the last place in town that might be expecting me that afternoon.

"I want to put some money down on that hat over yonder with the feather bird," I told the shop woman. "Want you to hold it for me."

She was a lot lighter than Sister and me. Could even pass, and had airs accordingly. "What's that you want?" She looked me up and down like I had a smell and seemed plum annoyed with the notion of letting one of her hats go without a fight. "You can't wear a fine hat like I gots in my shop!"

"Yeah? Why not?"

"Cause they're meant for ladies, not tub girls!"

I wondered how she knew I worked the tubs. 'Cause I was darker than her?

"How you know I work the tubs?"

"I see a laundress's hands comin' from a block away and don't want none in my place wastin' my time and crushing my hats with they's rough hands like they actually gonna buy one. They ain't never gonna buy nothin' here. Just want to pretend they's fine ladies and ride it on my dime. Ain't it so? Huh! Like I don't know no better! Anyway, you a child. These here hats are for women!"

"I ain't no child!" I said right up in her face. "I'm near thirteen and got breasts!"

"That so? Glad you told me on both accounts."

She came 'round her counter to look at my feet like she could confirm I was a tub woman by seeing if I wore shoes.

"Chile," she said again like I didn't hear before, "I got breasts when I was ten and a boyfriend when I was eleven! And nobody ever took me for some chile like I just done you!"

"Why I care? Maybe you a granny when you're twelve!"

"Granny, huh?" she barked. "I don't want your money and ain't gonna waste my time just so you can go tell folks you're a customer of this here fine shop."

Well, I guess Louvenia and me weren't the only ones who borrowed dreams from time to time.

"Who your customers?" I asked, figuring she beat them and tossed them out 'fore they bought something, 'cause there was sure not a single soul in there, 'less they was in the back getting their wounds tended from this woman's tongue-lashing.

"My customers, in case one day you're gonna open yourself a shop," she barely got those words out 'fore she was laughing like an alley cat in heat, "are the whores on First Street, and the best of them women bending the pews down with their fat asses at the First Street Baptist Church."

"You a whore?" I asked.

Sister always told me to never look into the face of one of them whores that hung round the mouth of Jesse's alley. So I never seen one up good and close.

"Do I look like one?"

"How I know?" I asked.

"I give up being a whore. Took my money and bought me this shop ten long years ago. I pay dear for rent, but I'm close enough to the whitey part of town where I need to be. Them white women venture over here so long as I pretend I give 'em a hefty discount for their troubles crossing the tracks. And I do their bills so they sure think so, too. Yeah, I charge them double and then give 'em a ten percent discount. Them white women pay dear for my hats, and that's all there is to that!"

"How you start your own shop?" I asked. "You got the money?"

"Honey, I stole my money back from my pimp!"

"Yeah?"

I had a vision of that woman and Jesse getting into it one night in some dark alley. He could sure sniff out our laundry money like some pimp!

"He don't come after you?"

"How he gonna do that now?" she asked.

"How? How he got your money from you to steal back in the first place?"

"No, chile" she said. It took her longer to get the word 'chile' out each time she hurled it at my face. "He a heartless man and he still back there countin' how much money he done stole from how many women. And he doing his numbers with my knife buried deep in his heart. See, it don't pay to be a heartless man, 'cause then a woman comes along with a knife and she jab it in there real good just to see if you really don't got one. Well, he lied 'bout that, too. He did have a heart and I cut into it like a rhubarb pie. I sure enough did. Just like he done to me all them years. Anything else you need to know now, 'fore you go on your way, lil' girl?"

"I didn't come in here 'cause I needed to know nothin'. I come to put somethin' down on that hat over there. Go fetch it for me."

"What? Go fetch it, huh? No, I ain't wastin' my time with you or your breasts, chile, 'cause I knows the only thing big on you is that mouth of yours! If I let you put a nickel or two down on one of my fine hats, then I got to save it till you come 'round wanting your money back, and all the while I could have sold it to some whitey! So, now off with you. I gots to make a basket of bows for them whores and them women at the First Street Baptist. And let me tell you something else: the whores and the women at the First Baptist, they all pray to the same Lord, and they be praying to be saved from the very same men! Now get on out of here. I got things to do!"

What could I say? I walked out thinking that if she'd asked me to prove she had a heart I'd for sure have to stick a knife in to see for sure. But I was not gonna let that woman put an end to Sister's bit of a dream. No, I wasn't.

I headed on over to the stables to talk it out with Jeffrey. It was summer and the sun was up till late so I could walk over there and still get back to the alley 'fore dark when Louvenia would for sure be headed up to the mouth of the alley to watch for me. And if I was late, she'd tongue-lash me all the way back to our porch saying things 'bout whores gonna interfere with me if I was out too late and all. "Don't go over to them whores," she'd say, "'cause they's callin' you sayin' they gots something you're gonna want to hear! You just walk on by 'em with your own mouth closed!"

Well, over at the stables I told Jeff everything. He smiled as he brushed down a horse. He asked me about the color of hat Louvenia had taken such a fancy to. I told him. He said he'd figure something out. Jeff's smile always calmed me down.

Next day, while his boss was gone and Alex was looking after things, Jeff headed over to the hat shop.

"Well, now look at you!" that woman said to Jeff as he walked in. "Ain't you an eyeful?" He said she looked him up and down and then in a certain place I can't say, but it was near the middle. "I think I see some dimples," she told him.

Talking like that I wondered if she'd done forgot she'd left her last vocation behind.

"I ain't here 'cept for a hat. One gots a feather bird up on it somewhere," Jeff told the milliner, who was still eyeing his manhood like she was armed with measuring tapes in each hand—and not to measure no damned head!

"You don't look like you'd fit one my hats. Ain't been a man in here for me to know how to measure a head that big," she told him. "I bet you got a big one, too!"

"Ain't for my head," Jeff told her.

"No?"

"I put some money down on it. You keep it till I get paid, then I come for it."

"Oh, I see. So, then you gots a lil' girl someplace that wants a big hat to look like a big woman? Huh?"

Jeff ignored her.

"Alright. Give me a dollar. Guess I put your hat with the damned bird in the back for keepin'."

"That's all I come for," Jeff said.

"Well, didn't I figure that out quick enough?"

Jeff probably let her see his dimples—always got a woman weak in the knees when he grinned—then nodded to her and then nodded again till she finally grunted and went to fetch that hat. That milliner probably felt a bit annoyed that Jeff's charm got her to do what she was sure not gonna do for a no-account tub girl.

For days I bit my nails to keep from telling Sister what we'd gone and done. Then one night my heart sank low. It sure did. We were coming home when Sister paused at the hat shop. But you see, the hat that shared her secret was no longer on the pedestal in the window and was nowhere to be seen. She stood frozen, as if one more dream had slipped her by to catch up with all the others long gone.

A look of sadness came over her as we headed off in silence. She didn't have much to say the rest of the evening. Sister said that she was tired and went to lie down on her cot. I pulled the cover up over her and she closed her eyes and rolled over to face the wall. She never asked me to read the verses she liked to drift to sleep with. Still, I knew she wasn't asleep for real.

Sister was quiet over the next few days as we worked our way through the piles of laundry stacked on the porch. At the end of the day, I'd try to work up a chat 'bout the church's big summer picnic where ever'body would meet in the square after the service. We'd all be getting dressed up and spend hours the night before, or early that morning preparing our best dishes to share with those sitting on blankets near ours. Jeff and Alex had been looking forward to the day for weeks, even though they'd come up with all sorts of excuses why they still couldn't sit through the sermon that morning.

The Friday before the picnic, Alex and me finally had enough put together to pay the milliner and Jeff planned to pick up Sister' hat. Could hardly contain my excitement as Louvenia had never had anything bought new just for her. No, she wore mostly castoff hats with an assortment of this and that sewed on by Lord knows how many prior wearers; a broken flower, a bent bow, they'd all been sewn and resewn.

The Sunday of the picnic Louvenia and I got up early to finish cooking and iron our dresses along with a shirt for Jeff. He was coming by to pick up the picnic basket with the chickens all fried up, peach cobbler all golden brown on top, collard and potata salads with crumbled hickory bacon all ready. Everything was packed carefully in a spare basket of Annie's with a big jar of sweet tea.

The morning of the picnic, Louvenia came out of the back room all dressed for church. Thank goodness Jesse was still behind bars 'cross town. He'd have given her a cursing if he'd seen that pretty dress Annie had given Sister. It was something one of the church-women had donated to the church clothes drive, and Annie knew it would be just right for Louvenia. Sister starched it to look like it just came out of a shop window. She was prancing about the kitchen in it when Jeff walked in. He set the fancy-wrapped package on the table where Sister tended to sit.

"Want your coffee now, Sister?"

"Mornin', Jeffrey. You had your breakfast yet?" Sister pirouetted so we could better see her special dress. "My goodness, what's in that package with such fancy paper?"

I handed her a mug of coffee with the extra cream her stomach needed.

"Miss Louvenia, this here was just delivered to your door by the delivery boy."

I went over the table pretending to examine the package.

"Yes, I can read the delivery label. Says it's for you. Best open it now, 'cause that might be chicken in there. You tell that butcher man to deliver an extra chicken for Sunday picnic, Sister?"

"Now, you know there ain't no chicken in that kind of fine paper with little pictures of blooming cherry trees. You ought not to be fibbin' like that on the Lord's Day! Anyway, He's got to be tired of hearin' your mouth all week and needs a day of rest from it, don't He, Jeff?"

"Amen, Lord, Amen, Miss Louvenia." Jeff nodded towards the ceiling like the Lord might be peeking through one of the cracks up there.

Sister looked at the big box suspiciously. Finally, she sat down and slowly peeled the paper away—just enough to see that little feather bird peeking back at her.

Not a sound came out of Sister for the longest time. Only a long sigh and a well-worn tear fell from the corner of her eye, one of joy as precious as a glistening jewel, as right there it looked as though her moments of happiness were no longer borrowed from someone else's dream. Sister stood there wringing her hands as she did when she was anxious and then slumped in that old kitchen chair and cautiously peeled the pretty wrapping paper back to reveal all of her prized hat.

She pulled her hand back and twisted it up in the other, and then sat there with her head shaking nervously as her foot tapped on the leg of the spindly chair. Tap, tap, tap, it went. Must 'a been to keep herself from grabbing at that beautiful hat like it couldn't really be hers, so she ought not to be touching it. Tap, tap, tap, little pulses beating out a drum roll saying what her soul couldn't fold into words. But I knew. There it was, that tiny little feather bird looking up at her—a tiny dream to feed her soul with joy.

Sister's obvious delight was greater than I'd ever seen—greater than any Christmas morning. None of us could say much, so we all went on to church in our quiet joy with Sister wearing her big hat just like the big-hat women. And they all smiled as we took a seat and couldn't seem to take their eyes off Sister's hat and nodded their appreciation. Still, Louvenia's shyness got the best of her and she could hardly look up to acknowledge their nods. She could only let a shy grin escape here and there.

After the preacher finally finished talking 'bout the devil—don't he know nothing else to preach 'bout? And don't Jesus always keep the devil locked up on beautiful days like that anyway?—we rose to leave. At the front steps the big-hat ladies were happy to see Sister and remarked how fine her hat was. I left Louvenia to chat while Jeff, Alex and I went over to the park to lay out our picnic.

What can weave a dream through a broken heart? Where could I borrow a few more for my sister? I remember asking Momma back on Orchard Hill what a dream was. For her it was a day she could fill her family's bellies. She was right; sometimes a dream smells like a hot peach cobbler. But then sometimes it's only borrowed, yet don't it still get us to the next day?

∽

That night Alex and Jeff sat at the kitchen table with big spoons finishing off the last of the cobbler like two big kids. While I washed up our picnic things, Louvenia sat talking about her hat and how it was as nice as any of the big-hat women's.

"Best in the world, don't you think?" she asked as her eyes caressed that feather bird.

"Yes, Miss Louvenia, everybody sure had their eyes on that new hat of yours. That's for sure, ain't it, Alex?" Jeff asked, not taking his eyes off that pan of cobbler 'cause Brother might get his spoon in there faster for the next bite. "You know, Miss Louvenia, I don't know nothin' 'bout women's things. No, I sure don't," Jeff said.

His gentleness always eased Sister into talking freely like she could with no other man.

"Like what color is that flower? That one right there. That blue?" he asked.

"No," Sister said as if she was the milliner speaking to a customer. "That there is called lavender. It ain't really pink and ain't really blue, that's how you know. I seen that color on a flower once. Yes, I did. Annie, she brung over some sweet peas from her momma's garden once. Little round flowers they was and they smelled so sweet. Yes, sweet and spicy. Thought it was the most beautiful smell in the world. Late that summer, Annie she gave me seedpods from her ma's sweet pea vines. Told me when to plant 'em."

"That's a good idea, Sister," I said, not ever remembering any flowers at Jesse's. "When you gonna plant them seeds?"

"Oh, Jesse, he seen them seedpods dryin' in the window and throwed 'em out. He don't want no flowers 'round him. Said it reminded him of the dead," Sister said. "Don't make no difference. Ain't nothing ever gonna grow in that alley. Not enough sun, and the soil's fouled bad out there."

"What color is that there bird, Miss Louvenia?" Jeff continued as he finished off the cobbler.

"That feather bird?" Her eyes got big—like a beloved pet, that bird delighted her so. "That bird's the color of a sapphire like prin-cesses wear. I know it is. Preacher said all the princesses in Pharaoh's court wear sapphire-colored gems in their hair. Guess it's the most beautiful color there is if princesses wear it. You think?"

"Yes, ma'am, I sure do," Jeff said. "And I know that color is red, ain't it?" He pointed to small roses tied into a posey with a pretty ribbon.

"Some folks call it magenta. I know that 'cause one time I was deliverin' some clothes to one of my women. Long ago it was. She was real nice to me. Always gave me some sweet tea to drink on her back stoop if she didn't have no company in her kitchen. Then one day when I started off, I seen a beautiful rose along the path to her gate. I bent over to smell it. Smelled like the finest soap that gots flowers in it like I smelled in the white folks' houses I used to clean. That woman, she came out and yelled for me to stop. I ain't pullin' up your roses, I tol' her. Then she come up with a knife. Said that rose was magenta-colored and it was her favorite, too. She cut it and tucked the bloom in the buttonhole of my blouse. Said she only wanted me to stop so's she could give it to me to smell all the way home. Don't even 'member anybody ever done something so nice. No white woman, I mean. I held that flower to my nose all the way home just to smell it. Always thought if I ever had me a baby girl, I'd call 'er Magenta. See that flower, just under the little bird?"

"I see it," Jeff said. "What color is that?"

"That's a special color. So special it don't have a name."

"You seen it on a flower then, Sister?" I asked.

"Maybe, but know for sure I seen it at church. See, there's a woman that has so many pretty dresses. She gots one that very color. Her husband takes her hand when they get up to leave and pats it as they walk all the way to the door. He looks so proud of her. Proud enough to give her all them fine things she wears, I 'magine. What color is that? Guess, I don't know. Oh, well. What difference does it make?"

Sister's voice had gotten so quiet we could hardly hear her. I never knew how much she so loved flowers. That night, around the table, her thoughts seemed to flow like torrents in a spring rain fixing to cleanse her soul of woes. Yes, there was a look of peace that came over Sister's face as she caressed her soft sapphire-colored feather bird with love.

FRED COMES CALLING

22

WITH JESSE IN jail our days delivered a peace that we so easily scattered smiles over. Running irons over those miles of old shirts, we talked about not hearing from Fred for days. Still, there were too many of those black dreams closing in on us when we fell over our cots at night from exhaustion. Yes, had to keep on the run, a step ahead of the man behind bars. We knew that Fred would try anything on us to chain us tighter to Jesse. How Jesse loved to brag in our faces about Fred getting fired from the county 'cause he was too damned mean to the folks that worked the ditches. Yes, we got his point, and the years living on that alley had only sharpened it.

Then one morning Fred came 'round reeking of desperation. I'd never seen him shake so. I figured he had to have caught it from Jesse; I knew that smell. It was the rank odor of Jesse's desperation for a bottle. That morning Fred was dripping sweat with big rings under his arms on a shirt he'd surely worn for days. He was looking for mercy in the form of money or anything he could get his hands on. These two who offered nothing to nobody had now found themselves begging.

You see, Fred had finally come clean as to why Jesse was in jail. Talk was that Jesse had some gambling friends who knew folks in the city jail. The guards over there would look after him till he squeezed money from some woman, else they'd be pleased to take him on a long drive from which he was unlikely to return. Folks said the Klan was sure to be down that road to nowhere, and coloreds who got lost out there were frequently found spinning from hanging trees.

Them city people coming down on Jesse didn't care 'bout some stack of empty whiskey bottles in no alley. They were merely helping good ol' Jesse pay up his gambling debts, and if getting down to business on Jesse meant a kick-back here and there, who'd care? That was life in the alleys; always whittled sharp. We talked about it. About when Jesse got out how he'd blame us for all his troubles as it was our duty to make sure he had no woes on his easy street where Fred was not the only squatter. Maybe Jesse been pacing that crowded cell looking for an exit to squeeze through like we'd been from that alley. Through it all, Sister and I kept to our promise; we'd not buy Jesse a ticket back with what little money we had. No, it would be our own freedom that came next. Or so we prayed.

And yet things were changing 'round Jesse's alley. At least the part where we'd finally begun to sort things harder than we did those piles of stinking clothes that waited on the porch. Things that Fred and Jesse couldn't keep an eye on, like our fears of their fists, were getting tossed out along with yesterday's garbage. Of course, I knew all along Fred was spying on us; he was Jesse's very own nigger dog. So, we decided never to let him in again. I tacked a note on the porch door reading we was out delivering ironing. We kept our kitchen curtains closed tight 'cept for peeks. But nobody could be out delivering that much, or then where's the money? Fred surely thought it had to be hidden in Louvenia's kitchen someplace. His thinking went sharp on him when he got to feeling that dry desert at the bottom of his whiskey belly and knew his brother had a similar condition as he sweltered over there in a cell across the hall from the whores he had unfinished business with—them wanting Jesse's bills paid up, too. Between these men, desperation was going 'round like a contagion.

Then once, when we was out buying canned goods, Annie said she seen Fred through her kitchen window as she did her dishes. He was down there pounding at our door even with the note there. Guess he sensed that his existence had to be getting perilously close to that bottomless well he was dancing on the crumbling edges of. He had to know that when Jesse came to the end of his final bottle, Fred's would be just as empty. That had them desperate with fear. We knew that somehow Jesse was sure to pry them iron jail bars open and then come put one to our heads. An iron bar, that is.

"You got some money? Huh, yeah? Huh?" Fred was there dancing on the other side of that latched screen door, gyrating like he had to pee ever so bad.

"No, Fred. I got nothing for you. Nope. Not a thing."

But he could see Louvenia had just put a nice breakfast on the table across from the open cupboards full of tins of food and mason jars of fruit the neighbor had canned and sold us.

"I need me a dollar," Fred whined. "I go take it over in the jail so Jesse can buy a decent meal. Yeah, give me a dollar then. No, two, like I say."

"Fred, I 'magine two dollar's only gonna buy you a bottle. Maybe two if you go across town. But Jesse, he say it ain't safe to go over there. They know you and your brother over there and they's likely to roll you."

At that I shut the door to Fred's pleading just as Jesse always did to Louvenia's after her head hit the wall again.

Despite Fred's dropping his needs at our door like they were his dirty laundry to be done up, there was yet a grace in our lives—that glorious lull from Jesse's curses. We enjoyed sharing the bounty our laundry money brought with Brother and Jeffrey, who started eating over most nights. That made their lives a bit better too. Had nothing but a hot meal to give them, and yet they savored every bite like it was a Sunday supper. The four of us, and sometimes two or three of Annie's kids, crowded 'round that little table for simple meals heaped with laughter. Jeff loved kids. He could tickle them with a grin when he aimed a finger at their tickle spots. Sister delighted in all the laughter and her joy spilled over to me as well. In those moments, thoughts of Jesse and his brother were all but forgotten. Gone like yesterday's tossed garbage.

∽

Saturday nights when we didn't have much ironing to finish up, Annie would bring her young'uns over to play. She said the peace and quiet back at her place helped the preacher prepare his sermons. Louvenia loved them kids so much, didn't she? She'd sit at the table chattering with them while stitching rag dolls together. One evening Annie brought over a box of brown buttons for dolls' eyes along with patches of old cloth for dolls' clothes. I baked batches of sugar cookies and every pan was gone near as quickly as I pulled it out of the oven. Annie, her kids, Sister, and I sat all evening eating cookies and sewing dolls and doll clothes. No sounds from that ugly alley ever penetrated these precious moments; no old man in the other room cursing away the nightmares that stalked him; the nightmare of him drowning under a desert of hot sand with not one bottle to be had.

Every day had gotten a bit better for us, but at the same time, every day was a bit closer to the day we knew Jesse would connive a way through his bars to go to one. At times that started to nip at my thoughts like a pack of nigger dogs. I wanted to slow the avalanche of fear rolling towards Louvenia, too. She couldn't suspend her notion as to what Jesse was gonna do to us 'cause we never paid off his gambling debts. Fred had made it clear that he was none too happy and sure as hell didn't take to the food I sent to the jail. Once in the dead of night I awoke to find Sister pacing about in the dark wringing her hands from worry. She didn't seem to notice me sitting up on my cot.

"Jesse not here, Sister, but ain't you still livin' in his hell hole if you keep it in your head like he is?"

She returned to her cot breathing heavy-like as she did on those nights when he'd come home drunk and went to bashing his words over our shattered sleep.

"He gots no power on you 'cept in your mind," I said. "You're still thinkin' Jesse can fly out of them jail bars and come hit you upside your head. If that's the case, haven't you done put them bars on yourself and given the keys to Jesse for keepin'? He ain't gonna do nothin' 'cause he can't survive without us when he gets out."

"He didn't know that all them times he put my head through the wall?" Her voice was tight, like he was right there squeezing her throat.

In the days ahead, Louvenia's every moment of happiness was stymied, wondering if Jesse knew the secret of his survival, which was no secret because it was only by Sister that he made it to the next swig. She wondered if that secret was just another distorted dream we'd already worn out by jabbing it too hard with our hopes all them years. Was it gonna be okay for us down the road someplace? Where, then? How far along the journey before I get me some? Could I hold out that long? Or if I did, would I even care by then? How easily our prayers so often turned into diluted pleas for mercy. The hardest place to sit tall ain't the pews at church; it's in the face of the curses hurled at your dignity.

Sister looked intense, but then sat up on her cot as though she was gonna try on her new hat. But she never said nothing for the longest spell. Still, I knew she was gonna try to be brave and let Jesus work his end of it.

"What's Jesse sayin' over there 'bout us not comin' up with the money to get him out?" she asked as if I could hear across town any better. How many times had he boxed her ears by then? Lord, she even ducked from the thought of him.

Towards the end of the night Sister's fears wore her out and she finally drifted to sleep. But the next morning she didn't drag herself up before dawn to catch up on the ironing that was, God only knows, never caught up. Not bothered by should Fred come calling, I got up and pulled the curtains open wide for the first time in days. It was a beautiful Saturday morning when Sister shuffled up for her coffee. As I ironed, she sat down at the table with her mug, looked over the rag doll we'd worked on the night before and smiled as she went through Annie's box of brown buttons to sort a matched pair for eyes. She stitched them on as we chatted. I still remember the look of serenity on her face as she gazed into the two brown button eyes of that little rag doll. I imagined that rag doll could see into Sister's exposed soul more than Jesse ever tried to. Lord, have mercy on him. If you have to.

"I want us to go downtown this afternoon," she said in that quiet voice that always reminded me of Daddy. "Want to get some paint; maybe a real soft color that's gonna remind us of Annie's sweet peas. We gonna paint this here kitchen where we been workin' day in and day out for too long."

"We don't gots lots of ironin' to deliver," I replied. "I'll finish that pile later. On the way back from deliverin' we'll get some paint if that's what you're thinkin'. Is that what, Sister?"

She rose and took the iron to finish my piece. "I'll finish here; you fry some of that ham so we can take sandwiches to Alex and Jeffrey."

Soon we headed downtown for paint. Sister met Annie down there and went with her to do some errands as I visited the men at the stables. Mr. Harold had not shown up that day, so things were good for us to talk about Jesse. Jeff said he was too old and weak to come home swinging no more. He figured Jesse was only gonna go find his bed and then reach for the easiest bottle he could get his hands on. Then he'd lie back in his dark bedroom catching up on old times with his captive bourbon buddy.

That Monday Louvenia seemed to keep her fears to herself and didn't say much. Yet even in her long silences, I knew things were different for her. We both felt it, just in different ways. When Sister had her work done, she went to painting our kitchen. She painted it a beautiful pale blue and put some bright green curtains up in the window made from fabric she and Annie had pieced from old choir robes. Hung in the same window where I'd planned on putting jars of pickled Jesse. Later that evening I read the Psalms as Sister hummed while she ironed our dresses for church. We'd worked hard for days and again put back some money in a place Fred or Jesse could never find. Or so we hoped.

Lurking in the Shadows

23

I RECALL IT BEING a warm evening. After leaving Jeff and Alex at the park I seemed to wander aimlessly. Had lots to think on and couldn't make myself head back to the alley. When the sun started down and I had no more shop windows to spend my dreams in, I drifted back to Jesse's taking the long way. But it could not have been long enough. The moment I stepped into that alley I could feel it: the presence of Satan. I knew the stench well.

Momma told me up on Orchard Hill that if you listen carefully an angel's gonna tell you when there's danger lurking. But most times I could hardly hear much of anything through all the screams in my life. But this time the angel sent word through one of Annie's little ones. Annie had little Nettie standing on a stool in her kitchen window to watch for me. At the sight of me, Nettie slapped at the window and waved and yelled for her momma. Annie dashed out drying her hands in her apron followed by her kids tugging at her. She yelled to the kids like they were in danger.

"Get back in the house!"

Her eyes said more than words. Something was lurking in the shadows of that awful alley!

"He's down there!" Annie blurted. "Jesse got home earlier."

Her words hit me like a kick in the stomach. Jesse home! She glanced down at my kitchen window as though Jesse might be watching for my return.

"No!" I resisted. "He ain't 'pose' to get out till late next week. Fred said!"

"Sister Louvenia said Fred's a liar!" Annie reminded me. "I know she's in there, but she never answered when I came to see if she's okay."

At that I knew that my prayer had gone unanswered; the prayer that Jesse's sins would end up storing him behind bars forever. It was not to be. Once again he'd squeezed through them bars as he'd squeezed through the many scrapes in his life. I knew that he would surely be waiting to inflict the revenge that Fred had so long promised.

"Fred brought 'im 'round earlier. Him cursin' like the devil himself," Annie said. "Guess they come from the bar. Fred, he just left. That man's so drunk he could hardly walk."

My heart fell into a tumbled rhythm as I sorted Annie's words. Then I realized that Sister was in there and not answering Annie's knock. Lord, have mercy. Annie wiped a tear.

Shaking, I walked up on the porch feeling my palms go wet from fear. Guess Sister had been hanging clothes across the porch earlier as they were still dripping in the stale alley air. I opened the kitchen door, and, there in all his glory, was Satan restored to his throne eating his supper.

Jesse winked like he'd been waiting for that door to creak open. He fondled his bottle like a trophy he'd just won. Jesse was used to winning. We had his trophies to prove it. A scar here, one over there and so many more where the wounds never stopped bleeding enough to scare over.

"You been expectin' me, huh, lil' girl?" he growled like a nigger dog. "Even got the place all fixed up for my homecomin', ain't ya?" His thick words were weighted under half-bottle slurs.

But where was Louvenia?

I suddenly realized there was a dead stillness, like an undertaker's parlor long after the candles are blown out and the last sobs put away. As that man stared and sucked the whiskey off his brown lips, I heard a faint whisper tap at my fears. Perhaps it was Minerva imploring me to hide them as I stood in the face of Satan himself.

"Got the place painted up here, ain't ya?" he said. "Lot better than the jail I been in. And then you gots enough food for the neighborhood canned up and waitin' on them shelves, ain't ya? But seems you can't get your hands on no money to get your Jesse out 'a jail. That be the case? Sure, it do seem, don't it? Now, what are we gonna do to set that right? Huh, lil' girl?"

"You out 'a jail if you're sittin' there," I replied. "Ain't that 'bout as right as you're gonna get?" I stood back, out of swinging distance from his chair.

"Yep, I sure is. Sittin' right here at my own table where I belongs. Thanks to my brother Fred who been lookin' out after you for weeks now, ain't he? And what's he gotten for it? Huh? He ain't got nothin' from the two of youse but grief and a smart-mouths deserving bustin'. So, I tell you, they done let me out early thinkin' I could get my hands on the money quicker. Follow my drift, lil' girl? Seems like ever'body knows there's money comin' back to my place. Ever'body but Louvenia. She don't know nothin', do she? That's what her story is back there. So I put it to her again and again, I did. 'I don't believe you, woman,' I tol' 'er. 'You're lyin' to me! You're lyin' to your own husband.' That's what I said to that bitch."

"Where's Louvenia? Where's Sister now?"

"Seems like she done had a bad fall over the news I was gettin' out. Must 'a happened right when the word got put to her ears a few times! You know her, she don't hear like she ought 'a. Then again, maybe she tripped over my foot when she went lookin' for my money to put things right between us. Don't think she's dead, but maybe. I ain't inclined to go back to see for sure. You know where that money is, or you want Louvenia to keep thinkin' where she put it with what's left of her head?"

Jesse guzzled his bottle and wiped the yellow drool from his mouth, then pulled from his pocket a wad, which he threw in my face. What crumbled at my feet were the pieces of Louvenia's little feather bird. I could hardly look as I knew what those shreds meant. Something was for sure bleeding to death. I jumped, aiming for Jesse's bedroom, expecting him to go for my throat. He only sat there on his throne knowing it didn't matter what he did; in his dominion evil won, no matter how far the fearful scattered. Nobody escaped, so why run from his fist because sooner more than later, he would exact his revenge and Fred would be nearby sniffing through the carnage for scraps to gnaw on. I headed around the table for the backroom.

Sister was sitting in the dark. She jolted when the door creaked open, as if somebody had jabbed at her ribs with a poker. She turned her head to that blank wall only a dozen inches from her face. Sitting there she held what was left of her hat with one trembling hand. The other arm hung down. Why did it hang that way? Like it needed to pick up a shred of felt from the floor, palm facing out limp-like and her other hand swollen ever so bad.

I glanced around a broken room where pieces of Sister's hat were mixed into the ruins with pieces of her face. No, Louvenia wasn't expecting a reunion with Jesse's fist that night. I'd never seen her so bad; that lip hanging all black and swollen. So distorted were her features that had she been on the street, I'd not known it was her walking past. She sat there rocking like her swaying head had given the struggle to stay balanced on her shoulders. She nearly could have held it in her lap the way it teetered that direction. Was it fear that kept her from looking at me through the swelling around her blackened eyes? Or did she see the silhouette of Jesse's fist coming at her again? Horror can distort every fear it hands you.

She held the pieces of that hat cradled to her, now no more than a knot of torn felt, smashed bows, crushed flowers and broken feathers. It was a dream murdered but not one she was ready to bury. Just the same, her sighs echoed a dirge. Thought she was about die, but then through the side of her badly swollen mouth a few words fell.

"He gots his bottle out there," she said breathing heavy-like over the longest pause I ever endured in my life. "When he get to the bottom…maybe I come out. You best go down to Annie's till he passes out. Hear?"

A broken piece of tooth followed her last words to join a piece of her face at her feet. She wiped her chin of blood and flesh.

Jesse's words from the other room were crystal-clear though. Like the old times, he cursed for Louvenia's attendance. Yes, Jesse was home again. His bellows heralded the occasion. "Hey, I done told you I want more tatas. Now's when I want 'em," he yelled from the table. "Get 'em peeled and fried up if you knows what's good for ya. But then it don't seem like you do, do it?"

His hollering could have been heard up and down the blackened brick walls of that alley. As broken as she was, Sister still wrenched herself up to get that ol' man more food. How many meals had he wrenched from her by then? Her eyes and that long sigh, like after a blow to the stomach, told me it wasn't only the pain from the beating this time. It had become the kind of pain that can only be eased with the thought that the Lord will soon come for you to take you away from it all and on to His Orchard.

"I go get that man's tatas on… Yeah, I do it…"

I pushed the debris off the bed and lifted her feet up to keep the swelling down. I reached to take the pieces of that hat off her lap. Still she held on to it tightly, held on to something that was no longer there. Louvenia caressed a bit of feather like it was the hair of a child even as Jesse rattled his threats. Guess he wasn't nearly as close to the bottom of that bottle as I'd wished. He was on another gambler's roll, him and his bourbon buddy. Yes, Jesse's good times were back, and his alley would soon be quaking for it.

"If you make me get up from this here chair, you're gonna see my fist again!" he slurred. "Jesse done come home and we gots some bookkeeping to deal with now." His fist hit the tabletop. He was drunk, but it was nearly an eternal hour of bellowing and cursing before Jesse finally teetered into his plate snoring.

As I went for a chip of ice on Louvenia's face I stood looking at that ugly ol' man and asked myself, "Where's that rusty pair of scissors, Momma?" 'Cause right there was his naked throat daring me to stab into it. I figured I'd leave his half-severed head in that plate till Sister walked back into her kitchen wondering why he wasn't yelling for her no more. He dead, I'd gladly inform her. He gone! Momma told me how to do it and do it quick-like. Got to have mercy on an ailing animal like Jesse. Yes, stone drunk he was lying in his own plate. He'd not had a drink for weeks, unless Fred somehow got him a bottle. Satan only knows they could pull a bottle out of nowhere.

Over the next few days all Jesse did was guzzle our lives down as we ran bottles in circles to Jesse's throat to keep him off ours. It was like running empty buckets to a raging fire.

In the days ahead, Jesse was truly back in jail again, however this one he owned. His cell was that dingy backroom where he'd spent endless hours in bed during those warmest of autumn days while Sister spent the same hours fanning him so the flies and acrid air from the alley didn't trouble his slumber.

So Jesse'd leave her be, I did Sister's work. Then she could keep to the fanning and serving. He never came for my throat. But I knew his revenge would come soon enough. How I prayed that when Jesse finally fell he'd drag Brother Fred with him. You see Fred was still sniffing for scraps and hounding Jesse for some of Louvenia's money, payment for keeping an eye on us all them weeks. Jesse had once again pulled us under the currents of his filthy alley as easily as if he'd simply dozed off for another nap. I was convinced the undertow would swallow us all if I did not act soon enough. Yet, what?

Well, it turned out Louvenia's good ironing hand got broken when Jesse drug her 'round the room that night trying to squeeze her head for where our money was hidden. Or did the room really spin her head so hard her arm got pulled out of the socket from the velocity? Head spinning, or the room itself, Sister told me the whole time Jesse pounded his revenge, Fred was there looking on with satisfaction, calling her the ugly bitch getting what she deserved. Nigger dogs like Fred can bark curses like their masters even as they salivate for the scraps. Strangely, under all that torture, Louvenia never told them where we'd hid our bit of money. Maybe somewhere deep in her addled soul there was still a bit of hope left. A seed or two perhaps. But even a tiny mustard seed can grow into something, someday, somehow, I kept telling myself and then asked the Lord if I was right. Yes, I prayed and hoped that if we lived through all this one more time, the money we'd hidden away might buy us a ticket out of there before it bought us a pauper's grave. Maybe even a ticket to a crumb of dignity. Likely somewhere we'd never heard of. But who knew where that life was? The next whistle stop? Right after the junction marked with our broken skulls; the spot staked by our splintered bones? Or a hundred years even beyond that?

Sister had long known she was living with her back against his slimy walls, but like she kept telling me, that alley opened to no place better for her. Like walnut shells, her hands were gnarled at the joints from the years of hard work that never let up. No laundry house was gonna hire her for a few pennies a week, as there were countless young women leaping onto them tubs to feed their kids. Even young, Sister was no longer young, and the scars Jesse had bestowed only made her older. Louvenia had no choice. She was his slave till she could figure a painless way out. In her darkest agony did she secretly look for a clean jump to the next life? How many miles up is the roof if our backs are broken first by that ol' man? Far enough away from Jesse? Close enough to the clouds? That do? Or make it all worse if I should survive the fall? Then, Lord will you finally hear our prayers?

Yes, as the days followed each other in an ever-deepening haze, Jesse kept drunk and we kept bringing him the chamber pot as we washed up his life to hold on to ours in this bitter peace between servants and master. Yet I figured somehow there was still enough of that brittle peace for me to renegotiate the terms of our surrender. I asked Jesus for help, even if I'd convinced myself that He'd gone deaf to our prayers. Evil spreads like swamp fever, and no waving of a stick will ever vanquish it. Yes, our lives were all getting lost again in Jesse's alley just as he and his brother had regained theirs!

Drowning Under My Days

24

THE GRIEF JESSE'S return brought to our lives rolled over our days like a crashing tide. I knew that it would soon drown us all. "Lord," I prayed, "help me to swallow the rush of my rage so the end comes quicker; another act or two of violence might be all it will take." We were sinking in an alley of hopelessness that we couldn't escape and Jesse was holding our heads under for all we were worth.

You see, it got to be that Alex and Jeff couldn't come by for meals. Jesse'd take it out on Sister if he even thought I'd been putting home-cooked food for the men on the porch while he slumbered back in his dark room where time was as stale as the air. Maybe he didn't want another man seeing him wallowing in his misery back there even if he relished rubbing our noses in it. Being hard-working men, Jeff and Alex ate what they could get their hands on. But they hardly got their wages, and what they got went for miserable food that should have been tossed out. At times I would think on that when I took Jesse's supper plate to him still in bed. He'd be too thirsty to eat any of it, so it would sit there long after he staggered off to the bars.

Through it all I worked hard to keep things going as best I could. Then one night, after Jesse had finally headed off, I went about preparing supper for Sister, Alex and Jeff. But Jesse was quick to make detours to see if I was holding food back for the men. I was taking a pan of biscuits out when he nearly knocked the door down to see what he may have missed.

"You forget somethin', Jesse?"

"Who them biscuits for?" he snarled as he scrutinized the room carefully like Alex and Jeff might have disappeared under the table. "You know I don't like biscuits!" He growled till bile seeped at the corners of his mouth. "Don't want nobody in my house!" he shouted from the porch as he left for the good times.

His house? Our money that paid the rent! The math on that was troubling.

❧

I helped Annie get her kids' clothes washed up even as Jesse cursed that I'd better get paid for it. Annie couldn't let her kids come over no more. Sister knew Jesse was the reason, yet still it wounded and made her hate the ol' man all the more.

I knew that things were closing in on Sister and she was slowly surrendering to it all; the darkness of hopelessness. Once in the middle of the night I awoke to her yammering and found Sister over at the table sitting in the dark.

"What are you sewin' over there, Sister? I can barely see you in the dark."

"It ain't dark no more 'cause I'm sewin' a real pretty hat to wear to church for when my face heals. Yes, gonna be the prettiest hat ever. I know it is 'cause Jesus told me so. You think my face's gonna heal one day? You think?"

I was thinking maybe not no more. Maybe no more times left. Hadn't we used them all up by then?

But I tell you, that was no hat Sister was sewing. It was another rag doll for the kids. She held it up for me to see, but it had no big brown button eyes. She mumbled something 'bout rag dolls ain't 'pose' to see the ugly of our days. But I knew rag dolls with no eyes saw only as well as ones with button eyes sewn on. My tears that night didn't keep me from wondering how good we were seeing things ourselves. I lay on my cot watching her look over that doll like a mother looks at her newborn. Time was running out for us. I had to save Sister somehow, somewhere before it was too late. But who would save me?

$\backsim$

The next morning I struggled up early so's I could get the piles of laundry going and Jesse's food made, so then Sister could sleep in. Every minute of rest Louvenia got made a difference. Sometimes she didn't fall asleep till nearly dawn, what with serving Jesse's needs and helping me with the ironing. She'd spend her sleeping hours fanning him when the air was thick and only the stench of that alley coming through the window was her constant companion. Or was that really Jesse we smelled?

He screeched at the sound of a peck at the door.

"Who's at the God-damned door?"

"It's just the boy bringin' my wash soap," I yelled back as Annie slipped in the door.

"How's Sister Louvenia?" she whispered. "We've been prayin' for her at church."

"She's comin' together slow this time. Don't know how many more times she's gonna heal up though. Don't even know if she wants to, no more."

Annie cried too.

"Who's out there? Hey? I'm talkin' to you," Jesse growled.

"I told you Jesse, it's the delivery boy with my laundry soap. He wants a tip; you got a coin for 'im?"

Jesse went back to sleep on that. He wasn't gonna get out of bed to give a poor boy a coin, that's for sure.

"This is all I got to share, Sister Sarah," Annie whispered. "You know my kids eat my cupboards bare."

Annie uncovered a golden crust apple pie still warm from her oven. With tears I took that pie over to the cupboard to hide it back 'fore Jesse smelled it. If he found it, he'd take it over to Fred's for their whores. I knew he would, too.

"Annie, Sister and me just can't cook nothin' decent these days. That pie is a bit of holiday for us. It is. Gonna cut it when Louvenia comes home from deliverin'. Later, I'll take some to the stables for the men, too. Thank you for this, Annie."

Annie hugged me like it might help heal my soul. Or maybe I was really hanging on to her to relieve my pain. Yes, I 'magine I stood there limp like a rag doll gots no big brown button eyes 'cause I don't remember her leaving. Fragments of our memories are carried with the smells of every day. For a few fleeting moments that morning life smelled like hot cinnamon apple pie that Annie's sweet friendship delivered to the door of my agony—a taste of hope that there's some goodness out there that knew us by name.

Annie was always good to us. We never felt as beaten down when she was near. And she always was, even when Jesse was on the rampage. She loved her husband—had five kids with him, didn't she? But he was gone long hours visiting his parishioners, and that left her alone to make do. See, the preacher was the only person 'round who would listen to or cared about our people. His work was dedicated to leading folk's minds away from the squalor and hopelessness of them alleys to something he had faith was on the other side of that alley, a Summerland kind of place. Had to be one, he kept preaching, which kept us on the lookout for something like hope. At times I guess we found a nibble of it and that fed our desperation enough that we could step over to the next day after all. The preacher would have smiled knowing that he had succeeded.

Yet I still wondered if the preacher's notions were challenged by all the wakes he'd done. My people died easy-like, but never easy. In the alleys most folks just fell over dead. Yes, those tubs could stack up on you when you weren't looking out for yourself and the fall could be fatal. Even though we didn't drag the chains of slavery, the vices of the alleys still chased and mauled us in more ways than any nigger dog overseer could have devised.

I always figured Annie gave to her people by taking care of the preacher so he could do Jesus' work up. Nobody knew at church what she did without so he could serve their needs. Just knew she was the preacher's wife and could read and write good. Seldom seen her at their home when somebody dying, getting married or being welcomed into Jesus' family at birth. But none of this would 'a happened if it hadn't been for this good Christian woman.

She made me want to be like her. I wanted to help my people. Maybe I couldn't help the preacher myself to lighten his load, but I could help Annie and that's what Louvenia and I talked on. We would put in extra time by doing her laundry. Till when Jesse got out of jail, Sister would bring the little ones over two or three at a time for Sister to bathe. Sometimes the kids sang along with her while she sewed dolls. Young Roy would stand on a stool and preach like his daddy while the others were getting soaped down. Louvenia was always filled with joy when them kids got out of the basin and wanted her to sing the church songs. They'd try to sing along, all mush-mouthed, clutching tightly the brown button-eyed rag dolls Sister made them. When their eyes grew heavy, we'd put them down on our cots till the preacher came for them. Then one by one he carried them back, him kissing their cheeks as if living depended on it.

There were too few days back then when Jeff and I could slip away to spend a few hours together. Since coming to live with Sister, I'd never really gotten out of town. Gone no place much further than a circle of blocks where we delivered. One bright Saturday morning Annie fried up some chicken livers with crumbled bacon and Louvenia made a sweet potata pie all for Jeff and me. He came by with one of the stable's buggies and we went off to the edge of Vicksburg, far enough away that the din of the city was muffled by the sound of a stream. The air was fresh out there. Happy was I to leave that dusty acrid air trapped between the ugly brick walls where they burned the garbage but only when it got piled high enough it could burn itself. It soon became a regular outing for us, as we both loved the countryside. Out there, we'd talk, laugh, eat, and then talk and laugh even more. Then sometimes we'd do nothing and Jeff simply held me. I had so much to think on, because the fog in my head could easily stir up the darkness back then. Didn't need any words with Jeff. His very touch or glance brought a calmness that claimed the moment and left it safely in my memories.

Sometimes, somewhere early in those bright moments of our love I got to counting again. Counting the days where I found new joys and the blessings they came from. How many times did Jeff bring this feeling to my heart? However, I guess it was 'bout then that things started coming down hard on Jeff and Brother. They barely got by at the stables in the best of times when there were plenty of customers coming in. Jeff told me his boss, Mr. Harold, lost himself to a bottle most days by noon, if he showed up at all.

"His wife mean-mouthed you, too?" I asked.

Jeff told me he'd seldom saw Mrs. Harold, but she was always nice and even baked a pan of cornbread for them from time to time. Things between Harold and his wife got so bad that at times she'd leave him and head for her sister's. There he'd go pleading for another chance. But when she was gone, Mr. Harold was overcome by his own demons and would get crazy on the men. When you're at war with your life there's seldom peace for anybody. Harold's rage set him against Alex and Jeff. Where else could he shovel it?

Jeff and Alex knew it was bad for Mr. Harold so they did the best they could to keep things going despite his abuse. When Harold was back in the storeroom sleeping it off, they kept the stable going and then took the money, even though Harold owed them weeks of wages, and handed it over to Mrs. Harold who had four or five kids.

When Harold come up from his dead drunk again, he'd say the men stole his money even when Mrs. Harold told him she had it fine. He was so mean he couldn't believe anybody could be honest. Harold's kids ate because of Jeff and Alex more than 'cause of their own pa. Even ate when the men hadn't.

Back then I was getting worried about my brother, 'cause you know he just had no patience with mean white folk. I was troubled that he might do something that might bring his life crashing down. "Please, Lord, watch over Brother," Sister and I prayed. Still, I got to thinking that maybe with all the screams and pleas coming from that alley, Jesus simply couldn't make out what we're praying on. Most times, neither could we. Ain't hopes frayed at the ends when they're near to being worn out? Guess that 'bout happens when they're gone for good. Seemed like every day we wondered what would come of us if another day did, and that made our dreams shudder.

Yes, blessings were running thinner by the day; about as thin as my hopes. But then times were bad throughout the South as plantations struggled against the competition they'd always strangled out. Vicksburg and townships around had throngs of colored folks squeezed off the plantations from what white folks called sharecropping, where nothing was shared but still divided—profits to the plantation owners and the debts and misery to the 'croppers. Suddenly cotton prices got so low it wasn't worth picking. We paid for the crop failures first. It was the only line we could stand at the front of, the lines for the empty-handed. It was the same old oppression with the same ol' bookkeeping for this new South. No, it wasn't just the alleys 'round Jesse's place, but all Vicksburg was crawling with desperation. I tell you, times were bad, but were they ever different for my people?

Mr. Harold's bitterness had to find a head to bash somewhere, and did so in keeping with the methods and devices of the South, right on a colored man. Seemed as though all his anger fell on Jeff and Alex, who wouldn't cower to his meanness. Sometimes Harold threw their half-pay at their feet rather than give them any courtesy.

Something had to give. The men started mumbling that there was no light at the end of their tunnel. "Lord, don't let violence come of it," I prayed, and for Jeff to calm his anger. I never told Louvenia 'bout nothing going on at the stables. Lord, she couldn't bear the weight of no more woes.

On the way back that afternoon, Jeff got quiet. When I asked him what bothered him, he said it was Alex. He'd been getting quiet of late and seemed to get lost in his own silence. That worried me, as Jeff and Alex always talked easily. During one of these late-night confessions about their hopes and fears, Brother told Jeff 'bout when he went off one night to the carnival that happened every year in Vicksburg. He'd never seen such a sight. Folks, white and coloreds, coming from all over and not bothering each other; just gawking at the lights and the swinging rides and games with pretty colored prizes that everyone seemed to win. Jeff said Alex's eyes lit up like a carnival just talking 'bout this adventure. I'd never been to such a thing and could hardly imagine it. Alex told Jeff he'd encountered some man moving crates and boxes. He offered to help him. He paid Brother a quarter when the task was done. Alex asked 'bout work. This man, he laughed in Brother's face, and told him nobody was gonna stop him from spending his money at the carnival, but not to bother looking for regular work. No, that was no more than a borrowed dream.

Still Alex saw carnival work as an adventure that might carry him to new parishes and counties. Maybe where a man was judged by the weight he could haul in life more than the weight of the white shadows that dragged on him.

Drifting to a Dream

25

LATE ONE AFTERNOON when I returned from my deliveries, Sister was there busy frying bacon. "This is near cooked. I'm makin' bacon sandwiches for the men." She moved about like a storm was headed our way. It was.

"What's you in a hurry for?"

She banged a fry pan on the stove like they'd had a bad quarrel.

"Don't give that fry pan no mercy!" I said. "It ain't Sunday and it's burned too many fried eggs anyway."

"Want the men to eat this before we go hungry."

I was puzzled. "But I ain't hungry."

"No?" was all she said as she wrapped the sandwiches in newsprint.

"You goin' hungry here fryin' bacon?" I swayed back and forth to stay out of her way. "What's the matter, Sister? Jesse ain't here is he?"

"No. He gone. Probably won't stumble in till I'm sound asleep. Him wondering where his bacon is and droppin' this here skillet on the stove for me to get up and get busy with it."

"That's all you're worried 'bout?" I asked. "Jesse wantin' more of somethin'?"

"Was at the grocer's this morning," she said. "Jesse, he been putting bottles for him and Fred on the bill over there. Seems like ever'body at the bar gots a bottle, too. Yeah, Jesse real popular these days. He done told the grocer I's good for the money."

"Lordy, so there ain't no more credit for food?" I asked. "How we gonna make it to the end of the month?"

"I don't know how we gonna make it to the end of the week! That bill's up higher than anybody gots money for. Oh, Lord we's in trouble now!"

She handed me a jar of sweet tea with no chip of ice. We were out of that too, which was why Sister decided to fry the bacon before it went bad.

"But don't start in on what you know I ain't gonna do."

"What do I already know, that I don't know, for all you know?" I asked.

"I'm not in the mood for sass," Sister said. "What you know is when our money's gone you always remind me there's a few coins put back. That money's gonna stay hidden. I ain't gonna use it for Jesse's bottle bills no more than we used it for his jail bail. That means even if we go hungry, and after this bacon gets eaten up, that's where we's at! You hearin' me now?"

I'd heard. I took the sandwiches, kissed Sister on the cheek for having the courage not to pull her escape money out, and headed over to the stables. There it seemed strangely quiet, like nobody was 'round. I stood there peeking in. The sun was hot against my back, but it was real dark in there and I couldn't see nobody, so I called out. Only the horses replied.

Then I noticed the longest shadow looming my way. It was the silhouette of a man I thought had to be ten feet tall. But it wasn't. It was Alex, looking pained and confused.

"Brother? That you? Why you over there in the dark?" I asked. "Didn't hear me call?"

"Don't know where I's 'pose' to be," he finally replied. "Ain't nobody called me. Nope. Been here all morning. Nobody called me for nothin'. Nobody."

"Why you hiding over there? Come on out."

"I got no place to go."

Alex didn't move. He stood there looking like a lost child struggling to hold back cries for his ma. I tugged at his hand and pulled him into the light near the doors.

"Here. Here's you a bacon sandwich Sister made. Annie baked the bread this morning."

Alex held that sandwich like he didn't know what to do next.

"Where's Jeff?"

"Riverman went to take Mrs. Harold the returns for the week. Reckon he be back soon," Alex replied. Then he looked me in the eyes.

"Mr. Harold, he say somethin' to you? Somethin' mean?" I asked.

"He say he don't want me here no more. Said he gonna do something to me if he sees me 'round."

"That why you're hidin'?" I asked. "You tell Jeff? He know 'bout this?"

"Riverman, he don't hear me no more. Anyway, I know what I gots to do. Got to move on."

"Move on?" I asked. "What's you mean? You gots no place to move on to."

"Get on out of Vicksburg, is what I mean. I got to."

"Where to?" I asked.

"Maybe go back over the river to Delta."

"The Burneys'?"

"It ain't that far, is it? Got to tell pa something."

"Brother, we ain't never goin' go back to the Burneys'. It's a ways on the train and then over the river to Delta. Don't you 'member?"

"Got to go home," he said. "Go fishin' with pa and Samuel."

"Daddy, he ain't there waitin' for you," I said.

"I been 'memberin' us out on the river bringin' in catfish. Got to see it again, don't I?"

"What did Jeff say 'bout you goin' off?" I asked again. "You and him, you got to talk it out. If you go looking for work, you go together like brothers."

"I got to move on."

Alex stuffed Louvenia's bacon sandwich in his mouth like it was his last meal.

We all knew what it was to fall lost under a shadow and it swallow you so quickly that even your grief would be invisible to the outside world if they ever came looking for you. You'd then be counted among the many who took off for something better but were never heard from again.

About then Jeff walked up. He kissed me and patted Brother on the shoulder like they were brothers. Jeff's look at Alex troubled me; their glances darted back and forth and then headed in opposite directions like they'd had a face down. Figured maybe they'd been talking again 'bout one day having some land and couldn't decide where it was gonna be, or what they was gonna plant. Whatever they'd talked on it didn't look like Alex was going along with it. I was sure he was feeling lost, and that frightened me.

"Hey, let's head over to the square," Jeff suggested. "Gots to be less horseshit to smell over there."

"Harold, he ain't gonna come back tonight," Alex said. His face at last creased with a slight smile. "I watch things till you get back. I will."

"Won't be long," Jeff replied and we started off.

It was early evening by then. I turned back and smiled at Alex. The smile he'd just given me had already slipped away as he was soon to do himself. Lord, how could I have known that I would never see my brother again?

∾

Jeff and I walked over to the square. He seemed to want to get away from more than the smell of horseshit. Well, I knew Mr. Harold was getting meaner by the day.

"That Mr. Harold, he always had it in for Alex," Jeff blurted after a long silence.

"Why did Harold treat Alex bad like that? Alex not a man, too?"

"What's you mean?" I asked.

"Ah, he's a white man. Alex and me, we're just another pair of mules to hitch every day."

"Him and Brother get into it?" I asked.

"You know your brother; he's got that strong pride is all. Ain't nothin' wrong with that. But that Harold, he thinks colored men 'pose' to tip our hats comin' and goin'."

"You tip to that man?" I asked.

"Sure, I do. But I got my fingers crossed behind my back and that means he smell like horseshit and that's all he is! Yes, sir, boss man pile of steaming shit standing there with nothin' to do but wave the flies off!" Jeff mocked. "So, Alex, he got into it with Harold and got told off. He been hidin' up in the loft while we figured out what to do."

"He got fired? What's Brother gonna do then?" I asked.

"No need to get worked up," Jeff said. "You Breedloves get worked up 'bout near everything."

"I got reasons to get worked up," I told him. "Brother goes lookin' for a job, the man gonna ask him where he been workin'? What's the name of his boss? What street that on? Then what's Brother gonna say? 'Ah, white man, don't get all worked up just 'cause I got no answers to hand you'?"

"Like I said, you Breedloves get worked up 'bout stuff before it happens!"

"Yeah? Did it happen for you this whole year? A year you worked for near nothin' but rotten apples and a place to sleep? That really never happen?"

"Me and Alex gonna get us a farm and divide the work like we been doin' all along. We figuring on growing corn for hogs. Then we ain't workin' for no horseshit white man no more!"

"That's how it's gonna be?" I asked. "And the bank done already come by with a bag of money for a mortgage on that farm?"

"I told you, we workin' on it," Jeff said impatiently. "We ain't got that far to know yet. But I 'magine you be the one bringin' the mortgage 'round, 'cause the banker man done give up and give you one 'cause you near smarted 'im to the point he sees no other way 'round it!"

"Who cares how it comes, smartin' or talkin' straight, as long as you gets your acre and seed?"

"Ain't nobody could figure out what you mean!" Jeff replied.

"That so?"

Over at the square we held hands till the streets got quiet. Then we circled 'round the park in silence before heading back to the stables. Standing there was a white man waiting. Him bringing his horse in for the night.

"Wait here till I take care of that man." Jeff dashed over to serve him.

"Where you boys been? I been waitin'." The man handed the reins to Jeff. "Thought you were closed."

Jeff yelled for Brother. "Alex! Alex," he yelled.

There was a quiet that I still hear.

BOURBON BLUE EYES

26

IT WASN'T LONG before our days seemed to settle back into the same routines as before Jesse went to jail. Some days Louvenia would deliver the ironing and then when she could, she'd escape for an interlude at the park where she'd watch the little ones at play. Guess she needed to see the joy and happiness in their bright young faces to remember it still existed. Sister spent so much of her life wearing Jesse's bourbon blues that she no longer cared what anyone thought about her broken face. Most folks that knew her already seen it all anyway. Bruises on bruises; some you see, some too deep to ever talk about, and sure as hell can't explain a single one. No, they all knew the denouement of her story. Fist by fist, they only mirrored their own, so who wants to hear it again. She lived in that deafening silence of 'It ain't my problem…sister'.

One day she returned as I was finishing the ironing. It always seemed as if Jesse was drunk or asleep till the very second Louvenia came home hot and exhausted from walking the ironing 'round town.

"Louvenia? Where you been? Get yourself in here when I call! Hey!"

But Louvenia didn't attend. No, this time she sat down at the kitchen table like he was no account. You see, she'd become expert at calculating the odds Jesse could bounce up swinging his fist by the thickness of his tongue.

"Oh, Lord, he's awake again," she commented, her eyes closing like her lids could shut him out. "Jesse, what's you want now?" she yelled.

In the past these words would have settled an empty bottle across her temple.

"Jesse gonna kill you 'fore you get out of here!" I announced like it was news I'd just heard in the alley.

"I got no place to go he can't get me. Lord knows, I got no place period," she reminded me.

But Jesse didn't need reminding who was slave and who was master. "Louvenia, don't make me get up!"

Yeah, Jesse was awake all right. Even in all the darkness of the moment it still hit us as funny. Jesse couldn't hold his pot to pee, yet we were bending to his threats of getting out of bed to put a chamber pot upside our heads. We buried our faces in dishrags so he couldn't hear us howling with mocking laughter.

"I best go get him a bottle," Louvenia sighed. "He been mean, real mean all mornin'. Mouth like the devil's. You get his supper on and don't start nothin' by droppin' a salt shaker in his tatas, hear?"

I nodded as Louvenia stepped out into the world that never heard her pain and went to buy Jesse his reprieve for another day. Or was it really our reprieve she was extending on credit?

I started getting supper on. Figured to put the best part of that cut of meat away for Louvenia and feed Jesse the gristle; that's all he paid for. I went to peeling my tatas, humming to myself and thinking 'bout meeting Jeff after I had my chores done.

Jesse was accustomed to me handing him a plate in bed 'fore he went out. 'Cept this time Jesse had a change of menu. He waited till he'd heard the porch door slam after Sister. Guess he didn't want her to know he wasn't that drunk, or she'd probably not leave me alone with him. Moments after she was gone, Jesse, he crept up and clapped his horny hand over my mouth as I stood cutting up that chicken. His cold acrid tongue on my neck made me jerk away hard.

"Huh! Didn't hear me comin' this time, did ya, lil' girl?"

The moment felt like I'd been dropped by my heels down that very well of desperation only to find myself up-side-down and face-to-face with Satan licking his chops to get at me.

"I could smell you, Jesse, a mile away!"

The butcher knife shook no matter how hard I held on to it.

"Feelin' handy with that knife, ain't ya girl? Yeah, well, you ain't no kin of mine!"

"I done cut up a whole lot of dead meat in my life. One slip from you, Jesse Powell, and I'll cut your throat so good your guts come up through your big mouth!"

"Listen to you!" Jesse slurred. "I'm tellin' you somethin', one slip and I gonna catch you, give you what's you're deservin' for not gettin' your Jesse out 'a jail, lil' nigger girl livin' off my table. That's what you been doin', too! Good for nothin' like your sister."

"Off whose table you say? What would be on your plate but flies if Sister didn't put it there? Can't feed your own wife and need somebody to hold your fork when she's not holding your pot to pee in, you ol' drunk!"

"Ain't you 'bout as high and mighty as I seen? Bet you never thought I'd come looking for my payday. But here I is, ain't I? Right here and now is Jesse's payday and I's hungry for some."

You see, from the heat that day, I'd unbuttoned the top of my blouse. Undoing his pants he stared through my opened blouse as if the buttons were all falling off. I froze with terror even before they dropped to the floor. He pawed to bend me over. I swung around with the knife to slash his face open. He pawed at me as though that knife was invisible and grabbed me stronger than I'd imagined any old drunk could. And the knife, my salvation, fell to the floor, where he kicked it across the room. He twisted my arm behind my back like it was an apron tie and brought me to my knees and did this gig walking on his pant legs dragging me.

It was then that I heard Louvenia's return with his bottle. Oh, Lord how many times can a bottle save us? The door swung open and so did Louvenia's eyes.

"Lord, Jesse! Stop! Here, I gots your bottle like you tol' me! Now, stop! Leave Sarah be."

She went to waving that bottle in his face as diversion.

"Here, here it is Jesse, here on the table," Sister pleaded. "Leave 'er be and come over here for your whiskey!"

"I got what I need right here!" he said. "You get out 'a here. Don't come back tonight! I got things I mean to get at and I gonna take my sweet time, too!"

He backhanded me hard when I sunk my teeth into his ugly arm.

"Gonna give this here lil' girl what's comin' to 'er!" he said and lifted his fist high over my face. "That's right! I's takin' what's owed me! I sure enough am. Gonna be right now, too."

Like I'd never seen her do before, Louvenia picked up that bottle and hurled it at Jesse's head. It shattered on the wall but stopped nothing. Not even his heckling.

"You think I's drunk, can't move on a woman and a bottle, too? I show you, bitch!"

I escaped his clutch and went for Sister, but he grabbed me at the table again. That ol' man dragged me, dragging Sister pulling the other way, along with the table leg she clung to. We dragged to his bedroom where he planned to catch up on his bookkeeping; Jesse, me, and Sister with the kitchen table as witness.

But grabbing on to every table leg along that alley could not have slowed the avalanche headed my way. I wrapped myself around the doorjamb as Sister beat at Jesse's hands on my throat—her kicking at him with everything she could muster. Still, he knocked her to the floor and yanked me towards his bed to perform his long-awaited deed of violation.

Oh, Lord, the fog in my head all but swallowed me, yet still I heard heavy footsteps on the porch. In a flash, I knew it was Fred coming for his cut. But, it wasn't. It was Jeff standing at our backdoor. He'd never come at that time before. Why that day? Did Jesus hear the prayers I was too dead inside to pray? Jeff looked over the room. Louvenia gasped as if she was having a stroke.

"Sarah, been expectin' you down at the stables." Jeff glared at Jesse who had one hand fisted and the other on my throat. "Mr. Jesse, I'm gonna tell you this but once: let her be!" Jeff looked as if he was 'bout to bust that growling ol' man to pieces.

Jesse snarled and grabbed my arm again. "Ain't none of your business what I aim to do here!"

"It's my business alright, 'cause I done ask Sarah to marry me. She said yes and I think she best come with me now."

All the cold fog started to evaporate as the Riverman stood there stabbing at Jesse with his eyes. "You're an old drunk, Jesse. If I come at you, I'll put you down for good. Now, let her free."

Her face bleeding, Louvenia ran to pull me out of Jesse's clutch. I was drenched in hot sweat and yet frozen stiff. It was hard for my mouth to let the words escape. Words that I thought one day I'd be saying with the purest of joy. "Sister, get your things. Hurry, now," I muttered. "We's goin' with Jeff now. We're leavin' Jesse's hell hole for good."

But she only stood there drowning in her own silence. Still Jesse's words were loud and clear.

"Louvenia, she ain't goin' no place! She do, I turn her in to the law! She'll end up in a chain-gang gettin' what she deserves, and then gettin' it over and over 'gain from the men!" Jesse blurted. "I done tol' her what it's like working the county roads."

Sister stood there like a hopeless rag doll with its brown button eyes ripped off struggling to see her way to the next breath.

"Come, Sister. It's time! Can't you hear me?"

I grabbed her to jar her frozen senses. But she couldn't move.

She was like stone, a grave marker standing there already looking all but forgotten.

"I said she ain't goin' no place, not ever, she ain't," Jesse yelled. "I'm the law in this here alley. She ain't goin' no place 'cause a worthless bitch like this ain't got no place to go. Now ain't that right, Louvenia?" That was Jesse's tender proclamation to the woman who'd kept him alive through so many whiskey-flooded droughts.

Louvenia smeared blood over her face, trying to wipe it clear of her eyes. Without looking at me, 'cause she couldn't without exposing her shame, she shook her head against me. "Best be gettin' on with Jeff, Sarah. You know he can't take us both on and make it. Go 'fore it's too late for you, too."

All I could do was sob on Jeff's chest till I near swallowed my tongue. I wailed at the very thought of leaving my sister behind to Jesse's mercy.

"Mr. Jesse, you ever hit Miss Louvenia again, Sarah say she's gonna to cut out your gizzard, fry it up and feed it to you while I watch!" Jeff said. "You hearin' me?"

"I ain't heard nothin'!" Jesse said. That was the only truthful lie he ever told.

"Go Sister, got to get out now," were her last words as Jeff led me through the wreckage.

"I'll come back for you!"

"Get out 'a my house! I'll put the law on you, too," was Jesse's farewell and thanks for all the years of cleaning up his filthy life, one bottle after another—enough bottles to fill a distillery he'd brewed of undiluted hopelessness.

Jasmine in My Hair

27

THE TUESDAY AFTER I left Jesse's, Annie came by the stables with her little ones in tow. I had to ask the kids why they were so quiet that morning. They opened their mouth to reveal melting lemon drops. The treat for me was Annie's message from Sister that she was getting by and longed for word on me. Annie told me that late one night when the alley was quiet, she heard Sister yelling at Jesse. I don't remember Louvenia ever yelling at anybody, not even that ol' man. According to Annie, Louvenia's hollered from the porch as Jesse headed for the bars. Sister followed clutching her rolling pen howling that if he ever hit her again, even raised a fist to her face, she'd kill him on the spot and then herself. Annie heard Sister say ain't no chain-gang ever gonna know the difference, plain as that. The words shook me. For Jesse this could only mean the power of his threats of turning her over to work the county roads had no power over her, even less than nothing, as he must have known that on most days she only wanted to die anyway. Guess she'd be more than pleased to push him into the very hell he was running from. Yes, one more swing at her head and his would land on Satan's lap.

Had Jesse finally gotten Louvenia's message? Seemed like after all the years together the lives of Louvenia and Jesse Powell had evolved into a truly bitter peace, but one that gave Louvenia scattered moments to heal some. Still, I knew the day would come when he'd box her again, if only to see if she'd really stopped buying into his threats. But for time being he had, and that's what mattered.

My first days at the stables with Jeff were spent mostly sleeping up in the hayloft as I was so weary of the hard work from near the day I landed in that alley. But after a day or two tossing and turning up there the straw had quickly become my jail. Mr. Harold seemed to be at the stables more after Alex had disappeared. Him not doing much but looking over Jeff's shoulder to see if the customers' money was going into his pockets and not Jeff's. While Harold was on the prowl, I stayed out of sight. Can't count how many times I thought it was clear to climb down when Jeff spotted Mr. Harold coming along. I longed for the late hours after Harold had stumbled off into his night. Then I'd make us a pot of stew on the little coal stove. We'd eat and talk about our days ahead.

Jeff and I finally got the day fixed for our wedding. It would be in mid-September, and the preacher would marry us. The whole church was invited to celebrate our union with a picnic under the shade of them magnolias on the square.

But it was the unknown of our days beyond that worried me most. My fears grew as the day of our wedding drew near. Perhaps knotted up in these concerns was my fear that I didn't want to wake up on this special day and find all my happiness had been a borrowed dream now claimed by someone better than me. I was thinking that unlike me this had to be a special girl who was really intended for Jeff. As those early days of September passed, I could tell that Jeff wasn't scared. Every time I looked frightened, he said he was too proud of me not to think ever'body should come and celebrate with us, so why wouldn't he be the one to celebrate the hardest. Sometimes when I couldn't figure if it was all real, that this man really loved me,

I'd look around the stables till the beauty of his eyes found me once more looking lost. He could always read my fears, I never could hide them. But then wasn't my soul bared to him from our first kiss? He'd look back at me, no matter what he was doing, stop everything it seemed, and smile till my expression yielded to his love that I was so tightly wrapped in. I knew there'd never be safer place in the world for me than next to Jeff.

The week before the wedding, Annie came by the stables on her way to the farmers' market. With a huge smile, she handed me a knotted up old rag. I knew that familiar jingle. It was Louvenia's money; seed money for her own escape. These were the coins she'd hidden back even when Jesse and his fists were on the hunt for them. She wanted us to have it to get started on. Here I was worried as to how I could somehow save my sister from that ol' man, and Sister had handed me her only chance of escaping him. Lord, how long had she gone without to save that money?

It was a few days before the wedding when Annie appeared across from the stables waving a kerchief for Jeff's attention. Guess she'd seen Mr. Harold in there and didn't want him asking Jeff what his business was with a colored woman. Jeff nodded her way and then signaled me with the broken tune he always whistled when Mr. Harold was prowling. I peeked over to see Jeff gesture to Annie. She stood out of the rain under the grocer's awning waving a piece of paper. When Harold finally disappeared to the storeroom, Jeff dashed through the pelting rain to grab it. Annie's note read that she wanted me to come by her place the following evening and she'd for sure have Sister there, too.

The next night after making Jeff's supper—tatas, some fried fish I got for a good price from the fishmonger—I ventured back to Jesse's alley for the first time. Nettie met us at the door and Sister soon followed. Annie's kids tugged at her like she was Santa with hard candy hidden in her pockets. She'd bought a nickel's worth every week to make sure there was.

"I got something for us tonight," Annie smiled.

I hugged Sister. She'd gained a few pounds, which meant she was eating better. She never could eat when her nerves had knotted her stomach up.

"So, don't you look like a bride to be?" Sister remarked. "Look at the shining smile. Now tell Sarah what's you got, Annie, or can you smell it?"

Annie pulled out a big pan of cake, with her kids hooting and hollering to get at it.

"Now you know it's too hot!" she scolded. "The grocer man had some pears. They's a bit bruised, so he give me a sack for a nickel. You know this is Ma's recipe for upside down pear cake."

"Gots pecans and buttered brown sugar on the bottom between sweet ripe pears just like Granny told me," Nettie announced. She was learning to cook.

"We gonna have a piece when it cools. But first we gonna see what I gots for you, Sister Sarah."

What I remember most about that moment was the gleam in Louvenia's eye. Couldn't image what they were up to. Then Annie returned from the backroom with a large box to show me. She opened it as Nettie brought down a stack of plates for the cake. Annie unfolded the paper and slowly lifted out a white gown. It was a wedding dress. She smacked at the kids' hands for touching it.

"Now, I told you, you can't touch it no matter how pretty."

There was lace on it and little pearls the size of seeds sewn on the front. Never in my life had I ever seen something so beautiful. I was afraid to touch it myself.

"This here is from one of the women at church. I was tellin' her 'bout you and Jeff gettin' started, and she told me that while she thought she'd never give her weddin' dress away, its value would double in blessings returned if some other woman shared the joy she did when she walked down the aisle wearing it. So, here it is. She done give it to you with her best wishes."

I didn't know what to say. The only fine dress I'd ever worn was the one Sister got for me to meet Jeff at the square. Sister hugged me and laid the gown over my arms. My only thought was that this beautiful dress simply couldn't be mine. Nothing so beautiful could be. Nevertheless, Annie said it was mine for sure, for my own wedding, and so much finer than any dress I could have somehow stitched from my greatest imaginings. Didn't matter none it 'a been worn once. The bride done had her baby when Annie told her 'bout me. The woman, Annie's friend, knew the answer to a prayer I'd not even had the faith to pray. She never knew me yet understood my dream, 'cause we all have it somewhere even if it's only as tiny as a seed waiting to unfold and take root someplace.

After we shared Annie's pear cake, and while the children were reading to each other, Annie asked me to go back and try on the gown. It was only a tiny bit too big.

"Lordy, Lordy, ain't you just a princess?" Sister remarked when I returned. "Who's the lucky prince takin' my sister off to a new life? Ain't he the luckiest?"

But then I suddenly wondered how Sister could get away from Jesse long enough join us. "How you gonna get away for the weddin'?" I asked.

"Joseph got it fixed for me," she said with a smile. "I reckon fixed right good, too. You know he's good with his hands."

"Joseph the locksmith?" I asked.

"I been helpin' his wife catch up on her ironin' to pay 'im. She sent Joseph over with a little bitty gift, and I been keepin' it safe on a string 'round my neck."

Sister pulled out a door key tied to a string hidden down her blouse. I couldn't figure out how that little key was gonna help her get to the wedding. But then Jesus don't always consult me on how He's going about getting prayers answered, even though I was sure most times I have better ideas than His. I looked at Annie. She smiled. Seemed like she knew 'bout things.

The Saturday of my wedding finally came. Jeff took off early for the church with the preacher so I could get ready. I kept thinking if he knew what was best he'd jump a boxcar and head off without me. I went to fixing up a washbasin in the storeroom and got myself bathed and dressed in my regular dress, 'cause Annie was taking my wedding gown over to the church for me to change. She'd been working on that hem till late the night before. She had a notion to fix my hair there at church. How could I not wonder what Minerva would have thought as Annie wove white jasmine, the kind that grew at Grandview, through my hair like a halo of fragrance.

I couldn't eat that morning 'cause I knew I'd throw up. But I decided I'd best eat anyway, 'cause I'd for sure throw up if I didn't. My nerves would see to it. What if Sister couldn't get away from Jesse's jailhouse? Or what if he came looking for her even at the church? My stomach churned at the notion. I couldn't think on these things and still manage to get something eaten, so I decided to let Jesus work on it from His side. But I later found out that Sister and Jesus already had something going. She said Jesse looked stunned when she walked into his backroom late that morning carrying a tray of food like the servant he thought her to be.

"What's that food for? I ain't hungry!" Jesse growled.

Louvenia set the tray next to his bed.

"You tryin' to poison me again? he barked. "Huh? I know you is! Look at you! You're lookin' too happy!"

"Now you gonna have a long day here, Jesse. So, don't get worked up and make it longer for yourself!"

"Huh? You got your hands on some of that nightshade to put me in a pine box? Put it in that there food, didn't you? Sure, you did. I can smell it!" Jesse barked again.

"You can't smell that stinkin' alley you lived in the last twenty years, but you say you can smell a teaspoon of dried nightshade poison ain't even in there?" Louvenia said, her damp hair still tied up in rag curls. "We out of salt and rat poison and I got no nightshade, so best eat it plain this time," Sister said.

"Huh? What'd you say's in that food gonna get me? You poison me and I'll tell Fred to get the law on your tail like that!" He snapped his fingers as he did when ordering his meals.

"Jesse, just how do you know I don't already got Fred poisoned up? Didn't I say the poison box was empty? And you ain't even seen your brother 'round for days, have you?"

"What? Huh? Why you crazy woman! What day is it? Where's Fred? Where you been all this mornin'? You been actin' strange for days, ain't ya? You gone crazy on me again?"

Jesse's brain was too bourbon-soaked by then to figure out much of anything. Night was day and day night and only the drops left in a bottle measured the good times. Yes, it seemed as though everything in Jesse's mind was starting to rhyme with poison.

"Why, Jesse, look here! See, your brother Fred been 'round, God bless his damned to hell soul, 'cause looks like he come by with your Christmas present. Sure he did! Two bottles of whiskey right here."

"My brother Fred come with them bottles?" Jesse drooled from shock. "But ain't it July, or August? I know it's September. Ain't it for real?"

"And if you think your brother would ever bring you a gift, then you're too sober! Here, let me pour some into your coffee then."

"Huh? Louvenia, what the hell do you have goin' on? I ain't goin' out till dark, and you already gots my supper. Ain't it just break-fast time anyway? Pull that curtain back so I can see what time of day it is. I ain't hungry. Why Fred bring me a Christmas present in the middle of July? Did I tell you to fix my supper? No, I never said nothin' like that. You see, you gone crazy on me when I wasn't lookin'. Fred always said you would, too! I got to get ready to go out. Yeah, gonna go find me some peace!"

"You ain't goin' no place."

"Why the hell not? I got folks waitin' for me over there at the bar where they's got a big Christmas party tonight!"

"'You ain't goin' to no party 'cause maybe that rusty lock on that door got broken and you ended up locked in here all day while I's out."

"Out? Where you think you're goin'?" Jesse demanded. "I'm tellin' you woman, you best not be spendin' my money on no God-damned Christmas presents for that sister of yours!"

"Now you sit back and take it easy. Shouldn't be hard, 'cause that's the only thing you know how to do, huh, Jesse? Yeah, ain't that the truth? You been practicin' sittin' back doin' nothin' since we been together."

"You listen to me, crazy bitch," Jesse snapped. "I know what you're up to! You're goin' shopping and wasting good money on Christmas things gonna get smashed under my foot as soon as I put an eye on 'em!"

"No, I ain't listenin' to you and there ain't a soul out in that alley that's gonna listen to you no more. They all had enough of Jesse Powell and even if they hadn't, they still ain't gonna pee on you if you catch yourself on fire. Now, I gots to finish gettin' ready. Or you want me to strike a match to see if your friends hear the crackle and run over here to dump their chamber pots on your head?"

"What's that again? Ready for what? Huh? Hear what?" Jesse moaned. "What's you got goin? I don't got to pee. Who you say gonna come dump my pot in the alley?"

Sister later told me Jesse looked scared to death as she walked out. He figured she had to have gone and poisoned up that food she set there so he kicked the little table across the room. Louvenia didn't care 'bout the food dripping down the walls none. She went about getting her things out of the drawers and pulled out her little door key. Yes, she locked that ol' man in that sweltering room so he'd not go hunting for her that day, and maybe even make his way to the wedding. He was locked in that hell hole all by himself with all his food scattered over the same walls where he'd scattered pieces of Sister's face over the years.

∾

At the church Annie helped me get dressed. I could already hear the folks arriving. Even above the din of chatter, I could hear Jeff's beautiful laugh.

Annie buttoned up the back of my gown so I couldn't escape. No matter how scared I was she knew I couldn't run fast or far in that big dress. Then a knock; seemed like Annie knew who was there. She opened the door and Sister slipped in. Louvenia, that woman had gone out and bought herself a new hat! And I'd never seen that dress before. Don't know how she got that way, so lovely, just knew it was for me. Sister brushed my tears away and adjusted the wreath of jasmine that held my veil.

"Got some good news. Did Annie tell you?" Sister asked.

"No, I never said a word." Annie winked.

Louvenia pulled from her pocket a pretty postcard. There was a picture of a big carnival on the front. She handed it to me to read. "I here. Alex Breedlove."

"Brother sent this to you?"

Sister smiled.

"But Brother, he don't know to how to write."

"He gone to the post office, bought a stamp and ask the postman to write on it for 'im," Annie said. "I know that's what he done. Sure it is."

"Then the postman brought it to me last week," Sister added. "I keeps it pinned up on my kitchen curtain just in the fold so Jesse don't see it. When that man gone, I open the curtain and look at it while I washing dishes. Alex, he alive! It say so right here!"

Sister took the postcard and kissed it.

"He there in St. Louis, right?" she asked. "He maybe works there at the carnival, don't he?"

"Don't know, Sister," I responded. "He sure may!"

"Sure he do! That means he gots work."

Only Brother being there would have made me happier than knowing he was somewhere and alive.

"Now, don't cry, Sister Louvenia," Annie said. "It's hard enough to keep Sarah's' eyes dry! Think we're ready. You best go take a seat up front there with the women. They's holding a place for you so's you can watch Sarah come down the aisle to her Jeff."

Sister nodded, dabbed at a tear, and headed down the aisle. Yes, Lord, it was for once a tear of happiness. She walked down that aisle with her chin high to take her seat with the other big-hat women. They patted her on the shoulder. About then Annie nodded through the door and the march began. Dressed in white with jasmine in my hair, I slowly walked down the aisle almost feeling like I was in a dream-like haze. Up there Jeff was no longer laughing. No, tears streamed from his eyes, the eyes that never left mine. As soon as he took my hand in his, a new forever had begun for us.

❧

Days after the wedding I met Sister at the farmers' market. She told me what had happened. Said that when she got home late after the wedding supper, she found Jesse had sobered up and forgotten their chat that morning. But then when he was ready to go out for the night, he'd found his door locked. Thank you, Joseph! He was still pounding at it with both fists when she returned. Louvenia said he acted as though he'd awakened just as the undertaker was sealing his coffin. As Jesse pounded away, Louvenia took her sweet time pulling off her special dress and hat and hid them under her cot. Said she went about getting the iron going as though she'd been working out on the porch, or perhaps if she needed it to put to Jesse's face. Anyway, what was time to Jesse, but something else to steal? I imagine it gave Sister pleasure stirring turmoil into that poor man's troubled bourbon-pickled head. Him back there pounding on the door and yelling out the window for the neighbors like his fate had finally caught up with him and he wanted to see if a bit of mercy could still be had.

While Jesse was back there yelling, Sister pulled out Joseph's key and unlocked the door to his purgatory.

"Jesse, that you makin' that noise, or that the neighbors again?" Louvenia yelled back through the unlocked door. "You want me to go tell 'em to shut up and stop botherin' you?"

He only pounded louder. His reality was too altered to know if he was coming in after a binge or maybe feeling Satan creeping up.

"What's you want now?"

Sister poured herself a jar of sweet tea. She no longer scrambled after or from Jesse's howls.

"Open this God-damned door! You tryin' to poison me again? I need the pot to pee bad!"

"I thought you said you didn't have to pee a while ago! Sure you did. Now I's busy finishin' up this here ironin' so you go pee in the alley."

Jesse slowly turned that old doorknob and opened the door.

"You locked me in there, ain't ya?" he said. "I know you did, too! Huh? Didn't you?"

"And you been sayin' I gone crazy! Lordy, Jesse. That was you hollering back there like a crazy man? Oh, Lord, they gonna come for you now! Well, I'll give them some sweet tea when they get here." It had been a beautiful day and she was now armed against Jesse's hot rage with a heated iron standing guard nearby. "Don't know what you're talkin' about, Jesse. You had a bad dream? You just opened the door, didn't ya? Still got the doorknob in your hand."

Jesse jumped as if that doorknob had chewed his hand.

"Anyway, you done lost the key to that door years ago. 'Member? After you locked me in there that summer for three days with no food and water while you were out runnin' with your whores on my wash money."

"Huh? What's that? Where you been? Where's Fred? He dead, too? You poison us both then?"

"Probably stiff by now. Wasn't he already half dead when I came here? You best go see if the other half's dead. And take the rest of that rat poison over to him. There's just a bit left. Tell the law it was the box you been feeding your brother from. Well, anyway Fred says he seen rats at his place, 'less he means you, Jesse."

Sister had a bit of power there what with that hot iron in her hand and Jesse not knowing if the earth had stopped spinning 'cause his head still was.

"It Christmas night?" Jesse asked.

"Yeah, it's Christmas alright. What did the Lord bring you?"

Sister said she tried so hard to keep from laughing at Jesse standing there speechless in all his coagulated misery. There he stood holding himself like he'd peed his pants before slamming the door shut again. For the life of him, he couldn't take a step ahead of himself for fear of getting there. Louvenia said he never came out till long after midnight, him still trying to figure if he'd had a rotten dream or Louvenia had really poisoned him and he'd joined the walking dead.

Well, that was the week I was married so very long ago.

Two days after the morning jasmine was woven through my hair, I turned fourteen.

UNDER HIS CHESTNUT TREE

28

WHERE IN LOVE are you when the rest of the world drifts by heedless to your colliding smiles? Wherever that is, it's not the same place you were before you met. The air is lighter, the colors brighter and everywhere you look there are more hues than the day before the sun broke through the clouds of your life at the end of an alley.

Some days back then, while Jeff worked with the horses, and when I was sure Jesse would be gone, I'd go pick up Sister's ironing and deliver it to her customers. Then on days I wasn't delivering, I met Louvenia and Annie down at the farmers' market where we chatted while buying our bread and produce. There were moments when it seemed that Sister's smile had almost returned. Later I'd head back to the stables with a basket of whatever was had that day for a good price and get a pot of stew or something cooking on that little iron stove. While eating supper, Jeff and I had long meandering talks about our times ahead and what those days might hold for us.

But sorting our ideas didn't come easy. There was much to sift and there weren't many folks who seemed to have the pieces of their own lives patched together well enough for us to follow. So where was the path to our dreams? In the back of my mind, I wondered if somebody ever made it that far before, to a dream of a better life? Or was it all just borrowed talk over borrowed dreams ain't nobody ever really owned?

Jeff groomed the horses while we talked. His thoughts seem to always drift like smoke from a candle and yet returned to this same passion: he had to have a piece of land one day to call his own. A place where the soil could keep a family growing. A man's dignity, he told me, was upheld by owning his own place. And yet as our days surrendered into weeks, seemed like any plan we worked out quickly fell to the same roadblock, the one at the end of our empty pockets. You see, we had no money to move on with even if we could work up a clear picture of where that might be. In fact, we didn't have much else in life but each other and a few things the church folks had given us at our wedding. These were special gifts of handmade kitchen towels, a soup pot and some well-used pans, a few mismatched and once silvered spoons and a precious small vase that belonged to someone's grandma. All these things I loved to pull out as Jeff reconfigured his ideas for our future. His vision was always large but he never had the opportunity to learn to read or get to understand the meaning behind some spoken words, so he was frustrated when he couldn't rightly express his passions. But let me tell you, when I needed a word to fill between his to understand his hopes, I easily found it in the song his eyes sang—eyes bright with passion and glowing with hope. His was a passion to make a family, and that family would be proud of him for his dedication to our happiness. Yes, he didn't have to search for hidden words; I'd read them in the poetry of his eyes.

It was a bright Saturday morning when Mrs. Harold came by the stables to speak to Jeff. I'd wondered why we'd not seen her for a spell. That morning she asked what his plans were, knowing we were just married. He decided it was time he told her about going off to make his way in the world and that he'd turn over the stable money whenever she wished. He'd kept this money safe in a tin box hidden high on a shelf till she came for it, as Mr. Harold might lose it at the tavern and his kids face hunger by it. Mrs. Harold knew how much the men had made her life possible by keeping the stable going. Mrs. Harold said she'd been thinking about her own situation and that of her children and that's why she'd come by to talk to Jeff. Don't let anybody tell you folks who speak in kindness can't come together and do it for the better of both. She explained that Mr. Harold had disappeared somewhere a few days before, and it would be for the last time for that as she was selling the stable—it had been her daddy's—and moving in with her ma in Charlotte. She thanked Jeff for his loyalty and told him to pick out a buggy and horse and he could keep them, as the rest were to be sold off.

I couldn't stop thanking the Lord for hearing our prayers. Two people, a black man and a white woman, came together one day at a place where there was no distance in their humanity.

Then, like she'd been saving it for just the perfect moment, she told Jeff about a place her neighbor had just outside of town: only a deserted two room cabin with a couple of cleared acres that he was looking to let. Out front, she added, was an old chestnut tree that would drop a pile of spiny nuts come autumn. Said that with a smile like she sure loved roasted chestnuts. Her neighbor had told her about the chestnut tree like it was the reason anybody would want to live out there. This neighbor would let the place for a fair price to somebody willing to fix it up. As this man was getting on in years, Mrs. Harold suggested that come a day, he just might work something out with Jeff on buying the place. Jeff's eyes revealed everything the moment she said this. The borrowed dream we'd been searching for a way to get to had been sighted just out of town. Mrs. Harold had pointed the direction, and waiting there would be a glorious old chestnut to mark the spot.

Well, the place was down a dusty lane off the county road leaving Vicksburg. Even at first sight, we truly thought it dream-like. No, it didn't have a white veranda with white-flowering jasmine cascading over the rail. Just a cabin barely visible from the road till the day Jeff cleared the overgrowth so folks coming from town could find us. Beyond the cabin was a tall row of cottonwoods along a stream. I easily convinced myself that the leaves of these trees turned silvery the moment I glimpsed them. No, I'd never seen leaves on a tree flutter and reflect the moonlight like pieces of tangling pewter.

And there, not more than fifty yards from the porch, was that great chestnut spreading its heavy branches outwardly as though it had been waiting to embrace us. At the first sight, I could already see our children playing in its shade while I hung laundry near the porch. Jeff said that chestnut had probably been there fifty years.

"See that tree?" Jeff asked.

"That's the chestnut Mrs. Harold told us 'bout?"

"That tree, come the first cold night in October, is gonna drop us a pile of chestnuts."

"Just a pile at our feet?" I asked. "Don't have to climb up and pick 'em?"

"Nope, just gotta roast 'em. My folks, when we was livin' along the river, they sent me down the road to one of the plantations to get us some so daddy could roast 'em all winter."

Jeff, he walked over to that big tree like it was a lost friend found again. He was at home under that tree already. Lord, I could never have known how much.

Even before we'd looked inside that old cabin Jeff had peeled off his shirt and led me down the slope towards those shimmering cottonwoods that always marked the line of a stream along their thirsty root—a stream that would rinse away the dust of our long day. There we let the cool crystal-clear water flush over us without words leaving our lips, just held hands down there. Cool and pure that water was. In only a few hours, it was as clear to me as the sky above how much that place meant to Jeff.

As the days passed and Jeff went to work taming the place, I reminded myself it wasn't ours. It was only a borrowed dream. We'd just rented it for next to nothing as nobody wanted to live that far from town. Yet for the moment it was easy enough to pretend. While watching Jeff as he paced about, I thought about my folks and their dreams of having an acre somewhere. And maybe one day a few fruit trees like the Burneys'—enough to make summer fruit jam for Sunday mornings.

§

Nobody had been living in that place for years, but it was better than it looked. Jeff said he'd spotted an old chestnut tree stump out back that somebody had probably felled to build the cabin. Wood from an old chestnut lasted forever, he said, and slapped the posts that supported the roof over the porch. So, after not doing much that first week but holding hands and splashing in the stream, we went about fixing the place up. Jeff set out to patch the holes between the timbers and scrape the fireplace flue. The raccoons were annoyed with the ruckus, but they'd be more annoyed come winter when we'd have a crackling fire going roasting chestnuts. I lugged pails of sand up from the stream bed and went to smoothing down those splintered old plank floors with it. A few days later, when I was back in town, Louvenia gave me some aprons she'd patched together from old shirts her customers had given her. One I saved to put up in the window to remind me of the curtain Momma put up every night so Isaac couldn't see in.

"What's ya got an apron up in the winda for?"

I couldn't really say. Later, when I dropped it down to keep the moon from peeking in, he asked again.

"Come on back to bed. Ain't nobody out here gonna bother us."

"I get to thinkin' 'bout Momma when I see that apron up there. She never had a piece of store-bought fabric to save her soul. Never even been in a store, I reckon. Made our things out 'a sackcloth like your ma. Even the curtain over the window was just an old apron— the same one she tied me to the bed with so's I couldn't wander outside and the dogs get me."

"You thinkin' 'bout your ma, huh?" he asked. "Ain't nothin' wrong with that. But don't get to thinkin' somebody's ever gonna get at you out here. I ain't gonna let that happen."

With the warmth of his words, I fell into a gentle sleep.

I still remember our first mornings out there near the chestnut tree. I seemed to always jump up early, wondering why it was so quiet. There was no din from the city that always awakened us past mornings; no farmers' carts rolling over the cobble and no tinkers barking their wares. It was only the birds chorusing in that big chestnut that I heard as I got the fire going in the stove for biscuits. Annie had given us three jars of wild berry jam her ma had put up, along with a couple of jars of peaches. I opened a jar of jam and put it on the table Jeff had resurrected from a pile of old furniture stacked out back. He'd placed it on the porch for us to eat as we watched the sun creep over the tree tops. That morning, as Jeff continued his survey of where he would break soil for a winter vegetable garden, I started a pie from the last of the dried stable apples I'd soaked over- night. Louvenia and I had gone out and spent her laundry money on flour, baking powder and a bit of sugar before we left town. I made comments to Jeff out the window as he wandered about, but he was too intent on his chores to pay much mind—that is, till he smelled the biscuits I'd placed in the window to cool. He quickly came to the table.

"This the jam Annie give us?"

"The same you were eatin' out of the jar last night with a spoon," I answered. "Her ma made it. Louvenia kept one jar and made me take the rest."

"You gonna feel all alone tomorrow when I'm gone?"

"No."

"No?" he asked with his mouth half stuffed with one of my biscuits.

"How can I get lonely with all this work I got here?"

"Men be comin' for me early," he said. "Down the road there's a man needin' some stumps cleared. I reckon 'bout four day's work for us."

"Then when are you gonna put up my clothes lines? Chop wood to keep hot water going for my laundry?" I asked. "I brought three piles of laundry tied up in white sheets still in the back of the wagon. I got to get 'em washed so Sister can iron 'em and we can get 'em delivered by Saturday."

"You watch out for that Jesse when you're visitin' your sister. I ain't lookin' to get into it with an old man already gots no teeth to punch out and nothin' worth listenin' to when his big mouth had 'em!"

"Louvenia told me to knock at Annie's door first when I come by. She knows when Jesse's home. Sees him out her kitchen window when he heads to the end of that alley."

"You know I don't want my wife working the tubs." Jeff scrapped his plate of scrambled eggs and spooned himself more jam.

"No? Who gonna wash your clothes then? A maid?"

"You know what I mean. Doin' tubs for white folks," he said. "It ain't right."

"What ain't right? I spend the day over the tubs and nights over an ironin' board? Or for you then, that your white man gonna pay you next to nothin' for clearin' stumps and that fixes what I got to do to help us get by. Which is right?"

"Someday I have this place turned out so we won't be needin' to work for nobody clearin' stumps or washin' clothes. Then when we do, I build a room on for Louvenia. Your sister's gonna leave that alley and never goin' back to that ol' man. Serve 'im right, too."

"When that someday comes, we all gonna have jam Sunday mornings. Just like Momma promised."

A few weeks later we were able to buy a couple of new tubs and a new washboard with his earnings from clearing stumps, and soon Jeff had everything set up for me. His dream that I not have to wash clothes was something we put aside for the time being. I still washed clothes, had five tubs soaking near ever'day. Some days when I was in town delivering, I'd eat something at Louvenia's if Jesse was gone and then go to night school to learn reading. It's what I promised Momma. Our lives were hard, but we were headed to a place we'd pointed out ourselves and it was on our own map, a place where our dreams could be built with one hard day stacked on the last.

Well, I guess things in town with Jesse weren't much different for Sister after all. The thing with that is, they were therefore worse no matter if there were fists flying or not. When you live for years at the end of an alley, even when things don't get worse, those never-ending days of no better eat at your soul like a slow-growing cancer. Yes, hopelessness can eat at you till there's nothing left. I think that's the way it got for Sister. She was walking through her days like a dead woman. Don't really matter which is gonna be the final step 'cause it's gonna be sooner or later but still just 'round the corner all the same. Which one is all that greets you every damned day. Monday or Tuesday, will I make it to Friday? Do I even care no more? Without me handling the washing end of things out in the country, Sister couldn't survive. I couldn't help fearing what would happen to her life if mine gave out first. But I knew. Hers would follow. Yes, the air between our tubs was always too thin to find a breath of relief. The thought that there was none to be had only fed the cancer.

From the beginning, Sister and I tried to work it out so our lives stayed tied. I got into town even when I was real tired so she'd know I was never so far away. She'd told me once. Said she'd not want to go on if there came a time when the distance between us grew so loud it shook her daydreams. All over again them pains of asking, "Where are you today, Sister?," ringing in our ears. Why would she, she added. Well, it was good that Jesse was gone most the time by then—him sleeping over Fred's 'cause he couldn't make it back home after drinking on an empty stomach that Sister no longer fed. He knew the people he called friends would roll him if he ventured alone into them dark alleys. His vision had become no more than blurs of days he'd already passed by. Everything was leaving Jesse behind and he knew it, especially the good times. Everything gone except them black dreams when he begged his sleep to leave him be. I reckon Jesse had started feeling the sharpness of those empty bottles stacked around his shaky days. Surely it sent shivers down his rotted-out spine. And then maybe all them sleepless hours he spent looking up at the ceiling, he could only hear what Sister had told him; that if he hurt her again, even one more time, she'd kill him and then jump off herself. Jump off that roof where she'd spent so many hours of her life listening to the shirts dry in the blistering heat just so she didn't have to listen to Jesse's mouth blister her.

Don't Need Nothing Else

29

ONE NIGHT AS I washed the dishes on the porch, Jeff came up from the stream carrying two canvas bags of water. I wondered if he was aiming to water the vegetable garden and save me the work on the morrow. But, you see, he was there pouring water over the hard soil where nothing grew. Made no sense to me. I dried my hands and went over to see what he was up to.

"What are you doin'?" I asked. "Toting water up the slope and then pouring it over that hard soil?"

Jeff looked sheepish. "Now how are we gonna get this hard-as-rock soil loosened up 'less I till it? How am I gonna turn it over 'less I get some water soakin' in it?"

"You done made the vegetable patch over yonder. You get lost looking for it?"

"Maybe I did and maybe I know where I's going and don't need you tellin' me where my feet is standing."

"Oh, no?"

"So, I'm gonna plant you a flower garden. Right here."

He pulled out of his pocket a twisted piece of paper he opened.

"Where'd you get them seeds?"

"Got 'em from Mrs. Harold." There was a twinkle in his eyes.

"Mrs. Harold been givin' my man flowers and even dried 'em for the seeds!" I teased like he been up to something with Mrs. Harold.

"Me? No, I ain't."

"Look me in the eye and tell the truth," I demanded, teasing-like.

"I am not growing flowers for no woman back in town!"

"No? Well, then I know who you're growing a flower garden for!"

"Go ahead," he said. "If you think you know everything."

"You, Mr. Jeffrey McWilliams! You like flowers and you're making a garden for yourself."

"Ain't no man makes a garden 'less he can't eat what comes from it."

"Do tell! Then what did you say you were totin' water up the hill for when it's near dark?"

He pointed me to the porch. "Don't them dishes need another dryin'?"

"Yeah, and I got a jar in there we could use for your cut flowers," I replied. "You want me to fill it with water, or you aim to plant them seeds first?"

Couple of days later Jeff started turning the moist soil for his flower garden. The following day one of his friends come 'round with a wagon of manure that they shoveled over the broken soil. Then soon afterwards a small fence of sorts found its way 'round his patch. Sure seemed like only a few days later those seeds started sprouting. Never had Jeff told me before that he would one day make himself a garden filled with flowers that would bring color and fragrance to our cabin.

"Now you know, when these flowers bloom we gots to have Louvenia out," he said. "Your sister, she knows the colors of every flower there is. Even knows the names of colors I ain't never heard before."

"She's gonna come out one day. I been askin' her every time I'm in town."

As the days followed Jeff worked to make the front porch into a better laundry. The well he and his men friends dug made it easier than going down to the stream. He even had so much firewood piled up I could keep my tub water hot all day. Because I heated the water outside, our place was never hot and sticky like Louvenia's kitchen had been and, praise the Lord, I didn't need to climb to the roof with my wet clothes to get to a clothesline. Jeff had lines strung from the porch where the hot sun and fresh air did its work. There were clotheslines everywhere. Made me laugh when he got tangled up in them as he made his way to the shed where he kept his tools. Never seen a man taken down by a clothesline before; ain't it a sight! Or least Jeffrey made it into one. I laughed at his antics tripping over my tubs and washboards like an ox learning to dance the polka in a web of clotheslines.

⚘

Whenever I was in town for night school I'd sneak into Louvenia's to pick up her ironing for delivery on my way to class. So that Jesse couldn't drink it up, Sister had me keep her ironing money except for the bit she kept back to eat on. She told him that since he near crippled her right arm she couldn't work the tubs and therefore couldn't keep him in bottles no more 'less he worked a tub and she do the ironing with her left hand. He didn't look on that deal favorably and so went to announcing that he just might go get himself a new woman. Sister said she didn't know where he went ever'night since he had no money. Guess he still went looking for at least a shot glass of peace down one of them alleys that curved and twisted 'bout like Sister's beaten spine. No, I couldn't think on what Jesse's life ran on back then, but I sure hoped it'd run out soon.

I stayed with her those evenings as long as I could and shared every detail of our new place. The last question she always asked before I departed was, "What colors did Jeff's flowers bloom in?"

⚘

Jeff understood my dreams even when I could barely sort them myself. Late one Saturday, when he'd returned from work, he came in shaking an old tin can which he emptied on the table. Out spilled dozens of peach pits along with a message clinging to his smile; one he'd memorized from the white woman who gave them to him. She had an orchard out back of her place. I made Jeff tell me over and over again how she said to get them pits growing into trees. Had to get it just right, didn't I? Put lots of holes in the bottom of some old tin cans. Mix plenty of sand from the stream bed in there so's the water won't stand too long, then add a bit of manure. Not too much; don't want to burn them roots when they get started. Jeff got so tired of telling me, he threatened to dig up one of the woman's fruit trees and plant it out front if I didn't quiet up. Well maybe, but when the day came it was Jeff who got on his knees, like when he asked me to marry him, and told me our peach trees had started to come up in those old cans. Twenty little trees lined along the edge of the porch to catch the morning sun. A few weeks later we planted them together, Jeffrey and me, in rows like they was gonna one day be an orchard—a place we'd follow the laughter of our children playing in the cool shade.

What color is joy? I wouldn't be able to describe all the hues I celebrated with Jeff that autumn by the chestnut. He had made another dream come true. One worked from the calloused palms of his hands and sprinkled with the sweat of his brow.

Those bright days were followed by long sweaty nights that have endured in my secrets to this day. We never wanted to go inside our cabin for nothing and seemed to mostly live on the porch, sat along the stream where we bathed, or enjoyed being under the canopy of his chestnut tree. From there we'd look over our newly planted peach trees like we could all but watch them grow in the moonlight.

On Saturdays, come early evening, Jeff would sometimes stop what he was working on around the cabin, and look for me between lines of sheets I was taking down. Sometimes I'd peek over my hanging clothes and watch for his glance. Yes, I was his woman and knew what he wanted. His shirt would already be pulled over his head by the time he made it over to me; him not wanting to waste time with no buttons. He'd carry me to the shade of the chestnut, lift me high and I'd hold his sweaty head between my breasts till he was finished. The taste of salty sweat running down his neck I'd catch in my mouth opened to his passion. Then he'd slowly ease me down till my feet touched time again. Then afterwards that stream felt so good. Down there we'd let the cool water undulate over us. Just my hand in Jeff's to keep me from floating away in all the bliss. He was always quiet when he'd finished having his pleasure, as though he lingered in the moment.

Even during the week we'd eat supper out on the porch in the moonlight. I'd fry up some fish Jeff had caught or a chicken one of the white folks had given him for his labors. That autumn Jeff started a fire near the porch to light our evening. I still hear the crackling of the burning leaves against the crisp air. He'd roll apples in sugar and then toss them in a can he'd place near the fire till they baked soft as custard. After there was nothing left to eat, Jeff would take my hand and walk me through where our peach trees were planted. Each time it was as though we were going somewhere special; a journey to some secret place, one that was no borrowed dream.

"What are you expectin' from them spindly little twigs we got planted?" Jeff asked. Asked me all the time just so I could dwell in our dream of an orchard. He pretended he was never tired of hearing the same story, 'cause he didn't really care 'bout my words, just the joy that came with them.

"Gonna be our orchard one day," I told him again. "Our own Garden of Eden just like the one Momma promised was up ahead for her family come a day she never saw."

As I look back to these moments I always see Minerva and Owen out in the dust of the Burneys' fields. And then, late at night, the look of Momma's weary eyes as she pulled up the bottom of that old

apron-curtain to look up at the big white house to see if Ella was signaling Isaac had capitulated to his bottle—the battle he never sought
to win, so we could finally head up to Orchard Hill. I remember
Minerva's gaze as sad but happy at the same time. Call it hope, or
whatever, even deep in her exhaustion her faith for the future of her
kids never dimmed.

"What's the matter, honey?" Jeff whispered.

"My momma, she'd take me up to the orchard late at night. I
'member lookin' up at them tall trees, branches touching over our
heads like angels' wings. Cool, the ground so cool to our feet where
they'd been waterin' that morning. Just me and Momma up there
close to the bounty that waited at the edge of the moonlight. Up
there where Isaac couldn't hear us talkin 'bout how it was gonna be
someday when we got away."

"Look 'round. You got away from the Burney place. All your
dreams are right here with me now."

"No, Jeff. Nobody ever gets that far, 'cause there ain't that far
to run to. Them plantation days are gonna follow us like a shadow
sewn to our heels. No matter how many miles we run, no matter
how many years we struggle to rid ourselves of the memories, they'll
still be chasing us down like the nigger dogs did our folks and their
folks before."

"Ain't nobody gonna be chasin' us! I see to it," he said.

But maybe he didn't understand my tangled thoughts. Still I
knew he felt the pain I had buried deep. His eyes told me so.

"You know, my momma, she tried to get away. Oh, Lord how she
tried. But every day things got fixed against my folks more than the
day before. No matter how hard they toiled, they still owed Burney
more and more, always more. You think that's why the Lord took
Owen and Minerva so young? He knew they didn't have it in 'em to
work them fields no more?"

"Don't know 'bout them things," Jeff said. "But I know you
keep your momma's dreams in you," he whispered. "I reckon that's

where the Lord sees your soul. Like our kids one day gonna keep our dreams with 'em."

"Momma would be proud I goin' to night school."

"When you get all the learnin' gathered up, you teach it back to me. Yeah?"

"When, Jeff? You're always workin' till late."

"Got to get my hands on some big money. See, I got plans, too. Yes, ma'am! Gonna buy this here acreage one day. That's what I been thinkin' on. A man's got to dream, too."

"Where you get that kind of money?" I asked.

"I got something going. Me and the men; it's all gonna work out fine. Sure it is."

"You're not talkin' 'bout no still, are you?" I asked.

Blood drained to my soles at the idea. You see, I knew that Jeff was real busy back then. He was out most days well into the night and then coming home exhausted. Yet I mostly didn't know what they were doing. Maybe a job here and there up and down the roads leading back to town. It scared me more when Jeff looked off as far as he could toss his thoughts. What was going on out there beyond his chestnut tree, I wondered.

"It's business," he announced in a tone that meant I was not a party to his schemes.

So many times he'd said it was a man's dream to care for his family and that could come to some messy dealings at times. Yes, I knew what that meant, didn't I? 'Cause I could read defiance in Jeff's eyes even if he was quick to avert his gaze to keep me off the trail.

"They don't care 'bout nobody's dreams when they come callin' with their lynchin' ropes," I hollered at his back as he headed to the cabin.

He turned sharply and walked back towards me. Our eyes were sparing. "I ain't afraid of no coward hidin' under his momma's bed sheets," he proclaimed.

But I was. Didn't matter where they hid, the lynching rope be in plain sight for ever'body to see but the law. Yes, that rope tied hard to one end of a tree branch and the other 'round your life and from then on every day tightening on the necks of your family.

"Well, you damned well better be scared, 'cause nobody'll save you if the Klan gets on your back! Then what 'bout your dreams for us? I mean me and the baby?"

"The what?" Jeff's eyes got huge. "What 'a you say, Sarah? A baby?"

"Just maybe you're gonna be a daddy now. Don't want this baby's daddy caught bootleggin' under the Klan's nose."

He caressed my belly like it was his child's head. "Ah, there ain't no Klan 'round these parts," he said. "You and me and now a baby! Don't need nothin' else. No, ma'am. We got our heaven right here under the chestnut tree."

And Then Annie

30

I TELL YOU PLAIN, summer is never a good time to be with child. Not in the thick humidity of the South and sure not when you got a porch covered with piles of somebody's laundry to get through, and you know as you sit there unable to move, that your husband's gonna come home hungry for his supper before you can even get up again. Yet the very thought of cooking makes you sicker than when he left at dawn.

One morning after Jeff had left, I'd barely gotten out to the porch before I collapsed from exhaustion. The best I could do was sit there looking at them piles staring me back. I was sure them rags were cursing me or maybe waiting for a word as to how they was gonna somehow get into my tub. I finally gave up on getting any loads done and figured I'd wander down to the stream to cool my feet. But then just the ordeal of standing up got me afraid of what might happen if I got sick down there. I'd sure never get back up that sandy slope before I rolled down into the mud along that stream. Lord, I was a sight!

That day I put my hand under my belly like I was lifting a load of laundry. Given how hard it had been for me to do absolutely nothing that morning got me thinking as to what in the world I would do when the baby came? I knew I needed Louvenia, and if it wasn't for Jesse, Sister would be right there pushing the heat back with a turkey feather fan and a bowl of her egg custard.

Besides worrying about my baby coming, it was thinking of my sister that twisted my thoughts into grisly knots. I worried 'bout what was happening in that alley if I couldn't keep up with the wash for her to iron in town. Even when I had a load or two done, Jeff had no time to be going into town to leave it off. No, some nights my man came home so tired he didn't know which way he was headed. Where did that leave Sister? Sick as I was, I couldn't help but worry myself sicker on how she'd eat without that bit of ironing money coming in.

Weeks later Annie told me that Louvenia could hardly sleep over worries about the baby coming. Sometimes, after Jesse gone off, Annie brought over a plate of whatever she had put on her table that night. They'd sit there in the quiet of the evening while Sister ate her beans and rice or pork and collards and drank a jar of sweet tea together. Annie was gifted in the way she could get talk going, which eased Sister's mind off the cycle of woes that had belted her that day.

"Now you know Sarah ain't the first woman to have a baby, Sister Louvenia. That's been goin' on for some time now. Just look at me and the preacher."

"I'm so 'fraid for her," Louvenia said, patting one of Annie's little ones on the head as the child eagerly tugged at the doll dress Sister had just finished. "What if she goes to have that baby when she's out there hanging the laundry?" Louvenia shook her head to rid herself of the thought. "Can't get that picture out of my head. That baby come and Jeff's not 'round. Lordy, what's gonna happen then?"

Annie said that Sister was biting her nails to the quick.

"Now, now. You know that child ain't gonna be born over no tub."

Annie said Sister went silent and looked ever so lost.

But I'm sure my baby being born while I was working my tub wasn't the worst thing Sister conjured; me, where the nearest candle is down some rutted pitch-black road. Annie said Sister's eyes bled with despair till she came up with an idea. She told Sister she'd get the preacher to hire a buggy and take her out to our place.

"I can't do that," Sister said, stifling tears.

"Poor thing, why not?"

"I leave here, I got no place to come back to," Louvenia whispered like Jesse was already at her throat. "Jesse see to it. You know he would, too. He'd bring the law down on me," she said. "Sure enough he'd tell 'em something bad on me and then Jesse, he'd stand there holding the door open till they come. Wave 'em on in to take me off, he would."

"What he say about you that could be bad?" Annie asked. "You ain't done nothing!"

"It don't matter none. Jesse tight with the men at the jail since he been paying 'em off with money his whores give 'im to keep the law off their backs."

"Lordy, that man don't know how lucky he is he gots you!"

"But he sure knows he gots me, don't he?" Sister replied. "Whore money he stealin' now," she said in disgust, knowing what it felt like all them years Jesse picked her own pockets. "The law, they come for me and put me in a work gang on the county roads. I'd be out there for a quarter a day. With my gout and cracked ribs, how could I make it through a day? So they'd drag me back till I give 'em a full day, then another one or two till I ain't got no days left." Sister sobbed. "Lord, I don't wanna go that way."

"I know, honey." Annie said. "That Jesse, devil gets his worst meanness from watching your ol' man. Don't matter 'bout him. I know what we gonna do! I'll get my sister-in-law to watch my kids. Then the preacher can take me out to Sarah and Jeff's place. She ain't gonna have that child alone. No, she's sure enough not, so you put your mind to ease on that."

Louvenia could only swallow back the tears by finishing the supper that had gone cold.

It must have been only a few days later when, sitting there on the porch, I seen Annie and the preacher with little Nettie. Didn't know they were coming. Annie told me that they'd be at our place sooner than a letter could arrive. I cried at the sight as their wagon turn off the road to our place with Nettie waving a bandanna.

"Sister Sarah," the preacher hollered as they rolled in, "brought you a visitor. Seems like she's figuring on gettin' away from the kids and me and come spend some time here in the country. How's that sound to you?"

I don't remember my reply; all I could think of was my house being a mess, the porch covered with piles of stale clothes and I was sure I was about to puke in front of them.

"Oh, look at that woman! Ain't she with child?" the preacher said. "You best work yourself into that chair over there on the porch, Sarah. Annie here knows a thing about birthing. Don't you, honey?"

"Now don't be worrying none," Annie said as the preacher brought their things in. "Nettie and me gonna get everything ready for you and the baby."

"Momma brought an apple pie," Nettie said grinning ear to ear. "I cut the apples."

"Yeah, but that's for the baby, ain't it?" the preacher added with a wink. "Annie wouldn't let Nettie and me have a crumb of that pie on the way out here."

Annie was a woman who could divide and conquer. No sooner had they unloaded than she had her apron on ready to get busy. "Nettie, go get wood from the pile and get the water heated for the tubs. Want to get these piles washed and hung," Annie said. "Maybe they be dry enough so your daddy can take 'em back into town for Sister Louvenia to iron."

"Momma, we can't wash all them piles in one afternoon!" Nettie declared.

"How you know? Think you're taking too much time making a list of the things you can't do. You got that water boilin' yet, Nettie?"

"Momma! Ain't got the fire started yet."

"Sarah, honey, where's your broom?" Anne asked. "While the water heats, I'm gonna get the cabin swept so we can get something on for Jeff's supper tonight. If he's like the preacher, he don't know how to fry an egg without half the shell left in there!"

As Annie and Nettie were getting things done, I got to wondering what Jeff would think when he returned. The thought made me chuckle. Most nights he'd came home with a face smudged with grime, him expecting to sit down to a supper of corn mush. But that night there waited a fine hot supper. I know that cooking was the best thing he'd smelled in a long time. He stepped in the door looking as if something was amiss. Not a word came out of his beautiful mouth as I filled bowls with potatoes and carrots and put my big platter with that pork roast in front of him.

"You too tired to say somethin' honey?"

Jeff stared in wonderment. You see, Annie had taken Sally down to the stream to bathe, so Jeff figured I'd cooked that supper. Given my condition when he left that morning it would have been a miracle from Jesus. Guess it was all the same!

"Yes, ma'am!" is all he could say as he looked over the table of plates and bowls of Annie's fine cooking.

"You best sit down and eat 'fore them black-eyed peas get cold. Go ahead now. You ain't dreamin'."

I put the cornbread on the table just as Jeff put himself in a chair. He'd no sooner lifted a spoon of black-eyed peas to his mouth than Annie and Nettie walked in, their moist clothes clinging and their hair still wet from the stream. Then he knew. Jeff grinned near as big as when I told him I was gonna give him a child. Annie cut the cornbread and we sat down to enjoy the Lord's bounty like we were all family.

"There's apple pie waiting for you, Jeff, 'less Sarah got to it already," Annie said as Jeff stuffed his mouth.

"No, I never ate Jeff's pie. Nettie went and hid it so I wouldn't."

"I brought some peaches I put up last week. Gonna make a peach cobbler for Jeff's breakfast," Annie announced.

Jeff could only sit there with a grin fixed on his dimpled face.

That night I felt better than I had in weeks. Nettie and I washed up the dishes while Annie rested with Jeff on the porch. He didn't light the kerosene lamp so the 'squeeters wouldn't bother us none. About then Jeff had gone to smoking a pipe. He struck a match to light his pipe which lit his beautiful face. Forever I will remember how contented he looked.

"You got it so good, Jeffrey McWilliams," I heard Annie say. "So quiet out here at your old chestnut tree. Not like that alley where there ain't one tree."

Jeff pulled down a jug of corn whiskey from the ledge over the porch posts where he kept his tobacco tin and sloshed some into their crock mugs.

"It's a fine life out here. Ain't none better," Jeff said. "Ain't never gonna leave this place. Not ever. Got my woman at my side. Got a kid comin'. Even got us an orchard out there. Ain't them trees a bit taller than when you were here last?"

"Them trees is comin' along fine," Annie confirmed. "They sure enough is!"

"Sarah keeps promisin' them trees gonna give us a peach cobbler soon. But I forgot how many soons from now that'll be!" he said. "I reckon 'bout the time we're too old to pick 'em. But I'll still be here me tellin' my kids how hard their momma worked to have all the peach cobbler they could eat."

"Ain't nothing prettier in spring than when the ground under a peach tree is covered with blossoms," Annie remarked. "It's sure something to behold and then your kids out in that orchard playin' hide-n-seek."

"Annie, you and the preacher best bring them kids out and join us country folks. Get out of town where you can breathe the good air."

"Jeff, you know we would, but the preacher, he's got folks depending on him back in town. Most can't read or write you know. So, my husband's the only one that can help 'em with their needs. But Lord, he's promised me when our kids are married and settled, we gonna do just that. Leave that city. Lord, bring that day 'round soon. Yes, I can hear my creaking bones remind me all the time."

"You know I can't read or write none like the preacher," Jeff said. "But Sarah and me, we got a bit of our dream right here. Gonna buy this place one day, and then our children are gonna get schoolin'. Don't know how I's gonna do it, but I aim to no matter. Sarah, she always figures a way to get things done so I know it'll happen. Puts my mind at peace knowing it. Just like I know that ol' sun is gonna rise tomorrow and smile on them peach trees again. Yes, ma'am. Come a day somebody ask me where my kids is I'll tell 'em, they ain't in no cotton field workin' for the white man. Nope, they's all be in school workin' for a chance at their own dreams."

I went out onto the porch just as Annie was coming back in.

"I done worked for my daily bread today," she said. "Gonna get some sleep now."

"Just made up the trundle bed for you and Nettie," I said. "Don't know how to thank you for comin' all the way out here to lift my burdens."

"Ah, I just come 'cause I needed rest from the preacher," she whispered so Jeff couldn't hear. "That man, it don't matter how hot the night is, he figures on making it hotter for me near every night of the week he can get some," Annie winked.

"You gonna take a walk with me, Sarah?"

With a glint in his eyes Jeff reached for a bar of soap off the shelf, pulled a rag off a hook and offered me his hand. He eased me down that sandy slope and into a cool stream of water where I knew we'd be followed by a chorus of chirping crickets and giggling toads. We kept an ol' bent tin for bathing down there. I'd barely stepped out of my dress when Jeff poured cool water down my back and over my breasts. He poured that stream water like it had turned into May wine flavored with sweet woodruff and every drop he had to sample with his tongue. Then he filled the tin and handed it to me to pour over him. We sat there as the water churned over our ankles and talked about how our hard work had brought us to that moment.

"Been thinking, in a couple more months or so, just maybe I have the money to put down on this acreage," Jeff whispered in my ear and caressed my swollen belly.

"Are we near to buying this place?" I asked.

"Don't hardly make sense to plant an orchard, water it ever'day, then head down the road 'fore we taste the jam from them peaches you been preachin' 'bout."

"No, that don't make sense," I said. "But can't think how'd we get the money to buy much of anything."

"It'll come. Just like a peach from your trees up there."

Jeff pulled me close to him.

"You know, I sure thought we'd put them peach pits in some manure and get us a big peach tree 'bout the next week or so. You never tol' me I had to wait near a hundred years to get some of that jam you always promisin'."

"Well, you must not have planted them pits like I tol' you or we'd be havin' cobblers by now. Yes, we would. We'd be pickin' them right off the branches. Anyway, even a hundred years ain't that long to wait for something good, 'cause holding on to a dream is like holding on to somebody you love. Ain't it?"

"You don't gotta be holding on to me like I'm gonna disappear one day," Jeff whispered. "It don't matter none how many years in front of us, I still be right here in our orchard waitin' to find you looking for me under that ol' chestnut."

HER DADDY'S EYES

31

FOR THE NEXT few days, Annie and me, with little Nettie's help, got my work caught up and still found a few moments here and there to sit a spell on the porch and talk.

I told Annie I was eager to get Louvenia out with us, as Jeff and I were getting by and there was plenty to eat most days, and on leaner ones we still had a bag of cornmeal put back for mush. It was far more than our momma ever knew. I was sure that having Sister near to help raise our child would be a blessing. I figured that Jesse couldn't last much longer, him having dived headfirst into too many empty whiskey bottles by then.

Louvenia and me, we never knew anything about giving birth. Nettie and I were hanging laundry to dry while Annie was down at the stream when the baby decided to come. I didn't know how long it would be 'fore the baby showed, so I leaned on Nettie, praying I'd get to the cabin first. Inside, I fell over the bed moaning. Nettie yelled for her ma to come quick.

"Well, guess it's time you start on a long walk," Annie announced.

"A walk you say? I ain't goin' no place till this baby comes! And you know it!"

"Yes, you are, honey. You can count on it!" Anne replied. "Now get up and get to walkin', Sister."

Then it dawned on me. There was no movement in my belly. I'd felt none all morning. I held my ample middle feeling for life that was not there. That baby had been kicking at me for weeks and suddenly I realized I'd not felt a kick since the night before. Oh, Lord, I prayed my baby wasn't dead 'cause I'd spent too much time bending over them tubs!

"Get up now, Sarah, and start walkin' like I say."

But I didn't want to move. I was certain I'd lost my baby and only wanted to wail myself away.

"Momma, Sarah looks like she's lost," Nettie yelped.

"No, she's not lost. Just doesn't know where she's goin' is all. What's the matter, Sarah?"

"My baby, he's dead. I can't feel 'im move no more."

"No, that baby's fine. Just bashful about showing his face."

"Oh, Lord," was all that would come out of my mouth.

"You stand up now and let's see you walk about the cabin," Annie said.

"No, I ain't gonna take no damned walk. My baby's gone!" I cried. "I ain't never gonna walk no place again!"

"That so? A baby only stops fidgeting before it comes. Just a little rest before what comes next is all. Now get up and grab on to my arm. Want you to waddle around so that baby knows you're getting ready for 'im or he may decide not to come till next summer!"

"What?" Nettie asked her momma. Having witnessed the birth of her siblings, she knew more about birthing than me.

"Sarah's got to move around till it's really time. She's just worked up, is all," Annie told Nettie. "You fetch some water from the well."

Nettie scrambled out the door.

"Annie, if I die, tell Jeff I love 'im."

I cried hard as Annie shuffled me 'round the table in a circle. But that only made me want to puke all the more.

"If you die, honey, I'll tell Jeff you took off 'cause what he put in your belly and you're waiting in heaven with a stick to put to his head for all his orneriness," Annie said.

At first I laughed, but then started crying. No, I howled. "I got to lay down," I begged.

"No, you got to walk about like I said. You been 'round the table this way, let's turn and head the other way to see if the view's any different."

"Oh, Lord… I'm gonna die!"

"No, you're not gonna die. Just gonna wish you were dead before the day's out."

I think Annie had me walk a mile in circles 'round that table.

"Now, I guess it's time you best lay down on the bed. You're beginning to walk like you can't get your feet far enough apart. That means the baby's head is working its way down."

Nettie helped me get my feet up off the floor. Guess it was hours I rested, but seemed like only moments when Annie started tugging at me to get up and squat near the bed.

"Now I want you to push that baby on out now, honey."

But why was she yelling in my ear? I know she was, or was it only the pain howling. "What? Right on this here floor?"

"You're thinkin' this baby's gonna march right out of you?" she replied.

Well, I had no idea. I'd seen piglets born on the Burney place but nobody ever told that sow to push. That hog just lay there till them piglets came then she went for her supper. I guess that was my notion. I'd have that baby, get up and get Jeff's supper goin' and then maybe wash a few loads of clothes while the baby teethed.

After an hour or so of Annie yelling in one ear and then the other for me to push, she stopped. What was wrong? She felt my belly again and whispered that the baby was twisted up in there. Maybe it couldn't get out. I could tell by her expression that things were going badly. I knew I was gonna die when Jeff walked in.

"Sarah, ain't never seen a face as red as yours!" he said.

Nettie reached over and blotted my face again.

"My wife gonna be okay?" Jeff looked frightened like I'd never seen.

"Jeff, you best go out on the porch. It's a hell of a lot cooler out there," Annie said. "You got to push, honey. Push, I say! You can't stay this way for days thinkin' on it. You got to do it now like I say. I been where you are and know what it means if this child don't come soon!"

But I had no push left. My body couldn't seem to do nothing more than writhe in agony.

Annie got up. "Nettie, keep her forehead moist and keep fannin', child."

There was a lamp on the porch so I could see Jeff way out there under his chestnut, that big tree where I figure we made our baby that hot summer night. He always drifted over there when he had things brewing in his head. Annie called him back.

"Your woman, you know she's really just a girl, Jeff. She's not yet fifteen. That baby she's carryin' don't seem to want to come," Annie said.

"I go get the doctor."

"Ain't no doctor gonna come way out here before it's too late," Annie said.

"What?"

"I tell you, this girl's worn out, Jeff. All them tubs of laundry back on that alley. Getting your place goin' here. She's weary like I never seen no woman deliver baby alive."

"She's gonna have that baby just fine," Jeff said. "It's our dream to have lots of kids. I ain't gonna lose one."

"You got to go talk to her then. Show her where she can find something deep inside herself to keep it comin'," Annie said.

"Find what?"

"Find the will to fight till she pushes that baby out. 'Cause we're gettin' close to a bad place where she's gonna give up. Then we're gonna lose that baby." Annie bent over to whisper. "Could even lose your wife!"

Jeff returned to the bed looking determined to get some business done. Yes, I knew that expression, as he'd had it the time he was pulling stumps out.

He looked into my eyes like he was searching for something he'd lost. Don't know if I was awake the whole time 'cause it seemed like hours he held my hand. I still remember them calluses on his. A ridge across his palms.

"Sarah, you 'member when I first came up to your porch at Louvenia's?" he asked.

I think I just moaned. Wasn't in no damned mood to chat.

"And you were sitting there at that kitchen table. Your hair all up in the air like…"

"My what?" I groaned.

"Sure it was. Your hair stickin' up like a scarecrow gonna scare buzzards away," he said.

"What?"

"Now shut up, honey. I'm talkin'. Before I got in the door, you'd stuck your tongue out and wagged it at me like a damned ol' dog! Didn't you?"

Jeff drew up close and then winked.

"Yeah, like a bitch in heat."

"Like a what? What'd you just say to me?"

"Yeah. That tongue of yours. Lick, lick, lickin' at me. Huh? That's all you could think 'bout when you set your eyes on me. Ain't it so? Yes, ma'am, you sure fancied me. Lick, lick, lick…is what your eyes told me."

"I'm gonna belt you for saying that!"

With everything I could muster, I sent my fist to Jeff's mug. Hit the palm of his big hand and he smacked me right back with those dimples.

"See, that's the thing. You're lazy as an ol' sow. You'll probably be there for days. I just hope you don't spend all day stickin' that tongue out like you's hungry for me. Don't want Annie and Nettie here seein' you at it, do we? Huh?"

At that I could only think of killing Jeff. I struggled to go after my skillet and put it to his head. I kicked as hard as I could, what with having a baby goat in me—kicked at that man while he held both my hands with one of his.

"When I get up from here!" I screamed.

"Honey, that's what we been talkin' about. You don't seem to have a notion to get up any time soon, you ol' sow! Lick, lick, lick. Yeah, you sure 'nough said it."

Well, Lord. That did it. I squirmed and twisted to smack that man, but something inside of me freed the baby, or the baby figured it best come out and help her momma, because out she came. A baby girl. Through all the joy of that moment I hoped she didn't 'member her folks cussing at each other.

"Yeah, you did it, Jeff. Got her all worked up. You best go back outside for now," Annie told him as our baby squalled at her daddy for talking to her momma like that.

Jeff went outside as Annie scurried around doing this and that. All I remembered was hearing them cry—out on the porch was my baby girl and my husband choking on his sobs. Yes, we had gotten through the birth of our first child because of Annie.

Annie and Nettie were with me for a few days after our baby came. Don't 'member now how many. When I was able to get up and walk a bit, I picked up our girl we named Lelia, and took her to see her daddy. He was out there next to the porch chopping kindling.

"This baby girl gots the best daddy in the world," I told my husband.

He reached for his tobacco tin sitting nearby and shook it hard. It rattled up a storm.

"What's you got in there? Peach pits?"

"Coins in here. Gonna be the education tin. Gonna save to buy our girl books and things she's gonna need for school," he said.

"That your dream?"

"A man's dream gots to be only what will bring happiness to his family."

Jeff took Lelia in his arms and held her up to kiss her forehead. I could see plainly that she had her daddy's eyes; two big brown button eyes that were already sewed tightly to our hearts.

Just for My Honey

32

Sister could only iron the things I left off in fits and starts. As she couldn't sleep well, she'd stay up late ironing in the still of the night when the alley was quieter. But that awful night it wasn't. It was long after dark when she heard Jesse howling his entrance to the alley between snorted laughs. Sister said some loud-mouthed woman echoed his howling. A trash-woman is what Sister called a whore. Yes, this time Jesse's whore was coming home with him. I wondered what kind of a woman could be persuaded to follow a man like Jesse down a dirty ol' alley? Lord have mercy on her and the likes!

Louvenia had taken ever'thing Jesse rubbed her face in, but in her mind, she didn't have to take having his whores in her home on top of it. Didn't Jesse love to flaunt his sins in Sister's battered face? He was always there to remind her he could do as he pleased, even as she put the money on the table to pay for it.

He walked in from the porch with this woman as though Sister wasn't standing witness to his transgression. But then to Jesse she was mostly invisible anyway.

"What? Who that? No, you ain't bringin' no whore in here!" She moved to block the woman from coming into her kitchen. "Not never. Get 'er off this porch."

To impress this woman of the streets, Jesse laughed in Sister's face and graciously led the woman into Louvenia's kitchen where he paused to begin his unbuttoning. She said he stank like he'd just bathed in alley water soaked with cigarette butts and whiskey vomit. Sister told me this woman looked about like she needed to know if that kitchen pleased her good enough. Her looking 'round with Louvenia standing there with a hot iron in her hand. Was this woman crazy, stupid or just drunk? Well, she was all of these, wasn't she?

"You best get to thinkin' on painting this here kitchen 'fore you move my things in. Hear, ol' man?"

Jesse was eager to please. "Hear that, Louvenia? You get to it tomorrow. Just for my honey, here," he said. "Paint it up the way she tell you to!"

"And I'm tellin' you, you ain't bringin' no whore in here!"

"Watch your God-damned mouth, tub woman!" the whore said, and then turned to Jesse. "Jesse, honey, this here do for now since I don't got a place of my own just now. But what 'bout her? You ain't keepin' her 'round if I move my things in, that's for damned sure, 'cause I don't like the mouth she gots on 'er."

"Honey, I got no need for 'er now I got you, so I put her out on the street if you don't want her takin' care of you. Is that what you're a wantin'?"

Guess Jesse had been thinking on the terms for a spell. Him figuring there'd be more pleasure for himself if he sweetened the deal by tossing in a maid for this woman who spent most of her time on her back. A live-in whore with no other place to call home all for an ugly old man not gonna get none elsewhere no more. No, Jesse's life was all poured down his throat and pissed back out in that alley by then. Yet for this woman seemed to harbor a notion she was moving up in the world by stepping down into Jesse's hell hole.

"You a whore!" Louvenia reminded her. "I seen you out there

hangin' on the corner of this here alley!" Sister reiterated as though the woman didn't know her place in Louvenia's hierarchy of sins. "You ain't comin' in my house, except one time. Then you're gonna be carrying your head right back out that door." Sister pointed the direction of the door as her iron heated on that old stove.

But the woman knew who she was. Still, to her, Louvenia was even less. My sister was an unpaid whore and a colored man's slave too. Maybe most days this woman was better off than us 'cause ever'body knew 'round them streets, you mess with a whore, get rough on her or try to steal her money, she'd break a bottle and twist the jagged end in your face till you looked like ground meat. Then you'd know not to mess with her again!

"You a whore! And you ain't comin' in my house! Hear what I say?"

But the woman hadn't. No, she was busy looking over the kitchen like she was figuring what color she wanted it painted.

Sister then told Jesse off. "Get this whore out 'a here, and I mean now!"

Don't know why Louvenia thought her husband would turn and apologize for profaning her home and then usher the woman on out to the streets where she belonged. No, that wasn't Jesse. "Now, huh? That's when you want it? Then I give you what you deserve!"

With his fist Jesse spun the room 'round Sister's head in that old familiar orbit. Leaving Louvenia on the floor, he fondled the woman back to his bedroom.

Louvenia said at first she didn't feel the blood dripping down her forehead where she'd collided with the corner of that table. Her head had been cracked open so often the nerves in her face were mostly dead by then. She lay on the floor bleeding, wiping the blood out of her eyes, unable to get up even as her head spun. But the sounds of Jesse fixing to copulate the whore started to jab at Sister's old wounds. She told me she could hear them as good as if they were doing it right over the table she lay beneath.

"No honey, like I tol' you, she ain't good for nothin'," Jesse told the woman. "But I tell her to fix your meals like you want 'em and take care of your clothes real good," Jesse affirmed. "Sure, I will. I make her iron 'em up real pretty the way I like youse to look." Jesse coaxed the woman out of her blouse. "That woman out there gots no choice but do what you tell 'er or she be out on the street cold," he snapped his finger. "Just for my honey here, I'll do it for you, sweetie. You know I will, too."

"I don't give a God-damned what you'd like me to wear, Jesse Powell. And I ain't your honey, you ugly ol' man! So, stop pantin' over me like some stinkin' dog runnin' between the legs!"

Guess the whore was not entirely disposed to the deal Jesse planned to squeeze wholesale out my sister. She slapped Jesse's pawing off and wandered back out to the kitchen again. Maybe she had second thoughts about the situation as she stepped over Sister like she was a bag of rancid flour fixed to be tossed. Then Jesse must have figured he could woo her into thinking he could get his hands on a bit of money to sweeten the habitation deal he was brewing with the whore. Louvenia would come through for his honey, wouldn't she? Cover his overcharges for the night's pleasures? Didn't she always have some money hidden back somewhere? Louvenia didn't need money to eat that week. Where was it this time? A fist or two would produce the reserve funds to complete Jesse's transaction and get the ball rolling in the backroom.

"I got some money comin' in," Jesse declared to the woman. "Got a bit here and there, enough for my honey, if you know what I mean."

Well, Sister sure knew what he meant. Hadn't her iron put out every coin that bought what she put on his plate and even them old used suits on his back?

The whore, who knew he was a wasted ol' man, had to buy into it because she'd run out of credit herself. You know she had if she wandered down to the end of Jesse's alley. She had nothing else going for her and no options, so she went on back to open her legs for him.

For Louvenia the moment had come. Living on the edge of hell for so long, she might as well head there and call it home. The only decision left was figuring what would deliver that fact to Jesse's head the quickest and split it open the widest. Well, I guess just knowing that man had lived his last day gave her the strength to crawl back up. She hoisted her skirt to wipe the blood out of her eyes and reached for a chair to climb to her feet. Jesse was already busy back there trying to mount the whore, but the woman kept coming up with deal breakers that frustrated his gyrations. Guess Jesse's working the whore's trade while abusing Sister added a bit of entertainment, so he left the door open for Sister to hear. But it wasn't to be the spectacle the ol' man had figured on. No, there was a tragedy unfolding on Jesse's very own dark stage, and there'd be little more light if he could open his coffin lid for another round.

Louvenia, propelled to her feet by Jesse's grunts and the whore's slapping at his back to get it over with, worked her way over to the counter where the other meat was cut up. Down under, behind some old mason jars, she kept the big knife. The one I'd pointed at Jesse when he came at me that time. Same ol' butcher knife, 'cept she'd been keeping it down there in a rusty tin filled with foul water so that even a prick, just a tiny one ain't nobody ever gonna see, would be lethal unless he was immune to blood poisoning. Yes, Sister knew the day had come; she'd been saving for it in that rusty tin.

Sister resurrected the knife and carried it back there dripping brown rust with one aim: to slit open Jesse's notion he'd have his whore in her home. How many past due bills of retainer were about to be settled? There'd be no trial. Satan was surely waiting for Jesse, and wasn't gonna fuss over the details of his final fall.

Despite her broken rib, Sister shuffled 'cross the kitchen he'd just bartered to the whore. Jesse was back there grunting like a mating hog and saw only pleasure coming his way. But there was to be more than he'd bargained for. You see, Jesse was panting so heavily he didn't see Sister also panting to get at his throat. She crawled 'round to the side of his bed and aimed the knife for the middle of his spineless back. Momma must 'a been there steadying her hand for the gut severing plunge that would put an end to Jesse. The woman, who'd been keeping her eyes shut to Jesse's ugly business, opened them only to see her own end coming down faster than dice hits a wall in an alley. In that flash, she could not have known if it was Jesse's mole-cursed back that would take the hit or if she'd end up with her thigh gouged. Not a good place for a whore to have battle wounds. And you know this time the woman finally realized she best jump to a respectful attention in Sister's presence. With the butcher knife in transit, she bounced so hard to rid herself of Jesse that he rolled over to the floor.

That knife missed Jesse's back but creased the whore's inner leg where it let blood. The woman now truly understood what the terms of Jesse's deal were, and that it was a slim chance she'd ever see any maid service from my sister in her future, which was now entirely uncertain. The whore got crazy at the sight of all that blood. Real crazy. Guess enough to clear up her whiskey head lickety-split. Suddenly she didn't seem to care no more 'bout how handy Sister might be in doing up her laundry and fixing her meals. No, getting butchered like a piece of meat was probably not as pretty as the picture of life on easy street that Jesse had smeared over her desperation to get the woman to stroll down his stinking alley with him. Sister told me the woman kept screaming and panting, but not the way Jesse wanted. No, she was panting gusts of terror. She had to have known that one-legged whores don't get much business. Those women only perform in alleys for enough raw cash to get to the next day, where things ain't never gonna be better. Wasn't she only a few steps ahead of them kind of women when she followed Jesse that night?

But Jesse's head was so bourbon-soaked and his eyes so

amber-jaundiced, he couldn't sort the real commotion till he realized that somehow the whore was up there on the bed and he was now on the floor. But as Sister went to pull the woman out of her house by the hair, he sobered up quickly. Yes, he could still pull his fist back to deliver it to Sister's splintered face. He sent her reeling across the room and up against that dented doorknob that had clashed with her head before. Even so, the whore was smart enough to know when a sister had turned the craps table over.

Yes, it was painfully clear that Louvenia had flipped the deal even if she was all but indisposed—her gasping and gagging on the blood filling her throat. But the woman must have figured that if there was yet another round, they might all end up dead, and sure enough there'd be no freshly ironed frock hanging over a chair waiting for the undertaker to fold her into. The blood running down the whore's leg was surely a reminder of how fragile life was. One minute you're the reigning mistress arranging the new home you relieved a tub woman of, and the next you're waiting for the undertaker to situate what's left of you in a pine box. Hadn't Sister told her that when she put a foot in her kitchen? Well, maybe not clear enough.

Jesse finally gave up on his next round of pawing on the poor woman because her screaming was distracting him from working his rhythm back. He went cursing over to the door to get Louvenia out of the woman's sight so the whore might stop howling. He yanked Sister 'round to drag her out by her feet so's he could get back to his honey again. He dragged her like a bag of garbage to be hauled off. Sister said she felt them uneven floorboards as her head dragged across the room. When Louvenia came to, she thought she'd been buried alive as her skirt was twisted over her head like a winding sheet.

Jesse, he left her in a pile at the backdoor. But she wasn't dead enough, was she? Somewhere inside, Sister found enough left to finish the deed. Surely it was a surge of Minerva's spirit that brought her back from the edge once again.

Louvenia didn't 'member what happened later 'cept she'd crawled over to the laundry pile for a rag to stop the bleeding. Said the whore stayed back there in Jesse's bed screaming ever' time he went to mount her again. She cowered and bawled her eyes out till Jesse had managed to pour enough whiskey down her throat to fortify her for more. Then when she got her bourbon guts back, she aimed herself for the road. 'Cept the only escape route was through Louvenia's kitchen and the very door Sister had warned her not to profane. Well, the whore should have thought on that when she was sweet-talking Sister 'bout her plans to redecorate the kitchen. Maybe this time she'd for sure listen to a God-fearing woman like my sister.

Yes, it was a mighty serious problem the whore had gotten herself into, 'cause the power had shifted and the lowly and badly bruised were raised and armed with a rusty knife and an iron was heating on the stove as backup. All Sister had to do was sit at her kitchen table and wait for the woman to muster enough courage to risk getting past her and it wouldn't be the same manner as her grand entrance.

Louvenia pointed her finger at the whore's face as soon as she dared to peek out. "Woman, did I not tell your sorry ass that you weren't comin' into my home? Next time I see your face it best not be anywheres on this alley. Else you're gonna get my iron upside your head and you're gonna keep gettin' it till your hearin' gets fixed!"

Well, the whore must have been good and soused 'cause her damned mouth got the best of her all over again. "You tub woman! You near cut my leg off. I got to go find me a doctor. He gonna sew me."

At that Sister got up to fix her mouth for good. "Honey, ain't no doctor gonna sew your head back on!"

With that Louvenia picked up her heated iron. Using her stronger left arm, she slung it at the woman's head.

It only grazed the woman's face but that was enough to slap some sense into her vacant head. At that she fought her way through the screen door to get herself out of Sister's kitchen alive.

Sister said she never saw the woman again.

END OF AN ALLEY

33

JEFF AND I had long talked about getting Louvenia out to the cabin for a visit. Still Sister could never see past that ol' man's threats as to how she might leave for even a day. I got to wondering if she could work something out with Annie's help, thinking that one night, when Jesse was out at the bars, she would head down to her place. Then Annie would go tell Jesse that Louvenia was real sick, needed tending and he best stay away or he'd catch it, too. I knew Jesse was scared of getting sick as he'd already been feeling the rough edges of his own coffin by then. Hating Annie's kids, I knew he'd never bother checking up on Louvenia even to see how long before she'd be back to cooking his meals and cleaning up his life. Then while Jesse was thinking that Sister was just down the alley, she'd be on her way to us. At Jeff's cabin we'd hug the ground till the fears faded as I knew Jeff could protect us from Jesse if he and Brother Fred ever showed to drag their meal ticket back.

It was dark early and seemed colder than usual when Jeff got back with the wagon and I took off for town. All the way I wondered if Jesse would be there and what he might do when the day came he found Sister was gone for good. Perhaps that's why I shivered on the way. Seemed like there was a cold chill licking at my every thought.

Maybe only a premonition, one that I was about to walk into a black dream. It was the night of the whore's visit.

Since I'd been with Jeff, Sister and I worked it so that Jesse was gone by the time I arrived or she'd be on her porch to warn me away. But that night was long brewed in tragedy before I got to the alley. I quietly stepped up on the porch, paused to see if I could hear Jesse, then went in. Louvenia sat there at the table frozen. I could hardly keep from crying out at the sight. Sister didn't cry. No tears, no sounds, it was all gone. Jesse had surely killed her, she just wasn't dead yet.

"Oh, Lord Sister, what happened?"

Louvenia was so head-battered she was delusional. Even her vision was scrambled from the blood welling in her blackened eyes. "Jesse, his whore come into my kitchen, didn't she? He brung 'er. That's what he done. She held me down while he did it. Killed her with my iron. Crushed her head open so's I could spoon her brains to Jesse. See, he was thinkin' on keepin' her on here. A whore, he was!"

"Where Jesse now?" I whispered, half expecting him to come at me from the darkness of his backroom.

"Where he mostly been. Back there passed out. Just maybe he ain't never gonna wake up again. Huh?"

She braced her head to slow the teetering.

"This time you gots to come with me. Jeff protect you from Jesse."

"Yeah, I go with you, but you best come for me after he gone. You know he won't let me out the door alive."

"I go tell Annie what we're gonna do," I said. "Down there I'll watch for Jesse. When he gone, we gonna walk to the end of this alley for the last time!"

I reached to hug my sister. In agony, she flinched at my very touch.

"Yes, you come back, Sarah. I be alright till then. Sure, I will."

Louvenia folded her arms on the table, turned her head away from me and laid it over them. Crying, I headed to Annie's.

But on the way I got to thinking that maybe Sister didn't really want me to read her eyes. Was that why she buried them in her folded arms? Maybe she was really determined to escape somewhere else. How many times had Louvenia told me she was praying for the Lord to take her? She was tired, she'd say, and in all her exhaustion she often called on Jesus to carry her over to Summerland, that place where there'd never be a wound that never healed. Hadn't Jesse cleaned her out of everything but her soul? Even that Sister thought he and the whore would sacrifice if she let them profane her home. And they would. Realizing what was in her head, to go looking for Jesus, I dashed back to Louvenia's. I was jolted at the thought that perhaps my sister would already be gone, that she'd cut her wrists or worse.

Truly, I'd never heard such dead silence. Not ever. My heart only stopped pounding when I walked back in to see Louvenia struggling to pull her things together. I took a deep breath of relief that she was still there, and, at least, half alive. I went to peek into Jesse's backroom. There he lay half slung over his bed, still gripping the whore's underwear.

Back in that dark bedroom, Louvenia went to filling a pillowcase with her things. I'm telling you, probably everything she owned wouldn't fill one. She paused to look about as she crept around his bed, like she was gathering up memories of the years those walls had been her prison. Jesse moaned but never opened an eye. If he knew she was headed out, he'd kill her before she got to the door. He'd little to lose, as death was already on the hunt for him. Yes, surely throbbing at his nightmare was a deafening chorus of crashing whiskey bottles. All empty. The very ones that Sister's rusty knife was surely hammering a hollow dirge on. Did she aim to break his head open on the downbeat? All the same, his would be a slow and painful death by whiskey starvation if she ever got out the door, leaving him to his own means.

When Jesse growled in his sleep, Sister ducked and bit the corner of the pillowcase like her broken rib was gonna come out her side. He groaned again and reached for his whore's thigh, but his hand only rubbed his old pillow. "Lily," he called out. He called them all Lily 'cause he never knew their names. To him they needed no name. Then, in his sleep, he cursed Sister again from somewhere that surely had to be too close to hell.

"Hey, I gots to pee, bitch," he mumbled to his dead bed and then passed out again.

His Lily was gone and now only Louvenia stood there. But it seemed as though the years of beatings had taken over. Her rage surged as she found more of his rainy-day half-empties hidden about. Bottles she'd paid for. Her staying up till dawn ironing to buy herself a moment of peace. One by one she toted them bottles to the kitchen and emptied every drop of whiskey into her washtub and then lined them in precise rows over her table, straight—one bottle after another like on a grocer's shelf. They soon covered the entire table as they'd long mapped out her life. Then she fell into a chair looking over her deed. I bit my lip to keep from crying.

Jesse wasn't tearful. "Hey, where's Lily? Huh? She take off? Go out in the alley and see. I got somethin' for 'er! Go on now, I said… Huh?"

He crawled out of his brown bed and stumbled into the kitchen like he had no memory of what he'd done, or it simply made no difference. His life was one long blur that didn't require apologies to punctuate his assaults. I stood in the shadows of the porch shivering at the sight of him staggering about like he was waiting for his thoughts to catch up with him. He snorted and choked on his own congested filth. Then he noticed the bottles lined up. Sister sat there with a faint smile on her busted lip. Her eyes fixed on Jesse's sacrificial altar in front of her, dozens of glistening whiskey bottles with every last drop of hope for his final binge drained away. You see, Sister had determined that Jesse would be going to hell sober.

"Why you're a God-damned bitch! You done drunk up the last of my whiskey, ain't you?"

He lifted his fist to punctuate his message on her face but stopped cold when he saw Sister's hand swing out. She'd been holding that knife on her lap. No, this time she didn't duck from his swing. She aimed it at his face and twisted it like she was daring him to swallow it whole. From her honey, Jesse, it was time to exact her own justice. The bottle had truly spun and now pointed to Jesse's throat. His luck had poured out.

Sister held tightly to the knife like she was fighting the Lord Himself for control. But then plunged it into the tabletop so hard the bottles tumbled and crashed to the floor. Her eyes glared back, and still she kept that grin fixed on her broken face. The grin of contempt. Jagged pieces of whiskey bottles covered the floor between them.

"You crazy bitch! I get you good for this!"

But not just now; he was still too drunk to do the deed proper. Later, for sure, when Sister wasn't expecting a blow, he'd come from behind like the man he wasn't. Just for another piece of his honey's head. With his mouth finally shut down, he looked over the broken glass. But all he could do was disappear back into his hell hole where the walls soon shook from his snoring.

Sister looked frozen in the moment; her hand still knotted to that butcher knife. I stepped back into the kitchen and whispered. "It's time now, Sister. I help you get the rest of your things and we get out 'fore he come after us."

She sat silently but then nodded. I pulled some clothes off a clothesline and shoved them into a pillowcase. Think they were hers, but don't know; maybe her customer's. Made no difference at that point. We were too close to some place not hell and surely not heaven to care. Sister worked her way up from her chair but froze like all the rest of her blood done drained to her feet. Her face was so ashen it looked as though a layer of poster paste had brushed over it.

"Sister, you sit. I finish gettin' your things," I said.

"Just one thing I left back there. I can hear 'im snoring so I go tend to it now. It 'a all be over then."

Her voice was hoarse, constricted like Jesse had just taken his hands off her throat. Lord, I prayed, she ain't got nothing left for him to take; it's all wrung out of her. I knew I had to get us on the road. Had to be on the run before things ran over. Maybe like a cauldron of boiling lye soap.

"Hurry now, Sister. Sooner we gets on the road the quicker we be safe with Jeff. Jesse ain't never gonna bother us at the cabin."

I went back to filling the pillowcase and looked over that room, knowing it was the last time my eyes would swallow the throbbing memories those walls had long served up. So many years' worth I could have gagged. Sleeping on the cot in that corner; washing heaven knows how many tubs of stinking rags. Living most of my life in a space not much larger than a shed and then begging Jesse to leave me be one more day.

Then, as I looked over that room for the final time it hit me cold: why had the snoring gone dead back there? And what could Sister possibly have left in Jesse's room that she'd risk waking him? My soul vibrated with her words from not long before" "Jesse, you ever hit me again, I'll kill you and then put the knife to my throat."

I scrambled over the broken glass and through the silence of what was surely Jesse's black dream in progress. Back there was my sister sitting on the edge of his bed with that rusty knife at his throat. His eyes bulged. Yet it was not like all the times when he was about to punch her broken face.

"I owe you Jesse Powell and there ain't enough pain for what you done to us. Ain't I only payin' you back?"

"Huh?" was all Jesse could utter. But she'd heard that lie before, hadn't she?

She was nose-to-nose with that ol' man, just like Momma had been that time with ol' Isaac.

She looked about for a ghost.

"Can you hear him?"

"I can't hear nothin' with that knife," he stammered. But that was only one more of his lies.

"Sure you can. That's why I put it there. Make sure you heard me good and clear this time. That's Satan callin' you. He wants what's left of you after I finish the butcherin'! 'Cause you're gonna die tonight. Satan…he been waitin' for you too long. Now I'm gonna deliver you to 'im myself!"

Her torture drew blood that trickled down his neck. One budge and she'd cut that bulging artery under his jaw. Then with a hard thrust she'd plunge the knife through his tongue till the tip lodged in his palette. From that bloody moment on she'd not hear his curses no more. Jesse lay frozen with terror as he surely felt Satan squirming for his take. Sweat poured down his cold face.

There are different kinds of justice in this world, and I reckon we'll all be pleading for one or two in the next life. That night I pled for my sister's soul. I grabbed her wrist to pull the knife back from Jesse's bleeding throat. But, Lord, she wasn't gonna let him live. I held on to her hand with all the strength I could muster and whispered against her yammering about killing that ol' man.

"You will, Sister. You be payin' Jesse back when you go, 'cause when you leave this alley there ain't nobody 'round that's gonna do nothin' for Jesse Powell. Don't let him walk your soul to hell with 'im! Leave the rest to Jesus."

Her chin quivered with rage. For what seemed an eternity, I struggled to loosen her grip on the knife. The moments chased after my beating heart. For the only time ever, Jesse's eyes pleaded with mine for mercy. I knew if I let her, she'd plunge it deep and his life would be relinquished to Sister's rage. But her soul would then pay for eternity for taking a life.

Then finally I got the knife back from Jesse's throat. I raised her off the bed still aiming that knife to his throat. Holding her shaking arm, I guided Sister into the kitchen and over to the sink where I shook her wrist over the dishpan. Her eyes were glued to the knife like she couldn't let it drop; the rage was yet spent. How many years had that been the dream that kept her barely alive, to rid her life of Jesse? I held her wrist over that sink to the sounds of cold silence coming from Jesse back there. He never moved to come at us. Even his curses had run their course. Sister's hand shook fiercely, the knife rattled against the side of the tin dishpan. Finally, she turned to me, tears streaming down her bloodied face and said: "I ready now. It's time." At that moment the knife fell into the dishpan.

Jesus had heard my prayer. Sister had relinquished her desire to send Jesse to hell. Yes, she had returned to God's grace and would not break His commandment not to kill. I took a deep breath. It was over and Sister was safe. She hadn't murdered Jesse; she would not spend eternity in hell with him. No, Jesse was doomed to go there without his honey and there he'd be left to stoke the flames waiting for Fred's arrival. We'd walked out his door for the last time. Truly, he must have known that his would only be an aimless stroll to his own end. Only a few more swigs left to count if he could find a bottle hidden somewhere, and then what? Wash and iron clothes for folks? Call in favors from the many he'd abused? No, it was over. That night, the night of the whore's visit, his world had become as dark as the inside of the coffin he'd soon be visiting. It was the place he'd bought on overdrawn credit and buried himself in.

Weeks later Annie told me that from time to time she noticed Jesse stealing a peek out of the kitchen curtains late at night. Him there watching to see if Sister was headed back to him. Yet he really knew he'd not see her again, as he never put a light on out there.

Now I faced my own black dream.

WHITE SHEETS AND THE BEYOND

34

THE STREET WAS wet. Louvenia waited in cold silence as I wrapped her ribs in a sheet I'd torn into lengths. Sister, who was always rail thin, shivered yet there was still a glimpse of a smile on her lip. She knew we were about to escape Jesse and his alley forever.

I couldn't get us away fast enough. Still, in all the fog of those tragic moments back at Sister's I saw visions of my husband waiting at our cabin door, him gazing down the dark road for my return. Louvenia was tired, not just weary from all she'd experienced that awful night with Jesse and his whore, but a bone deep weariness that had long dragged on her. On the road out of town she stared ahead but still at nothing. I chatted about everything I could think of to keep her from drifting to sleep and falling off the wagon. But my own weariness and the night's chill made it hard. Don't know how cold it is when somebody freezes.

"Sister…Sister, you say somethin' now," I demanded, or thought I had. "We got to stay awake on the road here."

"Jesse, he gonna come after me this far out?" she asked again, or had I only been reading her thoughts? Hers or mine, that is.

"No, he ain't," I assured her even as I searched for reasons to support my notion. "Where he gonna get somebody with a wagon to come this far? You ain't gonna see that man ever again 'cept in your thoughts till you wash 'em away. Every time you think of Jesse you gotta dump that brown water out of your tub on his head! He gone. You done handed 'im his ticket to hell an hour ago. He back there packin' for the fall!"

"What…What I gonna do…all day?" she wondered aloud.

Her voice sounded much like Daddy's most times, yet when she was tired her words cracked as Momma's did when she was exhausted. My sister, she never awakened to a day in her life that wasn't already breaking under the weight of the work piled on.

"Well, in the mornin', when you're ready to get up, you're gonna give Lelia her bath while I finish hangin' the loads I done washed."

"That all? Wash my baby?"

"Well, some mornings you might want to put a pan of biscuits in the oven. 'Course we don't have much jam comin' our way, but we sure will when our trees are growed! Yes, ma'am, we gonna!"

"You ever think about the Burney place?" she asked. "I mean, where our folks is buried and all."

"I do. I think about Grandview. I think 'bout Jackson and Ella. Wonder what they's doin' and if they ever think of us. And that always takes me to Orchard Hill. Our folks is up there. Ain't nobody but us cares, but we know they up there hidden under the weeds where nobody can trouble them."

"Ever' day…I pray for Alex." Sister said. "I wait for the day he comes back. Then we all be close again. Like our folks wanted it. We stay together from then on. I know we will."

We shivered as frost dusted the trees. Sister's eyelids grew heavier from the night air riding them down. But Lord, God, guess it was about then that she let out a holler that I figured my shifting on the seat had caused. She gripped her side like it was coming out, that cracked rib was. It was so foggy, couldn't really see where we were, but felt like we'd been bumping along the road for miles. I was frightened we'd taken the wrong road. I knew, with that broken rib, that every rut might put Sister closer to death. Her yelps at every bump grew more anguished. I knew she couldn't stand the agony much longer. I slapped at her to stay awake as my own weariness took command. I could hardly hold the reins no more.

"Hold on to me Sister. Don't fall out on the road. Back at the cabin, Jeff gots a warm fire going for us. You know he does."

Sister clung to me when she wasn't weaving in and out of agony. I kept thinking, was it our bitter peace to have salvaged our lives from Jesse only to perish from the cold? Where are you, Lord, when I'm on a road of darkness too thick to think on? Have the miles shifted out from under me? Am I headed in the wrong direction? A jagged corner of an abyss I've never been before? How far are we from Jesse's alley now? Not far enough…I wondered if my lips were turning blue. Sister's were, or was that only Jesse's fist following?

Time seemed to pause during the fleeting moments my dry eyes closed to escape the cold air. Thankfully, the horses did not drift from the road following my exhausted thoughts. Then I saw it. Way up ahead there was a light beckoning us. As we drew closer it got brighter and even whiter, like maybe Jeff seen us coming and hung lanterns along the porch, lots of white floating up yonder. I struggled to keep my eyes open. Then I remembered leaving them sheets out to dry that morning. Had to be them reflecting the light from the lantern that Jeff always set for my return. There was a heavenly look as them sheets danced through my blurred vision.

It was at that moment when Sister fell onto my lap moaning. Lord, I prayed, don't let her fall over onto the road—she don't really want to die. I knew the wagon's wheels would grind her before I got the horses stopped. Up there, almost in reach, hidden behind all them white sheets was the door that would welcome my baby's aunt for the first time. "Jeff is waiting," I whispered. In moments Sister could sleep in peace for the first time in her life.

It was then, and as I'd never heard before, even from the darkest corners of Jesse's backroom, when Louvenia let out an agonizing wail that snapped me from my daze like a bolt of lightning had penetrated my lip. I knew it had happened. Sister's broken rib had penetrated her heart. No words from Sister could follow that shriek of what she saw. You see, those weren't my white sheets fluttering on the clothes lines up there; somebody else's sheets, and somebody else wearing them. What my sister saw was Jeff. Him under his chestnut tree where we made our daughter. There, with arms bound like a slave and his beautiful face bloodied, he hung with a noose around his neck.

Jeff's eyes gazed back through all that fog. I know they did. It was as though to warn me that the horror of the white shadows had been visited upon us. It had come calling at the very place where we thought its horrors had been vanquished. Yes, the men who hide under white sheets had come calling: Knights of the White Camellia. Cackling like hyenas, they were dancing 'round Jeff with their whips. These men twisted their sin-worn ropes 'round and 'round Jeff like he was a maypole. Louvenia dropped over into my lap. She was dead.

I rode them tired horses like a demon to get to my husband. For fleeting moments, somewhere at the very drains of my hope, I conjured a notion them cowards were only scaring Jeff, playing like lynching 'cause they did nothing but laugh and hoot. I would kill them all the same! But it wasn't like that, was it? They stopped laughing and their faces bulged, so loaded with hatred were they. I galloped to strike back. Just as the wagon drew close, at the very last moment, they kicked the stool out from under my husband. Jeff looked at me to convey something beyond his love. What were these words, Lord? I leapt from the wagon—Sister fell to the ground. I ran to grab Jeff's legs to save him. I would hold him up so that rope could not squeeze his life away. I would do it. I would save my husband.

"Come on boys, still problem is broken in two now."

But it was too late. I could do nothing. The white men on their horses circled as I held my husband's ankles. Jeff's eyes looked down from his bent neck, but could not see me trying to catch his life before it escaped on the end of his last breath. Still his eyes, that would never see me again, stared back like they still longed to. The song they always sang for me was silent. There was no life to hold on to. Jeff had passed to the beyond.

Even as my husband's last breath evaporated, one of them came from behind and kicked me. First in the back, and then in the head. Don't know where else. I lay on the ground under my husband's dead feet. My last moments as I faced my own death was hearing the cries of my terrified baby girl screaming up on the porch and knowing they were surely gonna kill her too and I could do nothing. Nothing. It was beyond that, along with my husband's soul.

And yet strangely a moment of peace came over me. Somewhere in my last thoughts that night, I knew there'd be only a few moments of agony to endure. Then the slaughter would be over and we'd all be together in the Lord's Orchard.

Just before I fell to the fluttering white shadows, I heard their words echoing in the empty blackness that had swallowed me. "You find our money?"

It was all about money. Ain't it always?

"Yeah, enough to buy this here place," was the reply.

After stealing my husband's life and the savings he planned to buy that acreage with, the three men drifted away like a white cloud destined for nowhere. A cloud of pestilence.

Yes, white sheets had fluttered for me. Now I only want to be wound and buried in them.

A Bitter Place

35

I DON'T REMEMBER MUCH of the next few days, or was it really weeks that I'd surrendered to the clouds that rattled in my dreams? Truly, the days follow each other in an ever-deepening haze when you don't count them; can't find a reason to want to.

Like when my folks passed, the fog returned and steeped my thoughts till they blanketed my days like a shroud. Yet everywhere I turned in my despair Louvenia's dulcet voice pursued. Only her humming penetrated the numbness of those mornings fled, chased down by dead afternoons to be delivered to avoided evenings and finally the ever-dreaded lonely nights that only rolled me deeper in my misery.

In broken sighs I stammered back. "No! I won't come out! Stop!" Stop that chanting at my bedside, I thought as I covered my head with the pillow that he'd slept on moments before in my dreams. Yet her melodies seemed just as determined to break into my thoughts and weave them into new directions as I lay there under sheets gone sour from stale sweat. Let me find some peace in my sleep, Lord. Got nowhere else to go looking for some.

I still do not know how Louvenia got me inside on the night of the fluttering white sheets. Was it Lelia's crying, or the bitter cold of that night? For the longest time I could only imagine things in drips. How did Sister get Jeff cut down from his chestnut? Where did he wait to comfort me from my sorrows? Even now, I can barely glimpse back on those bitter days when I could only moan something about my husband to Louvenia ever at my bedside. "Where is he?" I asked the blank wall that stared back pitilessly. For days she sat fanning on the edge of my nothingness, softly admonishing me to let the pain bleed the wounds clean. Her words bled easily into the spirituals she hummed as she rocked Lelia. "Let it be for now," she said, and promised the pain would run thinner and thinner over the miles ahead. But I had no intention of going that far without him. She preached that I had to take the next step, yet I would not move in any direction. Where was my husband now? Where was Jeff? Where is that bitter beyond where he waits?

How I bless Louvenia that I did not have to face the sight of Jeff's crumpled body on the night of the fluttering sheets. Surely, my daughter would be one more orphan if it weren't for Louvenia, a frail woman who yet found the strength to save me as she'd done so many times.

Then late one morning Sister picked up the fan and flung it down and walked around the bed to see if I'd noticed. I turned my face deeper into my pillow only to see the same emptiness staring back.

"I ain't gonna fan you no more," she said. "So, when you get hot enough, you're gonna get up. That's what I think," she announced with words and eyes.

"Where is he, Sister?" I mumbled.

Moments passed in the thick silence before she picked up the fan again.

"I know I been askin'. But you been sayin' nothin'."

She went back to fanning, but her eyes darted about like they always did when there were things she didn't want to talk about. I knew she was hunting for those doors of escape. But I met her at every one. Even as I'd been hiding under my pillow, I yet knew Sister had been hiding from me because she couldn't reply for the longest spell. But then she finally told me and Lord, how I understood why it was so hard for her.

"You know how hard that soil is out there." Her words came like they'd torn her throat. "You know it is," she whispered and swallowed hard.

I waited and waited for more. "You got to tell me," I begged. "Where Jeff is won't let me be. Where is that place?"

"You don't 'member that night. Even after your head is healed from their boot kicks. I prayed for it to be that way."

I searched Sister's sorrowful eyes for her secret. "What, Louvenia?" I asked. "What's you need to tell me?"

"The soil was so hard where you said bury Jeff. Out near his chestnut, you told me. You know I just couldn't get the shovel in the dirt. Just couldn't." Tears streamed down her face like she'd forsaken me. "There was too much rock, Sarah."

"Rock? I don't understand."

Her dry mouth twitched like her words were filled with splinters. "Only place I could bury Jeff was…out there." She pointed out the window to some vague place beyond. Could I have seen where he was all along if I'd only looked through my misery far enough? Still I noticed that Louvenia couldn't look out that way.

"Sister…?

"Had to dig where the soil would take the shovel," she said.

"Yes. Where?"

"His garden. 'Neath the flowers he growed for you. That's where Jeff rests."

I reached for Sister's hand. She held mine tightly. We both choked on our tears as our thoughts ran wild looking for refuge from the calamities in our hearts. But our prayers were not granted.

"I understand, Sister. I know I do."

I fell back on the pillow begging for the fog to come quick and dangle my thoughts till the weight of them finally dropped off and released me too another long sleep. Still, all I could see was Jeff's smile on the day when he handed me that last fist of flowers he'd cut for me. When was that, Lord? What life did it still hang from?

"Don't matter that you turned his garden under. He be glad of it. To rest under the flowers he loved. I know he would," I remember mumbling to Louvenia as I stumbled off searching for the sleep that might release me from the pain of that moment. But it had revoked its promise and left me laying there more awake than I'd ever been. "Don't matter, Sister. Don't matter no more… Nothin' does…"

Days later we talked about the day she buried my husband. Sister finally told me that I came out that morning looking dazed. Like them men had kicked me in the head all over again. Or maybe like a dream had kicked me out of bed and I'd gone off to look for a hole to swallow the pain; my own grave near Jeff's. She told me that as she battled the hard soil to fill Jeff's grave, I could only gaze down at the shrouded body of my husband and sob.

"Pull down the shroud, Sister. Need to see my husband's face one more time."

But Sister shook her head. She wouldn't reveal Jeff's forever lost smile.

"No, he don't want you to see how sad he is for leaving you," she mumbled. "'Cause if you do, you'll carry the picture with you forever. No, Sarah. Got to bury the anger right here with 'im. I pray to God, you will come to, 'cause it will kill you if you don't. Then what about our baby?"

Louvenia went back to pushing the soil she'd dug into the hole. There was nothing left in me to fight with. No, I could barely get myself back into the cabin where I prayed for my bed to once more drown me and then deliver me to a bitter place next to my husband.

§

Because of my sister I arrived at a peace over Jeff's passing. It was a bitter peace, but not so for Sister having buried my husband in the garden he so loved. I no longer resisted Sister's admonitions that I not trip backwards to that cold night when I lost him. She pushed me to keep looking onwards, even if that was a vague empty place I did not want to step into. Truly for us, like all children of 'croppers, it was etched on my soul that I was a child born to slaves so at least I was certain that what may be out there for my child and me would be no more inhospitable than where I'd come from; that Klan-cursed soil I stood on. It steeped in my thoughts that there could be little ahead for us no matter what direction I drifted. Wasn't it all a profane lie that the mighty would fall and the downtrodden would rise and take a place at the banquet? All damned lies and nothing more. The mighty are not brought down and the weak raised. No, the nobodies do not become somebodies under the feet of those who hide under white hoods. Still, from somewhere in my heart, I knew that I'd spend the rest of my days and lonely nights spreading flower seeds over my beloved husband's place of rest.

One morning Sister carried my daughter over to my bed with a little rag doll she'd made from one of Jeff's old shirts. There were two mismatched brown buttons she'd sewn on for eyes, one little button eye and a big one. Who did she ever see with eyes like that? I looked at that doll and couldn't stop laughing.

"You think it's so funny? Then you get up and make a better one. That's what I think!" Sister's hands were on her hips, so I'd know she meant business on me.

"Is that what you think, Louvenia? You got a notion any child gots big brown eyes like that rag doll's?"

She handed my daughter to me so I could see for myself. The sparkle in my baby's eyes nearly blinded me.

"You think Jeff would be pleased if this child's Ma's in bed all day and then some?"

"Don't start in on me, Louvenia. If I'm in bed all day, that's 'cause there ain't *some* left to get up for. Just leave me be and go make us some biscuits. I ain't in no mood to roll in the dirt with you no matter how many times you stand there pointing to the ground you think it's time I stand on. Lord, don't I know it's time?"

Sister wasn't going to give in only to see me fade back into my pillow again. "Now don't rush none. No, if you're needin' some more sleep you can always take a bath next week or come another week… if you got a mind to."

"I said…don't start in on me!"

"Now ain't you feelin' sassy?" Sister remarked with a smile like she'd just won a bet and me getting out of bed was the prize.

So I got up determined to escape her. I took Lelia and her new rag doll and went looking for Jeff. Sister watched through the window as she rolled her biscuits.

"Yes, Jeff. Think you been sendin' Sister into me every morning. I know you have! The two of you been carpin' at me for days now. Well, you win! I'm gonna get up and take care of your baby girl."

Sister waited for us on the porch with a smile and a plate of eggs. On that bright sunny morning of yet another resurrection of my soul, even Lelia's rag doll had more faith than I had the day before that biscuit. I ate everything Louvenia put in front of me and fed Lelia the same time. When I couldn't eat another bite, Sister started cleaning up, and that meant me as well.

"You take the baby out to there where I got that tub of water warming in the sun and give her a bath."

I carried the basin over to the shade of the chestnut. It was under this same tree that I made love to Jeff—the very tree he was lynched from that I'd finally come to face.

What do I tell my daughter? I wondered looking up at branches Jeff had once climbed to shake down chestnuts. How do I explain to our child that men that never knew her daddy took him from us? Tell me, Jeff. "What 'a we gonna do now? I got to get on with it. Ever' day I just keep thinkin' 'bout you. God knows I miss you. If it wasn't for our child here, you know I'd come to you."

Just as Jeff did the day we arrived, I kissed the bark of that old chestnut. Then from afar I saw the preacher coming down the road with Annie. Over the weeks they'd been stopping by to visit and leave off food. Annie hugged me and kissed my forehead before walking inside carrying a basket of food. She knew the preacher wanted to speak to me. He looked deep into my sad eyes and nodded like he could read my fears.

"Where's a poor woman with a baby to go?" I asked. "Got nowhere to go and no man to wait for at night."

The preacher put his hand on my shoulder and bowed his head. But I had no mind to pray. Still he brought me along just the same.

"'Whether you turn to the right or the left, your ears will hear a voice saying, 'This is the way; walk in it.' Isaiah, chapter thirty, verse twenty-one."

I told the preacher that over the days I'd known spells when I saw little reason to go on and no strength to take me there even if I had. He kissed Lelia and nodded his understanding. Yes, the reason was in my arms kicking to get at life.

"'A man's heart plans his way, but the Lord directs his steps.' Proverbs 16:9."

"But what does the Lord do for a woman?" I asked. "I'm a tub woman. At the end of my day there ain't no air left between me and my days bent over one."

"I got no answer for that, Sister. Maybe nobody does. Still, keep seeking, and you will find it. That path that takes you to a better place. Amen, Sister. Keep knocking and the door will be opened to you.' Matthew, chapter seven, verse seven. Sister Sarah, you will take Jeff with you like you carry your folks' dreams for a life with dignity. He will always be right there with you, I promise."

&

During the ever-shorter autumn days that followed I cared for my daughter and tried to lose myself in my work so Sister could slow down from the weeks of doing my share. Yet in scattered moments,

I started to think on things. I came to know that I had to move on. Yes, I had to resist the desire to stay even a few months, even as the place Jeff and I had built up, along with our small orchard, had such a pull on me. But I knew if I remained long I could too easily postpone my farewells forever. Where would that leave me? Would there be decades of drifting along till the time came when I finally rested next to my husband? Would our daughter pick the flowers over our graves and be asking herself why her ma did nothing to make her life better while I was young?

For days Louvenia's eyes followed as I paced the cabin sorting my thoughts. For the longest time I never said a word 'bout moving on. Couldn't, 'cause I knew what her response would be. I thought on how I'd tell her, but still couldn't bring myself to that moment.

For the first time in her life she had some peace there in the country where nobody was crashing a whiskey bottle over her head looking to cut out a piece of her life to go after the next swig. I was so torn. Torn about us separating, yet didn't want Sister's peace to evaporate. I had to accept that she couldn't make it in a city again just as I knew Lelia could never have a life out there in the country where Southern hatred easily tethered lives with lynching ropes.

"Don't know why you got to leave," Sister replied when I told her. "Don't we have it good out here?" Her eyes filled with tears as she rocked Lelia.

"You know, like I know, that it's got to be," I said. "Lelia ain't gonna get an education livin' out here. White folks won't have it. I been thinkin' we gonna move on to St. Louis where there's got to be work." But was I only convincing myself? "Why can't you come with us? Maybe we can find Alex up there."

"I can't go nowheres. You know I don't have it in me." Her eyes were heavy with weariness. "I'm too tired for change. You know I don't got Momma's strength like you, and that's why you gots to go on. Don't you see? You been blessed bein' strong like her; you gots to use it to make a life for you and Lelia. 'Cause you're right; it ain't gonna be near this old porch and them tubs waiting out there."

Sister's words gave me the answer I'd longed for when she handed Lelia to me with a smile.

"Life's gonna let up on us! Don't die on me thinkin' it won't," I told her. "We ain't gonna die like our folks did thinkin' there's gonna be a day when white folks is gonna share the fruit of the orchard, 'cause that come one day ain't on no calendar." I broke down, leaving Sister in a gulch of tears.

"I ain't gonna die," she cried. With her worn hand, Sister lifted my chin and situated her nose in the air like she didn't approve of my weepy-woman stuff. "Anyway, who's gonna water them peach trees? I been out there ever' morning waterin' Jeff's orchard and getting right good at it. Them trees are near a foot taller than when I come. Sure they are! You think?"

I did. "Someday I'll come for you! I promise!" Still, I knew such promises can never be kept.

Sister averted her eyes as she knew as well. "I be prayin' for that day," she said.

For days we hid our fears separately in that small cabin where we shared everything else. I spent the next several days thinking on what I would do in St. Louis, 'cept I really had nothing to think on 'cause I had no idea what kind of life I could find for myself and my daughter beyond that chestnut tree. What could possibly be out there for a fatherless child and her tub ma—still not much more than a child myself? I wondered if the dangers of big cities could be greater than living on Jesse's alley. I was haunted with fear wondering if my notion of leaving for something better might carve up our lives.

To ease these fears, I lost myself in my work as we readied the place for my departure. I wanted to leave knowing Louvenia would be fine till I could get work and send money. We planted up the kitchen garden with winter vegetables and I prayed Annie and the churchwomen might come to visit and take some cabbages back with them.

Annie, always a blessing in our lives, knew a porter in her church that could get free train tickets for his family. She bartered ironing up his working shirts, dozens of them, and got a ticket for me to St. Louis. Sister didn't need Jeff's tools, so we sold them. Lord, I didn't want to, my husband wore his hands out on them wooden handles, but I had to. Sister met the man who came for them so I didn't have to watch Jeff's things being carted off. That same day, mostly in silence, as we knew our days together were few, we filled the emptied tool shed with chopped wood. When winter came, Sister could spend her evenings near a warm fireplace doing some mending for the churchwomen for a few coins. There near the fire her joints might not ache so bad.

Even with all the fussing dragging on the hours left to me at Jeff's cabin, the minutes still added up and the day I dreaded arrived. I had to stop preparing and face the very moment I'd step ahead on a new journey where there'd be no road maps and yet there was certain to be countless ruts along the way. I could only pray that I'd somehow make it over them.

"You know when spring comes and all the flowers bloom," I said on our last morning together.

"Yes, I'll cut the flowers 'round his grave and dry them seeds so's I can send 'em to you. I promise you. Then you're gonna know I'm here waitin' for your return."

I broke down. Sister held me briefly and then gently pushed me away from her bosom. She knew it was time for me to go.

Again, I was leaving my home feeling like an orphan. I packed Lelia's things and sat there at the kitchen table looking at Sister's biscuits. We seldom had biscuits except on Sunday. She knew the morning I'd for sure be leaving was upon us. I saw her out in the garden hanging clothes, her back to the window. She hid behind the clothesline so only the soil at her feet collected her tears among the drops from her wet rags. Lord, Lord, would I ever set eyes on my sister again? The silence of those thoughts was deafening.

I had our things at the door when Louvenia stepped back in, her eyes red but now dry again. She would be strong for us.

"I forgot something!"

"What could you forget? You been fussin' with your things for days now."

I dragged the chair over to the post that held up the beam under the porch. Up there, next to where Jeff kept his jug of whiskey was his tobacco tin.

"Lelia's education tin." I rattled it hard.

"That ol' tobacco tin?" she asked.

"Soon after the baby came, Jeff stopped smokin' and put aside this here tin to save money in for her schoolin'. Klansmen stole ever' cent Jeff saved up to buy this cabin. But they won't stop us. Yes, as I bend over the tubs, this child goin' to college!"

"College? You hear that, Lelia? Your momma sure can keep big dreams when she sets her mind to it!"

Lelia's brown button eyes smiled back.

"Our folks lived like animals. You know they did, Sister. I may be a poor widow and got no chance at happiness without my husband, but our child's gonna carry Momma's dream. She's gonna go to school and not be a slave to no tub. Even if it takes all that's left in me, I mean for it to be."

"Chile, can't you see? You already got the dream; it's in you like them peach pits you and Jeff planted out there. These coins in Jeff's tobacco tin means you never let a dream die with Jeff. And you gonna find that good soil to plant 'em in up there in St. Louis and grow a good life for you and your girl."

I kissed Sister. For the very last time she handed Lelia back.

"I got me a dream, too!" she confessed.

"What's your dream?" I asked.

"Well, I dream that you gonna keep up your learning to write and when you're real good, you're gonna write the president a long letter and tell 'im what these white folks been doin' to us. That's my dream. You're gonna write to the president one day and then thing's gonna get better for our folks when he knows. Just like when President Lincoln knew 'bout our troubles and broke our chains."

My eyes filled with tears. I couldn't hold them back no more so I bundled my daughter, picked up our things and walked out the door. From that first step I could feel my fears nipping at my ankles like nigger dogs on the chase of a runaway, yet I could not turn to say one more good-bye. But there never can be a last one.

On foot, Lelia and I disappeared over the horizon headed for Vicksburg and the Anchor Line that would take us to St. Louis. It was the start of a long journey away from Jeff's beloved chestnut, his garden of flowers and Louvenia.

END OF BOOK ONE

Continue Sarah Breedlove's extraordinary journey

THE AIR BETWEEN OUR TUBS

BOOK TWO
Nowhere to Somewhere

THE AIR BETWEEN OUR TUBS

BOOK THREE
The Weight of My Dreams

lewaroroad.com

ambition, who wants to be a film star – or, failing that, a novelist. She's about as predictable as a thunderstorm.

Alice is the girl next door and works for a literary agent. She loves Peter's writing – and Peter too. But will she find the courage to tell him so?

In a slippery tale of stolen hearts and purloined novels, secret loves and hidden ambitions, these lives become irretrievably tangled.

Who will end up with whom? Who will end up rich and celebrated? And will art – and love – win out in the end?

lewaroroad.com